STARKILLER
BY AMELIA ARVIE

STARKILLER

Amelia Arvie

To Evanna

Table of Contents

When the sun imploded, the world died within an hour.

Out of the darkness, A final society was born. The Imperial Republic of Raedon would build a civilization that mends all mistakes of the past, securing humanity's role in the future.

There will be no more corruption in the government, for we are fair and just rulers. There will be no destruction of our planet, for we are peaceful people. There will be no inequalities, for we are all the same human. There will be no turning away as our brothers and sisters die in wars they are too young to fight, for we are a society of tranquility. There will be no sickness or disease, for we have become masters of our bodies. And last, there will be no more mistakes, for we have become the embodiment of perfection.

Any ignorance of the regulations set forth by the Imperial Republic will be dealt with swiftly and efficiently.

Humanity will no longer be free to roam as it chooses; it will be leashed and controlled. It is the best way, the *only* way to ensure that we live beyond our predicted years and defy the boundaries nature has created for us.

The sun might have poisoned our air and suffocated us into the ground, but we will not continue to concede to its limitations.

Perhaps failure was the beginning of a new kind of success.

Perhaps the world would have to die before it could truly live.

-An excerpt of the first Supreme Leader's journal, extracted from the Archives of the Imperial Republic of Raedon

Chapter One

"Unde sol oritur ubi occidit."
- From where the sun rises to where it sets.

The name Wren Sitara meant nothing to anyone; she was a ghost.

It was one thing Wren enjoyed most about being herself. She didn't need to flaunt her name where it didn't belong, because she was already being spoken about. Everyone had heard of her, yet they had no clue who she really was. And the people that knew her by her given name feared to speak it.

She was nameless, and that was the way she liked things.

Positioned atop the block's highest rooftop, Wren focused her rifle's scope on the skyscraper that stood opposite her. Construction of the mass design was still underway and the loose tarp fabric hanging over the steel beams blocked her clear view of the interior. The pillars lining the skeletal structure gleamed underneath the starlight; the building was so high up that the light from the neon district below didn't reach it. But the top spire of the tower could almost touch the obsidian sky above, reaching for the stars and beyond. They had only plated the bottom half of the building in sheer glass so far.

The stars looked down on the assassin as she shifted the aim of her rifle, scanning the length of the floor through the tarps and beams. It was empty save for two purple velvet chairs set up in the center of the room, both remaining untouched and unoccupied. They faced away from Wren, looking outwards into the expanse of the metropolis beyond. Tonight, the district of Antares reminded Wren of small winking comets soaring across the sky.

She blinked into her scope, the tips of her eyelashes brushing against the glass lens. When she shifted to observe the far corner of the building, she felt the sharp edges of her silver knives brushing against the inside layers of her uniform. She let out a small breath, the warm air circulating through her mask. The hood pulled over her forehead created a jaded view of the rest of her face, taunting the stars that were begging for the slightest glimpse of her alabaster figure.

Wren was not the one summoned to the address that night; Raedon's most notorious assassin was. As far as everyone knew, Wren Sitara died when she was sixteen years old. The small barcode that used to be imprinted into her right wrist had been scratched from the record and given to someone new by the Republic. All that remained of it now was a line of scars on her skin. Her death had been staged and forgotten, just like everyone else who fell from buildings and pretended to die in order to keep themselves hidden from whatever they were running from.

Only Wren wasn't running anymore; she was the one people ran *from*.

A fraction of movement caught her eye on the left side of the building. Wren slid her rifle across the ledge of the rooftop to peer at the tall figure now standing in the opposite corner, miraculously appearing from the shadows. His hands were tucked behind his back in a proper way, although Wren knew he was anything but. His assigned civilian uniform fit squarely on his shoulders and was partnered with the assigned jacket, permitted to be worn when people got cold.

Even though Raedon was entirely temperature controlled in each of the seven districts and there was no wind or sun to heat or cool them, there were still those who chose to wear the jacket or long-sleeved uniform as a way to change up their lives every so often.

As if there would need to be any kind of change in a world that was already perfect.

Wren watched the man as he stood static for a few moments, gazing at the district with his back turned to Wren. She knew that he knew she was watching him. He was the one who had called her there. Wren would've found it insulting if he summoned her to the address and bothered looking for her. It insinuated that she was easy to find when they both knew that she could hide in plain sight without struggle.

It was part of being a ghost, after all.

A few moments passed by filled with fixed silence; the district below them was sleeping just like the rest of Raedon on the night cycle. With no daytime and no sun, it meant scheduled hours for sleeping and working each rotation. They kept the night the same, but they called the awake cycle "sol," which is short for solar day. Citizens were required to follow the protocols of sufficient working, eating, sleeping, and schooling hours each sol, meant to keep Raedon on its perfect schedule. It sounded more like a time bomb to Wren, but she knew that trying to interfere with it was pointless.

She did what she wanted to do when she wanted to do it without the consequences normal citizens received when they refused protocol. By any measure, she was far from being an ordinary citizen. She wouldn't allow herself to be one. If she did, it would mean that Raedon had blanketed her with its illusion of living in the perfect world when she knew that civilization was far from perfect after the sun imploded.

Wren listened to the faint clicking of her scope as she adjusted the sight, watching the lens move in and out of fuzzy and black-rimmed views. She didn't dare take her eyes off the man who was now moving towards one of the two chairs placed in the center of the room, stiffly lowering himself into one and crossing an ankle over a knee. He folded his hands carefully in his lap, sighing as he waited for her.

Wren took her cue when she'd confirmed that the man wasn't going anywhere else. She hoisted herself onto her feet again and slung the rifle over her shoulder, dancing dangerously close to the edge of the building. She felt gravity working against her as she tipped forward, looking downwards at the street miles below her.

Then she leaped off of the skyscraper.

She landed on a balcony two floors below in a graceful roll that gave her the momentum to jump again, this time bracing herself with bent knees. She arrived on a glass bridge connecting her building to the new one, with the man still patiently waiting inside for her. The bridge was not yet completed on one side, but it didn't matter to Wren as she ran across the top, her legs moving so swiftly that her feet barely had time to slip on the glass. When she reached the section where the bridge met scaffolding and eventually open air, she vaulted herself over the remaining portion of the street and landed with her limbs stretched between two steel pillars.

Then she began to climb. She held no fear of the open street below or how high she was in the sky; and getting higher. How could she be? She became fear itself the moment she'd donned her mask that night cycle and set out to the address.

The assassin moved quicker than she did on the bridge, scaling the side of the skyscraper with ease. She didn't need a harness or a rope to attach to her in case she fell; she knew she wouldn't. She disappeared in one spot and reappeared in the next, almost as if she simply teleported through space. One arm was always securing her to the building as the other one inched her upwards, pushing herself onto steel beam after beam until she reached the sixty-third floor, the level almost precisely across from her previous rooftop perch. Wren's body flexed as she propelled herself through the sky, catching onto a hanging tarp and swinging herself into the building through an empty windowpane.

The assassin made no sound as she approached the pair of chairs. She didn't sit in the empty one, instead opting to stand behind the already occupied seat. The sound of her breath barely reached the barrier of her mask before the man sitting in the chair in front of her spoke.

"Back from the dead again?" His fingers rapped against each other in a steady, rhythmic motion. "People are beginning to wonder if you really died in the first place."

"Ghosts don't die."

"That's obvious." His voice was cold, but not angry. It was the tone he always talked in; being her brother meant scolding her for everything she did.

"So then, why are you here?" Wren asked him, slowly rounding the empty chair. "According to the Republic, you're still alive. Shouldn't you be out pretending to be one of their perfect citizens?" Her brother's face came into view, lit up by the neon lights illuminating the city outside of the blank steel panes.

Eden Sitara was what Wren would describe as precise. Everything about him was calculated, as though he planned for one eyebrow to always be raised higher than the other in skepticism and for his face to always be set in a disapproving expression. He looked uncomfortable in his civilian uniform and tried to hide it by running a calloused hand over his dark hair to make sure it was tamed enough for his approval. He was older than her by three years and thought it was his duty to question everything that she did.

"I'm only here because of you," Eden said back, and Wren saw his eyes snap to one of the buildings adjacent to theirs. There was a large billboard screen attached to the side of the building, already giving news coverage of what she'd done only hours earlier. People would see it soon enough when the sol cycle began.

"Saw that, did you?" Wren tittered, finally dropping into the chair and finding it surprisingly comfortable. She leaned back and placed her elbows on the plush arms, lounging and stretching her limbs with a sigh.

"Everyone has seen it." Eden snapped. "Your work has been displayed on every news channel in Antares. Soon, the entire Republic will know what you did. It won't be long until the Rising Sun knows you defied them as well."

"They already know." Wren was sure of it. The rebels had eyes everywhere, watching every move the leaders of Raedon made. There wasn't one thing that they didn't know before the rest of the world did. But while Wren knew she'd gone against the Rising Sun's orders, she couldn't bring herself to care. "I assume they sent you here to scold me about it?"

"I'm here to collect the files." Eden sounded frustrated with her nonchalant attitude towards the entire situation. Working as the Captain in the Rising Sun's command, he was only one rank below the Commanders who ran the entire rebel operation. That also meant he was a complete buzzkill. "Please tell me that you didn't just make a mess out of this and did your job for once."

Wren ignored his jab and fished into the pocket attached to her thigh, her fingers brushing against the knives hidden within. She felt something cool fall into her fingers and pulled it out, tossing it to Eden without waiting for him to acknowledge it. He caught it anyway, flipping it in his hands and observing the silver flash drive like a precious jewel dug from the ground.

"Are you sure this is it?" he asked, still inspecting the drive between his fingers.

"Of course, I'm sure." She hissed, offended that he would ask such a question. "The names of all known rebels and rebel sympathizers according to the Imperial Republic itself."

The file only existed to five people: the Supreme Leader, one of the Supreme Leader's twelve Advisors, the Advisor's apprentice, and now Wren and Eden, both of them still examining the silver sheen of the drive. The rebels had gotten word of the document and sent her to retrieve it. Wren had stolen it from the very apartment that was still being televised on large screens all over the city. After she abandoned the poison the rebels had given her, she took matters into her own hands and assassinated the apprentice in her own way, one that ensured her work would be televised. It wasn't hard to find the file afterward, downloading it onto a flash drive and deleting the document from all Republic records.

Then she'd smashed the computer she used for good measure.

If the Republic suspected anything about the stolen files having to do with the Rising Sun, no one would be able to take action because the file was never supposed to exist in the first place. It was invisible and therefore she never stole it to begin with.

"You would be getting in less trouble if you used the method that was supplied to you."

"I prefer not to use poison." Wren casually dusted lint off the arm of her chair, unbothered. "It's too slow."

"It's also what you were ordered to use." Eden snapped, his head whipping to her. "How many times do you think you can defy them before they cut you loose?"

"Maybe you should ask them that, seeing as you're so high up in their ranks now." Wren didn't feel guilty about doing things her own way as much as Eden wanted her to. The assassin was notorious for leaving her mark and poison didn't fit the profile.

Certainly not a slow-working one that would kill her before the intended victim.

Eden was silent for a few moments, battling himself in his head. Arguing with Wren was pointless, they both knew. She would win regardless. So instead of scolding her about more things he couldn't change, he tucked the flash drive into his jacket pocket and said, "With this threat out of the way, the rebels have contracted another assignment for you."

"If it's about deleting the copies of records you made from the Republic's Archives, consider it done," Wren told him. She'd placed digital monitors onto the files of every database in Raedon using an invisible virus designed but never before used by the rebels. She didn't exactly have permission to use the technology, but the rebels didn't tell her not to use it either. Once a copy had been made of a document, the virus would delete it and any evidence that the database had been hacked.

"It's not about that, although I'm glad you did as you were told for once." Then he paused, his brow crinkling before he asked, "Would I remain happy if you gave me the truthful answer as to how you managed it?"

Wren smirked. "No."

"Then I won't bother."

Her smile widened. It wasn't often that Eden skipped over the gritty details of how she got things done for the rebels. Sometimes, he wanted every second of what she did on record for him to go over millions of times. There were countless reasons why he would want to listen to her description, ranging from analysis for the rebels to the fact that he was alone and miserable. Other times, he assumed that what she did was good enough to get him what he wanted and that in itself was worth not questioning her. Wren liked her brother more when he didn't ask for the details. Although she was a very detail-oriented person, it was bothersome when she had to recount everything she did.

It was part of the reasons she made things newsworthy all the time. If the reporters explained it in their glorious methods, she wouldn't have to.

"The Supreme Leader has formally invited the Phantom to the palace to arrange a deal with the Republic." Eden began again. "The rebels don't yet know the nature of the arrangement, but they do know that they haven't had an opportunity to plant someone on the inside before now. The Republic has yet to figure out that you work for the Rising Sun. Keep your caution up as a barrier on all sides. They'll be looking for you to slip up and reveal who you really are."

Wren squared her shoulders against the back of the chair, her gloved fingers curling into fists. She looked into the screen on the side of the building again, watching as Sanctum Palace appeared on camera. It was thousands of miles away from them in the district of Polaris. The Supreme Leader was probably huddled inside his fortress, looking at the news footage that had just disappeared from the screen. He, nor did anyone else in the Republic besides Eden and his close allies, know who she was.

"What makes you think it's not a trap?"

It was entirely possible for the Supreme Leader to hatch a plan to lure the assassin to his stronghold just to capture her and put her on trial. That would be a stupid plan, Wren thought, because they would never pin her down even if she was standing right in the center of their palace.

"If it was, you would already know by now."

Wren smiled underneath her mask. Eden was right; she was able to see everything coming for her and always seemed to be five steps ahead. In all her years of being Raedon's most notorious assassin, not once has she been touched by a single soldier. The only time they'd ever gotten close was because she was baiting them for a good laugh.

"What do the rebels want me to do? Steal a few more files and then disappear again?"

"You're familiar with the Supreme Leader's son?"

"Briar Atlas?" Of course, she knew who he was; he and his father's faces were constantly splashed upon every news channel and stealing her spotlight.

"Yes, him," Eden confirmed with a small nod. His jaw tightened; he didn't think highly of Briar either. "He continues to undermine his father and destroy the Republic's public image. He is treated as an outsider in their court but will come to play an important role in it too. He might be the key to getting his father to comply with the rebel's demands. Without the Supreme Leader paying attention to the Rising Sun, no one else will."

"What are these demands, exactly?" Wren finally asked, but instead of an answer, she earned a hard stare from her brother.

"They're classified with the Commanders." He informed her and in return, she rolled her eyes. Eden knew what the

Commanders wanted, but must've been ordered not to tell her anything. There was something about his rough exterior that made her simply want to punch through it and get all the answers she'd ever been deprived of.

When Wren drew herself out of her thoughts, she found Eden staring at her, his mouth set in a hard line across his face.

"Briar Atlas is not a target." He instructed. "He is an asset and should be treated as such."

Again, Wren didn't respond.

"Do what the Rising Sun is asking of you, and you won't find yourself in any more trouble than you're already in."

Wren stood from her chair, gazing at the neon palace on the news. Then she glanced sideways at Eden, allowing her eyelid to fall into a wink.

"I'm the Phantom." Her lips curved into a smile. "My name means trouble."

Even with 83% of the Earth's land scorched by waves of fire and poisoned by blankets of radiation, Raedon still uses their 17% of remaining land better than the 100% that was given to the world before the sun imploded.

To be more specific, 75% of the planet's landmass was taken up by large bodies of water, aptly named "oceans". These oceans were millions of miles deep and despite human development becoming far greater than ever expected, the depths of these bodies of water had never been explored. Despite their pitiful attempts, humans believed they could only go so far down into the oceans without being killed by the tons of pressure on top of them first.

That was a horrible excuse, and one that was illuminated when the sun imploded.

The radiation and scorching hot ripples of fire dried the oceans mere minutes after the majority of the human race died. It left vast valleys in between mountainous summits that were once continents. The bunker that survived the implosion was hidden within the earth's core, dug so deep it almost grazed the outer layer of the rocky mantle beneath.

It was named the Atlantic 1078, because of its location on the coast of the former Atlantic Ocean. After waiting millions of years for the air to become breathable again, humanity rose from the bunker to stand on the coast of a dried-up ocean.

The hollow depression between the two continents would become Raedon, and eventually, the Imperial Republic.
Humanity had been given a second chance; it would be cruel to waste it.

- An excerpt of the first Supreme Leader's journal, extracted from the Archives of the Imperial Republic of Raedon

Chapter Two

"Qui totum vult totum perdit."
- *He who wants everything, loses everything.*

Briar Atlas sat in the tavern with a certain poise that told everyone he knew people were trying to kill him at that very moment, and he didn't care.

There were many things Briar didn't care about, including the fact that there was a constant knife to his throat. But along with that also came things he did care about, like betting on cards, money, and cheap ale. He had been running from people his entire life and he didn't stop because he was ready to face them with a gun in his hand. He stopped because, quite frankly, he didn't like to run.

He was dangerous to his enemies, and that was the way he'd like to keep things.

Briar twisted the silver ring on his index finger, leaning so far down over the table his chin was nearly inches above the surface of the table. His stack of cards sat idly in front of him as he took another sip from the glass next to the pile, the drink being instantly refilled the moment he took the last swig. Around him, the underground tavern bustled with life. Briar enjoyed hearing the sounds of clinking glasses and cheering for odd reasons he couldn't decipher. He enjoyed being served glass after glass of lukewarm drinks, a different girl bringing them each time. He relished in laughing with other men, even if he didn't know what they were laughing about.

The circular table Briar sat at was as full as all the others. Five other men sat with him, all masterfully shuffling their cards in their hands. The room was dim, which made it complicated to tell if they were cheating as much as Briar was. The white lights rimming the ceiling and underneath the tables constantly flickered, a sign that Briar was definitely not where he was supposed to be at this time of night.

But where else could he go to gamble without his father finding out?

Briar rubbed his finger against the collar of his shirt. Out of his royal uniform, he was freed from the itchiness of the fabric against his neck and the constant discomfort that accompanied him every time he wanted to move. The shirt was plain and simple, nothing like the garb he had to wear daily in the palace. The pants he had changed into were loose and free, not only for Briar's comfort but for slipping gambling chips inside the waistband when he felt it was necessary.

And it seemed to be necessary every two rounds.

But even without the label his clothes constantly gave him, the other members at the table could not seem to keep their eyes off of him. Briar assumed it was because of how he looked; black clothing against his skin flattered him more than anything else. But what he wasn't thinking of was the fact that they'd seen his face on every newsfeed in Raedon and wanted his money out of his pockets and into theirs.

They were in for a real humbling treat, Briar thought, because he didn't have any money in his pockets.

All of his gambling chips had already been slid into the middle of the table with the rest of the enormous pile of winnings from the other five players. Briar had thrown out the large bet immediately, not caring how much he'd spent. Why would he, when it wasn't his money to begin with? Briar also had no idea how to play the card game that was afoot; all he needed that night was a drink, which he was heavily supplied with the moment he walked through the door, and a little bit of fun, something that was continuously sucked from him when he was attending his father's court functions.

Briar heard the shuffling of cards from across the table suddenly stop. He picked up his cards and held them to his chest, squinting at the pattern on the back of them. Then his eyes traveled upward to the man across from him, watching him and another bearded man put down two cards simultaneously.

Briar's general and extremely flawed perception of the game was this; once each player's turn came around, they could choose to challenge another player to a duel for the cards or skip the challenge, meaning that they would have to lose two of their own cards. The primary goal was to gain as many cards as possible by the end of the game, which was why each man challenged almost every time. A challenge included both challengers picking up a random card from their facedown deck. If the suit of the card is higher, then that means the player has won. If it is lower, then the other player takes both cards and increases their chance of winning.

Briar's eyes scanned the pair of men carefully, watching as both the younger player and the bearded man flipped their cards. He held his breath as they revealed the two faces and two numbers.

"Ha!" The bearded man erupted in victorious laughter as he slapped his hand on the table, taking the pair of cards. As he greedily shoved them into his rather large deck, Briar saw a glimpse of the corner of a low-number card from inside his sleeve.

Briar bit his lip and snickered with the bearded man. It didn't bother him in the slightest to see other people cheated out of their money. Hell, he'd been cheated too. But it seemed to be part of the regular behavior allowed here and Briar had no intentions of stopping it when it made him laugh so hard. Besides, it was part of the game. Who was he to change the unspoken rules?

Briar twisted the silver ring on his finger again, picking up his deck of cards. He shuffled them like the rest of the men around the table. Peering at the silver band, he saw each painted number on the cards he bypassed and put into the bottom of the deck. From what he'd seen, shuffling your own cards was completely on the table. In fact, Briar did it often to make sure his next card was the highest played and he would win the round.

"I'll take you," The man beside Briar pointed at the boy who'd just lost, challenging him again. They both played their cards and the younger man lost yet again, collapsing into his chair with a sour look as he gulped down the rest of the liquid from his glass. The girl who came to serve him whispered something in his ear, immediately making him sit straight up and plaster a smile on his face. Briar caught the boy's eyes, and he blushed, embarrassed that Briar had seen their exchange.

Then it was Briar's turn. He grabbed the stem of his cup with gentle fingers, tilting the glass into his mouth so that the last of his beverage disappeared under his tongue. Briar couldn't stop the smile on his face as the liquid burned a trail of fire down his throat and he coughed, unable to control himself.

"By the way you play, I would've assumed that this was your first time." The bearded man across from him scrubbed his beard. His voice was deeper than Briar expected from the shrillness of his victory laugh. "But by the way you drink, I know differently."

Briar dramatically placed the glass on the edge of the table. "By the way you look, I would've assumed you were dumber than the rest. Now I know differently."

The other men around the table laughed with Briar, and so did the bearded man. He asked through laughter, "Have you ever played this game before?"

"I'll figure it out," Briar responded, leaning back in his chair to brush the arm of a waitress passing behind his seat. The girl's skin immediately warmed as she took the empty glass away from him and practically sprinted across the tavern to replace it.

"Smart kid, smart mouth."

Briar smiled at the comment and pointed a wagging finger at him. "I'll challenge you, then."

The men around the table continued to squawk as Briar and the bearded man shuffled their cards. Briar concentrated on his ring, watching for a high number in the corner of his cards. When it came, he acted as though he was simply bored with the game and tossed the card into the middle of the table. It almost reached the pile of chips in the center as the bearded man threw out his own. Then Briar reached for his card and flipped it.

He couldn't help the smug grin that leaked onto his lips when he revealed a much higher number. Across from him, the bearded man slapped the table in good sport and slid his card towards Briar. The other four men looked at Briar with wide eyes as he tucked his cards into the middle of his deck, jealous of the growing size of his pile.

"Not what you were expecting?" Briar taunted the bearded man when he took a rather large swig from his heavy glass.

He licked his lips and brushed his gruff beard. "I was expecting a little more risk from someone with your reputation and all."

"What were you thinking?" Briar felt a nervous twinge creep into his stomach, but easily shoved it away when his eyes flickered to the pile of treasure sitting in front of him.

"Rapid five."

He said it loud enough for the entire tavern to hear. Around them, everything seemed to slow down as if time itself had warped, and was now listening to their conversation too.

From what Briar knew, playing rapid five meant two things; no more shuffling of the deck, and the game ended when the round was over. Each player takes five cards from the top of their deck and, as each is overturned, they see whose cards add up to the highest amount.

Briar sat up straight in his chair, feeling his interest beginning to peak. He cleared his throat. "What do I get if I win?"

The bearded man's eyes traveled from Briar to the center of the table, where all the chips were piled on top of each other in uneven, disheveled stacks. "All that," he said, unable to contain his gluttony.

"And do I get a cake to go with it?" Briar taunted, biting the corner of his lip.

"If you want."

The people around the tavern approached the table, waiting to see if Briar would take the bait or not. He could hear his heart beating twice its normal speed, but he wasn't nervous. He could feel the green desire spilling into his eyes like black ink into water.

How could he possibly say no?

"I'll give it a shot." He tried to sound casual, but he feared the yearning in his voice slipped past his efforts. Everyone else in the tavern cheered over his shoulder, confidently slapping him on the back. The waitress from earlier wormed her way toward the front of the horde, allowing her teasing hand to rub against the back of Briar's neck as she put his glass down in front of him. Feeling the insides of his stomach beginning to boil over, Briar downed the entire drink in one swift gulp.

Ahead of him, the bearded man was already placing five of his cards facedown. Briar followed his lead, slowly putting each of his cards on the table to add to the rise the room got when he did so. Briar moved with careful hands, not bothering to look at the reflection in his ring before taking the next card. What did it matter, anyway? There was no shuffling allowed when playing rapid five.

Both Briar and the bearded man flipped over their first cards at the same time. Briar's was the highest card in the set. His lips instantly parted in a smirk as the man across from him growled. When the second cards were flipped, Briar's was revealed to be a moderate number from somewhere near the middle of the deck while the bearded man's was a higher number, but not high enough to beat Briar's previous card.

The third card flip put the bearded man up by at least ten numbers. Briar scowled at his deck, cursing silently to himself. He glared at his second to last card, wishing he could see through the back and then threatening it to raise his score.

The cards were flipped. Briar was even with the bearded man now.

Briar's heart danced twice its normal exhilarating speed as they flipped over their last cards, revealing the same number in both corners.

Briar knew that the rules called for a final draw, a final flip of the cards.

The boy from earlier, who had lost twice in a row, got up from his seat, moving through the crowd to behind Briar.

"Not everyone's a winner, pal." He patted Briar's back in support, although Briar was sure he wouldn't need it. He only needed to win by one point; how likely was it he wouldn't achieve that?

"You would know, wouldn't you?" Briar chuckled, watching as the bearded man looked up from his deck across the table.

"Willing to wager more on it?" he asked, looking Briar up and down. "The rules state that — "

"I want you to give back everything you've stolen from the pile in the middle of the table." Briar took a brief pause, collecting his breath from where it had fallen onto the floor. "So that when I win, I'm not robbed of anything."

The entire tavern seemed to shift in response to Briar. The bearded man as well, lifting his arm and draining a pocket inside his sleeve of gambling chips he'd sneaked from the treasure mound earlier in the game. He wasn't shy about it either, which was what made Briar laugh to himself. The chips slid out of his clothing and landed with graceful clinks on the metal table before he was finished.

"You have yourself a deal."

Both he and Briar reached for their cards and flipped them in synchronized time with each other. The bearded man's face melted into a mischievous smile as he watched Briar's eyes go hollow, looking down at his cards.

In his fingers was the lowest card in the deck. In the man's, the highest.

Disappointed sighs and loud cheers echoed through the space. Around him, people flowing in and out of the bar reached to pat Briar on the back with pity.

Briar supposed he should've felt sorry for himself, or at least slightly disappointed. But in reality, he couldn't bring himself to feel any guilt for losing everything he'd bet that night. The rush of the loss was the reason he came. Even though it was money he wouldn't be able to spend the next time he played, the rush of losing it simply made him want to keep coming.

Briar supposed that was called an addiction.

He stood from his chair and brushed the hair out of his eyes. He would certainly come back again, if not the next night, then the one after that. Honestly, who doesn't want to be served lukewarm alcohol as they watch their money being taken away by a man with a bushy beard and crumbs hidden inside of it?

Just as he was turning away from the table and beginning to follow the crowd towards the door, Briar heard the skirl of a gambling chip being flung into the air. He turned around just in time to catch it.

"Come back sometime soon. And hey," the bearded man nodded mockingly towards the chip, "Don't feel bad, a ton of people waste their money on challenging me."

Briar sighed, allowing his shoulders to sag as he pretended to feel sorrowful. "I would love to insult you right now, but I fear nature has taken the opportunity from me." He dropped the act and replaced his frown with a light smile. "Have a pleasant night."

Briar departed the tavern accompanied by boisterous laughter and the lingering sensation of inexpensive alcohol trickling down his throat. He left the underground tavern and ascended the concrete steps to the sidewalk, the neon lights of Polaris illuminating the road for him. He looked up into the dark sky above his head, sighing at the stars that laughed at him as he crossed the street.

Billions of years ago, there was a yellow star in the sky called the sun that imploded and sent the Earth into a spiraling disaster. Radiation and heat plagued the planet, killing all life and drying up every pint of water there was. The explosion of the star caused a mass extinction of all those who weren't selected by elite government officials to survive in an underground bunker hidden off the coast of what was once called the Atlantic Ocean.

Briar rarely cared about the history of how Raedon built itself up when the bunker became too cramped and society was forced to resume life above ground. However, there was nothing to resume because everything was reduced to particles of dust. Briar hadn't paid much attention to his lessons on history when he was younger, but had enough of his own thoughts to know that humanity was better off now than it was before the sun died. Everything in Raedon was built to be perfect; there were no mistakes, except for Briar accidentally locking the kitchen quarter door behind him after he'd snuck out earlier that night. Avoiding his father's wrath was the thing he always seemed to mess up.

With that thought in mind, Briar knew that there was no other way he could get into Sanctum Palace unless he wanted to scale the sides of the platinum and black walls and plummet to his death.

Deciding not to die before making a show of it first, Briar approached the Arc, a bridge that separated the city of Polaris from the palace. Peering down at him, the structure gleamed with the blazing lights it omitted. It was like a beacon for the rest of the city, an overheating light bulb but blue; and better.

There were cameras mounted on the glass bridge that would recognize Briar's face, but he tucked his chin into his chest anyway, shoving his hands into his pockets as he walked along the sky bridge. The cameras followed him through motion sensor technology until he approached the large doors, guarded by a legion of his father's soldiers.

They all stared at him as he drew nearer, but said nothing as one stepped forward with a small device in his hand.

"Don't bother," Briar said casually, lifting his chin so they could see his face. The soldiers wouldn't need to run a facial recognition scan on him; only he would walk back to the palace through the front doors at a time like this smelling of cheap alcohol and sweat.

Briar waited for the doors to open and waved to the soldiers, pressing his lips into a thin smile. "Just pretend I wasn't here," he told them. "Like a ghost."

Then he made haunting sounds with puckered lips as he strutted down the rest of the hallway, twirling a single gambling chip through his fingers.

It is impossible to govern a group of people, no matter how relative in size, without guidelines. Humans are wired like machines; they function the same way but with different needs. They have admirable skills in different situations, yet they have the same list of necessities needed to stay alive. They lust for attention and constant eyes on them, no matter where it is coming from.

But they are also like machines in how they are circuited to crave more out of their lives. Studies in the Republic Archives have shown that one in every five humans turns towards rebellion to quench that craving. It is like a tickle in their mind, an itch that cannot be scratched. It is a truly dangerous thing to concede to a poisoned mind, telling you that you can have everything you want; and more.

This leads to more advantageous crimes and more unstable actions that in the long run, will make them even more thirsty for what they cannot have. Kindling the flame of rebellion in one's mind is a mistake. Telling a human that he may have those kinds of thoughts was the first misstep that one makes when trying to suppress revolt. Any attempt at insurrection must be stomped out before it becomes a true flame in the mind, one that would burn far worse than it would itch.

There is a limit to how much one man can restrain himself, and that limit is growing ever so thin.

So, if a man cannot control himself, other men will do it for him.

- An excerpt of the first Supreme Leader's journal, extracted from the Archives of the Imperial Republic of Raedon

---

Chapter Three

"Vivimus quoniam morimur."
- *Let us live since we must die.*

Briar reached up to his neck, shoving two fingers in between the collar of his royal uniform and his skin. He could feel a red mark blooming as he itched the space, groaning at the flame beneath his fingers.

"What the hell happened to our clothes being made of the finest material?" He whined, scrunching his nose as he tried to peek down at his neck. "They're so scratchy."

"Perhaps if you wore them more, they would feel more comfortable." Next to him, Achlys Sonnen reached a pale hand to slap Briar's fingers away from his neck.

In the electric blue lights of the palace, Achlys reminded Briar of a white sheet. His skin was paper pale, and he moved so fluidly between motions that Briar believed if he wanted to walk into a wall, he could coast straight through. He had tried to get his friend to try it multiple times, but Achlys seemed hell-bent on the idea of not breaking his nose.

Which made sense to Briar because Achlys's nose was quite straight.

"I'd rather not." Briar countered, turning the corner and finding himself in a hallway of windows on their left side. The walls were paneled with black and silver steel, strong metals that were found in the ground after the sun's radiation hit Earth. It's what almost all the buildings in Raedon were made of; strong materials for a strong Republic.

Looking out of the windows, Briar blinked at the stars that constantly watched them. This sol, he woke up to a blinding headache and remembered the night he had before and how those very stars giggled at him all the way home. He would scold them, having much practice being scolded himself. Briar even made a bet with the celestial lights, telling them that he would drink another bottle of champagne if his father reprimanded him that sol and two bottles if he didn't.

Briar was hoping for the latter, but knew he shouldn't get his hopes up.

"You're right." Achlys drew Briar's eyes back to him with a flick of his ring-littered hand. "You'd rather wear civilian clothing like the rest of the help around here."

Briar shrugged his shoulders and grunted. The royal uniform Briar was being forced to wear was made from coarse fabrics that fit him so tightly, he felt like his arms were losing more circulation by the minute.

"At least I can move in other clothes," Briar argued, although he didn't need to put much effort into annoying Achlys. It seemed to happen naturally for him, like a long-lost art from the days before the sun collapsed on itself. "I can barely walk in this." Then Briar suddenly stopped moving in general, standing stick straight in the center of the hallway as Achlys continued moving. "Oh well. I don't think

I'll be able to make it today. I might as well go back to my room and — "

"Go back to your room so you can sneak out again?" Achlys snapped, grabbing Briar's arm and pulling him along. "I don't think so."

Briar cursed, but kept pace with him. "Next, they'll have me wearing a mask so I can't move my mouth."

"That would be wise." Achlys rolled his pale eyes. "You'd save your father the embarrassment of roaming to gambling halls and taverns all night." His eyebrow lifted as he turned to Briar and asked, "Exactly how much money did you lose this time?"

Briar clenched his teeth and sucked in a breath, hissing at the question. "Bold of you to assume I would count the amount."

He reached into his pocket and pulled out the single gambling chip the bearded man had flung at him the night before. Briar twirled it in his fingers and tossed it between each hand before throwing it sideways to Achlys.

"What is this?" He scowled, inspecting both sides of the chip.

"I won that." Briar flashed him a winning smile. "Keep it."

"I don't want it." Achlys shoved the chip back into Briar's hands so fast that Briar would've thought there was an uncured disease festering on it. Then his head snapped back to Briar as if the confusion had just set in. "You won *one* gambling chip?"

Briar bit the corner of his lip. "Technically, I lost a lot more, but it's a long story."

"I don't want to hear it."

"Smart choice."

"Did you at least cover yourself up?" Achlys raised his voice, hoping that Briar would give him the response he wanted to hear.

"If you're asking me if I had a shirt on this time, then yes. I did." Briar puffed out his chest proudly.

"Making bad decisions and drinking at the same time won't help your public image, Briar." Achlys berated him how Briar imagined a mother would reprimand her child. He had that same look to him, the one that made Briar think it would, in fact, be easier to slam his own nose into a wall.

"Not to brag, but I don't need alcohol to make bad decisions."

Achlys might've been one of Briar's last remaining friends, but he didn't share Briar's mischievous nature. Achlys would rather follow his own father around learning how to become one of the Supreme Leader's Advisors than run behind Briar as they evaded soldiers running after him for stealing weapons from the training room.

"You constantly set my expectations low and fail to achieve them." Achlys slapped Briar on the arm as they turned the last corner, approaching a set of tall iron doors. They were guarded by soldiers, ones that Briar passed without a word as the doors opened.

"Whoever told you to be yourself gave you bad advice." He winked, leaving Achlys behind in the corridor as he sauntered into the throne room.

It was an enormous space, packed tightly with his father's court. The walls were taller than the ones in the corridor and the chandeliers were somehow grander, lighting a blue pathway up to the dais and Supreme Leader's throne in the back of the room. The seat was made from cold spires of bleached metal, adorned with carvings of stars just above the crown of the Supreme Leader's head. Behind the seat was another mural of windows, looking out into the blinking sky beyond.

The entire court turned to face Briar as he strolled through. He could hear their murmurings about him, mostly about how he jumped from the highest balcony in the palace to one only a few levels lower not too long ago. Briar raised his chin while hearing the rumors, glad that word had spread around. He was sincerely proud of himself for landing as smoothly as he did and only fracturing three fingers in the process.

As he got closer to the dais, Briar saw that Achlys had already entered behind him and found his place near the front of the pack. He glanced at Briar with a suspicious gaze, as if to tell him he'd better hope his father didn't learn where he was last night.

Standing next to Achlys was Quinn Vega, the Captain of his father's guard. She too had on a uniform, although this one looked far superior to Briar's and seemed to be padded on the inside for extra build. Her chin was raised high, looking at the Supreme Leader on top of the dais. Her copper hair spilled down the length of her back and she had a scar on her jaw, a small thing that was stark white against her sandy skin. There were weapons strapped to her hips like jewelry on a noble, ones that made Briar shiver to look at. He'd seen her in the training room throughout his years in Sanctum Palace and didn't want to think about crossing her like he had the soldiers in her command.

So, considering his caution, Briar ignored the Captain and took his first steps onto the dais, immediately catching his father's daunting eyes.

There he sat, leaning sideways on his throne, his court humming around him like the star at the center of their system. Dorin Atlas peered at the screen Advisor Sonnen placed before him, hands curling into tight fists. His skin had the same honey tinge as Briar's, but he was aged enough to have a beard on his chin and wrinkles in the corners of his eyes. As soon as Briar reached the side of his throne, though, he waved Achlys's father away with a finger and looked at his son from the side of his eye. Reluctantly, Briar stepped closer and leaned down to hear what he had to say.

The Supreme Leader's voice was icy as he asked, "Where were you last night?"

Briar closed his eyes for a moment, already ready with a simmering lie. "I was with Achlys the entire night. My maid can prove it."

"You cannot pay someone off with money you gambled away." His father snapped, keeping his voice low enough that the Advisors standing behind them wouldn't hear, but fierce enough to hit Briar like a blunt weapon. "Achlys was with his father and me all night in a meeting,"

Briar growled, his eyes flickering up to Achlys to see the man's shoulders bouncing with laughter. He'd caught Briar in a lie and set the trap simultaneously. Beside him, Quinn lifted her eyebrows and pressed her lips together, trying her best to hold in her chuckle.

Briar cursed when his father spit into his ear again. "I'll ask you one more time. Where were you?"

"Here and there." Briar shrugged, standing up straight again to lean on the side of his father's metal throne. It was something he'd gotten scolded for millions of times, but he didn't seem to care; he thought it was comical when other people were annoyed with him. "Mostly there though."

"You might not care for your image as my son, but care for it as the future Supreme Leader." Briar's father sat straight himself, looking outwards towards the court. By now, the doors on the end of the hall had shut again and there was a polite buzz of talk around the room. It echoed off the silver walls, but Briar couldn't hear anything but his father despite trying to zone his voice out multiple times. "Raedon will be your responsibility, and I suggest you take that more seriously."

As his father said the words, Briar mouthed them in unison. When he was finished, he realized his father had been watching him do so the entire time. Briar chuckled, running a hand through his hair before lazily pointing at the court. "I won't make it to thirty. They're all yours."

"I want you to take this with a mature attitude." The Supreme Leader turned his head away from his son, shaking it as he did so. "The alarms sound more often than they used to."

Briar rolled his eyes. There were cameras scattered throughout the city; not one corner of a building or shadowed area was left unseen by invisible eyes. The sirens went off when someone was up past curfew and spotted by the cameras. From what Briar had heard, the interlopers were rebels who wanted to overthrow his father and the Republic.

He'd also heard that they were publicly executed moments after being spotted.

"The rebels have gained a foothold in Antares. It won't take long before they come to Polaris as well." The Supreme Leader continued.

"Send out your soldiers." Briar flicked a hand towards the perimeter of the room. Then he glanced directly at their Captain, now speaking with Achlys and avoiding his gaze. "You've got plenty of those to spare."

"They're not things to *spare*. You will learn that soon."

Briar couldn't help but roll his eyes again. He didn't respond, trying to seem as solemn as he could. But inside, he was holding back the laughter bursting in his throat.

The rebels had been trying to tear down the Supreme Leader and his Advisors for years. What made his father think that they'll suddenly have the power to overthrow him now out of all the times they'd tried? They called themselves the Rising Sun, something Briar thought was a piece of poetic trash seeing as there hadn't been a sun to occupy their sky in billions of years. Regardless of their lyrical title, they seemed to strike fear where their name was said.

They've been running raids, stealing from trains going from Polaris to other districts in Raedon. It seemed to be their primary goal to cause chaos; they did it almost everywhere. Running through streets with fire on torches, screaming about how the Supreme Leader was lying about the sun. Briar didn't know what his father was holding back from Raedon, and he didn't want to know either.

This was the first time Briar had heard anything about them in Antares. Antares was one of the northern districts in Raedon; what possessed the rebels to take a stand there over anywhere else in the Republic? Briar thought it was a completely amateur move to settle on the place farthest from Polaris and his father.

Not that he would willingly give tips to them in the first place.

The Supreme Leader had gone back to talking with Advisor Sonnen by the time Briar escaped his thoughts. Looking around the court, he could spot the faces of enemies he had already made. Most of them were members of his father's council on different levels, but others were regular members of court. Briar had been caught fooling around too many times by the guards only to be later scolded by his father in the company of Captain Vega.

But what difference would a good impression make if he might be dead by the next sol cycle?

"They need to be put down." Briar heard his father say quickly to Advisor Sonnen next to him. He was as pale as his son. "They will only get stronger if we don't figure out where they're coming from."

"We have areas marked, sir." The Advisor was saying. He pulled up a screen on his tablet and gave it to Briar's father. "Cassiopeia, a small section in Rigel, and-"

"They're everywhere." His father concluded with a grim look at the rest of the throne room. They still hadn't been told why they were there, and Briar was becoming slightly restless about it too.

"Do they have a base?" His father asked, moving images and words around on the tablet.

"Not that we know of yet, sir. They seem to appear in random places, but when they retreat, they never go to the same spot once."

"They can't hide everywhere all at once."

"I realize that, sir." The Advisor bit his lip. "But I-"

Finally, his father interrupted him. "There's no point in trying to continue ignoring them. Send troops to the locations; not to capture, but to scout. I want to see what they think they're doing." The Supreme Leader handed the tablet back to the Advisor and cleared his throat. "Hopefully, this solution will fix a few things. Open the doors."

At the other end of the throne room, the grand silver doors split in the middle once more. The entire court, including Briar, looked at the center aisle as a lone figure walked down it, the chamber becoming an eerily kind of silent.

The figure walked with lethal elegance, their hips swaying as they swept across the floor. Their uniform was bone white, threaded so tightly there was no inch of skin left exposed to the open air. Briar seemed to be in a trance when he saw the silver rifle strapped across the figure's back, the top of the scope just peeking over their white hood. There was a mask secured to their face too, rendering their identity a restricted privilege.

The Phantom marched towards the dais, spreading fear through the court like blood bleeding into woven fabric.

Briar had heard of the ghost assassin on various occasions. He'd listened to his father and the Advisors discussing the soulless creature in many of their political meetings and gossip around the court. The Phantom was rumored to be nameless. Their identity switched everywhere they traveled, never being the same person twice. The assassin never appeared on any of the Republic's databases besides being all over Raedon at a moment's notice. The ghost never took off their mask, leaving their face a mystery to those brave enough to wonder what they looked like.

The entire court remained soundless as the Phantom reached the base of the throne, bowing their head. The Supreme Leader looked down on the assassin with cruel eyes, watching as the haunting figure stared straight back.

Briar found her voice surprisingly female as her aquamarine eyes tilted up in a smile underneath her mask.

"It's been a while since I visited Polaris."

In a perfect world, there is no need to search for something better. Everything is already as it should be. There are no more solutions because the problems that humanity used to face have been erased. Scratched from our memories, like extracting a diseased cell from a body.

Yet there are still small moments where mankind doubts itself and its ability to thrive rather than simply survive.

They call themselves the Sun Searchers; believers that a fraction of the sun remains and is burning on the other side of the world. They left Raedon, the safety of the known, to explore the unknown.

That only explains why they never came back and why people cast away hope for another yellow star.

It's impossible, of course, one of the few things in Raedon that is truly non-viable. When the sun imploded, it contracted into itself and became a white dwarf star, so deprived of its energy it could barely function.

The event left the sky in permanent darkness, an everlasting night. It polluted the air with poison and drained the oceans until they became monstrous valleys in between highlands. There would be no more rain, no more clouds. There would only be what humankind used to call a phoenix rising from the ashes.

The Imperial Republic would be that phoenix.

The sun was a representation of an old world, a
dead world.
Why would anyone want to bring back the dead?

- An excerpt of the first Supreme Leader's
journal, extracted from the Archives of the
Imperial Republic of Raedon

Chapter Four

"Oderint dum metuant."
- *Let them hate, so long as they fear.*

"I'm glad you received my message." Supreme Leader Dorin Atlas peered down at Wren, where she still stood at the foot of his dais. His cold voice cut through the absence of sound. The entire room remained motionless, paralyzed by Wren and her sudden appearance in their throne room. "You're a very hard person to track down."

The corner of Wren's lips ticked upwards. She liked it that way. It was one reason she had picked white for her uniform. Not to solidify her name with her image, although that helped in striking fear wherever she went. It was because the color white was so rare in Raedon that she couldn't resist. She wanted people to talk about her and spread her lies around the world for her. It wasn't hard to seal her story in stone when she first became the ghost assassin, and it wouldn't be complicated to correct those rumors if they were incorrect.

If she wanted to correct them, that was. The lies that kept spinning around the assassin kept her safe in a web of mystery. No one was close to knowing who she was, and no one ever would be.

She was the Phantom, after all. She almost didn't exist.

"I would've liked to keep it that way, but you made this engagement sound so imperative," Wren answered, feeling the court at her back tense. They could only see her from one angle and hear her from the echoes bouncing from the walls. She'd made sure her uniform was perfect for them, seeing as they would only get one first glance at her.

The fabric making up the entire garment was a thick form of white leather, protecting her on all sides like armor without the iron. Her hood and mask were constructed of the same material, molded to fit her perfectly. She wore gloves and knee-high boots, both of them the same milky white color as the rest. The white strap stretching across her chest held the rifle secured to her spine, the shine of the scope flashing behind her head. There were thin pockets in the sleeves, pants, and back skirt that stopped at her knees, hiding small knives she'd sharpened just for this occasion and a gun she'd loaded right before she walked into the room.

It was amusing to her to watch the faces of the soldiers outside the throne room doors as they listened to the sound of her clicking the ammunition into place. They didn't know whether to stop her or run.

"I am grateful you found it just as important." Dorin continued. The Advisors dressed in deep purple robes behind his throne looked everywhere but in her direction.

"Don't be grateful until you know what my answer will be." Wren already knew what he was going to ask her and what her answer was, but that didn't stop her from drawing out the exchange to further instill the fear of her unpredictability.

"I hear that you have a reputation around Raedon." The Supreme Leader spoke with a magnitude that would shake anyone he was talking to. Well, all except Wren. "You never seem to stay in one place at a time."

Wren looked up into Dorin's face, remembering the image Eden had shown her not too long ago with the Supreme Leader and his son's faces plastered on the front. They looked almost identical, with one sitting and the other standing next to him. All except for Briar's auburn eyes; his father's were black and beady.

In Briar's expression, Wren found no evidence that he knew who she was or that she had pulled up every file and news article ever written about him last night. She scoured all the Republic's databases and left her tracks untraceable as she did so, observing every piece of information there was on Dorin's son and clinging onto it like it was her last lifeline. In fact, Briar seemed confused at her unexpected arrival, much like the rest of his father's court. He simply stared at her with unblinking eyes, his upper lip curling into a snarl.

"I get bored easily and have ears everywhere," Wren replied with a slight curve to her voice, taking her eyes away from Briar. "Travel is the pinnacle of my job, after all."

"What you occupy yourself with is *not* a job." Dorin snapped from his throne, white-knuckling the arms of the chair. "It violates all the Imperial Republic's laws."

Surely not everything Wren did was against the law. Yes, she went about climbing buildings in the night and assassinating people on the Rising Sun's hit list, but she didn't do so without sanitizing her hands before getting on a public train to get there.

"Am I here for you to charge me?" Wren said, letting a bored scoff roll off her tongue.

The Supreme Leader sucked in a breath. Wren was digging deeper under his skin by the second. But finally, he said, "No, you are not."

The court around them buzzed with conversation. How could Dorin not charge her? She was an assassin, after all, an unsanctioned one roaming their streets with a rifle strapped to her back and knives twirling around in her hands! Surely, she should be put into some kind of high-security prison.

Wren chuckled at their remarks, knowing that even if someone managed to place her in a high-security prison, she would be out within the hour.

"You say you've traveled around my Republic, have you?" Dorin spoke over the discussion in his court and eventually, all talk came to a close.

"I have."

"Then I assume you've been to Polaris enough to know that we do not bring weapons into places of formal gathering." he looked directly at the gun fastened to her hip and the long rifle parallel to her spine. "It's a sign of disrespect."

Wren didn't answer, letting her eyes wander around the perimeter of the room. She noticed that people in the crowd shrank away from her gaze when she looked in their direction, creating a perfect line of vision toward the soldiers surrounding the entire room. Their black uniforms matched the ones outside the door, although these guards were armed with knives as well. Then Wren's eye caught on a specific copper-haired soldier standing in the front row, nearly inches away from the stairs on the dais. Her withered gaze was trained directly on Wren, and they locked eyes for a moment before Wren opted to look away.

"Your soldiers are armed with weapons." Wren turned to face Dorin again. He seemed to watch her the entire time. "I'm not clear about what separates them from me."

"These soldiers are a part of my guard." He extended a hand to the left wall of his throne. People's eyes followed his hand as an excuse to avoid looking at Wren. "Their job is to protect my court and me."

"Aren't I here to do the same?"

Dorin took a moment to pause, halfway in between a response and awe that he could contradict himself. "Of course," he said, slowly nodding his head. It was obvious to Wren that he didn't enjoy being corrected and it made a kernel of laughter burst inside her chest. She enjoyed watching the Supreme Leader of Raedon correct himself for her; it reminded Wren how human he was.

And along with that, how easily he could be brought down.

"My son, Briar Atlas." Dorin waved a hand at Briar and his son's expression changed from curious to annoyed as he stepped closer to his father's throne, listening to his formal title. "My second in command and future Supreme Leader of Raedon and the Imperial Republic."

Before Briar had a chance to speak for himself, which he wanted to do by his expression, Dorin slightly jerked his head in Wren's direction. She watched with glee as Briar pressed his lips together, forbidding himself from snapping at his father as he stepped down from the dais, meeting

Wren at the end of the center aisle. He made it a point to stand as far away from her as he could, keeping his heels connected with the bottom stair of the dais.

"There's no point in introducing myself now," he grumbled. "If I do anything from this point on to offend you, know that it's intentional." When his eyes finally met her own, she saw a spark of interest flare through his expression. His hair was cedar colored and disheveled, falling into his face at odd angles. The freckles dotting his cheeks and nose made him look even more childish than he was acting. Briar looked her up and down with his chin raised, squinting when he reached her face as if he was trying to see through her mask. She sneered at him under the fabric, unbothered by his previous comment.

"The radicals that call themselves the Rising Sun have become a minor threat to our safety," Dorin spoke with a booming voice, no longer talking to just her but the entirety of his court. Everyone listened, embracing his words with awe. "They are constantly trying to expand in our largest districts. But they are failing."

It took all the energy in Wren's body to keep herself from bursting into laughter. The Supreme Leader knew nothing about the rebels, and what he thought he knew was false.

The rebels had people in all seven districts of Raedon, but they weren't just in the largest ones; they were everywhere. They kept themselves a secret and didn't want to be heard about, allowing the Supreme Leader and his Advisors to receive only the information the rebels had planted for them. The only reason the Republic thought they were spotting rebels in their streets and sounding alarms was because the Rising Sun wanted them to think that. Despite Dorin's confident stature when speaking about the Rising Sun, he had no idea that they were not failing, and no idea where they were mainly located.

But Wren had been there; it was where she came from before escaping into Raedon.

The rebels called it Novus. It was outside of Raedon and away from the Imperial Republic on the ground that everyone believed was still decimated by the sun's radiation and no longer habitable because of toxic air. There was a society built there, but one majorly different from Polaris and the other districts under the Supreme Leader's rule.

While Raedon's skies were dark and strewn with stars, Novus had a piece of the imploded Sun still shining in theirs.

"The Rising Sun is not a danger to our lives," Dorin continued, desperately trying to grasp at the lies he was spreading. "They set fire to only our name and run rampant through our streets. They cause no damage despite false statements and the power outages that leave our homes dark in the night."

Wren held her eyes in the same position to resist, rolling them towards the back of her head. The rebels had nothing to do with the power outages around the cities. It was Raedon's own dwindling power supply. The only reason the rebels hadn't put a stop to the rumors yet was because it gave them more attention. If people were afraid of them, they would become more powerful.

That was one reason Wren was in the throne room at all. Getting Polaris to collapse was just one cut on her long list of things to do to bring down the Supreme Leader.

Someone shifted in the crowd to the left of Wren. Her eyes snapped towards the movement, finding a man with eyes so pale they looked almost silver standing next to the soldier with the copper hair. He was not staring at Wren, but at Briar.

When Wren dragged her gaze from the man to Briar, she found him looking at her rather than back at his friend. His eyes didn't flicker like people's normally did when she gazed at them. Instead, he stared at her through his long eyelashes, barely blinking and breathing so slowly she thought his heart might stop entirely. When his father spoke again, he finally blinked and snapped out of his possessive trance.

"But despite the feeble attempts of the rebels, they have been able to get close to the lives of my son and myself." Everyone in the room gasped as if it was a shock to them that someone would want to kill their dictator of a leader. "It is of utmost importance to me to keep our bloodline secure during these times of turmoil."

Below his father and away from his eyeline, Briar let out a long sigh and mouthed his father's words like a speech he had memorized in his mind. Wren had to admit he was very well rehearsed.

"So, I will offer you a deal, Phantom." Dorin's mouth twisted in reluctance to say his own words. His brow was already creasing in conflict. "You will become my son's guard and, in return, I will pardon you of all your crimes."

Wren had been waiting for Dorin to drop the grenade. Behind her, the entire court erupted into chaos. She listened to them as they complained, even wailed at the prospect of her protecting their Supreme Leader's beloved son. She heard every word they said and still ignored it, instead focusing on Briar, now whipping backward to face his father.

"What the hell is this?" He howled over the havoc. "I don't need a personal guard following me around like dead weight!" Briar's stare flickered back to her for a moment, surveying her from base to top for the fifth time. "Look at her! You said it yourself, she's a murderer!"

Wren snickered under her mask. It didn't bother her what people said, especially right to her face. In truth, she liked it when people gossiped and spoke about her behind her back. To her, it meant that they were too afraid to confront her directly.

"Silence!" The Supreme Leader's voice boomed across the chamber, echoing off the silver walls so loud he could be heard minutes after he spoke. Only when it was completely silent did he calm, furious at the outburst of opinions.

"What makes you think I would pay for my crimes in the first place?"

Dorin did a double take, and the Advisors froze.

The Supreme Leader pinned Wren down with a deadly stare that she had no quarrels returning. "Excuse me?"

"You've never caught me before. What makes you confident that you could do it now?" With his father at his back, Briar could let his face contort into something satisfactory as Wren insulted Dorin. His mouth tilted into a downward smile, trying his best not to let his body bounce as he choked in laughter. He might not like the idea of her, but he enjoyed seeing someone else put his father down for a change.

"I-- " The Supreme Leader stuttered, shocked once more that she would impose such a question on him. "You are surrounded by the most elite soldiers in the Republic. I could have you arrested in front of my entire court in the blink of an eye.

Wren allowed herself to scoff out loud. "Those imbeciles?" She jerked her head towards the perimeter of the room again. "Not a chance."

In the corner of her eye, Wren saw the copper-headed woman shift and felt the weight of her heated stare. She must be in charge of the soldiers Wren had just insulted. She'd been here less than an hour and was already making enemies.

"Will you take the offer or not?" The Supreme Leader's voice tightened like a rope pulled between two corners. He stared at her with knives in his black eyes, fisting the arms of his throne so hard he began to visibly shake. "Mind you, you only get one chance to take it before I order you to be executed in front of the entire Republic."

Wren tilted her head to the side, pretending to think about the offer. While she did enjoy public spectacles that practically handed her all the attention, she didn't quite like the idea of being shot in the back of the head.

Besides, this was why the Rising Sun had given her this assignment in the first place. How could she do anything but comply?

Wren Sitara felt hundreds of eyes aimed at her when she spoke again.

"I accept."

Nothing kills a man like himself.

It is a curious thing when the body works against itself. Beneath the skin, there are over 200 bones, 639 skeletal muscles, 78 organs, and over 30 trillion cells. These components work together like an engine. They assist one another in creating new ways for the body to adapt to its environment, doing their best to ensure the safety of their sanctuary underneath the skin.

The right side of the human heart collects blood that is low in oxygen levels. It pumps this blood into a human's lungs, where it gathers a fresh supply of new oxygen. When the blood returns to the left side of the heart, it is ready to be pumped into the brain and the rest of the body. The heart is the central node of the entire human being.

It was a shame when disease began to tear it apart. According to the Archives of the Republic, a disease is a severe disorder in the function of the human body that can cause several symptoms and anatomical changes. These diseases occur when viruses and bacteria enter the body and begin to multiply at a rapid rate. When the 30 trillion cells beneath the skin are damaged due to the infection, the signs of the specific virus begin to appear. Scientists used to pathetically believe that there was only so much that they could do to help a person diagnosed with a specific disease, the risk of saving them became far too complicated and expensive.

But risk did not exist in the Atlantic 1078, therefore, neither did disease.

When individuals were being selected for the few hundred allowed in the bunker, many ill patients were immediately put on the list. When humanity was sure that it would not die due to the conditions of the world above them and the scarcity of supplies below the ground, they began to experiment.

I am not a scientist myself, but I have run enough tests and diagnostics to know one thing; man is more likely to succeed in saving humanity when they know that they can die just as easily as the rest. It only took 25 years before humanity became immune to sickness. The genetic makeup of the human body was a limit, one that had been broken when scientists developed a cure to create a permanent barrier around all 30 trillion cells and prevent any ailments from ever destroying a human life again.

The only thing that could kill a man now was himself.

How ironic.

- An excerpt of the first Supreme Leader's journal, extracted from the Archives of the Imperial Republic of Raedon

Chapter Five

"Specie fallax."
-The appearance of things is deceptive.

Briar was used to being the target of assassination attempts. It didn't faze him that rebels were getting closer to Polaris because not once did they succeed in hurting him or his father. Sure, there had been that one incident when Briar was bowed over the dinner table clawing at his throat because he had gulped down poisoned wine. And then that other time when he'd almost gotten shot because he was fooling around at a press meeting. But other than that, he'd never been touched by the Rising Sun.

Briar itched his neck underneath his collar, slamming the doors to his room shut. He ran a clammy hand through his hair, feeling his face beginning to burn more scarlet by the second.

It was ridiculous for his father to think that he needed a babysitter following him around everywhere he went. How would he live? He would be watched more than he ever had been in his entire life! Even though Briar enjoyed the attention people brought him when they did watch him, he didn't need the eyes of a murderer stalking him at all times!

Hell, she was an assassin! Who's to say she wouldn't be going out at night to kill people right under his father's nose?

Briar wiped the back of his hand across his face, breathing heavily. He stepped further into his darkened room and leaned on the edge of the desk in the center of the space, not bothering to turn on the lights near the door. He needed this moment alone. He needed to figure out what to do; how to get rid of the Phantom before she ever stepped within another five feet of him.

Briar scrubbed a hand down his face, letting out a heated breath as he began to claw at the fabric on his neck again. But before he could take it off, he heard a small shift in the corner of the room. Briar's eyes immediately darted towards his armoire on the left wall, searching the shadows.

He saw the silver reflection of her scope before the rest of her.

"Here to kill me too?" Briar's face flushed scarlet as he set his lips into a hard line.

The Phantom stepped out of the darkness. Closer to her now, Briar could see the intricate details of her uniform. He wondered if she crafted it herself.

"Not yet." Her voice was softer than it was in the throne room.

Briar chuckled and then scoffed, stopping suddenly when he realized she was being genuine. "I saw what you did on the news."

The Phantom didn't respond for a moment. She took another step further into the middle of the room to reveal herself fully. Briar could see the small pockets lining the inside of her uniform's short train that was filled with silver knives. The assassin looked at him through piercing aquamarine eyes, scoping down his length like invisible blades.

"How do you know it was me?"

"Who else would make a performance out of a murder?" Briar's voice was clipped. The news coverage he'd seen last sol before escaping to the tavern was truly gruesome. She'd killed the apprentice of an Advisor and left a mess to prove that he put up a struggle. Briar couldn't help but shudder, remembering the scene even though most of it had already been cleaned up so the footage could be aired across Raedon.

"I thought you would appreciate my presentation." A tremor seemed to shake the ground when the assassin met him at the desk, leaning on the other side of it.

His bedroom was a large space lined with black metal walls that now displayed dark reflections of them both. The lights were still off, yet Briar could see, watching the Phantom's gaze travel around the room. He didn't think there was much for her to see, unless she was looking to climb into the bed dawned with silk sheets on the far wall or glance around his desk at the papers strewn there. He had yet to complete those documents for his father, and he never would. He had an armoire and a closet that the assassin's eyes were veering dangerously close to, and Briar wondered if her goal was to intimidate him by looking in his sock drawer.

"Isn't there a bullet you should be jumping in front of right now?" He retorted, crossing his arms over his chest.

"Yes." She hissed. "One meant for you. Perhaps I should let it fly."

"Go ahead. Wouldn't be the first time someone tried to shoot me."

"I'd made sure it was the last."

Briar surveyed the assassin with jaded eyes and sucked in a breath. She smelled like polished steel and blood. "The rumors say you're nameless."

"Do they now?" The Phantom sighed passively, looking down at the surface of the desk to ruffle around his papers as if she were bored of him. He didn't know what she was looking for; perhaps she wanted to give him a paper cut instead of killing him. Briar would much rather be murdered than brave a cut from one of those horrid documents.

Briar's eyes flickered between the ruffled pages and her face. Once she was finished, she threw them to the side and began to prowl around the desk. Briar followed her.

"What should I call you then?" He asked, stepping around the other side of his desk to sit on it, propping himself up with his arms.

"You may call me Ebony."

Briar snarled, trailing the assassin with his eyes as she circled his room. "You dress in all white. Maybe Ivory suits you better."

He heard her snicker. She stopped walking for a moment and Briar remained still as well, planted to the edge of the desk and wondering if he somehow pulled the trigger that would cause her to turn her rifle on him. Instead, she spun around on the heel of her boot, her hand moving fluidly towards her mask as she unveiled herself.

She had an unusual color of olive skin that was flushed with pink underneath. Her hair was still tucked into her hood, but beneath the white fabric, Briar could see coils of mahogany brown braids wrapped around her head. When her fitted mask was completely lowered, Briar found her face carved, sharp, and stern as she peered at him through her long eyelashes. She didn't dare blink and miss his reaction.

"Call me whatever you like." She told him with a sigh, her voice no longer muffled by the mask. "Just don't get in the way of my job."

"What is your job exactly, besides the occasional murder?" Briar inquired, hiding how pleasantly attractive he found the assassin. But her appearance did not change the fact that she still had two guns on her person and many more weapons hidden in her uniform. Or the fact that she was capable of using any one of them to kill him.

"To keep you from getting killed." Ebony shrugged casually. "Though I'm not too inclined to keep you alive, either."

"Then why are you here?" Briar spat, ignoring her second comment. He was disgusted with the amount of time his eyes spent roaming her face. "You could be anywhere in Raedon right now and you chose to obey my father's summons."

"Because the Republic has something I want."

Briar scowled. "What is it?"

"I would tell you, but I can't trust you to keep your mouth shut."

"You'll have a lot of free time," Briar informed her with a jerk of his chin. She had still yet to turn back around and continue searching his room, something Briar found more appealing than yanking his eyes away from hers every time she looked at him. "The Republic will be more secure now that you're here and the rebels haven't tried to kill me in a while."

"They should try harder." The way Ebony laughed was something a person wouldn't want to hear when they were unarmed in an empty bedroom with a notorious assassin inside.

Briar's breath hitched. "What do you know about the rebels?"

"Why do you want to know?"

"Pretend I'm curious."

"I know they'll kill you or the Supreme Leader at the first chance they get." Ebony teased him as if what she wanted to say was, "I would join them if I had the chance."

"Let them try." He chided and swatted the thought away. He remembered her comment from the throne room earlier when she told his father that she had ears everywhere. Maybe that was how she seemed to know more than everyone else. Either that or she was seriously good at faking it.

"Believe me, they have been since the moment you were born." Ebony reached up to pat the side of his face twice. He shoved her hand away, and she chuckled, turning back around.

"What else do you know?" He asked again, ignoring the burning red rising on his face as she began to wander his room. "Surely someone like you knows more than you're letting on."

The assassin licked her lips and stopped walking. She wasn't hesitating, more like trying to sort out what she would tell him that would be most advantageous to herself.

"The rebels say that they have a piece of the sun on their side of the world."

Briar immediately burst into laughter.

Everywhere outside of Raedon remained decimated by the sun's radiation waves. It was inhabitable and has been since the yellow star imploded. There had been people, Sun Searchers, who separated themselves from the new society in hopes of finding the remainder of the sun. They were never heard from again, killed by the poisonous air that the other side of the world held. Only Raedon was safe from the sun's eternal venom.

When he finished laughing, Briar looked at Ebony again. She wasn't smiling, merely blinking at him as if caught off guard by his laughter.

"You believe the rumors?" Briar asked, his brow crinkling in disbelief.

"They were true about me." She responded, pressing her lips together.

"The sun is gone," Briar confirmed.

"Is it?"

Briar's throat bobbed. She was a liar; liars lied, and that was what she was doing now.

"Get out." He sidestepped her and pointed to the door. "Don't come back."

"I would take you up on that offer, but I recently struck an accord with the Supreme Leader. I'm not going anywhere."

"If you're here for the recognition, by all means, leave me alone. I'll be talking to the news about you if that's what you want. I'll pay you too." Briar towered over her, but she couldn't have looked less intimidated by his stature.

"You'll be talking about me regardless, but it's good to know that you're desperate." She sidestepped him on her way to the door, talking over her shoulder. "And all the money you lose in those pitiful gambling halls isn't nearly enough to keep me away."

Of course, she would already know about everything he did in his free time. Was there any bit of information the assassin couldn't get her hands on?

"How do you — " he began to protest, but she flashed him a toothy grin that caught him off guard and reminded him of a beast in a nightmare that would chase him until his feet were raw.

"Careful where you wander off to at night. You might end up walking into one of my next murders." She warned him playfully, although there was nothing childish in her eyes.

She cracked open the door and slithered out into the hallway. The door finally clicked shut and Briar stood there with his eyes still locked on the knob.

How the hell was he going to get rid of her?

When they are born, each citizen of Raedon is given
a serial number and a barcode.
The number is embedded in the barcode that is
permanently implanted into the skin. It is done
when the child is young and asleep so it cannot
remember the pain or feel it. We aren't monsters,
although an opposing party might argue
oppositely. The barcode is not a tattoo because the
ink from the art form was discovered to be toxic to
the body, but a chip inside the right wrist of each
person.
Some might think that this method is inhumane.
That we are numbering humans like cattle getting
ready for the slaughter. There are only a few things
wrong with that statement. First, there are no cattle
because all animals died when the sun imploded.
Second, they're not being sent to the slaughter
because that would badly affect the population
numbers. And third, we do it to protect them.
The amount of people in a society depends on the
amount of resources Raedon can provide. If the
population expands to a point where we can no
longer supply sufficient rations to everyone, the
population must decrease and therefore fewer
children must be born. The barcodes and numbers
allow the Republic to track how many people are in
Raedon and therefore estimate the number of
resources that need to be used and harvested every
year.

When the barcode on the wrist is scanned, it transfers money into different accounts for a person to purchase something. It allows the Republic to see who is taking substantial amounts of supplies and who is abusing our generosity.

When a human dies, their serial number and barcode are given to someone else. Recycling the numbers and barcodes allows the Republic to see a steady line in growth and decline; for every human that dies, a child is born to replace it. Although no person could ever be forgotten because of relationships and family ties, the barcode completely erases any information on the person that hadn't been uploaded to the Archives for further inspection. It is rare that we see a case where a person's entire life is uploaded and looked at closely. Most of the time, the only information that is transferred is when they were born, when they died, and the age that they were when they passed.

There have been rumors that a tracking chip is placed in every wrist hidden within every barcode. They think the Republic wants to track their every move. While that isn't a far-fetched concept, it would be a waste of material. There are cameras on every street and in every corner of every building. There are heat signature sensors and fingerprint scans on every door. There is not a single place a human could go in Raedon without their movements being tracked. We don't need implanted technology to do that; we've already

created a system that provides everyone with a safe
environment to be born and eventually die.
We are not cruel creatures for doing what we do.
We simply ensure that everyone in Raedon truly
belongs there.

-An excerpt of the first Supreme Leader's
journal, extracted from the Archives of the
Imperial Republic of Raedon

Chapter Six

"Multi famam, conscientiam pauci verentur."
-*Many fear their reputation, few their conscience.*

"She just shows up everywhere."

Wren watched Briar whisper to the pale man next to him, barely paying attention to the papers stacked in front of him. He was in his royal uniform again, wearing the same jacket Wren had seen thrown across his bedpost a few sol cycles ago. He kept running a clawed hand through his hair, causing the cedar strands to fall lazily in his eyes.

"Like a ghost." The pale man responded blankly, obviously not giving much time to Briar and his complaints.

They were in one of the Supreme Leader's meeting rooms. There was a long table in the center of the chamber surrounded by men dressed in deep purple uniforms; some too young to be deciding for the Republic, some too old to be trusted to blink without closing their eyes one final time, but all of them wearing serious expressions as they ruffled papers around in their hands. All except for the Supreme Leader, sitting at the head of the table looking at the documents handed to him, and Briar continuing to bypass everything he was given to instead speak with the pale man.

Wren had quickly learned who he was; Achlys Sonnen, son of the Supreme Leader's head Advisor. Achlys reminded Wren of one of her knives. He was tall, slender, and shining all over with the many rings and earrings he wore. He was the kind of person she saw everywhere in high-class Raedon; money, status, a reputation to feed off of, and so much bling Wren had rendered herself blinded. She noticed how his eyes constantly fluttered to his father before copying the Advisor, making sure he even stacked his papers the same way Advisor Sonnen did.

Meanwhile, Briar continued to fuss, not bothering to pick up the ink pens he'd knocked over while dramatically flourishing his hand and grumbling.

"She keeps looking at me." Briar flinched away from Wren's direction like she'd aimed a weapon at him.

"Maybe she can float through walls, too." Achlys jabbed with a lift of his white eyebrows, reluctant to speak to Briar. He whispered out of the corner of his mouth as if he feared his father would see him.

"I hope your life is filled with people like you," Briar spat, rolling his eyes at the Advisor's son.

"Fantastic," Achlys replied in a dry tone. "Maybe then I'll find someone more agreeable to talk to than you."

Even Wren flinched at the harsh comment as Achlys stepped sideways to speak into his father's ear. Briar stayed at the corner of the table, pressing his fists into the edge as he scowled at a pile of documents before him.

Wren remained in the back of the room, ignored by everyone. She didn't mind that people weren't looking in her direction because she knew they were still thinking about her. How could they not?

She was adorned in her ivory uniform again with her hood pulled high onto her forehead. Her mask was secured tightly to the bridge of her nose again; she'd surprised herself when she took it off last sol when she'd spoken to Briar. If Eden was so sure that Briar was an asset, she might as well catch him off guard once in a while if she wasn't able to kill him. She needed him to trust her or get as close to trusting her as possible. Knowing that no one had ever seen her face after she became the Phantom, Wren hoped that this would make Briar feel slightly less guarded when she was around. Clearly, it was going to take him a while.

She leaned on the silver walls with crossed arms, planting one foot on the floor and the other on the wall behind her. She allowed her knives to be seen in her white skirt, flashing their silver blades at the Supreme Leader's soldiers standing by the door. Wren's eyes never stopped moving, masterfully gazing at each paper assembled in front of the Supreme Leader.

There was a map of Raedon placed to his left, so close to Wren that she could spot red markings on the parchment, yet too far away to see exactly where they were. She could read the boundary lines between each of the districts in Raedon; Cassiopeia, Antares, and Fortuna in the north and Xadon, Polaris, Asura, and Rigel in the south. Wren could also easily spot the blacked-out land surrounding Raedon, the world that everyone believed to be decimated and poisoned after the sun exploded.

Wren smiled underneath her mask as an Advisor whisked the map away again. Dorin was no closer to pinpointing the location of Novus than he was to figuring out that she worked for the very rebels he'd hired her to protect his son from.

Last night, before the first hours of the sol cycle began, Wren took her own time to place a few markings around Polaris. Mainly, Sanctum Palace.

She didn't sleep even though she had been assigned a room near Briar's. She didn't open the door to her new chambers, determining it a complete waste of time. She doubted she would spend any hours there anyway and decided to rather roam the halls. Besides, she was in no danger of being caught. The Phantom belonged in Polaris now. There was no place she couldn't go that she wasn't permitted to be.

Well, besides the archives deep below ground level. She'd have to find a way to those later.

The corridors were empty and silent save for the pounding of her boots against the floor and the echoing sounds of other soldiers patrolling. Wren only spotted them a few times, marching down the platinum hallways shoulder to shoulder in pairs, completely avoiding her eyes when she looked their way and saluted them as equals. They wore padded black uniforms with a purple seal on the sleeve, the colors of the Republic.

If she needed to, it would be easy to throw a knife at one of them before they could even think about reaching for one of their firearms. That was one thing she liked about her blades in the first place; they were small and faster than a bullet, but only when *she* threw them.

Wren turned corner after corner, burning a map of the entire palace into her head. She climbed up staircases and explored every inch of the walls, remembering where the armories were as well. The map was her guide, last night being the only time she might've had to memorize the hallways before the Supreme Leader and his son were called to a meeting. She knew how to get to the meeting chamber; she'd passed it while she was walking back from the training rooms.

"I can feel her eyes burning holes into my skin," Briar whispered into Achlys's ear, although his voice could be heard without Wren having to strain her ears to listen. She was indeed watching him, never once blinking, even though he was partially turned away from her.

"Perhaps she'll do me a solid and disintegrate you," Achlys suggested in a casual tone, picking up a paper and handing it to Briar. He simply let the parchment fall out of his hands and onto the floor with a snarl.

"You'd like that, wouldn't you?"

"I certainly would." Achlys beamed.

"She's a murderer." Briar spat, jerking his thumb behind him and towards Wren. "Do you know how many people she's killed? Do you know what she said to me last night?"

"Stop talking," Achlys ordered in a stern tone, going back to his father's side. "I don't care what you and her were doing last night, and I certainly don't like where this conversation is headed. Besides, she can probably hear you."

"She can't." Briar battled with a scoff.

"I'd shut your mouth if I were you," Achlys warned his friend, clicking his tongue. "She'll throw a knife right into your skull."

Wren chuckled from her shadowed corner and Briar whipped around his shoulder, glaring at her through blunt eyes. She only smiled underneath her mask, something she knew he could see, as she lifted her eyebrows in confirmation. She had been listening the whole time, and she thought it was amusing Briar assumed she couldn't hear him.

She heard everything, including the soft steps of a woman approaching her from the door as Briar turned back around with a curse.

"You must be the Phantom I've heard so much about." The woman stopped before Wren, allowing the assassin to survey her from the top down.

It was the same woman Wren had seen in the throne room last sol cycle. Looking at her now, Wren realized she must've been from Cassiopeia; her bright rust-colored hair wasn't common in any other district of Raedon. She wore a soldier's uniform, padded with armor on the interior. Her sandy skin was slightly unusual too; normally people from Cassiopeia and the northern districts had paler skin. She stood with a confident yet sophisticated poise, something that told Wren she had status among the soldiers who stood with her by the door. Wren assumed she was Captain of the Guard or the Supreme Leader's bodyguard.

"I suppose my reputation speaks for itself. Although most people seem to know me better than I know myself sometimes." Wren responded, ignoring Briar. He had nothing else to offer her and the papers on the Supreme Leader's table were of no use to her anymore. She'd gotten the information she needed within the first few seconds of entering the room. Now she was only there because it wouldn't help her if she drew attention to herself by leaving too early.

"No one even knows your name." The woman pressed her rosy lips into a thin line and leaned against the wall. She remained relatively far from the assassin, and Wren noticed the ticking of her jaw as she spoke. Even leaning against the wall, Wren was taller than her and more muscular in her ivory uniform.

"You may call me Ebony."

"Ebony." She repeated, letting the name roll off her tongue. "What an unusual name."

"I don't repeat the titles I've already used."

"Of course." She nodded her head, still watching the table in front of them. "You change your identity wherever you go."

Wren opted not to respond. The girl had all the answers she needed, and Wren found no excuse to be asking for more. The Phantom was meant to be a ghost, an invisible figure to anyone brave enough to look for her. Her name never remained the same when she traveled around Raedon, even if she visited the same district twice. It wrapped her in a safety net, a web of false masks to protect her when someone like the woman began to dig too close.

"But why choose a name so unforgettable?"

Wren supposed it was a good question if the woman wanted to slowly sink her teeth into the assassin's skin. Good thing she was wearing armor.

"No one would ever forget me." Wren finally told her.

The woman seemed to take her response as Wren planned. She didn't speak for a moment and Wren saw her biting the inside of her cheek from the corner of her eye, trying to sort out what her answer meant.

"So, what are you to be called?" Wren brushed away their previous questionnaire with ease.

"Quinn Vega. Captain of the Supreme Leader's Guard." Quinn reached her hand towards Wren with a smile. It wasn't the expression Wren expected but took the Captain's hand anyway, giving it a firm shake before dropping it. It was not a friendly gesture.

"Captain of the Guard." Wren parroted, watching Quinn's lips split into an even prouder smile. Not boasting, but pleased to hear the title. "That is no small feat for someone so young."

"You flatter me." Quinn snickered.

"Where are you from?"

"Cassiopeia."

Wren's expression tilted with glee. She had been right so far, why not keep going? There was plenty about Quinn Vega that Wren knew already, just from looking at how she held herself when standing against the wall.

She was trained in one of the top academies for soldiers in Raedon. Those were only in the larger districts like Rigel, Antares, and Xadon. Wren guessed that Quinn's family was either wealthy enough to send her to one of those schools without having to apply or Quinn had signed up on her own, soon becoming top in the class. Wren assumed that by the way she kept her hand close to her gun, she was taught to be prepared for an attack at any time.

Standing next to the Phantom, the situation warranted an extra bit of tension on her trigger finger.

"You went to school in Xadon?" Wren took a guess, earning a nod from the Captain.

"I did." She told her. "How did you know?"

"You hold your gun differently than your soldiers." Wren explained. "People who go to the academies in Rigel and Antares are taught to hold the gun in their non-dominant hand to make sure the impact doesn't damage their important arm. Alternatively, you use your dominant left hand because you don't trust your right."

Quinn's eyes widened as she looked at the assassin. "You're good." She admitted. "So, where did you train?"

"I learned on my own."

"I doubt that," Quinn argued in a way that was familiar to Wren. She wasn't playful at it like she wanted to gain the Phantom's trust, which, by the way, was not given out lightly. Instead, she slyly scoffed at the lies Wren told.

"Someone with your capabilities doesn't just learn how to do that on their own."

"I suppose that makes me a prodigy." Wren liked that word. It was used to describe her when Eden and the soldiers in Novus had first trained her to be one of them. Everything came naturally to her; shooting, throwing knives, hiding in plain sight, spying. She stood out amongst the groups she was assigned to and even moved up training levels with the advanced students. There wasn't a single thing that Wren was not good at within the Rising Sun's ranks.

Yet she left. And now, the Rising Sun seemed to be incapable of forgiving her entirely.

"Impressive." Quinn looked away from Wren and to the Supreme Leader summoning Briar to his side. He seemed hesitant to go but slumped to the other side of the table anyway, leaning in so he could hear his father's words. "I also find it stunning that you've carried out all these assassinations on your own without ever being caught."

Wren smiled at the sharp edge of Quinn's voice. "Stunned, you say?"

"Very." Quinn's mouth split into a toothy smile that resembled fangs as she took her eyes away from the Supreme Leader. "How did you manage that?"

"I'm not one to reveal the tricks of my trade, Captain." Wren felt Quinn digging and stopped her efforts by putting an iron shield around herself. She was used to people trying to pry into her business. Normally she spat lies about herself to throw them off, but Wren knew that the Captain of the Guard was not the kind of person to follow a fake trail twice.

"You're proud of yourself, aren't you?"

"It wasn't hard," Wren said casually. "I know everything that happens in Raedon."

"I heard." She raised an eyebrow. "You have ears everywhere."

"I do."

"I would be interested to know who these ears belong to." Quinn bit her bottom lip. Wren knew she wanted to seem more casual than she was. She was wary of the assassin. "There are many people in the Republic, you know."

Wren snickered and glanced at Quinn with a crooked smile. "Are you inquiring because you're my friend or the Captain of the Guard?"

They were the furthest thing from friends.

"A friend," Quinn suggested anyway.

"Shame." Wren clicked her tongue and uncrossed her arms. She picked out a knife from her belt and picked at her nails with it. "I'd rather have enemies than friends."

"Why is that?" Quinn observed the knife, slicing along Wren's skin so close that one wrong move would sever the tip of her finger.

But the Phantom made no wrong moves to begin with.

"Friends are forgettable," Wren answered, sliding the tip of her silver knife across the edge of her nail. "Enemies are not."

The world population was precisely 10,349,323,038 people when the sun imploded.

The inhabitants of Earth were unequally spread throughout 195 countries. The territories were not identical, nor were they all comparable to one another. The land was constantly being divided and borders were regularly reestablished. Some of these countries were ruled by what was deemed a democracy, others by a dictatorship. Customs and rules varied depending on where a society was located amongst the expanse of all 195 of these countries.

Scientists concluded that natural resources would run out in the year 2365. Surprisingly, humankind lasted five years after the death date, only to be incinerated by the radiation waves emitted from the sun's implosion.

By that time, the world population had reached its limit; the death rate had been increasing and the number of births in each country was not enough to sustain life for the next ten years.

It was not a hard decision to select who was eligible to hide in Atlas 1078. Essential personnel were hand-picked from the finest societies around the world and leftover tickets to enter were bought for billions of dollars.

To control the population, a limit was placed on the number of children women could bear. Along with the curing of all diseases and the development of cleansing for all sicknesses, no child would die due to natural causes.

Any child born or elderly dead would be tracked on an Imperial database that allowed the progress of civilization to be constantly monitored. The barcodes implanted in each citizen's wrist allowed the numbers to be tracked and calculated. Raedon could not sustain an overpopulated society and therefore, for every birth, there must be a passing. To defy nature was one thing, but to defy death was another.

-An excerpt of the first Supreme Leader's journal, extracted from the Archives of the Imperial Republic of Raedon

Chapter Seven

"Pars magna bonitas est velle feri bonum."
-A great part of goodness is to want to do good.

War was a term used to describe intense combat between two or more parties, characterized by violence, military, and mortality. Historically, battles ended with a treaty and an agreement between two or more states, but left a gaping hole in national relations. Nothing after bloodshed was ever the same again.

That was the Archive's definition, at least.

It brought on the slaughter of humankind. It shredded any form of humanity from a human being and revealed what was inside them, deeply hidden behind wasteful things like peace and friendship. Those kinds of things like hope and tranquility were lost when a gun fired and began a revolution. They were lost when a dagger pierced a heart and an empire fell to the hands of tyrants and when men were pitted against men. It was a cruel thing, combat, and yet war was a term used until the sun imploded and the sky turned black.

In Raedon, there was no bloodshed.

Anyone who disobeyed the rules found themselves erased. There would be no mourners to begin an insurgence because no one would grieve for the losses.

Well, at least until the Rising Sun appeared. A golden dawn over the black horizon of the Republic.

Wren chuckled to herself at the thought of it as she turned the corner and sauntered into the length of a new corridor. The only sound that embraced her was the falling of her own white boots on the platinum floor. During the night cycle, everyone slept soundly, save for the soldiers stationed in specific spots around the palace. Put there by Quinn Vega, who Wren had the pleasure of meeting earlier, and most likely stationed around specific areas to keep the Phantom from going anywhere she didn't belong.

Which was a pathetic effort, Wren knew, because anyone who *tried* to keep the assassin away from anything ended up dead.

The Captain of the Guard was a person of interest to Wren. She was powerful and influenced the Republic, not because of politics, but because of her skills. If she wanted the Supreme Leader to die, which was an impossible scenario, she could snap her fingers and it would be done. Quinn could also snap her fingers and order Wren to be followed around all night. Introducing herself to the Phantom was a smart idea on her part, Wren admitted. It practically handed the Captain a validated reason to watch the assassin.

And it only gave Wren all the more reason to put on a show.

The assassin drifted towards a fork in the road, choosing the hallway on the furthest left. If she was meant to be scouting the area and gaining a lay of the land, she might as well wander towards the downward levels as well.

Wren found herself at the top of a grand staircase as she turned the corner. When she descended, she found her eyes wandering the length of the walls. There were portraits of former Supreme Leaders hoisted on the walls in black frames, watching Wren as she passed by each one. She knew they were meant to look daunting, powerful even, but in their royal garb with undeserving metals plastered to their chest, Wren thought they looked like greedy children instead of the leaders of Raedon.

As Wren stepped onto the landing between the two staircases, her eyes continued moving upwards until she found a small black device hoisted into the dark corner of the wall before it folded into the next hallway.

The assassin beamed at the camera from underneath her mask. There were surely soldiers behind a screen and watching the stairs at that moment, but instead of watching the Phantom stare back at them, they were seeing an empty staircase.

When the Republic rose and the first Supreme Leader came to power, a system of networked security was placed around all seven districts of Raedon. It wasn't simply cameras on the corners of streets, although there were multiple that Wren could identify just by looking at Polaris from a balcony in the palace. There were listening devices, heat-sensitive identification methods, and facial recognition scans for every square inch of land in the Republic. They were constantly measuring each face and retinal scan to identify anyone who went anywhere in Raedon.

When Wren designed her uniform, she knew she would be recognizable the moment people saw what she was capable of. There would be cameras all over the Republic, constantly tuning in on the smallest of details to spot her in even the most crowded areas. That wouldn't do, especially when her personal appearances to the public were exclusive. If Wren had walked by the camera, even with her mask on, the technology would not only know where she was and give away her location but also find out that Wren Sitara wasn't dead and that she had found a flaw in their system.

When Wren had come across the dilemma in her design, she found an old friend to assist in the making of her uniform. It was built not only with armor underneath the fabric and pockets for hidden knives but also stitched with a kind of scrambling technology that temporarily disabled any camera as she walked past.

So, when the Phantom reached the base of the stairs and looked over her shoulder at the camera, it aimlessly blinked back at her invisible figure.

Smiling to herself, Wren left the hall of portraits and found herself in another corridor of windows. The sky outside was beautiful, sparkling with stars. Wren had always believed that the skyscrapers in the districts gave her a magnificent view of the sky, but even the lowest levels of the palace gave the steel towers a run for their money.

The Phantom went everywhere in Raedon but had never officially been invited into Sanctum Palace. Sure, she'd been to Polaris a short time ago and had seen the massive platinum structure from a distance, but looking at it from inside and knowing that she might cause its downfall was simply another welcomed rush of adrenaline in her veins.

Wren gazed into the sky of stars, feeling her breathing synchronize with the pulsing of the lights. Only, this time, the sound coming from her was joined by another.

Wren looked to both sides of the corridor. There was no one there, yet she knew her senses had not betrayed her. They couldn't. When she was trained by the rebels in Novus, her senses heightened, and she became more aware of everything around her. She could feel the density of the surface she was standing on and determine what it was without having to look down at it. She could taste poison in her food with one lick of the steam rolling from it. She had perfect vision and could see things in immense detail. She could smell the scents of things and remember them years later, and she could hear the small hesitant click of a trigger finger from miles away.

But now, all Wren could hear was the set of lungs that had been following her the entire time.

The assassin turned on her heel, walking away from the windows as the stars begged her to come back. She reached the end of the hall and turned into the next, only she didn't continue walking; she stuck herself to the wall and unsheathed a dagger from her belt. She was completely silent, making sure her sudden shadow never left; she didn't want to scare it away before she had the opportunity to *really* frighten it.

Soon enough, the sound of nervous breath got louder as it approached Wren's corner. It was accompanied by a small footfall from someone light on their feet but not graceful.

Wren waited until her assailant reached the other side of the corner before she pounced, marking her target with precision. She landed with her knife pressing against their hand and her finger looping around a chain hanging from their neck.

The girl screamed. Wren realized she couldn't have been over sixteen years old. Her midnight hair fell into her face in panicked tangles, the braids scattered through her scalp swinging. Her heart-shaped face was twisted in surprise as she gasped for the air Wren had knocked from her lungs. Her skin was pale with fear as she blinked up at Wren through her gray eyes, looking between the assassin and the necklace pulled tightly between her gloved fingers. Wren looked down at the pendant for a moment, drowning any thoughts of hurting the girl when she saw it.

It was a silver sun, embellished with a ruby jewel in the center.

"These kinds of sentiments aren't usually worn in Raedon." Wren's voice was icy as she pulled the necklace tighter. It made a red rash around the girl's neck. She was oddly familiar, but Wren never forgot a face.

"Please don't kill me," the girl squeaked, squeezing her eyes shut as if this were a nightmare. Her chest rose and fell rapidly, and Wren could almost hear her heart beating two times the normal speed.

"Why shouldn't I?" Wren pressed the knife further against the girl's smallest finger, pinning her hand to the wall beside them. She leaned forward into her face, so close that the tip of her mask and the girl's nose almost touched.

She didn't respond, holding her breath instead. Her eyes were still closed, and she was slightly shaking her head, convincing herself that she wasn't pushed against a wall with a knife dancing over the top layer of skin on her finger.

It obviously wasn't working, so Wren pressed the knife into her skin.

"Fine!" The girl gasped, looking down at her finger from the corner of her eye. It had begun to bleed but Wren barely made any damage. "My name is Nova Solaris. The Rising Sun stationed me in the palace to aid the Phantom with anything she needed. It's only my first mission and I would honestly appreciate it if I came back with all ten fingers."

She talked so fast, Wren barely had time to register what she had said.

Solaris.

The Rising Sun.

Wren felt a flare of anger underneath her skin as she yanked the girl from the wall, dragging the squirming creature by the ear until she found a small closet at the end of a hall and shoved her inside, slamming the door closed behind them.

It was a supply closet, filled with brooms and mops and different cleaning devices used by the servants. This one was obviously used frequently; the containers of cleaning chemicals were running low. The light inside was dim and almost so dark Wren could barely see Nova as she fell into the supplies hanging from the wall, grabbing onto a broom handle as she tried to catch herself. Instead, she collapsed against the floor as a rack of rags fell onto her head.

"Holy-- " She began, but Wren didn't give her the chance to finish before she yanked Nova off the floor by the collar of her shirt, which she was now realizing was a servant uniform, and pushed her against the wall. Nova gasped, holding her head where the rack had hit her. "I'm thankful that you didn't sever my finger, really," She ranted again, speaking faster with each word, "You have no idea the trouble I would get in if I had to sew my finger onto a keychain to take back home."

Wren lunged again, jabbing her forearm against Nova's neck.

"Where is 'home', exactly?" She asked as the girl clawed at her arm. Wren's uniform stopped Nova's nails from ever reaching her skin.

"Novus, of course." She choked out, annoyingly beginning to hyperventilate again. "Where else did you think the rebels were based? I thought you worked for them."

"I work for no one." Wren glared at her, finding it difficult to speak to Nova when her eyes were constantly darting around the supply closet. "I— "

"They warned me that you were going to be mean, but I didn't know you would be this aggressive." Nova interrupted, her throat bobbing underneath Wren's arm.

"Excuse me?" What the hell was she thinking Wren was going to be like? Did she assume they'd meet and braid each other's hair whilst they talked about different weapon ammunition?

Yes, I would love it if you passed me the .357 Magnum bullet.

"The Rising Sun told me you would not be happy about working with me but put me here anyway to give me at least a shred of experience before they hand me a gun," Nova explained, and Wren's anger climaxed.

"They sent me a *novice*?"

Nova gasped. "That comment hurts, but I'll let it slide."

"I don't care what hurts you." Wren snapped, rearing back and dropping her arm from Nova's neck. She coughed and tried to hide it with her hand. "Go back to Novus."

"I can't go back." Nova shook her head furiously. "The rebels practically dropped me off with a to-go bag and told me to stay until the job was done." And under her breath she muttered, "Whatever that means."

"You're telling me that the Rising Sun sent you into the field with no training?"

"Well, no. I've had training and everything." She flourished her hand like it was nothing. "My sister isn't happy with any of this, but hey, what am I supposed to do about it?"

"Your sister," Wren paused her to clarify, realizing now why Nova's face had looked so familiar. "is Vesta Solaris."

"How did you know?"

Wren's gaze hardened. "You look the same."

Nova's smile widened and her eyes glowed. "I get that a lot."

Vesta Solaris was a soldier in the Rising Sun. She specialized in a medical position and was also a part of Wren's brother's personal team. When Eden was selected to be a Captain, he was permitted to put together a special task force to assist him in completing his assignments; they were his to command. Vesta had been a part of the force since the beginning, chosen with two other members who were skilled and dangerous enough even for Eden's standards.

Wren looked back to Nova, noticing that she was waiting for what the assassin would say next. Bracing herself was more like it. Nove curled her hands into nervous fists at her sides, her shoulders raised so high with tension that they almost touched her ears.

"Tell me," Wren stepped forward even though it was impossible to have space in between them in such a small closet. "Was it Eden Sitara who gave you this assignment?"

"No," Nova shook her head so fast her braids almost hit Wren in the eye. "It was the Commanders." Then she bit her lip, glancing bashfully at Wren through her eyelashes. "They obviously don't trust you very much."

"I don't care if they trust me or not." Wren snarled. "All they should know is that I get things done and I don't need an amateur following me around everywhere I go."

Was this how Briar felt when he heard the Phantom was going to be his personal guard? No, Wren thought. She was not an amateur, nor did she *follow* anyone. She was too good for that.

"I'm not an amateur." Nova insisted, raising her voice higher than she should've and immediately lowering it. "I won't follow you around."

"Really?" Wren sneered.

"Yes." Nova huffed, raising her chin and crossing her arms in front of her chest. "Really."

"Then what were you doing so obviously in the corridor a few minutes ago?"

Nova's face fell with her arms. "How did you know?

"You breathe rather loudly."

"Well, that's not something I can turn off, but I'll definitely work on it for when you need me later."

"I won't need you later. I don't need you at all." Wren's lips curled as she looked at Nova from base to top. She seemed entirely too small for sixteen and far too weak to pass the most basic level of rebel training. She had no muscle to her bones and Wren believed that if she simply blew on her, Nova would fall over again. It was clear that she had no weapons on her person; she would've used them to defend herself when Wren attacked. That was, if she knew how to use weapons at all. How the hell did this child make it past basic training?

"You obviously do," Nova argued. "Why else would the Rising Sun put me in Polaris in the palace at the exact time you were invited here?"

"First, be careful about when you throw that name around. It'll get you killed, and I'll be blamed for it." Wren bit out. "And second, have you ever thought that perhaps they sent you here to get you out of their way?"

Nova's mouth fell open. "I'm not a liability, if that's what you're thinking."

"It is what I'm thinking, and you are. Go away."

"I'm not leaving, and no one is going to bully me into doing so, either." Nova stood her ground and her jaw ticked in frustration.

Wren growled. "You will leave Sanctum Palace by the beginning of the next sol cycle, or you will, in fact, be going home with more than a finger on a keychain."

Nova immediately shoved her hands behind her back to hide them from Wren,. "I'm not going anywhere."

"Fine." Wren crossed her arms as well. "Then tell me, if you would, how are you disguising yourself here?"

"I work in the kitchens." Nova picked at her uniform. It was far too big for her, and the itchy black fabric was obviously irritating her skin. "The Rising S- rebels gave me a key card to get in. I'm one of the helpers downstairs."

"And what do you do down there?"

"If you're expecting me to not know how to cut a vegetable, I have news for you."

"What do you do down there?" Wren asked again, becoming more impatient. "Are you poisoning the food? Or placing digestible trackers in the soup?"

Nova swallowed a lump in her throat. "I don't even know how to do that."

"Exactly my point; you don't belong here." Wren's anger was building. It was insulting that Eden questioned her on everything that she did, but even more so that the Rising Sun had placed a novice rebel in the palace to monitor her.

"I belong everywhere a real rebel belongs." Nova spat back, her brow furrowing. Her gray eyes were shadowed with distress.

"So, is this how you're going to do it, then?" Wren asked, listening to the edge in her voice. "Is this how you'll prove yourself to the Commanders and become a Captain?"

"What's so wrong with wanting that?"

"Being in the Rising Sun doesn't mean shooting guns or sneaking around," Wren told her and found Nova retreating. "People get killed."

"I -- " Nova was the one to stop herself this time.

"You wouldn't be able to stomach the least of what I do." Wren narrowed her eyes. "You'll be dead weight."

Nova's mouth twisted in vexation. "I won't."

"You're right." Wren's skin burned with resentment. "Because you'll be gone by the next sol. And if you're not, I'll kill you myself."

Before the sun imploded, there were two sides of nature: possibilism, and environmental determinism.

They were a dark duet, lingering on the opposite concepts that describe how humanity has fared so far with the horrible hand we've been dealt.

Possibilism describes the fundamental belief that humankind makes its own decisions about how to survive; that society is not based on what the environment has given us to work with and rather on what we have chosen to become on our own.

Environmental determinism explains the dominance of nature, how it controls *us*, and how *we* bend to its will.

If there is one thing that the world no longer does, it is to bend to the will of a higher power.

We are the higher power now.

We have defeated death by disease and illness. We have lived beyond the point of all other extinct creatures. We have industrialized the planet to a point where there is no longer any need for conflict or uncertainty. We have assured that our people will live until the end of time.

We do not look at nature the same way we used to.

Nature is death.

And we are all fighting against it.

-An excerpt of the first Supreme Leader's journal, extracted from the Archives of the Imperial Republic of Raedon

Chapter Eight

"Semper en fide."
-Always loyal.

Wren was used to people fearing her.

It was one reason she had created this persona for herself. If they were scared, they wouldn't question her. They wouldn't ask about her past and they wouldn't inquire about what she was going to do next.

The Phantom wasn't just an alternate identity she had drawn up in her head. The assassin was a symbol. When people saw her white uniform and the silver rifle strung across her back, they knew to be afraid. A faceless, masked creature was something no one wanted to learn about beyond the layers of rumors. Horrified was all they were ever taught to feel when passing by her or seeing her hiding in the shadows of a room. There was always the scent of fear in the air when the Phantom would appear.

It was Wren's favorite smell, after all.

The soldiers patrolling the palace at night weren't any different from the rest. In their black uniforms, they blended into the night while Wren made herself stand out. They shrank away from her when she strutted by, walking in the opposite direction than them and still not earning any double takes or questions as to where she was going.

Wren had a reputation surrounding her. She used the fear she crafted to build a wall around herself. She had been doing it her entire life; it was practically indestructible now. No one had been able to get past her wards unless she allowed them to. Even that regard had a dwindling number attached to it.

Wren allowed herself to walk as slow as she wanted. As she turned the corner and in the electric blue lights lining the paneled walls, she could see herself walking down the corridor in the platinum reflection. Her rifle flared at her back as she made her way down the last corridor and towards the Arc.

A bridge of steel and glass, the Arc separated the palace from the rest of Polaris. It was warped in a shallow arc-like shape, stemming from the main entrance to the palace and landing on a street in the city. The interior was lined with blue lights until Wren made it to the end, stepping into the neon illumination of the capital district.

It had been five sol cycles since she'd caught Nova following her in the hallway, and the amateur fiend had yet to leave the palace like Wren had instructed. Eden must've contacted her somehow and ensured that she stay put, along with giving Nova the message to relay to Wren that he needed to see her that night. So, Nova had found Wren last sol to tell her that Eden was waiting for her in the city. Afterwards, Wren promptly told the girl to go away and leave her alone.

But despite her anger towards the entire Rising Sun, Wren had a job to do.

She kept to the shadows as the wandered the streets, avoiding neon lights. The cameras plastered around the district didn't awaken any alarms as she strolled by them, yet she could feel eyes on her. In fact, there were more than one pair of eyes watching her, but as she ventured deeper into the city and away from the palace, those curious gazes seemed to vanish. Once Wren was positive she was no longer being watched, she turned a corner to come across an alleyway that immediately drew her attention.

Wren saw the grate outside of the alley first. There was a small piece of red fabric tied to the metal circle in the ground, limp and dirty against the pale pink lights shining from the two skyscrapers next to it. She reached down to untie the shred of a crimson scarf and fisted it in her hand, slipping into the darkened alleyway until she came across a stone stairway leading underground.

In most Raedon cities, the alleyways between large skyscrapers were not put to waste. To the Supreme Leader's knowledge, they were used for storage of materials for the skyscrapers above. But deeper into the city, the small bunkers were emptied and instead built as taverns and illegal gambling halls for citizens.

Wren knew that this specific bunker was used as a wine cellar as soon as she reached the floor of the cave. She could smell the tangy essence of red alcohol before she saw the barrels lining the walls.

Stepping into the silence, Wren spoke with a clear voice. "Did you have to be so obvious about where we were meeting?" There was a shift behind a pile of barrels. Wren's eyes snapped to the side as Eden stepped out of the corner.

"Anyone could misplace a red handkerchief on the street." He explained. Eden was dressed in his civilian uniform again, but still had the Rising Sun's scarf tied around his neck. The fabric was blood red, a color that wasn't common in Raedon either. It had a half of a sun rising from the corner of the triangle, surrounded by yellow rays that reminded Wren of pointed spears.

She let her eyes roll to the ceiling in response. "No. No one would lose a scarlet handkerchief on the ground and also find it exactly where they lost it, tied to a grate in the middle of the street." Wren passed by Eden's shoulder, patting his back. "Nice try."

"Did you find anything useful?" Eden turned to watch as she roamed the small bunker, touching every barrel with the tips of her gloved fingers. Even with the fabric covering her hands, she liked the way the wood bumped against her skin.

"Take that ridiculous scarf off." Wren ignored Eden, her back to him. "You'll make yourself stand out."

"What do the Supreme Leader and his Advisors know about us?"

"I see you're skipping the formalities. Not even a 'hello, how have you been these past few sols?' Did you even miss me?"

Just as Wren turned back around to face her brother, she felt him grab her wrist and yank her towards him. "We don't have time for formalities. Commander Rheas is waiting for your information." Eden's voice was deep, grave even. It made Wren snicker when she twisted her hand out of his grip.

Nixx Rheas was one of the head Commanders of Novus. There was no Supreme Leader to lead the rebels, only a group of advanced soldiers that were descendants of the original Sun Searchers. Wren seriously doubted their ability to get things done efficiently, especially when all they did was annoy Raedon with their constant, useless attacks.

Commander Rheas, though, was behind an ambush a little while back that involved the lights of the Xadon district going out while the rebels raided supplies from multiple food stores around the city. That seemed to be Rheas's style though, causing blackouts followed by utter chaos.

Eden was also under the control of the Commanders. He seemed to think he was more important than Wren because he had previously led a successful raid against a train running to Polaris. The rebels didn't need the food in the first place; there were plenty of supplies in Novus. The only reason they did it was to cause a distraction and make people think the rebels were weak.

Only it didn't work. Instead, Raedon as a whole was more scared of them and what they were planning on doing next despite the Supreme Leader's effort to calm them down.

Wren bit her bottom lip to mock confusion. "How is Rheas getting information anyway if his pet is in Raedon with me talking in wine storages beneath the street?"

"There are multiple people in the city and outside of it that are working with us." Eden ignored her jeer and continued. "They pass the information between each other until it gets to Novus."

"Is that why you've placed Nova Solaris in my way? To relay information?" Wren was bitter on the subject, even if it meant taunting her brother.

"I hope you didn't get rid of the girl too early. She could be useful at some point." Eden warned, but Wren didn't care for his cautions. Not tonight, not ever.

"Yes, at some point. But for now, Nova is in my way."

"It wasn't my choice; nor was it her sister, Vesta's," Eden countered. "The Commanders agreed it would be wise to begin field training for rebels at an earlier age."

"Why?" Wren hissed, "So that they can learn to shoot a gun and steal weapons before they turn five years old?"

"You're overreacting."

"Nova will only get in my way."

"Then take another path."

"Shut up." Wren sized her brother up. "Stop pretending to be wise."

"I'm not pretending." Eden's eyes flared.

"Then answer this; how are you sure the information you, Nova, and the rest of your rebel posse transfer is secure?" Wren said in a singsong voice. She knew it annoyed Eden, so she kept doing it. "It's a long way from here to Novus."

"You stick to your line of work, and I'll stick to mine," Eden snapped, frustrated with Wren now. "Get on with it; what did you find?"

Wren sneered at her brother but complied. "Dorin and his Advisors are still indecisive about calling me to Polaris, and it shows. None of their soldiers talk to me, save for the Captain of the Guard, who has ordered her men to watch me at all times."

"Were you followed here tonight?" Eden sounded wary of her.

"I'm not an amateur." She snapped back. "I'd know if I was being followed, just as I knew who told those soldiers to monitor me."

"What about the Captain of the Guard? The rebels barely have any information on her."

"You'll find some if you look at the military academy records in Xadon," Wren informed him. "Her name is Quinn Vega, most likely top of her class, and accepted from Cassiopeia. It's probable she graduated early and became a member of the guard in Polaris before being appointed the role of Captain."

"Looks like you have some competition," Eden chided, and Wren scowled, pinning him with a lethal stare.

"I compete with no one." She said sourly. "The only reason she hasn't been killed yet is because she's attached to your asset."

"*Your* asset as well." Eden corrected. "What does Briar have to say about it all?"

"Hostile, as expected. He's resistant to anything his father does to protect him and worms his way out of anything he doesn't want to do." Wren paused a moment before saying, "He tells me he wants me gone, but can't help talking about me when I'm in the room."

"So, he's an idiot."

"An idiot who's smarter than he lets on." Wren wouldn't let Eden underestimate Briar. She'd seen the slyness in his movements when studying him throughout this sol and the last. He knew what he was doing, even if others thought his actions were meaningless.

"Nonetheless, get him to trust you," Eden directed, his jaw ticking. "Briar Atlas could be our only way to get close to Dorin."

Wren nodded her head. As much as she disagreed when she first received the assignment from the Rising Sun, she knew Briar as more of the asset Eden insisted he was. He might've been childish and sneaky, but he was predictable.

"What does the Republic know about the Rising Sun?" Eden asked, switching topics now that he'd heard all he wanted to hear about Briar. Wren was still convinced that he bypassed the man's intelligence, but she would let it slide for now.

"Dorin and his Advisors have meetings daily. I listened to as many as I could, or at least the ones Briar was required to attend." She allowed herself to speak casually about it and taunt her brother as much as she could. "There were maps of Raedon everywhere, documents, contracts, the usual. There were red marks on the map the Supreme Leader always had by his side. I believe they're predictions where the rebels are hiding."

"Where is that?"

"Almost every city, mainly Antares, Fortuna, and Rigel."

Eden's lips broke into a small smile as he chuckled. He crossed his arms in front of his chest. "They have no clue."

"They were speaking about the blackouts as well." Wren went on. "They're blaming it on the Rising Sun."

"That doesn't make sense. We've only done two blackout raids in the past." His expression shifted from angered to curious as he wiped the corner of his mouth with his thumb. "Unless the rest have been real power outages."

Wren nodded, linking her thoughts with her brother's. "I think the solar power that was saved is running out; it's why the slums are never lit for over an hour a sol cycle."

"That would explain the circuitry on the power stations underneath the city." Eden agreed, forgetting about Wren's mocking. "The rebels found less power being pumped into the slums each hour. They're making it the rebel's fault to ensure people stay loyal to the Supreme Leader."

"I'll try my best to find where the sun's power is kept by the next time we meet." Wren had already been thinking about it the moment she heard the topic of blackouts and rebels coming up in the meetings. There were a few places she could go, already pinned on her mental map of the palace. Now all she had to do was find out how to get inside. Surely, they would be heavily guarded, but that had never been a problem for the Phantom before.

"We won't see each other for a while," Eden said, already thinking ahead. Wren could see the gears in his mind ticking. "Get whatever you can."

"Do you know who you're talking to?" Wren scoffed. "I'll get everything."

"Before I forget," Eden's forehead creased, "expect an attack on the palace soon. Commander Rheas likes fast progress."

"Then you better deliver. Dorin won't stand for many more squeamish attempts before going full force on the Rising Sun. He's already trying to hide the impact you're making on the Republic." Wren began to turn around when instead she found herself tucked carefully into Eden's chest.

She could feel his warm breath against her skin and feel his heart pounding in his chest. Eden wrapped his arms around her back and whispered against her scalp. "Be careful. These people are monsters."

"I am a monster, remember?"

Eden stepped back and held Wren at an arm's length, locking eyes with her. His jaw ticked. "You are far off from being anything of the kind." Wren could feel a pit in her stomach when her brother said the words.

She knew he was wrong; they both did.

Nevertheless, she nodded her head and separated herself from him, walking backwards towards the base of the stone stairs. "Tell Commander Rheas I said, hello."

"He'll kill you one of these times."

"He's been saying that for years." Wren climbed the stairs, still speaking with Eden as she exited onto the street. "I'm still waiting for him to make good on that promise."

When the sun imploded, the Earth's global temperature was 72 degrees Fahrenheit and 22.2 degrees Celsius. Humans could survive the open elements for only six hours in 95-degree temperatures spanning the entire width of the planet.

We were only 23 degrees away from burning ourselves to death before the sun did it for us.

The rising levels of carbon dioxide in the air have been a concern for society since the year 2029, when the temperature rose rapidly due to advancements of humanity. Things like cars not running on electricity, burning oil and fossil fuels, and cutting down forests to use for industry. Even the plants, no matter how big or small, emitted carbon into the air.

The Earth heating rapidly was an unavoidable dilemma. All until the yellow star imploded.

In Raedon, there are no gas run vehicles among the advanced electric cars in our streets. A new design for a car that limits the number of resources used and also runs on saved sunlight has been created specifically for the purpose of saving the Earth. In our society, we do not burn fossil fuels like coal and oil. That is because there is almost none left and if we did, we'd be following in the same footsteps as humankind before the sun imploded. We do not cut down plants because we have none to deforest.

It is a perfect solution for a perfect world.

By the time Raedon reaches its carrying capacity, which is several billions of years away, the global temperature of the Earth will be at least 30 percent lower than the temperature of the planet before the sun imploded.
Perhaps the sun should've exploded sooner.

-An excerpt of the first Supreme Leader's journal, extracted from the Archives of the Imperial Republic of Raedon

Chapter Nine

"Saepe malum petitur saepe bonuna fugitur."
-Often is evil sought, often good is shunned.

Thousands of years ago, when humanity was reduced to the size of hundreds of people in an underground bunker, someone had the bright idea to cure all diseases.

Why wouldn't they? The scientists who were saved from the sun's radiation poisoning had all the time in the world. At that point, the underground society still had hundreds of years before they would resurface and build Raedon and the Republic to govern it. No one above ground in the time of the sun had been able to cure one disease forever, much less all of them. Being in a dark, below-ground metal container sounded like the perfect place to save the world.

In the Republic archives, the curing of all diseases expanded over twenty-five years. It had taken scientists aboveground hundreds to simply cure one sickness, much less every ailment to ever plague humanity. According to the records, almost everything scientists and doctors knew before living underground was false.

The barcodes printed into each civilian's right wrist displayed the immunities. When they were scanned, a log of information would appear, showing the genetic makeup of each person's body and how safely they were guarded from disease.

Well, all except for the one sickness that seemed to spread through Raedon like wildfire. Which was odd, because Briar had never even seen a wildfire in his entire life.

Overnight, the Rising Sun became all anyone in Raedon could talk about. The rumors of their most recent blackout raid in Asura had broken out of Republic confidentiality and spread through Polaris and the other six districts faster than Briar had ever seen any news spread, and that was saying something. The last time he'd been on the news was when he bought six sapphires the size of his fist for six girls he had his eye on in his father's court. The reporters had tried to capture a time when Briar was alone to interview him about the scandal, but his father and the Advisors thought it best to pretend the incident never happened and ignore all news connected to the topic.

Which, for Briar, was a serious problem. He was banned from going to any court functions for months and couldn't even see the six girls he'd promised the sapphires to.

In response to the raids, the Republic had publicly executed three more rebels they had in custody. The entire show was televised and planned perfectly; a quick display of the power the Republic held over any rebels who dared to defy them.

The alarms in the cities seemed to go off more often than they ever did before.

Walking behind his father, Briar could already see the reporters gathered outside of the Arc waiting for them. He saw cameras flashing and heard microphones buffering as they were set up on a stand directly outside of the sky bridge. People were lifting their chins to get a look at their party as they marched across the bridge and towards the starlit district.

Two rows behind Briar, Advisor Sonnen was already coaching Achlys on how to behave. Briar listened in and tried his best not to roll his eyes when the Advisor guided his son on the correct way to stand behind the Supreme Leader.

"Raise your chin and tuck your hands behind your back." He told Achlys, and Briar heard him slap his son's hands away from each other. "You fiddle with your fingers enough as it is."

"Yes, Father," Achlys grumbled behind Briar, folding his hands politely behind his back.

Slightly in front of them marched Quinn Vega and another high-ranking soldier. Neither of them said a word to each other, but Briar could feel their eyes roaming the space ahead of them, constantly searching for potential threats and dangers coming the Supreme Leader's way. Briar had seen Quinn discussing something with his father earlier, the Captain having been quite reluctant to let his father lead their brigade down the Arc without other soldiers in front of him. Quinn seemed insistent on higher security protocols, but Briar's father had shut her idea down immediately.

"We are not afraid," he had told the Captain, who was biting back her protests. "The rebels will do nothing to harm us if we continue to downsize their existence."

After that, the Captain loaded her weapon with more ammunition than Briar had ever seen put into a firearm and told her soldiers who would act as crowd control to do the same.

The citizens and reporters at the end of the Arc stood on their toes, recording their entrance as they reached the final glass segment of the bridge. Briar set his face into a smug expression, knowing that the footage and photos taken that sol would be aired on screens all over Raedon in the next few hours. But when the next round of cameras flashed, Briar got the feeling that he wasn't the only one being photographed.

Swaggering beside him with her polished ivory uniform was the Phantom. Out of the corner of his eye, Ebony reminded Briar of a marble statue set out for display in a museum. Her face, the parts of it that weren't covered by her hood or mask, was set in a hard line like there was something sour stuck in between her teeth. Her eyes masterfully traveled across the crowd even before they stepped out of the bridge, scanning the area like Briar assumed Quinn was, although distinctively faster than the Captain. It was like she was waiting to be attacked by a horde of angry reporters and journalists, bombarding them with microphones and camera equipment.

Briar mindlessly followed his father out of the Arc, facing the mass beyond them. There were hundreds of people; not just in the section of reporters itching closer to the platform with their recording appliances, but regular citizens, too. They all stared at Briar and his father, waiting to hear the answers they had been deprived of by the Republic.

In truth, Briar also wanted to know why his father and his Advisors were keeping the raid a secret from the rest of Raedon. Wasn't it their primary goal to keep everyone informed about what was going on with the most current problems they were facing? Although Briar couldn't comment on that topic himself. He was so rarely informed of anything that wasn't court gossip that if an entire block of Polaris crashed down from an explosion, he wouldn't know until a hundred sol cycles after the event.

Maybe Ebony had been right when they'd spoken in his bedroom. Perhaps he didn't know everything like he pretended to.

The stars above their heads observed the scene as Briar filed into a space meant for him on the right side of his father. Ebony followed him and took up a position near the end of the platform. Briar made it a point to take a small step away from her when she stopped moving, hoping that the cameras trained on his father captured his movement even if it was slight. On the other side of the Supreme Leader, Achlys and his father ceased their previous conversation and stared straight out into the crowd. Quinn continued to look for threats, although Briar doubted she'd find any. Unless, of course, she was looking for the violent journalist Briar had dreamed of moments earlier.

Perhaps he'd be stabbed by a pen and spared the misery of the speech his father had spent all night preparing.

Finally, the staccato chatter around the Arc silenced as the Supreme Leader put his hands on either side of the podium. Briar could tell that his father was opposed to giving any statements about the status of the Rising Sun. In fact, he didn't appear fond at all of speaking about it with his Advisors much less in public in front of hundreds of cameras and journalists. He seemed to think that if he ignored the problem completely, it would simply erase itself from people's minds.

"I have been called to speak for the Republic today," The Supreme Leader began in a hostile tone, "regarding the movements of the rebel organization who call themselves the Rising Sun."

Murmurs traveled through the crowd at the mention of their name. Briar saw many faces in the crowd turn to frowns, others into hard expressions of anger.

"Their title alone is an insult to the Imperial Republic and our history. Billions of years ago, the sun imploded and destroyed all life on earth, save for the few out of them all who survived in an underground bunker. We were reduced to nearly nothing but a group of scientists and officials who saved us all." The Supreme Leader paused, and cameras flashed. Then he began again. "When humanity resurfaced, we discovered that the sun had been erased from our future; but it remains unforgotten in the past." Many whistles and cheers of agreement rose from the crowd. Beside Briar, Ebony shifted on her feet.

"The Rising Sun organization aims to do one thing; repeat the past and upend our perfect world. They mock our hard-earned progress, from being reduced to a size that barely survived the sun's radiation, to a society with no flaws. But it seems, not all flaws were erased from our genetic code."

Briar's father allowed another moment of support from the crowd. All around them, Briar could already see the large screens on the sides of buildings displaying the live image of them on the platform. Briar saw himself and his bored expression, along with his twitching fingers behind his back as he withstood the impulse to reach up to his neck and itch the red skin boiling beneath the collar of his royal uniform.

"The traitors of the Rising Sun are not a new fault in the Republic. They have come in many shapes and sizes, addressed with many names. With perfection comes resistance to comply. The laws set in place to keep our society functioning without defects have been challenged in the past, like they are being challenged now. But never before has the Republic seen as much disgrace as these renegades who call themselves reformers exhibit now."

"You have no doubt heard about a feeble attack the Rising Sun had orchestrated in Asura meant to chip away at our powerful barriers. The raid they attempted to run was conducted on an entire city block. They vandalized stores, homes, and places of business to catch the attention of the Republic. I tell you this now; you have my attention."

Briar yawned when a flicker of movement caught his attention from one of the news streams being broadcasted on the side of a skyscraper.

Ebony's gun holster clicked as she drew the weapon from her belt. Briar jumped, afraid that she was going to aim the weapon at him. But instead, the assassin took a step to her right, balancing one inch away from the edge of the platform. Briar made a move to grab her arm, but decided against it.

"Where the hell do you think you're going?" He whispered through clenched teeth, looking back and forth between Ebony and the reporters. Their eyes were still trained on his father.

"Don't follow me." She ordered sharply, loading the weapon as she spoke.

"I wasn't going t-" Briar began, but Ebony had already jumped off the platform.

"Mark my words, the Republic is investigating any actions made by the Rising Sun. Any steps they take towards further terrorism will be dealt with." Briar's father continued to say. "Which is why my Advisors and I implore you, the citizens of Raedon, to inform the Republic of any suspicions you have about these rebels."

Briar's heart reached a speed faster than it ever had before as he frantically searched the crowd, squinting to see a white figure amongst everyone dressed in uniformed black. Ebony had submerged herself into the crowd; she was gone.

Beside him, the Supreme Leader looked directly into a camera and spoke into a single microphone as he said, "I speak to the Leaders of the Rising Sun now; these minuscule attacks on my people will not go unnoticed and will not be tolerated."

Briar blinked, wondering if the stars were playing tricks on his eyes. No one had seemed to notice the absence of the Phantom from his side except him. Now he was thinking about jumping off the platform to find her himself.

"A crime against a single person in Raedon is a crime against all of us. An act of treason against a single person in Raedon is an act of treason against me." As Briar's nerves reached their highest point, Briar's father was also reaching the climax of his speech. He felt his breath hanging from his lungs like a rope from a noose.

"I swear, on all who came before and all who will come after me, that any member of the Rising Sun that is found guilty of disloyalty to the Republic will be publicly executed — "

A gunshot rang out from the center of the crowd.

Briar ducked down to the ground, feeling the weight of a soldier throwing their body over his own.

A scream erupted from the crowd and then another, followed by a chorus of gasping that could be heard by the entire district.

After a few moments of utter silence, Briar lifted his head. He blinked the blurriness from his eyes, gaping sideways to see that Quinn had shoved the Supreme Leader under the podium in the moment of panic. They were both frozen, waiting for another blare of danger to reflect the gunshot they'd all heard. Both Achlys and his father were on the ground as Briar was, protected by more soldiers who ran from the edges of the crowd to shield them.

"Get off of me." Briar snapped to the soldier on top of him, half shoving the man away. He heard his father and the Captain of the Guard yelling for him to get back down as he stood, but Briar couldn't keep his eyes off of what he saw.

Standing in the center of the crowd surrounded by a ring of people was Ebony, and at her feet, the body of a man with a large, bleeding gash on the back of his head.

All sense of fear was emptied from Briar's mind as he watched the assassin tuck her firearm back into her belt, listening as the barrel clicked into place. In her other hand was a pistol, one that Briar had not recognized on her earlier. Beside him at the podium, both Quinn and Briar's father had risen to watch silently as Ebony leaned down and reached into the pocket of the man's uniform jacket, pulling out a single red piece of fabric.

More gasps surfaced from the crowd surrounding the Phantom as she unfolded the piece of fabric, holding it out in front of her to reveal a single yellow symbol bleeding through the scarlet scarf.

All cameras pointed towards Ebony as she held out the scarf with a rising sun painted in the corner. Briar could only gawk at the assassin as she marched forward, the crowd around her immediately splitting to make a path. She reached the platform and then the podium, balling the fabric up in her fist and handing it to the Supreme Leader.

"Please continue." She said before wordlessly walking back to regain her position beside Briar.

Humans were cowards in how they spent their final days on Earth.

When the news of the sun's coming implosion was leaked from the Federal Government of the United States, a country known for having fifty unified states within it, people didn't know how to react. It had been broadcasted on the television, a bright red headline that read the words *BREAKING NEWS: Say your final goodbyes.*

For one hour, everything was calm.

Within the next, chaos erupted.

How could society live longer than the five months predicted until the sun destroyed the planet? How would the government choose who was selected to stay in the bunker? Who would sacrifice themselves in order to keep their family safe? Did the rest of the world know what was going on too? How long had the government been hiding this information? No one had answers. At least no one was willing to *give* any answers.

Questions formed from panic are historically followed by havoc. This explains why humanity tore itself apart before the sun rose on that final, fateful day.

Humans, the vengeance-hungry creatures that they were, set out to settle scores. They took groups with them, gangs of men and women who allegedly held weapons and screamed slurs in front of the residences of their enemies. The rest of society that did not take part in these destructive actions sat by

and watched, knowing that stopping the anarchy
falling upon the planet would do no good.
Why end up dead in the hands of your neighbor
when you're fated to die within the next hour?
I tell myself that it is a shame that more could not
be saved in the Atlantic 1078. But another part of
me knows it would've been dangerous to allow
poison to slip through those airtight walls.
Because anarchy would've killed us far faster than
starvation or disease.

-An excerpt of the first Supreme Leader's
journal, extracted from the Archives of the
Imperial Republic of Raedon

Chapter Ten

"Crudelius est quam mori semper timere mortem."
-It is crueler than dying to always fear death.

The last time Briar had slept so horribly, it was because he broke three ribs trying to climb the chandelier in the dining room without a ladder.

This time, it was because of some lousy rebels and an assassin who he couldn't seem to erase from his mind.

Briar tucked his collar into his uniform and stepped out into the corridor. He gritted his teeth as he passed the soldiers standing outside of his door. Ebony was not there, and he hadn't heard from her since his father's speech from the previous sol. Perhaps he'd gotten lucky, and a falling skyscraper hit her last night and he was finally rid of her.

Unfortunately, that seemed to be the least likely situation.

Briar turned the corner, coming across the wall of windows and ignoring the stars staring at him from outside. He took no notice of their laughing of him and quickly passed through the hallway, biting his lip as he turned the corner.

How had Ebony known about the rebel that was hiding in the crowd? She was practically standing in the same spot

Briar was, and yet he had seen nothing that would possess him to go jumping into a throng of people with a gun. Provided that Briar would never be allowed to *touch* a gun, nor would he voluntarily go near anyone with one. Sure, he wasn't the most observant person in Raedon, but he wasn't entirely blind, either. Wouldn't he have seen something move before Ebony jumped off the platform and disappeared into the crowd?

Beyond that, how was she certain she had the right guy? Was it a hunch, a gut feeling in the pit of her stomach that drew her to the man holding the pistol beneath his jacket like Briar was drawn to certain court events that hosted attractive girls and good food?

But there was one thing that bothered Briar more than getting shot in the head; what did Ebony know about the Rising Sun?

The rebels say that they have a piece of the sun on their side of the world.

How could the Phantom know anything about the sun? She was no one. And beyond that, how could there be a surviving piece of the star? It was gone and has been for over a million years. Hell, if there was even the possibility of the world having another yellow star, why didn't Raedon have it as well? Why did it belong to the rebels instead of the Republic?

It was entirely impossible, and Briar tried to convince himself of this as he came across a grand pair of doors guarded by four soldiers. The Advisors did not disturb his father's private offices, giving him time to work on his own documents or whatever boring problem he was dealing with.

That could wait. Briar could not.

Briar approached the doors, and without a word, the soldiers opened them for him. He brushed a sweaty hand through his wild hair, sucking in a breath before stepping inside.

The Supreme Leader sat at a large platinum desk in the center of the room. He was surrounded by shelves of folders and flashing televisions that reminded Briar of the security quarters he'd once broken into on the way to steal an electricized spear from the armory. The room was brighter than the hallway, illuminated with an intimidating white glow instead of a blue one. There were no windows, and only one set of doors.

One more chance for Briar to change his mind and escape.

Instead, as Briar heard the doors shut behind him, he stepped up to his father's desk and folded his arms carefully behind his back. His fingers were fiddling inside his fist.

The Supreme Leader ruffled the papers in front of him and tapped a pad implanted into his desk. Without looking up, he growled, "Whatever you want to do, the answer is no."

"I --" Briar hesitated, stopping himself. His father had still yet to look up at him, and in some ways, that caused a small hole to open inside Briar's chest.

"I don't have time for this."

Briar bit his bottom lip, still reluctant to say anything else. Was it still a good idea to ask his father about the attacks on Asura when he'd been so hesitant to tell the rest of Raedon? Was it a good idea to bring up the executions of three rebels without a trial? Was it even a good idea to ask him about the sun? He'd reprimand Briar regardless, and he was already used to being scolded about stupid things he asked.

Looking down at his shoes, Briar knew that if there was even the slightest possibility that the sun was still alive and burning, his father had a good reason for keeping it from him. Hell, the Supreme Leader knew everything that happened in the Republic.

The sun was gone. Everywhere but Raedon was toxic, deadly even. If Briar's father was hiding something, he must've been doing it for a good reason.

When Briar blinked again, he found his father glancing up at him from under his furrowed eyebrows. "Were you planning on telling me anything, or are you just here to continue wasting my time?"

For the second time, Briar felt the pit in his chest expand.

"I earned back the money." He lied, attempting to school his voice into somewhat of the usual swagger it had. He allowed his mouth to split in an over exaggerated smile, one that he was used to pasting on his face. Briar, feeling ignored by his father and being alone in the room, managed to find some satisfaction by giving himself something to feel smug about.

The Supreme Leader scoffed and double tapped something on the pad before crinkling a paper in front of him. "It's about time you took responsibility for your pathetic actions."

There was the pit again.

Briar waited for a moment in front of his father's desk, waiting for him to say something else to him. After a few minutes, he realized it was a fruitless attempt. Briar's lips tilted downwards as he bowed his head, knowing his father wouldn't see it, anyway. He slowly backed out of the room as if he was escaping something monstrous, escaping into the hallway with a small huff of relief.

Only once he'd walked for some time away from his father's office did Briar allow his mind to race.

He didn't understand many things, but this was one question that had always been tucked in the back of his mind; why was it so hard for Briar to speak to his own father?

He'd grown up in Polaris and in this palace, never afraid to do what he wanted because he was used to getting in trouble. Who would do anything about it? He couldn't be thrown from Sanctum Palace or banned from Polaris. He was free to do whatever he wanted whenever he wanted.

Except for filling his father's Advisors cups with white vinegar instead of wine. The last time he had tried to do so, his father threw him in the cells below the palace for three sol cycles straight.

What was so different, or even harder, about asking a question?

Briar shook his head and ignored the stars outside the glass windows. They were screaming at him now, taunting him on his walk of shame back to his chambers where he would most likely remain for the rest of the sol, drowning in his own stupidity over the simple task he'd failed to do. Briar felt his cheeks burning red with embarrassment. He tried to scrub a hand down the length of his face to rid himself of the crimson tinge, but it remained.

Why was he so self-conscious about what small bundles of fire thought all the way up in the sky? They were only delusions in his head, after all.

Briar cleared his throat and brought a hand up to his neck. His collar itched him uncontrollably now, so much so to the point he wanted to rip the fabric from his uniform. But the moment Briar brought his second hand up to his neck, he heard a blaring scream.

No, not a scream.

A siren.

The neon blue lights in the paneled walls changed to a blinking red. Briar remained frozen in the center of the corridor, the thoughts previously racing around his head slowing to a halt. There was only one word he could think of now.

Rebels.

By the fourth screech of the siren, everything had erupted into chaos.

Briar slammed his palms against his ears as a shriek echoed towards him from somewhere down the hallway. Then another shrill, and full of horror. They followed him as he scrambled away from the sounds, only to find them rising from the hallways ahead of him as well.

At the first sound of gunfire Briar heard, he threw himself to the ground and against the wall.

With his head banging and his ears blocked by his hands, it was impossible to tell where the sounds were coming from. He huddled himself into a ball, curling his fingers into fists so hard his palms bled. He listened as bullets were shot from their guns not far from him and ripped through the air. Glass from the windows above him shattered, as if the pure sound surrounding Briar was cracking them on their own.

Briar cursed, feeling the rain of shards fall on his back. He tucked his head into his chest before rising to his hands and knees, crawling and dragging himself away from the demolished windows.

At every gunshot, he flinched. Once Briar had gotten to the opposite wall and hoisted himself up, he looked towards both ends of the corridor.

It was empty, for now.

Letting out a long string of curses, Briar sprinted. He didn't allow his legs to stop, pushing them faster with each pace. He was no stranger to running, but it wasn't often he was being chased by people who were aiming to kill him instead of bringing him to his father to be scolded.

The rebels had wanted Briar dead since he was born. There was a target on his back, one that the Rising Sun had failed to hit last sol. But this time, they were trying again, no matter the cost.

Briar's breath tore from his lungs as he skidded around a corner, leaning against the wall for support. He didn't stop until he found his father's study again. Only there were no soldiers standing guard outside.

Briar groaned in frustration as he wiped a bead of blood from his cheek. A piece of glass must've sliced him. Briar scampered towards the Supreme Leader's office as fast as he could, peering inside the open doors for just a moment, hoping his father and his soldiers were still waiting for Briar to come back.

Instead, Briar found the space abandoned.

They had left him.

His heart thundered in his chest as the siren in his ears got louder. He could feel panic beginning to take root in his chest, sending a searing pain across his entire body. The blinding red lights flashing in between the silver walls gave him a pounding headache and Briar held a hand to his temple as he moved away from the office.

Whenever Briar heard a scream followed by a gunshot, he ran the other way. He listened as best as he could, waiting to hear the barking of orders from the Supreme Leader's soldiers. If he could find them, he would be safe.

He wiped a drip of sweat from his brow, wishing he had had the chance to rip his collar from his uniform. Now, the fabric was grating across his skin and only making things worse as he swerved around corners.

Finally, after running for what seemed like hours, Briar tumbled to a stop. He placed a shaking hand on the wall beside him, resting his forehead on the cool wall next to him. He needed to think.

After one trembling breath, Briar found it hard to breathe.

After the next, he felt a brick slam into the side of his head.

Briar fell to the ground beside the wall. The edges of his vision blurred together as he felt a mass climbing on top of him, holding a black brick against his temple. No, not a brick.

A gun.

Briar gasped, throwing his hands in front of his face as the gun pressed deeper into the side of his head. From above him, a man with a scarlet and yellow scarf tied around the lower half of his face shouted at him. Briar couldn't understand him over the roaring in his mind.

The Rising Sun was finally going to kill him.

This was it. There were no more second chances or waking up in the infirmary after pulling a dangerous stunt and blacking out.

They were going to kill him, right there, right now.

The rebel barked an order again and this time Briar yelled in protest, flailing one arm to knock the gun from the rebel's hand and the other to shove into his face. The rebel was prepared for it, allowing the gun to be knocked from his hand but grabbing a knife from his belt and pressing it against Briar's neck.

Briar's senses smashed into him the moment the silver blade cut his skin.

There was a throbbing pain in his head where he was hit and where he fell to the ground. He couldn't breathe, feeling the rebel sitting on his lungs and pinning his arms and legs to the ground. Above him, the man with the scarf laughed in Briar's face, his wild eyes flaring with fire. He wore a black uniform, but it didn't look like a uniform at all. Rather, it was made from scavenged clothing dyed dark colors.

"You're dead, boy." The rebel's vengeful spit splattered onto Briar's chin, and he cranked his neck sideways, trying to put distance between the knife and his neck. The rebel only pressed it into his skin further, cackling above him.

"Get off of me!" Briar yelled again. He bucked his hips and kicked his legs, but it was no use. The rebel was stronger than he was. Briar could barely hear the screams from the other hallways and the gunshots over the laughter booming above him, the rebel slowly cutting Briar's skin until he could feel blood leaking from his neck.

Just as the rebel threw his head back and lodged the knife further into Briar's skin, a gunshot louder than the rest echoed in his ears.

Briar's ears rang.

The rebel's limp body crumpled on top of him.

He couldn't move. He *wouldn't* move. Everything inside Briar turned molten, leaking out of him in one long wail. When he finally lifted his head from the ground, Briar found a small red circle on the back of the rebel's head.

"Briar!"

The edges of his vision fogged again when he, spotted an ivory figure sprinting down the corridor towards him.

The Phantom.

She had a gun in her hand, pointed firmly in front of her as she crossed the corridor towards him. Her hood was pinned to her head and her mask remained secured to her face. She ran with incredible speed, closing the distance between them in less than five seconds. When she got closer and kneeled down next to him, Briar found the parts of her face that he could see set in stone.

Her aquamarine eyes were not widened in fear. Her breath was not fast-paced as Briar's was. Her hands were steady and calm as she dragged the rebel's body off of him, grabbing the back of his neck to help him sit up.

"Are you alright?" Ebony knelt by his side.

Briar could feel emotions bubbling inside him, but only one was able to surface. "Of course, I'm not alright!" he yelled, throwing his fists at her. She wasn't taken aback, rather let him hit her on the shoulder. Despite his anger, she didn't fall off balance. "You almost shot me!"

"Trust me, if I wanted you dead, you would've been so the moment I got here." Ebony's voice had gone solid again. Her eyes moved up and down the length of him. Checking for injuries, Briar soon realized, until she came across the obvious cut across his neck from the glass and knife. Briar's own hand moved to touch it, the slight amount of pressure from a single finger sending a rippling sting into his body.

"Get up." She instructed, standing and moving behind him to anchor her elbows underneath his arms. Briar struggled against her help, his face burning impossibly red as he tried to stand on his own. The blood on his fingers made him woozy.

When he was finally on his feet, Briar found that Ebony had been speaking to him again. Her mouth moved, but it seemed like no sound came out.

"What?" He asked, his eyes still whizzing around the corridor for other rebels. If there were any, he thought, Ebony would've already gotten rid of them.

"Focus. I asked you where the nearest safe point was." She repeated, loading her gun without looking down at it. Briar blinked at the motion and how unfazed she was by what she did in the small movements she made.

The safe points in the castle were designed specifically for attacks, rebel or not. They were built into the walls and the floors, opened by the touch of a button or the pull of a wall panel. They were a secret, their locations only known by people who were deemed important enough to be saved in their hidden locations. The servants and help would have to fend for themselves, but the Supreme Leader, Briar, and the Advisors were all assigned special safe points to seek refuge in together.

But unfortunately, Briar's father and his legion of soldiers had left without him.

Briar himself had used the safe points many times, but not for rebel attacks. Once, he stole a rather expensive gold and amethyst pin from one of his father's Advisors and hid himself inside the paneled walls. The soldiers ran after him for hours but never found him, even though they passed his safe point multiple times. He still had the pin hidden in his armoire in a small box of other trinkets he'd stolen.

Briar snapped himself away from his thoughts. He swallowed a lump in his throat, pointing to the direction Ebony had come from. Her face twisted from something uneasy to something determined as she stepped towards Briar, putting her gun out in front of them for protection.

"Do you trust me?" She asked him, her finger already on the trigger.

Briar flinched as he heard a chandelier crash. "Of course not."

"Then don't let go."

An hourglass is used to measure the passing of time.
Sand from the top side of the glass spills down into the bottom, creating a mound that, when flipped over, will eventually leak back into the other side. They're beautiful inventions, in my opinion at least, and I've come to discover that they resemble our planet and its history.
I like to think that the top of our hourglass was the planet before the sun imploded. It was plentiful in resources and beauty, but it was running out of time, hence the falling sand. But where was it falling to?
Raedon, of course. The time that was slowly slipping away from the Earth went into the bottom part of the hourglass, saved up for Raedon when the time came for it to rise out of the ashes. If the sun hadn't imploded, humanity would've lived for millions of years more, and the hourglass would slowly reach a point where it could no longer spill. Then time would stop, and we would all cease to exist.
But that is not how things worked out. The sun imploded and the leftover time was given to Raedon.
I consider it a gift hidden within a curse.
We have no idea how much time is left for us.

-An excerpt of the first Supreme Leader's journal, extracted from the Archives of the Imperial Republic of Raedon

Chapter Eleven

"Serva me servabo te."
-Save me and I will save you.

Wren was no stranger to chaos. She'd created a monster out of it, after all; the Phantom was chaos. She was dangerous and everything that stemmed from it, including panic.

So, when Wren heard the first gunshot of the rebel attack, she found herself disappointed.

There was absolutely no flare to their efforts. The grenades they threw into the corridors did nothing but spark and flicker out. The lights that they'd wired to black out were still blaring red through the corridors. They ran around in their makeshift uniforms with minimal ammunition in their weapons like the dead waking up one random sol and deciding to walk out of their graves.

If Eden planned this advance on the palace, his title as Captain in the Rising Sun should've been revoked. What sort of idiot tried to cause this much havoc and failed so miserably at it?

Wren had to hold back the eye roll she had been aching to express as she made her way deeper into the palace. How could there be such minimal effort into the performance of it all?

Being the Phantom, Wren made a scene out of everything she did. She would leave small, haunting messages at her crime scenes and made sure they were noticeable enough that people would know it was her. No other rebel or petty criminal would take credit for her work. After all, plagiarism was one thing Wren hated most.

So, when Wren found Briar underneath one rebel, she had no problem shooting him in the back of the head. It didn't matter to her what side she was supposed to be on, only that she had a job to do and a part to play. Anyone who impeded that would pay a price.

And besides, the Rising Sun could consider that loss payback for the disgrace that was their attack.

From beside her, Briar winced. Wren knew it wasn't because of the slice on his neck, continuing to gush underneath his fingers. She noticed quickly that he flinched every time a bullet was shot from a gun, and they heard the echo of it as they traveled. Even the sound from Wren's own weapon bothered him, turning his eyes in a different direction each time she pulled the trigger.

Their arms were tethered together elbow in elbow; Wren wouldn't risk letting Briar run behind her on his own. He yanked her along, moving as her guide towards one of the safe points closest to them. They weren't the last ones trying to find one either; there were still plenty of shouts vibrating through the hallways. Even though Wren had dismissed her, she couldn't help but think about Nova as she made her way through the palace.

Eden had warned her of the attack, right?

He wouldn't leave Nova in the dark, especially as new to this as she was. So Wren cast the thought from her head, hoping instead that Nova was hidden away well enough to be excluded from the details of the attack so she didn't ramble on about it to Wren later.

Wren's arm that wasn't attached to Briar ached, partly from holding her weapon outstretched in front of them and because of the long cut on her shoulder. She could feel the dribble of blood leaking into the sleeve of her white uniform.

She hated when her crisp white fabric got blood on it. It was near impossible to wash crimson out.

They'd only traveled through six corridors when Briar finally stopped pulling Wren along. She let him out of her grip and listened to him behind her, cursing to himself as he backed up against the wall. Wren glanced over her shoulder, still holding the gun out in front of them.

"Hurry!" She yelled, watching Briar search the wall. He shouted something back that Wren couldn't hear before his hands finally came across a spot near the crack in between platinum panels. Briar pushed on it and the panel popped open, revealing a dark space inside.

Wren grunted in relief, feeling the sting on her arm beginning to sear hotter than before. She didn't bother to watch out for the hallway behind them as she whipped around, shoving Briar into the room, letting the door lock behind them.

Instantly, the lights flickered on.

Wren released a small breath and let her arm fall. The sounds from the corridors vanished, trapping them in a shield of silence.

All until Briar let out a string of curses and pulled the assassin from her momentary relief. She turned in a circle, observing the small room. The walls were silver and bulletproof and the lights rimming the perimeter of the ceiling a dim kind of white. There were two shelves on the far wall stacked with food and water packages, a medical kit, and thin blankets.

Wren didn't bother waiting to see what Briar did before marching towards the shelf, grabbing the medical kit and unzipping it. She holstered her gun with one hand while the other searched the kit, ruffling through the different compartments and pockets. She could hear Briar over the sound of crinkling bandages, listening to his heavy breathing and muttered curses. She took a roll of gauze out of one pocket.

"Here." She turned around and threw him the roll. Briar's head snapped up, and he caught the bundle against his chest. There was blood running down his neck now, staining his royal uniform.

"You almost killed me."

"But I didn't." Wren bit out, biting her lip to combat the sting in her arm as she grabbed a pack of disinfectant wipes, throwing them over her shoulder. "Catch."

"I thought you weren't supposed to get shot, being the Phantom and everything," Briar said from his corner, holding the bandages and wipes to his chest as Wren retrieved more from the pack for herself. He watched as she backed up against the wall below the shelf and slid down it, unstrapping her rifle and laying it carefully beside her.

"I wasn't shot." She glared at Briar from across the way. He copied her and slid down his wall. The room was not big enough for both of them to stretch their legs out entirely; Wren moved hers diagonally to avoid Briar's. His eyes were fixed on her arm as she peeled away the fabric surrounding the wound. "It was a knife."

"My mistake." He snapped. "I'd hoped for too much at one time."

"I saved your life. You should thank me," Wren growled. In reality, she was calmer than the time the Rising Sun had asked her to take out an entire car full of Republic officials. She did it perfectly, of course, and by the end of it learned how to rig explosives.

"You almost shot me." He repeated, as she lowered her hood and unzip her uniform. She could smell the metallic blood rusting around the wound. There were layers to her uniform that kept her skin immune from prying eyes. Unfortunately, that meant peeling back at least three layers of clothing until she finally revealed her shoulder and arm, stripping the top part of her uniform off.

"But I didn't."

"That's not the point."

A strip of Wren's uniform grazed the outside of the wound and she flinched. Briar's gaze hardened until the assassin's shoulder relaxed, realizing that she hadn't split the cut further.

"I didn't need your help." He went on.

"Lying to yourself is a bad habit."

"You would know, wouldn't you?" Briar clenched the roll of bandages in his fist. "Giving yourself a new identity everywhere you go."

"At least I have enough personality to become other people."

"Well then, if you're going to be two-faced, at least make one of them pleasant."

Wren didn't respond. Not because she was at a loss for words, but because she needed to focus. She was no stranger to sewing herself up on her own; she did it when she trained herself after leaving Novus. Eden hadn't come with her. He stayed with the rebels to rise in their ranks. It always seemed to be his greatest aspiration to become a Commander. Wren never saw the benefits in the position, not even when she got into trouble in Raedon and the rebels were forced to bargain for her back.

Working for the Rising Sun after all those years meant becoming a ghost. The Phantom, to be exact.

To pay off her debt for the rebels saving her, Wren had to get rid of herself and create someone new. Someone faceless, a dangerous assassin that targeted people on the rebel's hit list. They were the officials in office closest to the Supreme Leader, but she never got so close to killing one of his Advisors. She would add in a few random assassinations here and there, but those were only to throw the Supreme Leader off her trail. No one could know who she was and who she was working for. That meant being alone, solving her own problems, and cleaning up her blood as she did it.

While Wren enjoyed the secrecy and fear that she stoked in people, she knew she could never go back to being the old Wren Sitara. That girl was dead.

Wren held her breath as she poked the tip of the needle into her skin.

She could feel Briar's eyes on her as she looked up, the needle midway through the first stitch, and caught him off guard. "Stop drooling."

"I'm not." He insisted, pressing his back flatter against the wall as he twirled the bandages in his hands. He seemed to completely forget about the cut on his neck now that he had seen the condition of Wren's.

No one had ever seen the Phantom without her uniform on. The people who knew her as Wren Sitara before becoming the assassin knew her face, but to them, she remained dead. Not even her brother had seen her skin since she adorned the role of Raedon's most notorious assassin, save for the times when she opted not to wear a mask. She did not care whether Briar saw her, either. He'd already seen her face; perhaps this was just another step in the right direction of getting him to trust her. Now she was completely exposing herself to him with only her undergarments to cover her.

"The look on your face says otherwise." Wren took a disinfectant wipe from the package and cleaned the wound as she went.

"You're the one sewing your own arm." He was right, but she was only halfway through. Her skin was still shredded, and she could tell Briar was close to gagging.

"Careful." She warned, clicking her tongue. "It's dangerous to use your entire vocabulary in one sentence."

"Spare me the lecture." Briar hissed through his teeth. "All you know how to do is threaten people."

"It works, doesn't it?"

"I'm not scared of you."

"You should be."

Briar's mouth snapped shut. When he said nothing for a few minutes, Wren paused her stitches to observe him this time, looking at him from base to top.

He was a wreck. His hair, normally disheveled but neatly, hung over his forehead in sweaty strands. His skin was doused with dust from distant grenades and the neckline of his uniform had been torn away. He blinked every second as if there was something in his eye and it annoyed Wren to see nothing there, yet his eyelashes fluttered anyway.

In a way, she admired the spark of fire in his auburn eyes when she challenged him.

It balanced her own.

"What?"

Wren blinked. She realized she'd been gazing at him for a long time without knowing he was watching her, too.

"What?" She asked back, faking stupid. Briar didn't buy it; they both knew she was anything but clueless.

"You were staring at me." His brow furrowed for a moment before his face lifted into a sly smile. "Were you checking me out?

"Excuse me?" Wren blanched, almost ripping a stitch.

"You were totally checking me out." Briar's grin widened as he nodded his head, laughing to himself. "You can admit it; I know I'm hard to resist."

Wren visibly gagged. "You're arrogant and pathetic."

Briar's smile vanished instantly. "You've used 'pathetic' before. Have some originality."

"Well, if you insist. How about," Wren cleared her throat, "take my lowest priority and put yourself beneath it."

"Oh, please." Briar rolled his eyes and scoffed. "If I'm so low on your list of things to do, why did you save me?"

"So, you admit you needed saving?"

This time it was Briar's turn to choke. "I didn't -- "

"You said it, not me." Wren's lips split into a grin as she went back to her stitches, not feeling as much pain in her arm now that she'd gotten a boost from arguing with Briar.

Or perhaps she was just numb.

"I didn't need your help," Briar insisted, sitting up straighter and pointing a stern finger her way. "You put words into my mouth."

"Well then, if you're so sure you don't need me, next time I come across a rebel palming a knife to your throat, I'll simply tell them to get it over with faster."

"That's perfect." Briar's hand fell onto his leg. "I'll never have to see your face again."

"I can arrange that," Wren said, finishing her stitches with a knot as she hoisted her uniform back onto her shoulder. There was still a slit in the sleeve where the knife had snagged the fabric, but she would stitch that later when she wasn't planning Briar's demise right in front of him.

"You can do it now if you'd like." Briar's eyes flickered tauntingly towards the knives sheathed on her thighs.

"I would've thought you wanted an audience." Wren tilted her head and crossed her legs at the ankles, showing more of the blades hidden around her boots.

"This is fine enough." Before Wren could register what was happening, Briar had lifted himself to his feet and stalked over to Wren's wall. It only took him two steps before seating himself next to her outstretched legs and taking a knife from her thigh, handing it to her with a teasing smile. His fingers brushed across her gloved hands as the knife settled into her palm.

Wren weighed the blade between her fingers for a few moments. Briar nodded towards it, encouraging her. Then she lunged.

They landed on the floor with Wren's knee pressed against Briar's chest, pinning him to the ground with the knife resting against his already bloodied neck.

"Has anyone ever told you that you've got a smart mouth?" She asked with a tilt of her head, waiting for Briar to retreat and struggle under her hold.

But he didn't, instead chuckling so that her knife bounced against his throat. Fire danced in his eyes. "All the time."

"Add me to the list." Wren snarled.

"Will do." He smirked.

For a moment, neither of them spoke. They didn't need to; the breath that met between them and disappeared was exchange enough, especially for Wren.

"I will slit your throat." She pressed the blade against his skin but knew it wouldn't cut.

"Fine," Briar smirked.

"Fine." She said sharply.

"Fine."

"Fine."

"F-"

Briar was interrupted by the opening of the safe room door. Immediately, Wren's hand grabbed the gun strapped to her belt and pointed it at the opening, one hand still pressing a knife to Briar's throat with her knee pinning him to the floor. Neither of them moved as light leaked into the room from the corridor outside. Wren could only see silhouettes of people until she heard the Captain of the Guard's voice shouting orders to the soldiers behind her.

"It's him! Alert the Supreme Leader!" She yelled, but her relieved expression was traded for a confused one when she saw the blade Wren had palmed against Briar's throat. Her hand twitched on her gun.

"No need," Wren said quickly, flipping the knife so the hilt was pointed towards Briar instead of the blade as she lifted herself to her knee and stood. "We were just having a pleasant talk between friends."

She reached a hand sideways to help Briar up. Only when he took it, she yanked it so fiercely he nearly stumbled forward into her grip again.

"Yes." Briar nodded, dusting himself off and clearing his throat as he regained his balance. Then he glared sideways at Wren and through gritted teeth bit out, "Pleasant."

Quinn's eyebrows raised in skepticism for a moment before deciding it was not worth unpacking. "After the sirens alerted the guards, the rebels tried to turn off the power and raid the security quarters for weapons." She explained. "The attack only lasted for a few minutes before we were able to capture most of them. The rest left with nothing."

Wren listened carefully as she watched the soldiers outside of the safe room. They were still tense, wary that the rebels had left people behind. They had, in fact, and she was standing right in front of them.

The attack sounded like another one of Commander Rheas's distraction missions. No wonder the Rising Sun's efforts came off so pathetic.

"We found many rebels in the hallway that led us here." Quinn stopped her briefing and looked to Wren. Her expression darkened. "I suppose we have you to thank for that."

Wren smiled at the Captain's cautious expression. "Thanks would only be necessary if I saved him out of kindness." She jerked her head sideways towards Briar. "I only took him to be my shield."

"Look how well that worked out for you." Briar jabbed, playfully hitting the wound on Wren's arm with his hand. A spear of pain shot up her arm, but she ignored it through clenched teeth. Briar seemed to notice and sneered.

"Right well -- " Quinn began again, but Wren interrupted her.

"I'll need an entire brief on the attack by next sol." She informed the Captain, reaching sideways to pick up her rifle again and sling it across her back. When she saw Quinn's questioning face, she added, "For reference purposes."

"Of course," Quinn said, still unconvinced. But before she could question Wren on anything that had happened in the safe room, the assassin was already passing by her shoulder to speak to one soldier instead.

"Get a better disinfectant." She told him, nodding towards the medical kit on the ground. "Maybe one that sedates me next time."

Before the sun imploded, humankind used to
believe that a person could only survive one week
without substantial food or water.
Such stupidity.
It took 47 years inside the Atlantic 1078 until food
rations dwindled. There wasn't enough for
everyone, and withholding food from a certain
portion of the remaining civilization would do no
good. Keeping the young alive would later improve
the population when they reproduced, yet that
would only create more mouths to feed. There were
too many essential personnel to pick out who was
more efficient in their work and who sat in the
corner doing nothing.
But when society is reduced to merely hundreds of
people living in a small underground bunker while
the air above them poisoned the entire planet, the
impossible becomes possible.
Scientists before the sun imploded discovered a
method of splicing, a process in which one helix of
DNA would join another segment of a different
DNA strand to create an entirely new source of
product. Scientists above ground did not get far in
their studies until they were obliterated, but with
the research already done, scientists in the bunker
could experiment.
Not with human DNA, but with food.
The research explained that all plants and animals
had genes. Therefore, they all had perfectly
adequate DNA to splice. When taking a strand of
the double helix form of DNA and chemically

combining it with another, new food groups were created that surpassed all nutrients of regular nourishment.

A person could eat slaughtered cow meat, or they could eat the spliced technology and gain the same protein as beef but also intake the nutrients of different vegetables, fruits, and grains all spliced into the food but rendered invisible under the mask of meat. They could eat one carrot, or they could eat a carrot combined with fifteen other nutrients and health benefits derived from other vegetables and fruits.

It only took one strand of DNA from a food source to splice it, meaning that millions of strands could be taken from one source before it was used up. The DNA taken was planted and grown, creating an endless amount of food for the next hundreds of years. The technology didn't stop when the Republic came to power either, increasing the production of technological food by one million-fold.

Humans used to have a saying for food that was combined with other foods. "Mystery Meat," they could call it.

How stupid indeed.

-An excerpt of the first Supreme Leader's journal, extracted from the Archives of the Imperial Republic of Raedon

Chapter Twelve

"Ira furor brevis est."
-Anger is a brief madness.

Briar stabbed his fork into his potatoes.

"I believe that if we increase the production of weapons in Antares, we will be able to send them to Rigel and Xaden for further military training."

Briar chewed slowly, vaguely listening to his father's Advisors. He speared another potato and shoved it into his mouth, leaning on his fist with his elbow perched on the edge of the table. No one was paying him any attention, and, in some ways, Briar felt like that was a good thing. His mind was too concerned with other things to also have to deal with the Advisors seated around him. The Supreme Leader sat at the head of the table with Briar at his side, speaking to Advisor Sonnen, who was across from Briar. The rest of the Advisors tuned in on their conversation but were obviously excluded from it; and currently trying to be included.

The competition between them sickened Briar. He resented the idea of having to deal with twelve idiots in purple robes when he became the Supreme Leader. But hopefully, Briar thought, the rebels would get to him sooner and spare him the torture. The Supreme Leader was just a man, one that had left Briar behind when the rebels attacked six sol cycles ago. If he'd been with his father during the duration of the ambush, he wouldn't have needed the Phantom to save him.

Briar looked around the table, ignoring his father and Advisor Sonnen. Beside his father, Achlys listened closely, his pale lips twisting when he heard certain bits of information. Briar could always tell that Achlys wanted his father's position when he stepped down from power, just like Briar would become Supreme Leader when his father died. It made Briar's blood boil, simply thinking about having Achlys as one of his Advisors.

As the only son in his family, thanks to the birth rate restrictions on the population, Achlys was always following his father around. Briar wanted nothing more than to split them up and yell at Achlys for becoming yet another brainless fool trying to control the Republic like the rest. There was no point in vying for the position when he was already set to win it. Briar was annoyed watching him and he didn't even know what the topic of conversation was.

Briar's emotions flickered back and forth between irritation and anger. On one hand, he saw the Advisors and wanted to slam his head into his plate. On the other, there was a constant voice ringing through his head that belonged to a certain assassin that made him want to smash more than a plate.

Six sols ago, when the rebels attacked the palace, Briar didn't know what to do with Ebony. He needed to get rid of her, and fast, but he didn't know how he was going to go about it. Was he going to summon her to his balcony and throw her off the side of Sanctum Palace? No, that wouldn't have worked. She could probably climb back up. But that didn't change the fact that he was constantly thinking about her and never entered a room without checking all the shadowed corners first.

But after the attack, sitting at a table stabbing things with his fork, Briar felt that feeling beginning to spill over and flood.

I will slit your throat.

Was it a threat? Yes, most definitely. But did she say it to spite him? Also, yes.

There was a moment where she was on top of him with a knife to his throat. She was trying to make him squirm only to realize that he wasn't afraid of her. He couldn't bring himself to be. The only reason there was a blade at his throat in the first place was because he had told her to put it there. If Briar had never prompted her, Ebony wouldn't have done it. Briar didn't know the Phantom like she seemed to know everyone around her, including him, but he knew that it angered her to realize that he'd gotten the best of her.

But his celebration only lasted for a few seconds. The Phantom let him believe he won until Quinn Vega opened the safe point door and interrupted his victory. Ebony stood, dusted herself off, and walked out of the room like he didn't exist. Like the rise he'd gotten out of her never even happened. Like the feeling of rare and momentary success he'd gotten from seeing her eyes burn with fire meant nothing to her.

She didn't even have the common decency to be embarrassed by him.

Briar's eyes darted to Quinn Vega on the other end of the dining hall, standing silently in between the closed platinum doors. Her copper hair was swept into a braid, and she had her hands tucked carefully behind her back. Her eyes swept the room and even though he knew she could feel him watching her, she never met his eyes.

Get a better disinfectant. Maybe one that sedates me next time.

That one burnt more than Briar would've liked to admit. The worst part about it, though, was not the sting of the aftermath, but the amount of hesitation she had when she said it. Which was none. Briar felt the room tighten as the soldiers inside the safe room waited for his reaction. Only he couldn't bring himself to give one.

No one had ever thought so lowly of him before. At least not out loud and to his face. And he wouldn't be letting it happen again soon. If the Phantom was going to make his life a living hell, he'd be stupid not to return the favor.

Briar looked down at his plate, realizing he'd been stabbing an empty spot. He moved to his wine, noticing that his cup was also dry. Looking around the room, Briar found a servant carrying a silver pitcher. She was noticeably younger than all the other help around the palace.

He snapped his fingers at the girl, and she jumped, the braids scattered through her midnight hair swinging gracefully as she made her way to his side of the table, leaning over his shoulder as she poured the wine into his glass. Briar watched her hands as she did so, noticing how they shifted nervously around the pitcher as the weight of it decreased. He heard the gulp of her throat when she finished, quickly backing away from him before her gray eyes could betray her and look at the spot of red wine she'd spilled on the tablecloth.

Briar rolled his eyes as he took a large swig of wine and slammed the cup down on the table. Even when the glass made a loud sound, no one seemed to notice him sitting on the Supreme Leader's right side.

"The rebels who attacked the palace six sol cycles ago have been apprehended." Achlys's father was saying, switching to a different topic. "They're scheduled to be executed before the --"

"I don't want to be babysat anymore," Briar spoke louder than any of the mumbling Advisors. The entire table was still, silence ringing over their heads.

The creaking of a chair broke the stillness and when Briar looked to his side, he found the Supreme Leader staring at him with burning eyes.

"What did you just say, boy?" Briar's father's lip curled. He spat the words, and they made Briar's jaw twitch.

"I said," Briar repeated firmly, "that I don't want to be babysat." The Advisors around the table seemed to shrink away from father and son.

"I was speaking with one of my Advisors about a pressing subject." The Supreme Leader spat. "Keep your words to yourself and don't interrupt again." He turned away once more, but Briar wan't finished yet.

"No," he said, his back pressing against his chair.

The Supreme Leader seemed to stop breathing entirely. The entire room slowed to a halt as if time stopped at Briar's father's command. He stared at his son, his lips tightening into a straight line.

"You wouldn't need a babysitter if you weren't such a child."

"I've been taking care of myself for my entire life with no help from you," Briar retorted. "Why are you putting restraints on me now?"

"You are out of control, boy." The Supreme Leader turned fully to face Briar again. It seemed to send a tremor through the entire room, and the soldiers standing around the perimeter shifted. "This stops now. No gambling halls or taverns. No more going out into the city and messing with things you do not understand."

Briar began to snap back when this time his father interrupted him. "It won't be long until you've become the Supreme Leader." Briar could hear the cautious edge to his father's voice. He hated arguing with Briar in front of the Advisors. It was part of the reason Briar had begun this spat in the first place. "You need to take responsibility for your actions."

"I am taking responsibility!" Briar let his grip on his self-control fly. "I know what I do, and I'm fine with how it makes me look."

"This isn't about your image. It's about your safety."

"Spare me." Briar hissed. "The likelihood of me living to see the title adorned on me is slim. You can't seem to stop the rebel attacks, and it's about time they came to kill me again."

"You have no room to discuss these matters." The Supreme Leader raised his voice to match Briar's. But Briar wouldn't stop.

"You've been lying to Raedon. Your fake promises mean nothing if the Rising Sun takes over and kill everyone here.

Hell, you're killing the rebels! They're only going to keep coming."

"You know nothing!" Briar's father slammed his fist on the edge of the table. It sent a shock through the room, banging the dishes and cups together. Briar refused to flinch. "You know nothing about what is going on!"

"It's not my fault you failed to tell me anything."

"I don't tell you because I cannot trust you." The Supreme Leader's skin changed to crimson. A vein protruded against his forehead. "You're too immature and childish to handle it and I will not have you going off to become a drunk and sharing things about the rebels that will only scare people."

"I'm not a drunk!"

"You're well on your way, aren't you?"

Briar blanched. He clenched his teeth together, grinding his jaw. His eyes floated to the rest of the table, watching their gazes wander everywhere but the head of the table where Briar and his father sat. His eyes immediately darted to Achlys to find his friend silently staring at his plate with his hands tucked in his lap.

Briar's chest was suddenly filled with a blazing agony, causing him to falter in his words as his father raised a hand.

"Do not embarrass yourself, boy." His father said. "You've said enough."

Against every bone in his body, Briar obeyed. He sat with his back rigid against his seat and his face burning scarlet. He watched as the Advisors and Achlys continued to stare towards the center of the table in silence. At the head of them, the Supreme Leader continued to eat.

"In the recent events of the rebel attack on Polaris," He continued with his fork halfway to his mouth, "My Captain has informed me that she found you hiding in one of the safe points. You were injured."

Of course, he knew he was injured. Briar could still feel the sting of the cut along the bottom of his neck where the rebel held a knife to his throat. Since then, it had been healing quickly, but Briar didn't understand what that had to do with anything. But his confusion was clouded with fury as he glared sideways at Quinn, still standing by the door and ignoring him.

"I want you to learn to defend yourself. It is in your best interest should any other attack from the radicals strike Sanctum Palace." The Supreme Leader looked down the table as if he was simply talking about what star was the brightest in the sky.

"Isn't that what your soldiers are for?" Briar growled through his teeth.

"I requested that the Phantom take charge of your training."

Briar's entire body erupted. His knee jerked and slammed the bottom of the table, rattling the dishes again.

"I can't train with her!" he protested, outraged that his father would even consider something so horrible. "You should hear how she speaks to me."

The Supreme Leader ignored Briar.

"She's the most dangerous assassin in Raedon and you think it's a good idea to put her and me in a room together where she could kill me?" Briar shook his head feverishly. His palms began to sweat. "She'll murder me like all her other victims."

"As part of our deal, the Phantom was pardoned of all her crimes." Briar's father explained in a subtle tone. The

Advisors around the table didn't seem to agree with his deal but it was made, regardless. "You could learn a thing or two from the soldier, seeing as she has more honor than you ever will."

Briar stared at his father even though he wasn't looking back. The Supreme Leader turned away from his son and leaned back towards Achlys's father, beginning their conversation again. The Advisors surrounding the table who were once close to cowering beneath it rose again, their backs straight against their chairs as they resumed their mumbling. All twelve of them miraculously ignored the fact that Briar had spoken at all.

Briar himself sank backward instead. He gripped the arms of his chair so hard his knuckles turned bone white.

He had called her a *soldier*. She was nothing of the kind. She had no place in Raedon, no real name to her face, and certainly no honor that Briar would be interested in learning from.

Briar felt someone staring at him. His gaze moved upwards to find Achlys glancing at him from across the table. His friend shook his head, a strand of white hair falling into his face. When he brushed it away, Briar could see Achlys rolling his eyes as he went back to listening to his father.

Briar felt something inside him vibrate, like an oncoming earthquake rattling his bones.

Not even his friend would defend him now.

Briar's chair screeched across the floor as he stood. He scrubbed a hand down his face as he stormed away from the table, listening as the Advisor's murmuring changed from politics to him. Normally, he craved attention. He bathed in it, letting it sink its dirty claws into his skin and drag him under a shield he could hide behind.

But now, as his back faced the dining hall and with his head tucked into his chest, their muttered words seemed to claw at him until he was raw and exposed.

In the world before the sun imploded, censorship
was a term used to describe the intentional blocking
or covering up of information from the public in
order to serve the unfair needs of higher powers.
I have one thing to say to that; life is no longer fair.
It is important to control the flow of information in
Raedon. Too much knowledge to the people means
too much power to them. Power to the people will
lead them to believe that they are equals to the elite
when they are the furthest thing from mediocrity.
I do not want a standard citizen to see the reforms I
make to improve their rationing each year. While it
affects them, it is none of their business. All they
need to know is that I am helping them rather than
harming them.
What goes on in the news is only what needs to be
there. Anything other than that is confidential
information, and releasing it could mean confusion
and anarchy for the rest of the Imperial Republic.
I am not censoring information. I am protecting it.
And therefore, I am protecting humanity from
itself.

-An excerpt of the first Supreme Leader's
journal, extracted from the Archives of the
Imperial Republic of Raedon

Chapter Thirteen

"Alea jacta est."
-The die is cast.

Wren found her talent of switching personalities both disturbing and quite masterful.

She'd always been able to school her face into a certain expression when it was needed; like putting on different masks for a masquerade party. It was almost like she had transforming skin or scales that could change color depending on the surrounding environment. She was a prodigy at watching body language and matching it flawlessly, making her the perfect person to be put into any kind of situation.

In the time before the sun, there was an illness referred to as 'identity disorder'. Wren had considered it in herself a few times before she realized it was impossible; first, because there was no sickness or disease in Raedon, and second, she was completely aware of all her distinct personalities. She was two-faced, but had one brain controlling the entire operation. It only made sense that she had multiple completely different identities and still, no one knew they were all connected.

This sol, Wren adorned herself with her real name. No one in Raedon knew she still existed; according to the Republic records, her barcode number was given to someone else when she died. She'd given up all ties to herself when she scraped the marking out of her skin, permanently erasing herself from history.

Since she didn't exist, Wren found it easy to slip on her civilian uniform and sneak into Polaris. The streets were so crowded under the dark sky that no one paid attention to her like they did the Phantom; Wren Sitara was just another name in another crowd.

It made Wren smile to think that no one knew Raedon's most notorious assassin was walking amongst them like an equal.

As the Phantom, Wren adored the city of Polaris. It was her playground; the skyscrapers were just tall enough for her to scale and close enough to the street for her to still watch the flurry of life. The Phantom was never seen on the street or spotted on the penthouse floors of the enormous steel and glass buildings, despite practically sitting there for hours. She enjoyed being invisible. It made the most sense, after all; no one would see her if they weren't looking, and no one wanted to look for the saint of death looming above their heads.

There were no distractions so high in the sky. There were only the stars and her, the ones that she believed would willingly take her into their warmth if she reached out a hand to let them.

But without the Phantom's mask to obscure her face, Wren was forced to become herself again. She moved across the streets with the rest of the crowds beginning their sol, heading to university or the other jobs they occupied. Everyone in Raedon had a place to be, and it made her feel even more different from them.

Wren felt a small brush against her elbow as she turned the corner onto a new street. She glanced sideways and found Eden walking with her, his eyes staring at the path straight ahead of them as they crossed the street. He, too, was in his civilian uniform, but didn't seem as out of place as Wren did.

"Why are you here?" Wren asked him with a straight face, keeping her voice low despite the hum of conversation embracing them. No one was interested in what they had to say to each other, but regardless, Eden insisted on them acting like the suspicious rebels they were trying to avoid being.

"I'm checking up on my asset," he responded in a gruff tone that made Wren's blood spark.

"Why?" She snapped, louder than she should have but yet she didn't care. "Are you thinking of pulling me out after I took out a few of your rebels?"

"No, although the Commanders are not happy with the stunt you pulled."

"Seven stunts." She corrected after counting the number of casualties in her head. "And the Commanders are never happy. Especially not with me."

"Those are seven soldiers who can no longer fight in our ranks." Eden had to take a deep inhale to calm himself down. Meanwhile, Wren let her anger burn inside her like fuel.

"You told me to gain his trust." She snapped. "I'm doing that."

The rebels caught in the palace would've been executed, anyway. She was doing them a service; anyone killed by her was considered mercy compared to the Republic.

They crossed the street with a mass of others. Wren dipped her head low, and Eden casually looked sideways, knowing that the cameras on the neon light posts had facial recognition technology. If Eden was spotted, he would be passed up like any other citizen. But Wren was not in her uniform; if her face was identified from any angle, the Republic would find her records and hunt her down. She'd never heard of the Republic having to capture someone because their records were deleted, but she supposed that came with the danger of being the Phantom.

"And does he?" Eden lifted his chin again when they were back on the sidewalk.

"Does he what?"

"Trust you." He glared sideways at her from the corner of his eye. "The answer better be yes. Otherwise, I'll make sure you hear from the Commanders about your 'seven stunts'."

"I'm getting there," Wren growled. She didn't like to be questioned, especially not by someone who wasn't in Sanctum Palace himself. Eden knew nothing but what Wren had told him and so far, her odds were not leaning the right way.

But that was another skill that she had mastered, along with switching her identity. Fate meant nothing to her when she could control her own.

"Let me do my job without being stalked and then maybe you'll see some favorable results."

"I watch you because you're unpredictable and don't follow the orders you're given."

"You sent me to Polaris to infiltrate the Republic and get Briar Atlas to trust me in order for the rebels to gain power. No one gave me the specifics of how to go about doing it."

Eden glared at her as if to ask if she meant to say it as loud as she did. "I assumed it was obvious. Get in and feed us information."

"Why else do you think I'm wandering around the city risking my ass?" Wren countered.

"Start talking, then."

"I found where the solar light is preserved in the palace." She said in a casual tone. Eden's eyes illuminated at the words, but she withheld the rest from him until he asked for it.

"Well?"

Last night, while the rest of Raedon was asleep, Wren went exploring once more. It wasn't hard to find the solar rooms; she knew they must be underground if they were so powerful. They were also guarded on round-the-clock soldier rotations that weren't hard for her to sneak past. It was almost as easy as the time she snuck into a high security archives building to retrieve the blueprints of an underground train station for the rebels.

When Wren finally entered the solar rooms, she wasn't surprised to find millions of tiny, deactivated consoles stacked on top of one another connected by electrical wiring of all colors and thicknesses.

It was almost as if the Supreme Leader *wanted* the rebels to have an easy time cutting the power to the entire city.

Only some consoles were lit; those were the ones working to light Polaris and the palace on the floors above Wren. There must've been years' worth of sunlight reserved on the small devices, and there seemed to be millions more where they came from. Wren assumed that by the size and makeup, each console held at least five years of power. A small grouping of at least one hundred devices would last Raedon another two thousand years. Plus, if there was a solar room connecting the power to the palace, there must be others around the city that were all interconnected.

It was a hive mind of power waiting to be tampered with.

When Wren explained it to Eden, she saw the dark pupils of his eyes grow wide.

"All we would need to do to cause a total blackout would be to sever the connecting wires from the panels," Eden explained breathlessly. "The city would be a complete dark zone."

Wren nodded as she looked across the street. Two groups of people were crossing simultaneously from opposite sides. To Wren, they looked like animatronics with the same uniforms, the same barcodes, and the same dull expression.

"A technical engineer wouldn't even be needed."

Wren agreed with a hum. How hard would it be to find one red wire amongst millions and pull it out of the server? Although, the risk of it would make more of an impact than the blackout would. As well as the hundreds of consoles, there was also a large power basin in the center of the room. If it became unstable, the power it held inside would become radioactive and detonate.

"If that's what you're planning on doing, be careful," Wren warned. "Those wires are attached to a million different panels. One wrong move of the solar devices could have everything go up in smoke." Literally.

"If we're going to shut down the power, we'll need people who know the city in and out, better than the rebels do." Eden went on, glancing up at the skyscrapers towering over their heads.

"Leave that part to me." Wren bit back, unable to help the sinking feeling digging a pit in her stomach. Getting the help Eden and the rebels needed required something she dreaded doing, even when she was in a good mood.

"How was the latest rebel attack?" Eden moved on quickly, but Wren could see the rest of the gears still clicking in his head. "How did the palace respond?"

"The palace responded with chaos, as expected. Everything went to hell when the lights flickered. People knew it was the Rising Sun the moment it happened." Wren couldn't withhold her snarl as she said, "But I thought there could've been some improvements."

"Of course, you do." When she looked sideways at her brother, she saw a look of satisfaction seeping onto his face despite her criticism. She was right; he had a part in planning it. No wonder it had no excitement.

"What about your personal task?" He asked next.

Wren bared her teeth. "Briar remains unhappy about the arrangement his father made with the Phantom." Wren talked about herself as if she didn't know who the assassin was. She liked the sound of it coming from her own mouth, as if no one truly knew who she was. "He despises cooperating with her and tries to get a rise out of her any time he can manage it."

Wren avoided the details of their interaction in the safe room when she had a knife pressed against his throat. He hadn't even flinched when the blade almost split his skin.

She'd let him get the best of her, that was for sure. But she wouldn't allow him to have the last word; so she'd walked away like it had never happened.

Avoidance seemed to be the best solution.

Eden chuckled, but to Wren it sounded more like a scoff of disbelief. He must've thought Briar was a fool for not realizing who Wren really was the moment he saw her. It was easy for him to say, though; he grew up living in the same bedroom as she did in Novus. All until she ran away. After that they became strangers turned acquaintances.

"Briar taunts her too much for her liking, but she casually reminds him who is the better shot out of the both of them."

"I wouldn't believe it if you told me you held yourself back." Eden cracked a small smile and Wren snickered to herself.

"Dorin asked the Phantom to work with his son in combat." Wren resumed. "To train him to defend himself after he almost got killed during your attack."

"You saved him?" Eden fully turned to Wren, and she shrugged.

"Trust is a hard thing to gain from someone who rarely gives it out."

"Believe me, I know." Eden looked back down to the ground, his expression fading. Wren swallowed a lump in her throat.

When Wren left the rebels, she didn't just leave their ranks and the rest of her life they had planned for her as a rebel soldier. She left Eden there as well, in the hands of the Commanders and teachers that had taught them how to shoot a gun for the first time together. It was years before they spoke again and even then, their relationship had become a fragile glass statue.

Wren trusted Eden with everything she had, and Eden trusted her with all he could offer her. But with the Rising Sun backing Eden and Wren working mainly on her own, the divide between the two widened by the year.

Wren couldn't miss what they used to be because she had forgotten a long time ago. She had yet to bring herself to ask if her brother remembered either.

"This could be good," Eden spoke up from the silence gaping between the two of them. He scrubbed a hand down his chin and Wren had the feeling he had been thinking about the same thing she was. "You could weaken Briar, so it'll be easier to get to his father through him."

Wren would've forced Eden to stop walking if there hadn't been a large crowd in front of and behind them. "He's resilient. He won't fall just because I hit him a few times." She snapped, grabbing Eden's forearm instead. He looked back at her with wild eyes, shoving her hand away from him.

"Why do you care?" He scoffed. "He and his father are the same. If you exhaust one, you exhaust them both."

"I don't kill without a reason, Eden." Wren pinned her brother with a lethal stare.

"The Phantom does."

"The Phantom and I are separate." She snarled.

Eden glared at Wren. "Are they?"

Before Wren knew it, her brother had disappeared into the crowd.

When the sun imploded, it left very few resources behind for us to use. Therefore, Raedon is made entirely from the most viable, long lasting, and practical materials.

Almost every building in Raedon is made from the same things and is almost the same height. There are some instances where the use of glass for walls is impractical, but on those rare occasions, the rules are bent. Steel and iron are valuable and strong, so they are used for the support of most skyscrapers in Raedon. Glass is plentiful and can be molded into millions of different shapes and sizes and is therefore used as walls in between the steel and iron beams. Things like concrete and stone bricks are used as the bases for all architecture.

Not only are all seven districts of Raedon sturdy and made to last, but they are also pleasing to look at. There are no run-down apartments or alleyways that need sweeping. The tar on the streets is not faulted or cracked in certain areas of distress. Everything is aesthetically pleasing and, as studies have shown, makes humans happier as well. What is the point of having a perfect society if it does not *look* that way as well?

-An excerpt of the first Supreme Leader's journal, extracted from the Archives of the Imperial Republic of Raedon

Chapter Fourteen

"Libenter epulamur iis qui nobis subire volunt."
-We gladly feast on those who are willing to submit to us.

Wren slid a white cloth over the top of her silver scope.

She went nowhere without her rifle. The weapon was always loaded and strung across her back, easily accessible and practical. The Phantom was the best sharpshooter in Raedon, after all. Even if someone had the chance to take a shot at her, she'd hit them before they put their finger on the trigger.

Wren sat on the edge of one of the training mats, her eyes wandering the silver surface of the weapon for any smudges or fingerprints. The training rooms in the palace were only a few levels above the solar rooms; they weren't meant to be seen by the court. They were mostly used as the barracks for the Supreme Leader's personal guard and military. It was where they fired their weapons and threw their knives when they weren't patrolling the hallways or doing a lousy job protecting their Supreme Leader.

The space was large, bigger than the throne room was. It had a large glass domed ceiling like every other room in the palace. The silver paneled walls were held together by black steel beams, another thing that Wren recalled seeing in many other palace rooms and buildings in Polaris. The center of the floor was covered in training mats, lined with boundary zones for when the soldiers would combat train. Racks of weapons and targets littered the space beyond the mats, anything from rifles to long scythes.

Wren was familiar with all the tools surrounding her; she knew how to shoot arrows and throw knives at the speed of sound itself. When she had first walked into the room, she expected something more guarded. Perhaps with soldiers inside to protect the millions of rounds of ammunition or even the loaded guns lying on the racks. Instead, she found the space abandoned. It was completely silent until her footfall echoed. It reminded Wren of her nights wordlessly looking at the stars and her conversation with Eden last sol.

Wren didn't know what to think about her brother's reaction to her explanation of the rebel attack. He was proud of himself, she could tell. His eyes didn't light up often, but when she said the word 'chaos', it was almost as if she had told him he was being promoted to Commander of the Rising Sun. Wren knew Eden took part in planning the rebel attacks and raids, but she didn't think he had so much say in them. Perhaps the minor attacks on the trains running northward to Antares and south to Rigel were his idea after all, instead of Commander Rheas's.

Wren never agreed with the rebel cause, or how they went about things. Of course, she liked the chaos it created; it allowed adrenaline to run through her veins. But she wasn't also completely on Raedon's side either. No one seemed to be innocent in the matter, and it bothered Wren beyond belief.

Both the Rising Sun and the Republic were equally flawed.

Wren rubbed her thumb across the bottom edge of her scope before polishing it with the towel. She'd been sitting here for at least half an hour and Briar was late to their first lesson. She wasn't surprised in the least bit, though. He wasn't keen on taking anything seriously. Truthfully, Wren wasn't either until Eden brought it up last sol.

Wren knew it was dangerous to keep Briar alive; he could either help the rebels destroy Raedon or work on his father's side to continue building the Republic. He would take his father's position once Dorin was dead and be molded into something the Advisors could control. Eden had told her that he would be no different from his father. So why were the rebels insistent on keeping him alive? Why was he ordered to be treated as an asset instead of a target?

Wren rubbed away a splotch of dirt on her scope when, a moment afterwards, she heard the large doors on the other end of the hall break open. She expected to see Briar stomping through the opening, but she found Nova bouncing across the floor.

"What are you doing here?" Wren bolted from the edge of the mat as Nova approached her, a beaming smile spread onto her lips. "You should be down in the kitchens."

"How did you know Quinn was following you?" Nova squeaked, holding her hands to her chest like an eager child receiving a gift. "How did you sneak away without her knowing? Do you know how many people she sent after you?"

"Nova — " Wren tried to stop the girl, but she was still going.

"Wait," Her shoulders fell as she looked at the rifle in Wren's hands. "You didn't just send me out to get me out of the way, did you?"

"Of course not." Wren snapped, pulling the rifle away from Nova's wiggling fingers and slinging it across her own back. She hadn't spoken with her about why she'd dressed Nova up in her Phantom's uniform while she herself went into Polaris to meet with Eden last night cycle. Although, getting Nova out of the way by giving her tasks wasn't such a bad idea. Wren would have to keep it in the back of her mind for when she needed it later. "Now go away. Briar is going to be here soon."

Wren doubted that. He was already late; she assumed he was walking extra slow on his way to the training room on purpose.

Nova only shrieked louder. "I saw him in the dining room, the other sol!" She told Wren, jumping up and down on the mat. "He was having breakfast with the Supreme Leader and the Advisors. They were fighting about something, but I wasn't paying attention." Nova spoke so fast it was hard for Wren to tell what she said next under her breath. "I didn't realize he would be that attractive in person!"

Wren's eyes rolled towards the back of her head as a blush spread across Nova's pale face. She was falling for the same stupid charm as everyone else in Raedon did. It was infuriating. No, more than that. It was maddening.

"He calls you Ebony, doesn't he?" Nova swayed on her heels.

Wren flushed, remembering her and Briar's interaction in the safe room. She hadn't meant to encourage his banter, but she did, and it ended up with her knife to his throat and their extremely close proximity.

"So?" She opted to say instead, pretending that the memory of Briar hadn't brought her any embarrassment.

"You never told me what to call you."

"What the hell were you doing in the dining hall in the first place?" Wren snapped, switching the topic and drawing her focus from Briar. He'd earned enough of her thoughts already; he wasn't worth any more. "You're supposed to be working in the kitchens."

"They needed an extra servant, so I volunteered." Nova shrugged, seeing no errors in what she'd done. "I carried a pitcher of wine and did an excellent job pouring it."

"Fantastic," Wren said sarcastically. "Maybe next time you'll be able to poison it."

"Does that mean I'll be able to help you murder someone else?" Nova jumped up and down excitedly and her pendant necklace hit her in the mouth. She didn't seem to notice it.

"First, keep this hidden. Or better yet, take it off entirely." Wren took the sun pendant and shoved it under Nova's loose uniform. "If someone sees you with it, you'll be killed."

"I never take it off." Nova looked down at her shirt where her necklace used to be. "My sister has the same one."

"I don't care." Wren grit her teeth together, settling her hands on Nova's shoulders to stop her from bouncing. "And I don't *murder* anyone."

"You seem to use that term lightly."

"You don't belong here, Nova."

Her shoulders fell and her gray eyes widened. "This is what I've been training for my entire life. I deserve a chance to prove myself."

"Proving yourself doesn't mean getting killed," Wren told her, clenching her jaw. "Vesta would come after me if anything happened to you."

"But -- "

Nova was cut off by the sound of doors opening again, only when Wren looked over Nova's shoulder, she found Quinn Vega entering instead of Briar.

Two for two; Wren knew this would not go well.

"Go away." Wren looked back at Nova, snarling at her from beneath her mask. Nova changed personalities as well, playing her role better than Wren would've expected. As Wren pretended to treat her like a servant, Nova nodded her head obediently. "I'll send for you when I need you."

With her back to Quinn, Nova smiled brightly at Wren before whipping around on her heel, practically running away from the mat as if the Phantom was aiming a gun at her back and her trigger finger was itching. Quinn paid no attention to Nova as she stepped onto the edge of the mat, eyeing the assassin up with suspicion.

Wren waited until she heard the doors shut, and a few moments after to make sure Nova had truly left to say anything.

"Have you finally come to train with me?"

"Have you been waiting?" Quinn asked with a sly smile, not passing the outer rim of the mat. She wasn't entering, rather declining Wren's invitation.

"I'm always waiting for something," Wren responded and taunted her again. "Grab a knife."

"As much as I would love to," The Captain began, "that's not why I'm here."

"Then why are you here? Have you finally realized that sending your soldiers into the city to follow me around was pointless?" Wren tilted her head, mocking curiosity. She knew Quinn was suspicious of her after her assault during the speech and finding her with Briar in the safe point. The Captain did not trust her. But it was a good thing that Wren didn't build relations on trust; she built them on fear.

"How did you know?"

"I always know." Wren winked at the Captain and Quinn snarled.

Wren knew she was being watched; she wouldn't expect anything less from the Captain. In fact, she'd counted on it. She'd given Nova her uniform last night and told her to walk around Polaris for an hour so she could meet with Eden. It was hard to convince the girl to do anything without bribing her first, so Wren had promised to give Nova one of her knives once she completed the task.

Nova practically screamed when she held one of the Phantom's knives in her hand. Wren shoved her back into the kitchens before she could make any noise and even saw the imprint of the dagger shoved into Nova's servant uniform a few minutes earlier.

She'd have to teach her how to hide her weapons better.

Wren strolled down the completely opposite streets as Nova and it seemed to her like Quinn didn't suspect a single thing. She hadn't yet asked who she was talking to, and if she did somehow miraculously send two scouts, she wouldn't have known who Wren was amongst the other crowds.

"Of course you do," Quinn responded. "The Supreme Leader ordered me to monitor you. He seemed to believe it would keep you from going against the terms of your arrangement."

"Going into the city should hold no threat to him or to our deal."

"So, why were you in the city in the first place? You don't look like the kind to enjoy walking around crowds of people." She asked, looking at the rifle behind Wren's back. Her reflection danced on the tip, contorted by the lines of the weapon.

She was right, of course. Wren hated crowds that weren't watching her pull stunts as the Phantom. So instead, she repeated the answer she provided to the Supreme Leader. "Again, my reputation speaks for me. I haven't visited Polaris in a long time. Despite what people say about me, I quite enjoy strolling around the loud streets."

"Were you looking for anyone?" Quinn's voice wasn't trembling like most did when they spoke to the Phantom. She was fierce, unthreatened by her persona, which made Wren scowl. That was twice now that someone hadn't been affected by her bravado.

Perhaps that meant she needed to try harder.

"If you're assuming that I was secretly traveling around Polaris in the middle of the sol cycle to meet with the accomplice of my evil plans, you'd be mistaken."

"No, I -- " Quinn began, but Wren interrupted her.

"You were curious?"

"To put it simply, yes." Then Quinn glanced at Wren's uniform, specifically the knives tucked into her pants. Wren considered offering them to her to throw when the Captain spoke again. "How did you know about the assassin in the crowd?"

Wren didn't allow her face to change, although her lips ached to smile. She had been right; the only reason Quinn had sought her out in the first place was to question her about the assassination attempt she'd stopped. That was good to hear; Wren was hoping she wouldn't ask about the scene in the safe room with Briar.

"I saw him," Wren said, letting the ghost of a smile appear on her lips. "I went after him. Then I stopped him."

"Right but -- "

"From my angle, the shine of his pistol reflected off of the lights around the Arc. It caught my eye because my own weapon gives off the same glare." Wren tapped her rifle lightly on the ground. Quinn looked down to inspect it.

She couldn't let Quinn get too close to the truth. She had, after all, stopped an assassin from killing the Supreme Leader and his son, but the only reason the man had been there in the first place was because Wren planted him. She hired him secretly through Nova. She paid him money that would return to her when the job was finished and told him to tuck the pistol into his pocket but not to use it. The Rising Sun's scarf hadn't been there when he entered the crowd; Wren put it in his pocket when she reached to grab the gun from him and reveal his traitorous actions.

And her plan had worked, as they usually did. No one suspected a thing besides the rebel's desperate actions to kill the Supreme Leader. The Phantom would remain unscathed and still completely separate from the rebels.

"Ah, I forgot." Quinn nodded. She was still miles away from becoming confident in Wren's answers. Any lies the assassin flawlessly told wouldn't be so easily brushed away.

Sometimes, it was truly refreshing to be as good at one's job as Wren was.

"Did someone tip you off, perhaps?" Quinn kept digging.

"I don't need people to tip me off." Wren spat the last words like foul tasting food. "I simply do my job. Now go do yours and leave me be."

As easy as she was for Wren to manipulate, Quinn was not an idiot like the rest of Raedon. She wouldn't fall to white lies or pretty smiles, and Wren could tell she was dancing on the edge of a very fragile cliff.

Unfortunately for Quinn, Wren had fantastic balance.

"You are my job." Quinn retorted. "I am responsible for everything in this palace, which now includes you."

"I see." Wren clicked her tongue. "Your soldiers didn't watch me close enough to your liking, so now you assign the task to yourself."

The Captain shrugged, but it was the furthest action from casual Wren had ever seen. "Something like that."

"Then tell me what you think you'll catch me doing, if I'm so worthy of watching."

"Something incriminating, I'm sure. You have a reputation."

Wren had found a weak joint. Now all she had to do was hit it.

"Are you afraid of what I might do to hurt Briar?"

Quinn bared her teeth. "I'm not afraid of you in the slightest."

Wren kept herself from smiling. Briar had told her the same thing. Everyone was afraid of something, especially the Captain. Wren guessed she was afraid of losing control, especially over something she had no doubt worked so hard to gain.

But a loss of control was what Wren was best at. No control meant chaos. And Wren had a sweet tooth for that.

"Briar said the same thing to me until he flinched at the sight of me."

"I'm looking at you now." Quinn glared at the assassin. "Do you see me flinching?"

"Not yet."

"You're so determined to make everyone afraid of you." Quinn finally stepped onto the mat and closed the space between her and Wren. "What makes you think you're not the scared one?"

"I don't get scared." Wren lifted her chin, allowing Quinn to look into her eyes since she couldn't read the rest of her face.

"Not yet."

Wren didn't respond.

"You're not a threat, if that's what you think of yourself." Her eyes raked across Wren's uniform.

"You wouldn't be watching me if I wasn't a threat."

"So, you think you're intimidating?"

"Are you intimidated?"

But before Quinn could say another word, the doors on the other end of the room cracked again.

"Was I interrupting something?" Briar stood by the wall, allowing the doors to slam close with a loud echo behind him. He wore his royal uniform but without the usual jacket. Today, it was just a tight fit long-sleeved shirt and trousers. It made him look taller and leaner than Wren first noticed.

"The Captain was just leaving." Wren held back the bite in her words. Couldn't Briar have been late some other time?

Quinn said nothing as she turned around, following Nova's path towards the door. She slammed them behind her when she was gone, surely storming through the corridors in a rage of loss. Wren couldn't keep herself from laughing.

"What the hell was that?" Briar scowled as he twisted his shoulders to face the doors and then back at Wren again. "If I interrupted something that would've been a fight, I would've just stayed silent."

"You're erratic." Wren snapped, still high from her conversation with Quinn.

"I prefer exotic." Briar flashed her a toothy smile.

"Let's go." Wren turned away from him and stepped back onto the middle of the mat, crossing her arms as Briar slowly came to meet her. Up close, he stood taller than her by at least a few inches. He copied her stance, crossing his arms as well.

"Look," he began, and Wren instantly let out a sigh. This was their first time together since roughhousing in the safe point and he was already complaining again. "I don't want to be here and neither do you. So, if we could come to an agreement that would allow me to do absolutely no work and also make sure my father thought I was training, that would great."

"Yes, sir."

Briar blanched, and his hands fell from his chest. Lifting his eyebrows in pleasant surprise, he nodded his head slightly. "There's no need to call me 'sir', but I'm glad you've finally learned your place."

Wren uncrossed her arms as well. "It wasn't a formality. I was mocking you."
Before Briar could retort, she curled her hand into a fist and punched the Supreme Leader's son in the nose.

Beauty is a complicated subject.
Every human has a distinct genetic makeup that causes them to see things differently than one another. Whilst one man might look at a portrait of the sun and call it a marvel, another might stare at the same painting and call it horrifying.
Perspective was a concept that humankind before the sun that described someone's opposing or edged view on a subject. It was the reason *why* they thought what they were thinking and allowed other humans to understand their situation and display a common human feeling; empathy.
But what was beautiful then is certainly not beautiful now.
If a painter had depicted the explosion of the sun, the poisonous waves of air expanding from the sky and the extinction of all living things, he would be put to death. No array of colors or shapes could convince a person to not look deeper within the painting; past all the brush strokes and canvas layers to see the intended message.
While the destruction of our world was not beautiful, it was necessary.
What is considered a beauty in Raedon is not what would've been alluring billions of years ago.
When I look at the skyline, I do not see a society of crystalline glass windows and impeccable architecture. I do not see a thriving expanse of cities and, with success, woven into every aspect of human life.

I see control.
Control is the one thing that will always amaze me
above everything else.

-An excerpt of the first Supreme Leader's
journal, extracted from the Archives of the
Imperial Republic of Raedon

Chapter Fifteen

"Omne quod movetur ab alio movetur."
-Everything that moves is moved by another.

There was blood running out of Briar's nose like the wine he once purposefully spilled on one of his father's Advisors. Although this stung more than that scolding ever did.

He bowed over in the center of the training mat, holding his nose with both hands. He could feel the blood rushing from both nostrils and leaking through his lips. He grunted, wiping a bloody palm on his pants before looking up at the Phantom.

She'd circled him now like a hunter looking at her prey. In her eyes, he could see the laughter blooming behind her mask. It made the blood leaking from his nose burn hotter than fire.

"What the hell was that for?" He spit out a drip of blood that fell into his mouth. It was metallic and tangy and now all over his front teeth. It stained a splotch of red into the neckline of his uniform.

"If I have to look like I'm training you, you should at least come out looking like you put up a good effort." She reached a spot behind him and he heard her chuckle. She was laughing at him. Again.

She hadn't been this confident when they were in the safe point together. Sure, there was a knife pressing against his throat, but when wasn't there? She might have been holding the weapon, but he was the one who encouraged her to do it; out of a joke, of course, but it took him taunting her to finally lunge at him.

Briar felt his face burning up as he wiped the back of his hand across his lower face. There was scarlet stained into his skin now, all over his chin and lips. But he didn't care because it hid the blazing red color now rising beneath his skin. He would get the best of the Phantom again.

"You could've warned me," he sniffed, his jaw flexing. Ebony was back in front of him now, her hands placed in a taunting position on her hips.

She leaned to the side, jeering at him as she said, "That wouldn't have been as much fun."

Briar growled, gritting his teeth together as he lunged towards the assassin. He let his fist fly, but it never made purchase. Instead, he looked up to find it trapped in Ebony's own palm and her other hand jabbing to strike him in the ribs.

Briar stumbled backward, clutching his stomach. He coughed, not imagining one small fist could hurt so bad.

"At least rough up your fists a bit," Ebony teased. "Make it look like you tried."

"Anyone who told you that you are a delight to work with lied." Briar spat blood onto the mat, feeling it boiling in between his teeth.

"I work alone."

"That explains a lot."

"You would make everyone so much happier if you and your attitude would just leave the room." Thankfully, Ebony didn't throw another punch at him as she said it.

Briar straightened and tried to ignore the bruise blooming on his abdomen. It hurt to breathe and yet he still said, "It's a good thing I wasn't put on this earth to make you happy."

"You're right." She countered, tapping her foot impatiently on the ground. "Your only job is to convince people not to have kids." Then she held out her hands with her palms facing Briar. "Now, hit me."

Briar rolled his eyes and scrubbed a hand across his mouth. He curled his fingers into a fist and took in a deep breath. Then he lunged.

Ebony had deflected his hand with a lazy wave of her wrist. "I said hit me, not love tap me." It was like she could barely feel any impact that hit her, almost like she was wearing a bulletproof vest underneath her uniform.

Briar would gladly test that out after their lesson.

"I would never 'love tap' you." He spat. "Ever."

"My mistake." Ebony shrugged, and the relaxed nature of it made his blood simmer right down to the bone. "I meant to say, 'hit me as light as you can'."

Briar jerked his chin in her direction. "Fine. If you're so perfect at it, show me how it's done." he held out her hands as she did for him. "Hit me."

"I'm afraid I already have." She cast him a dismissive look. "Multiple times."

"Well then, try again." Briar set himself up to take the hit, but Ebony remained in her current position, snarling back at him.

"I can only explain it to you. I cannot understand it for you, too." her upper lip curled, and Briar felt his entire body beginning to heat with fury.

"I hate you."

"I tolerate you."

Briar roared and lunged toward the assassin again. Instead of catching his fist, she ducked under it with ease, jumping onto his hips. Briar suddenly found himself unbalanced and distracted as Ebony jammed her elbow into his ear and flipped him over her head.

He landed with a loud crash behind her. He groaned, unable to move any part of his body. Seconds later, his head throbbed with a horrible headache. He'd hoped to catch a break from the Phantom, but the next time he blinked, he found her sitting on top of his lungs with a knife pressed gently against the side of his neck.

"This should feel familiar." She used her legs to pin his arms down beside him. Her other arm was pushing against his chest so he couldn't even attempt to rise.

This was three times now that he'd found himself under a knife since meeting her. Although, the second time was his fault, and he wasn't ashamed of it either.

Ebony's masked face was so close to his that he could almost feel her breath cascading down his neck. It was like a ghost of a touch, something he could barely feel but knew was there. The tip of the knife she had pressed to the side of his throat felt the same way; he could only slightly feel the cold silver caressing his skin where his previous cut had only just scabbed. When Briar finally let his eyes stop wandering, they met Ebony's crushing aquamarine irises.

Her pupils flexed. She seemed to realize she held the weapon that could end his life and leaned in closer so he could hear her voice. It was coarser than he'd anticipated

"I'll cut you a deal." She said, "I'll go easy on you and make sure your father never hears of your slacking."

Briar grumbled. "What do you want out of it?" His voice was strained.

"I want you to tell me everything you know about the sun and the solar energy stored around Raedon."

Briar would've laughed if there wasn't a blade being pressed to his throat by the most unpredictable assassin in Raedon. But he was unpredictable as well and still managed to snicker in her face.

"You can't be serious." he laughed, feeling the knife remain steady against his skin despite his bobbing throat.

"You don't want the deal?" The Phantom was either genuinely confused why Briar hadn't immediately accepted, or she was great at lying. He'd guess it was the latter.

"Knowing about the sun is useless." He spit. "It's gone."

"This deal won't work if you're lying to me." She seemed more serious now. The heels of her boots dug further into his wrists, and he defied every bone in his body to keep himself from flinching.

"I'm not lying to you. There would be no point." He replied. "What's your obsession with the sun, anyway? It was just a star." The Phantom mostly worked at night; he knew that from the rumors circling her. What use was it to her to know about a bright yellow flame when she already seemed to know enough to do more than just survive?

"It was more than a star, you idiot." Ebony's tone cracked like a whip. "You're not pretty enough to be this stupid."

"I'll have you know my face has been deemed perfectly symmetrical." Briar snapped back, watching Ebony's mood turn from serious to annoyed.

"Being told that by your grandmother doesn't count."

"She's dead."

"I would be too if I gave birth to the thing that created you."

Briar felt a jolt of anger inside him. He jerked his head forward and bared his teeth at her, but she moved the knife across his skin. It didn't cut, but the icy whisper threatened to.

"Take the deal or leave it." The Phantom told him. "I could make your life a living hell, or I can subdue the flames. It's your choice."

Briar chortled. Wasn't she already making his life a living hell? Instead of voicing his opinions, he clamped his mouth shut and spoke through clenched teeth. "Fine."

"Excellent." Ebony twirled her knife against his neck. "Now, push me off."

"What?" Briar tried to glance down at the knife, but Ebony jerked his chin up with a small slap.

"Push me off." She repeated. "I'm an attacker trying to kill you. Push me off."

"I'm not sure repeating the statement will do anything to help me. And wouldn't you have already killed me by this point?"

"Let's assume I opted for torture and stared at your face a little longer than usual." And just to spite him, she said, "Push me off."

"I feel like -- "

"Just do it!"

Briar yanked his wrist out from underneath her heel and jammed his fist into her elbow. Her arm buckled, and she fell onto his chest, giving him the chance to roll out from underneath her with a surprised gasp.

"That wasn't hard, was it?" Ebony chuckled, still lying on the floor beside him. Briar was more out of breath than he'd imagined he'd be, but that might've been the rush of shock flowing through his veins.

Did he just escape the Phantom?

Beside him, Ebony lifted herself to her knees. She twirled the knife in her fingers before slipping it back into the pocket of her uniform. Briar seemed to be unable to take his eyes off the other knives until the Phantom stood before him, reaching out a hand to help him up. Briar found it unusual and blinked slowly. Finally, he took her gloved hand.

He knew it was a mistake the minute their fingers interlocked. When he was halfway off the floor, she swiped a leg underneath his feet to unbalance him, twisting him in a storm of arms until he found himself locked between her elbow and her face. She squeezed his neck until he clawed at her forearm.

That was the second time he'd fallen for that move. The first time wasn't so painful, though.

The Phantom's mouth was close to his ear as she whispered, "Never accept help from an enemy when they offer it."

"Is that what we are now? Enemies?" Briar choked out, struggling to get a full breath. He found Ebony's arm crushing him against her and he felt her heartbeat underneath the layers of ivory fabric.

"We're certainly not friends."

Ebony released him and shoved him away from her. He grabbed his neck with both hands, relieved to feel the air continuing to flow through his body. When he glanced up, he found the assassin glaring at him with jaded eyes.

"Lesson one." She stepped towards him and grabbed his chin with her hand. She lifted it and he hissed. "Know who your friends are. Most importantly, know which ones can destroy you."

The word "happiness" was relative.

No one person is ever truly happy, and that was something that humanity thought could never be cured. The human mind, no matter how complex or how organized it was, how tangled or simple it seemed to be, would always find something wrong with the world. It was like spotting a crack in the glass and tapping on it endlessly until it finally broke beneath your fingers, spilling shards of glass onto the floor around you.

Then humans would step on that glass and give themselves yet another thing to complain about.

But how could there be anything but happiness if everything was already perfect? How could anyone even *think* about not being happy when each aspect of their lives was purposefully built to bring about the maximum level of content? It was like a painting, the hues masterfully concocted and combined with delicate brushstrokes to create a world without exception to this rule.

It was a mathematical equation solved with only one answer: faultlessness.

There were no cracks in Raedon because it is not as fragile as glass, and the Republic certainly didn't step on any shards.

-An excerpt of the first Supreme Leader's journal, extracted from the Archives of the Imperial Republic of Raedon

Chapter Sixteen

"Plena hominum nulla amicitia."
-Full of men, no friendship.

Briar's entire body ached. Even his mind seemed to put the least amount of effort into everything he did. Walking down the corridor was a challenge and this time it wasn't because he'd climbed onto the dining hall chandelier and flipped from it to land on the table. That had hurt excruciatingly because his attempt to do three flips instead of two failed. It also happened to be in front of a group of girls.

After the Phantom hit him in the nose, flipped him over her head, pressed a knife to his throat, and held him in a chokehold, she taught him hand-to-hand combat training. There were no weapons involved; something that Briar was enormously thankful for after having a blade against his neck for the third time in only a few sol cycles.

Ebony was strict about it despite their deal to go easy on him. She was constantly correcting him; his stance was floppy, his arms were weak, and he had the reaction time of a blind man. But despite her constant insults, Briar had the sense to shut his mouth through most of it. Sure, he had made a few backhanded comments and cursed so colorfully when she'd punched him over and over, but mostly, he knew that the moment he did something wrong she would take it out on him.; whether that meant shooting him in the head or telling his father. They both seemed to be an equivalent punishment.

In the few hours they spent together, Ebony taught him a sequence of basic movements to defend himself and a few on attacking. It was harder than he thought and going into the training room, Briar assumed he could shoot a few rounds of bullets and leave. Unfortunately, there was a certain way he was supposed to hold his fist when punching and a specific way Ebony taught him to stand to give the strike more impact.

It was nothing like the maneuver she pulled when she flipped him over her head. Even though it hurt like hell as he walked and even more at the moment she did it, he still wanted to learn how she managed to do that when she was three-fourths of his size.

In the time they spent together, Briar was sweaty, his entire body ached, but he had landed exactly one punch to the side of Ebony's jaw. He could tell she wasn't expecting it, but didn't flinch when she touched it, either. Briar felt an enormous sense of accomplishment and giddiness when he saw the bruise next to her eye becoming darker, but his expression instantly melted when she pointed a stern finger his way.

"Savor this feeling." She said to him, "It will never happen again."

Everything inside Briar still throbbed, but it didn't bother him as much as he thought it would. There was also a bonus that came with their deal that didn't include getting beaten to a pulp; Briar's father hadn't scolded him for the past few sol cycles.

Briar turned the corner and approached a set of doors guarded by two soldiers. Even with the blossoming aftermath of his training with Ebony, he still couldn't forget what she had told him.

Know who your friends are. Most importantly, know which ones can destroy you.

It made Briar's mind tick, and not in the way he enjoyed when he got a new idea for a stunt to pull in front of his father's court. It disturbed him how much her words resonated inside his head like a chip implanted into his skin.

His argument with his father came flooding back to Briar's mind. He remembered looking across the table at Achlys, wondering if his friend would say anything. Instead, he refused to meet his eyes and ignored him. It was usual for Achlys to ignore Briar when he was talking about random things, but this was different. It felt different to be ignored now, and Briar was confused. He had so few real friends, and he'd always thought his best one was Achlys.

Maybe that wasn't the truth anymore.

Briar came across a new corridor and stopped in front of a set of doors. He jerked his head to order the soldiers to open them. They did without a word, and Briar immediately spotted Achlys standing by a table draped with clothing.

Achlys's back was facing him. His bare skin was exposed on his upper body, but the rest was covered with his black uniform pants; buckled with an onyx-colored belt. His skin was shining with water droplets that reflected the neon blue lights of the room as Achlys turned around. He was wiping his face with a cloth when Briar approached him.

"Do you walk in on everyone when they're shirtless?" He asked. A strand of wet, milky hair fell into his eyes.

The doors closed behind Briar, and he scoffed. "We both know you have no problem being shirtless around anyone."

"Says you, who I remember ripping off his shirt in a gambling hall as part of a bet."

"That was a good time." Briar grinned, remembering the incident clearly. "You should've been there."

"You lost the bet," Achlys said blankly.

"Not entirely. I gained a few girls, mind you."

"Sure, you did." Achlys hummed and nodded his head, then cast Briar a confused glance. "Where are those girls now, exactly?"

Briar's lips ticked upwards. "I got bored with them."

Achlys chuckled. "You? Bored? Never."

Briar smiled, satisfied with the way the conversation was going. In front of him, Achlys shrugged and looked down at himself. He was handsome. Or at least, all the girls in the court thought so. Although, they seemed to be fonder of Briar, even with cracked ribs and only two flips in his repertoire.

Achlys turned back away from Briar, wiping the rest of his damp face with a cloth before gracefully strutting towards the open bathroom doors on the other wall. His bedroom was much like Briar's but without all the grandiose decorations and stolen items. Briar followed his friend to the doors and once Achlys passed the threshold into the tiled room, Briar leaned against the doorframe.

"Would you like to shower with me as well?" Achlys jeered, leaning down into the sink to run his face over with more water. Briar didn't see the point of it; he was already glowing.

Briar felt a pang of familiar emptiness in his gut. It was the same feeling he had when he approached his father in his office the other sol; the time when he conveniently forgot to mention anything about the sun. Only this time Briar felt surer of himself. It was an odd feeling for Briar to have; true confidence rather than faking it with a smile plastered on his face.

Determined to reach his point this time, Briar glared at Achlys and set his face in a hard expression. "Why didn't you defend me?"

Achlys, still bent over the basin, picked up a bar of soap next to the sink and held it up for Briar to see. "I have this lovely soap to try. Apparently, it smells like," he glanced sideways at the label and shrugged. "'The Stars'."

"Achlys," Briar said more firmly, catching his friend's attention. "Why didn't you defend me?"

Achlys's hand slowed as he scrubbed the length of his face. Water dripped from his pointed chin as he looked at Briar through the mirror's reflection. Briar could tell his friend was thinking about his response, but didn't know if that was a good or bad thing.

"I didn't interfere because it wasn't my place." he finally said, his white eyelashes dripping tiny beads of water. Underneath them, Achlys's pale blue eyes widened. "You should know that."

"To hell with anyone's place." Briar spat, although he wasn't truly mad. "I — "

"No, not 'to hell with anyone's place'." Achlys countered faster than Briar thought he would. "Don't you hear yourself?"

"Of course, I do." Briar felt his brow crinkle. "Being deaf doesn't exist anymore."

"Then, listen." Achlys turned around to look Briar in the face instead of at his reflection. "You're the son of the Supreme Leader. My father is one of his Advisors. I can't just let my mouth run like you allow yours to."

"My mouth doesn't run." Briar insisted.

"You're right. It sprints."

Anger flared inside Briar's veins, more so than it did when Ebony insulted him in the training room. "What is wrong with you? I thought we were friends."

Achlys laughed, an airy sound of disbelief. "Please, Briar. Stop with the hallucinations." He said, still high from his outburst. He reached for a shirt draped across the marble counter and stretched it over his arms and chest. "We aren't friends."

"What the hell is that supposed to mean?" Briar didn't understand what Achlys was saying, much less what he meant by all of it.

"Look around." Achlys gestured to the space of the bathroom, but Briar didn't let his eyes wander from the man in front of him. "Raedon is getting more dangerous with every sol cycle. The Republic is becoming more fragile than ever. There are rebels at large trying to kill you."

Briar swallowed a lump in his throat. Raedon seemed fine to him; as perfect as ever, really. And what was wrong with the Republic? What were the rebels doing that Briar's father was hiding from him and the rest of the world?

"But they haven't killed me yet, and they never will," Briar said instead, keeping his questions to himself. For every mystery that came to him, more followed until there was an endless well of questions in his mind.

Who was lying? Achlys, or his father?

"Briar, we're not kids anymore. We can't waste time pulling stupid pranks on your father's court anymore!"

"You have no room to talk." Briar smiled, trying to lighten himself up. He waved a hand in dismissal. "You never took part in any of my plans, anyway."

"Get it through your head, Briar! You have to grow up!" The bite of his words sunk into Briar's skin like the teeth of a beast. He was frozen in the doorway, staring at Achlys.

"What?"

"Eventually, you'll be too busy trying to find the humor in everything, and by that point, it'll be too late!" Achlys responded. "You'd have already messed everything up."

"I didn't mess anything up." Briar snapped back.

"Look at yourself." Achlys's tone became more demanding. It made Briar think of his father. "You are the future Supreme Leader of Raedon and I will be one of your Advisors. I have to stay in my place, and you have to learn where yours is."

"That doesn't mean we can't be friends." Briar countered, pushing off the door frame with his foot. The anger that flickered inside him seemed to be snuffed out. Now, there was only a pit in the middle of his stomach, the same one he felt when standing before his father, wordlessly accepting his stinging rejection.

"Think, Briar." Achlys tapped his fingers to his temples. "Remember the meal with your father? Did any of the Advisors look like friends to you?"

Briar didn't respond.

No. None of the Advisors looked like they were anything close to friendly with each other. In fact, they looked like they would willingly kill to be one of the others who talked to Briar's father. It was a competition between all of them and the Supreme Leader was the prize.

"What does that have to do with us?" Briar shook his head in disbelief.

Achlys ran a hand through his hair, combing back the wet strands. "Everything we do matters. Every step we take and every sentence we voice will be put into the news and seen by everyone in Raedon." His tone changed from firm to something softer, like he was telling a child right from wrong. "There is no room for mistakes for me."

"I don't understand."

"This is a race, Briar. I can't focus on anything but winning."

"Is that what your father tells you?" Briar snapped, hearing the waver in his voice. "I hear the way he talks to you."

Achlys blinked and looked down at the ground. "He just wants what is best for me." His hands mindlessly tucked themselves behind his back.

"Why does it have to be that way?" Briar waited for Achlys to respond, but he remained silent, passing by Briar's shoulder with a small shove. Briar turned to watch him walk back into the main room, slipping on his uniform jacket and continuing to ignore the question. He walked towards the doors, adjusting his uniform on his shoulders. Briar watched him get further away until he reached the doorknob, turning it with one final glance back at Briar.

"Grow up." He said, locking eyes with Briar for a fraction of a second before opening the door and slipping out into the hallway. "There are no friends here."

Briar listened to Achlys's footsteps escape down the hallway. When there was silence again, he felt something in the very core of him. It felt like it had been festering for a long time now, but this was the moment Briar could feel it beginning to explode.

No, not explode.

Crumble.

Emotion is one thing I will never understand.
No human can live without feelings. It's what
causes us to make the decisions we do. If I am
driven by love, I am more likely to make sacrifices
in my daily life to be with the person I care about.
But if I am driven by greed, I will do everything
within my power to make sure I am the only one
who gets to say that they succeeded.
Humans are emotional creatures. We cry, we laugh,
we hug, and we fight. It's a part of our nature.
But if we've defeated nature, haven't we also
defeated emotion?
I emote just like the rest, but that does not mean I
agree with what I feel. I am not driven to decide
based on my emotions. I find them rather
distracting. Being upset about a certain thing will
overshadow my decision-making about another.
Feelings are like curtains drawn in front of clear
windows, obstructing our view of what we need to
see.
Emotions are weaknesses.
And there will be no weaknesses in Raedon.

-An excerpt of the first Supreme Leader's
journal, extracted from the Archives of the
Imperial Republic of Raedon

Chapter Seventeen

"Optimum est pati quod emendare non possis."
-It is best to suffer what you cannot improve.

Briar was used to distracting himself. In fact, to him, it seemed to be an art form. Whether that was thinking about his next scheme while his father was talking to him about important matters of the court or playing with spoons and forks at court meals where the conversation was so boring Briar wanted to gouge his eyes out, he considered himself a master at it.

But this time, Briar couldn't seem to control his racing thoughts like he normally could.

Briar sat against the railing of his balcony. He tucked one leg into his chest as he rested his elbow on it while the other lay idly out in front of him. He held his head in his hand, tapping his fingers against his scalp. There was no noise surrounding him, yet his mind was screaming. From the edge of the balcony, Briar could see all of Polaris. It was the best view in all of Raedon, or so he thought, until now.

There are no friends here.

Briar and Achlys had known each other for so long that he was hesitant to call them anything but family. They grew

206

up in the palace together, playing with toy swords and shooting guns that had absolutely no ammunition in them besides the small spitballs Briar occasionally rolled into the barrels. Briar would come up with brilliant ideas of how to trick the court next, and Achlys would ignore him. Briar would complain about things that had nothing to do with either of them, and Achlys would continue to ignore him. Briar had gotten so used to the dynamic of Achyls casting him aside that he hadn't realized why he was so attached to the man in the first place.

Things were never stable in Sanctum Palace, almost like the stars were constantly tipping the scales of fate just to throw him off balance. In one moment, his father had hired a babysitter to keep him alive and in the next, he had to hold a hand to his bleeding neck because a rebel had tried to kill him. Stability wasn't a concept that was familiar to Briar and as much as he faked hating the idea of it, it was the only reason he still held onto Achlys.

But now that Achlys had left him, Briar felt more isolated than ever.

Briar drummed his fingers against his temples. He needed a distraction, something to take his mind off of his argument with Achlys.

Fortunately, he saw the glimmer of the Phantom's ivory uniform just in time.

Briar's curiosity sparked just as the assassin reached the middle of the Arc. He stood, instantly pushing Achlys from his mind. He squinted as the Phantom strutted until she reached the end of the bridge, looking back at the palace. Her shoulders were bent unusually, and her chin was tilted downwards as if she was avoiding looking anywhere but ahead. Briar saw her fingers twitching at her sides. When she turned around again to face the end of the Arc, she pulled her gun out of its holster and continued into the city.

Where the hell did she think she was going without him?

Without thinking, Briar raced back into his room and wrenched open his armoire. He grabbed a coat and hoisted it onto his shoulders, pulling up the hood as he dashed out into the hallway. He didn't know where Ebony was going, nor did he particularly care. He needed to get out of his head, and perhaps following her through the city whenever she was going was just the thing he needed.

It wasn't hard for Briar to escape the palace. The soldiers he passed looked him up and down with his hood, but determined he was no threat to them. They could see his face so they knew who he was, but his expression dared them to stop him. Instead, they marched on and allowed Briar to practically walk right out the front doors of the palace.

When he reached the Arc, she was gone. Briar could feel his heart beating in his chest, both from his sprint out of his room and his curiosity. Where was she going? Why did she need a gun for it?

Was it a good idea to follow her? Probably not, but Briar continued anyway.

Briar hurried the rest of the bridge and out onto the street. The alarms that usually spotted rebels hadn't gone off, which Briar thought was unusual. It was well past the curfew; what had shut them off?

He walked along the main roads until he came across a fork. There were four streets in front of him, all lit by the neon lights lining the sidewalks and buildings. None of the roads seemed to be something Ebony would go down, but then again, he probably didn't know her as well as she'd led him to believe.

What if the reason she was going into the city at this time of night was to assassinate someone? She was the Phantom, after all. Making an agreement with his father didn't mean she'd completely abandoned her hit list. Perhaps Briar had just earned a front-row seat to the demise of her next miserable victim. It didn't appeal to him in the way that wine barrels did at his father's court gatherings, but Briar moved on. Following Ebony as she stalked her prey was better than thinking about anything else that had happened to Briar that night.

The moment Briar took a step towards the leftmost street, he heard a scuffle from the one furthest to the right. Intrigued and somewhat eager, Briar stopped his pursuit down the left street and walked towards the right. He checked to make sure his hood was fully covering his face, even though there was no one around to see him. There were security cameras on each street. Surely he would be spotted and later scolded, but the exhilaration he got from following Ebony wasn't equivalent.

Briar walked in the center of the street until he found another split in the road. The avenues had become dimmer and continued to be that way until Briar finally stood in the middle of the slums.

Briar had heard about the slums of Polaris, but he'd never actually been to one of them. From the looks of the street ahead and behind him, they were exactly what he imagined them to be. The term perfection only applied to the elite.

The road was dark, and the pavement was cracked. The lights from the rest of the city had become a rarity, flickering or entirely snuffed out on the sides of buildings. The road was rather lit with lanterns and candles, hanging above shattered door frames and kicked in doors. It seemed like a complete ghost town, somewhere the Phantom would belong but never actually visit. The cracked pavement, littered with trash and other substances Briar didn't feel at liberty to question, ran on the sides of the street at uneven angles. The entire place smelled like sewage and smoke and reminded Briar of what must've been the aftermath of the sun's first wave of radiation.

He'd only been standing in the street for a few seconds and already wanted to go home.

Briar pulled down his hood to run a clawed hand through his hair. He looked around the street and up the sides of buildings, seeing no evidence that anyone had been there at all that night. Why would Ebony come here? Most importantly, why did she need a weapon in the slums?

Briar walked down the street, letting his eyes wander. He was too distracted by an oozing green liquid running from one of the trash cans to see the ghostly figure of the Phantom jump out from an alleyway and slam him against a brick wall.

Briar's head hit the rock so hard he felt his skull vibrating with the impact. He cried out and before he could panic further, Ebony held the barrel of her gun against the corner of his jaw.

"You shouldn't be here." Her voice was colder than Briar had ever heard before. He blinked, pain echoing through his head.

"You were right." he ground out, blinking furiously to get rid of the pain. "I do have the reaction time of a blind man."

"You shouldn't be here, Briar," Ebony repeated, pressing the gun harder against his skin for emphasis. Her finger was on the trigger, but she hadn't made a move to press it. Through her mask, Briar could see her eyes widening.

Why was she scared?

"What are you doing here?" Briar looked past her gun and towards the end of the street. It remained empty. "Decided to go for a little nighttime stroll and kill someone?"

"If it comes to that, I will." She growled back. Briar couldn't tell if she was kidding with him or not. He decided to bet safely and determine the latter.

"Slow down there." Briar held up his other hand in surrender. She didn't release her hold on the gun. "My father pardoned you for past crimes, not future ones."

"Go back to the palace, Briar."

"I'm not going anywhere until you tell me where you're going." Briar retorted, panic suddenly settling into his bones. What was she thinking?

"You will not want to see this." Ebony pressed the gun harder against his jaw but still didn't move to pull it. "Go home."

"What the hell are you talking about?" Briar snapped, looking around the street. "There's no one here but us."

"Good." Ebony spat back. "No one will know you were ever with me."

"Wait a second." Briar closed his eyes and sighed, attempting to regain the sanity he'd lost when he'd been slammed against a wall by a girl who didn't have time to play with him. When he opened them again, he found Ebony glaring at him. "You expect me to go back to the palace and move on with my dandy little life while you stomp into the city to kill someone?"

"I wasn't planning on it, but now that you've given me the option," Ebony removed the gun from his jaw, only to back away and point it straight at his forehead. "Leave me alone or your brains will be splattered all over this street." She cocked her head to the side and Briar could practically see the venom dripping through her mask.

"Ebony, wait a minute-" Briar started, now holding up both hands, but she interrupted him before he could go on.

"If you saw the substances on the street, you'll know that no one will question the blood that comes from the bullet." She threatened. "Or the sound."

While that was true, Briar also wasn't in the mood to die with no one watching. "You won't shoot me." Briar dropped his hands and took a step towards her. She took a step back to match his distance.

"Watch me."

Briar took another step. Ebony didn't back up anymore, pressing the barrel of the gun against his forehead now. Ebony flinched.

"Get out of my way, Briar."

"Let me come with you." He argued, his eyes flickering from the gun to her eyes.

"You don't even know where I'm going." She countered, widening her stance. It was the position she used when she was shooting, Briar knew that much. But what he didn't know was if she'd actually shoot him. They both knew that she could cover it up as easily as she could pull the trigger.

"I don't care," he replied, keeping his voice calm. "Anything is better than where I was."

"Where we're going?" Ebony shook her head. "I doubt it."

"We?"

Ebony's narrowed eyes locked with his. Then she cursed. Her gun dropped, and she cursed again, louder this time. Briar chuckled and grinned at her, crossing his arms over his chest.

"Where to now, partner?"

"We aren't partners." The assassin snapped at him, holstering her gun with a click. Then she spun around on her heel and continued to walk down the street. The road only got darker as she went along.

Briar shrugged and followed her with a slight skip to his step. He had been called worse than that before.

"Where are we going?" Briar caught up to Ebony and walked by her side. When he watched her from his balcony, her entire body seemed to be bent the wrong way. Now he found it rigid and tense. It was completely unlike her usual state, which had now turned from prepared to positively paranoid.

Briar scowled. "Are you going to ignore me now, too?" Even though Achlys was neglecting him and so was Ebony, it didn't feel the same when she did it. It felt like she meant to be jeering him into conversation, even though Briar's dwindling amount of common sense told him that was not the case.

"If I offered you money, would you leave?" She didn't look at him when she asked it, rather surveying all aspects of the street.

"Quit being yourself for once." He snapped back as they turned a corner. She had yet to look at him since she held a gun to his head and Briar was beginning to think that it was on purpose.

"I'm the reason you're still alive." Ebony glared at him from the corner of her eye for a fraction of a second. Or maybe she was looking across the street at the crosswalk she was avoiding using. "I'd suggest thanking me for my generosity."

"No way." Briar's arms swung casually by his sides. Compared to Ebony, he seemed like a wet noodle being dragged down the street next to her sharpness. "I'm not thanking you for anything."

"You'd be dead without me."

"Believe me, if your face was the first thing I saw every sol, I'd pray to die."

"I'd be tempted to stuff a bag over your head," Ebony stopped walking and finally faced Briar. "But we're here."

Briar's interest peaked as she said it, but immediately plummeted when he looked left and saw a small corner shop awaiting them. Briar tilted his head to look through one of the broken windows.

"Are they having a sale or something?"

Ebony growled and shook her head, once again leaving Briar behind as she stepped up to the door. When she opened it, a bell rang above her head. Briar quickly followed as she tried to shut the door in his face, but he caught it with his foot instead. But before they could take another step out of the doorway, Ebony whipped around and he nearly tripped.

They were so close to each other that Briar's chin almost touched the top of her head and instead of speaking to him, she was shoved uncomfortably into his chest.

"Don't say a word." She told him and didn't seem to be bothered by their closer-than-normal proximity. She reached up to put his hood back on and her gloves brushed his temple. "Follow my lead."

Before he could ask what she meant, Ebony spun around again and walked further into the store. Now that he wasn't shoved against her, Briar could observe the rest of the shop as he followed Ebony through the shelves.

The entire place smelled like rotting food and chemicals. Briar didn't understand why; regular civilians weren't allowed access to any chemicals that would make the store smell like it did. The white lights flickered above them and Briar swore he could hear the faint buzzing sound of something broken. He wouldn't be surprised if the entire ceiling of this place came down on them the moment he reached up a finger to touch one of the broken ceiling tiles. The food on the rusting shelves, packaged in ripped plastic, was so rotten that everything else around it was going bad too. There were scratched-off price stickers on each shelf, but nothing seemed to be bought in years.

Briar swallowed a lump in his throat as he looked away from a stale loaf of bread. He didn't think it was supposed to be the color it was turning. He'd realized that the people living in the slums couldn't pay for electricity, but he hadn't realized they didn't have healthy food either.

Briar could feel a small guilty pit opening in the core of his stomach as Ebony led him towards the back of the store. There they found a young boy who looked years younger than Briar, sitting with his legs resting on the counter in front of him. He was reading a torn magazine that looked like it had also been hit by the sun's radiation. There was a TV hoisted on the wall behind him that broadcasted the news from earlier today. Briar saw a headline that read, "Rebels gain a larger foothold with train raids in Fortuna and Xadon districts."

Ebony approached the counter with her usual saunter. When she saw the boy, she immediately slapped his feet off the counter. His legs fell to the floor, but the boy caught himself, slamming a hand on the counter and instantly looking up. Briar could tell he was about to yell at her, but when he saw the Phantom standing before him, he suddenly halted.

"Do you still supply teardrops?" Ebony asked the boy, regaining her usual confident stature. Behind the counter, his mouth fell open. But it only took him a few more seconds to realize who had asked him a question to slightly nod his head, still staring at Ebony as he reached below the counter. When his hand appeared again, Briar saw a small vial with light blue liquid and a dropper inside.

Ebony took the bottle when the boy gave it to her, immediately unscrewing the top and squeezing it to collect the liquid. Briar watched her beside him as she tilted her head back, using the dropper to carefully dip the liquid into both of her eyes. When she finished, she blinked twice before looking at him.

Briar took the bottle but did nothing with it. He inspected the contents inside but had no clue what it could be. As far as Briar knew, it didn't smell like anything it shouldn't. He glanced sideways at the boy behind the counter, waiting for both of them to finish whatever they were supposed to be doing and then back to Ebony. She slowly inclined her head, encouraging him to follow her lead.

Reluctantly, Briar took the dropper and the liquid and let it fall into both his eyes. Immediately, he felt dizzy. But the second he did, it was gone again. Briar blinked. Once, then twice, before looking at Ebony again without a word. She reached for the bottle and took it from him, handing it back to the boy. When it was tucked behind the counter again, the boy reached further down. Briar was expecting him to pull out another vial, but instead, he heard a button clicking.

"Kiran requires his guests to be at least the slightest bit high when they enter," Ebony explained like it was a warning before turning to face the bare wall beside the counter. Only it wasn't bare anymore, rather sliding open to reveal another room.

Briar could only see the blinding, colorful lights before Ebony took his hand in her gloved one, guiding him inside.

Humans are born greedy.

We might not all have green eyes, but we have green hearts. We lust after the things we wish we possessed. We take more than we are given, more than what we *need*.

I am not talking in the sense of food, water, or money. Food and water are distributed in rations and no amount of stealing or hoarding will change that. Money is no longer a problem in society because before the sun imploded, it caused the depression of the entire world and the near collapse of multiple governments. Therefore, the Republic controls the flow of most currency now.

But what we lust after now is more dangerous than what we wished we had before the sun imploded. Instead of wanting money in the form of power, we simply go straight for the gold.

The only way to advance oneself in this society is power. Some achieve it by displaying their intelligence and becoming a valuable human to the rest of the world. Others are not born with the same strengths and therefore rely on their cunning and sneakiness to slither their way up to the top. Because once they're there, there is nothing more they have to do but maintain status.

We over-consume power and hold it in our greedy hands. We are all green monsters in our own way.

-An excerpt of the first Supreme Leader's
journal, extracted from the Archives of the
Imperial Republic of Raedon

Chapter Eighteen

"Non timebo malum."
-I will fear no evil.

Normally, Wren didn't mind getting her hands dirty. Sometimes, she enjoyed it. A little mud here, a little blood there. It was all a part of the daily routine and without it, she felt a little out of place. But in this case, Wren would rather give up everything she owned than have to enter Kiran Sabik's threshold ever again.

The circular room was built underground and shaped like an amphitheater. When the sun was still in the sky and millions of years before that, circular theaters were used for entertainment of all sorts. Sports games, gladiator fights, and sometimes gatherings for music. Wren never found much interest in the ongoing events before the sun exploded; most of them died when the sun did. There were hundreds of people stacked onto the bleachers carved from rock, all of them facing the center of the cavern. Wren herself could barely see anything as she led Briar through the crowds. The flashing neon lights blinded her, and the thundering music blanketed too many of her senses for her liking. The people on the bleachers hollered as Wren heard a roar come from the center of the room.

She glanced through moving bodies to see what they were all cheering for; a caged pit dug in the lowest point of the center of the amphitheater, with two fighters beating each other inside.

Wren quickly looked away and glanced behind her, finding Briar's eyes locked on the scene before them. His hand flexed in her palm as his throat bobbed. Wren held onto him as she pulled him away, weaving her way through the horde. They heard whispers of her name through the crowd as they moved further into the underground auditorium. Some people even stopped watching the fight to glance at her, puffing smoke from their small handheld devices as she passed by. The sound of clinking glasses and sloshing chemical drinks rang in their ears, synchronizing with the blasting music.

Wren yanked Briar closer to her and his attention snapped from the cage to her. "Don't take anything from anyone." She instructed, and he nodded. She held his eyes for one moment before turning back away, moving through the uneven path ahead of them.

It wasn't hard for Wren to create a walkway for the both of them; people separated as soon as the wave of whispers reached them. She kept walking until she was approaching the very back of the coliseum, coming across the tallest seat in the entire arena.

Kiran Sabik sat in the center of the bleachers in a chair made from welded scrap metal that reminded Wren vaguely of a throne. He puffed smoke from a small purple device in his hand, breathing in the colored substance from his mouth and exhaling through his nose. His skin was surprisingly tan for someone Wren knew spent all of his time buried deep underground. His sandy hair was a mess on top of his head just as Wren remembered it, but the usually unkempt goatee on his chin was now cut to a short stubble. His muscular stature looked out-of-place lounging on his throne like he did, all until the whispers seemed to reach him and his eyes snapped open, his body suddenly sharpening. His dark emerald eyes grazed the crowd until he finally spotted Wren and Briar approaching them from the midst of the arena.

Instantly, Kiran stopped talking to the people surrounding him. Those were his elite; his most talented fighters and best friends, if Wren would call people who constantly lived in fear of him severing their tongues friends. They all seemed to take the hint and sat down in their seats around his throne, watching Wren with piercing eyes as she approached their cluster.

She stopped directly in front of Kiran's throne. Briar stopped beside her, his eyes still wandering around the room. Wren let go of his hand when Kiran spotted them. Now he stood closer to her than he had before, his arm occasionally brushing her shoulder. Wren was determined to not let Kiran see, so she took a subtle step away from him, causing Briar to clear his throat and glare downwards at his feet.

Through the strobing lights, Wren watched Kiran bring his device up to his mouth. He took another puff of smoke. Closer now, Wren noticed the chemical was not only purple, but smelled fruity too. Kiran exhaled again, observing Wren as he blew the smog straight into her face.

"It's been a long time since the legendary Phantom has graced my arena." Kiran's voice was hoarse from years of engineered chemicals. The drugs he got and sold in his operation were no longer made by the Republic for medical use; they hadn't needed them since all diseases had been cured. Kiran acquired the recipes for the medicines from old archives, mixing in new ingredients meant to cause an adrenaline high or dopamine drop demanding on what the buyer wanted to feel. They were chemically induced thoughts and emotions, meant to have customers continue coming back until they simply couldn't anymore.

Wren herself had been convinced to try a few before she became the Phantom. They never satisfied her needs and even if they did, they would kill her before she finally felt the need to stop trying.

"I would've liked to keep it that way," Wren hissed, speaking loudly over the cheering and whistles ringing from the rest of the amphitheater. "Unfortunately, I require your assets for a job of mine."

Kiran's eyes widened, but before he could respond, a figure stepped out of the shadows behind his throne.

"No one will make any deals with you." The figure's voice was familiar to Wren. "Leave before I sever your head from your neck."

The female stepped into the neon lights, finally revealing herself to Wren. Her chocolate skin seeped with fury as she glared at the assassin with eyes as sharp as razors. Her arms were crossed in front of her chest, revealing small throwing knives strapped to her sleeves. There were more sheathes all over her tight black clothing. Her dark hair was tied behind her head in a chopped braid, framing her hollow face like the skeleton of a starved creature. She was taller than Wren and noticeably more muscular. The piercings lining her ears shimmered iridescently as she tauntingly cocked her head to the side.

"Artemis." Wren pressed her lips together in a tight line. "Your welcome has been a long-awaited pleasure."

Artemis Neoma bared her teeth like a feral monster. She reminded Wren of a hungry creature prowling the night for prey, only to find that everything had already run away from her.

"I'll make you bleed." She snarled.

Wren's jaw ticked.

When Wren had left Novus and her brother behind, she found herself alone and powerless in Raedon. Specifically in Antares, where she met Artemis for the first time. Artemis had been in the district on a run for Kiran, delivering a few of his manufactured smoking devices to another underground operation when they met. Wren was stealing from Kiran's buyer without knowing who he was and who was coming to meet him that night. Artemis, posing as the seller, caught Wren and deemed her skills valuable to Kiran's business and took her to Polaris in exchange for keeping her unfortunate misunderstanding a secret.

By that point, Wren Sitara was still alive and well and in the Republic's Archives. It only took a few years of running errands across the city under the Supreme Leader's knowledge for her to realize she'd gotten into more trouble than she'd originally bargained for. Being a runner for Kiran meant sticking her neck out where it could get chopped off by the Republic. It paid well for the first few years, and Wren was assured that she wouldn't become one of the pit fighters trapped in the underground arena forever.

Only, it was hard for Wren to resist the countless amounts of money Kiran brought in from selling his goods. So instead of keeping her mouth shut and her hands to herself, she decided that one small cut of the pay would do Kiran no harm when he'd already created a massive empire. Unusual for her now, but Wren couldn't have been any more wrong.

Kiran found out about her thieving and stripped her of her job as one of his runners; she would become a permanent fighter in his pit. Artemis was no longer a runner either and had voluntarily gotten roped into the arena after almost being arrested by the Republic multiple times and cutting backhanded deals with Kiran. But it wasn't long before Wren came around again and fought in the arena, becoming one of Kiran's best fighters.

Wren supposed she took Artemis's status, name, title, money, and pride from her when she began winning every match Kiran scheduled her for. She used her training from the rebels to help her and eventually became the champion of every fighter Kiran put against her.

How could she help herself? It wasn't Wren's fault that she was better than Artemis at practically everything.

"You couldn't cut me if you tried," Wren told the fighter in a singsong voice. "Oh wait, you did. And failed."

Artemis growled and took a step forward when Kiran put a hand on her shoulder to stop her. "Now, now," he cooed, "save it for the arena ladies. I'd much rather wash the blood off of the floor there than in front of my seat."

Artemis obeyed and took a step back. Wren smiled underneath her mask, wiggling her eyebrows to further taunt the girl. She knew it took every inch of Artemis's unraveling self-restraint, which didn't seem to be bountiful anymore, to hold herself back from lunging at Wren.

Above them on his throne, Kiran puffed another cloud of purple smoke and jerked his chin towards Briar. "Who's your guest?"

Wren looked sideways at Briar, finding him blinking feverishly in the lights. He kept rubbing his eyes and swaying from side to side. When he realized all eyes were on him, he squeezed his eyes shut as if to pretend none of this was real.

Unfortunately, it was.

"It's his first time." Wren sighed, slightly embarrassed. She should've left Briar in the middle of the street after he insisted on following her. But then again, his curiosity would've won him over, and he would've found his way into the amphitheater, eventually. Perhaps she should've gone with her original plan and forced him to go back to Sanctum Palace.

Kiran threw his head back in laughter, and the rest of the group around him copied the gesture. All except for Artemis, who continued to glare at Wren with a lethal gaze.

When Kiran had finally calmed down, he took another puff of smoke from the device. Then he turned to the group of men beside his throne. His face suddenly turned cold. "Occupy the boy," he ordered. "I have business to discuss."

The men from the side of the throne obeyed as well as Artemis did. They slowly rose from their lounged positions and retrieved small devices and bags of a chalky substance from their pockets. Wren surveyed them carefully as they approached Briar, speaking to him with sweet words as they moved towards an empty group of seats not far away from the throne. When one man reached to nudge Briar in that direction, Wren palmed a blade and pressed it against his wrist.

"Touch him again and it'll be the last thing those fingers ever feel."

The man froze for a few moments before his throat bobbed and he nodded, cautiously taking his hands away from Briar to instead follow the other men to their seats.

Briar went with them, looking back at Wren for confirmation. She nodded her head, slipping her knife back into her belt. Briar allowed himself to be carried away, feeling Wren's eyes on his back until she knew he was completely out of earshot and wouldn't hear a word any of them said. Then she turned back to Kiran.

"We need to talk."

"Indeed, we do."

Control or be controlled.
It is as simple as that.
Have power, or not have power. Become an asset or become a liability. Have integrity or have no honor. Move mountains or dig valleys. Become a leader or be a follower.
One does not get to choose where they fall in between. They are either the controller or the one being controlled.
There is no shame in being controlled. Stepping back does not mean weakness, but rather strength. Knowing your assets and faults is a valuable thing in our world. Some people are simply better than others, making them a higher societal benefit. Others are regrettably less than perfect and become a liability holding us back.
Yet that isn't to say that the liabilities, few and far between as they are, cannot be molded into assets as well.
Everyone has a place in Raedon, and whether or not you belong is the question. Everyone in Raedon deserves to be there; without their ancestors, humanity would've died inside the bunker off the coast of the Atlantic Ocean. Fitting in is not the problem.
Accepting assimilation is.

-An excerpt of the first Supreme Leader's journal, extracted from the Archives of the Imperial Republic of Raedon

Chapter Nineteen

"Aut viam inveniam aut faciam."
-I will find a way or make one.

There was a game that people played before the sun imploded. It was set up on a black and white board with small figurines that were carved to look like different structures in ancient lands; knights, castles, bishops. Each piece had its own set of rules to play by, like only moving one square at a time or only being able to shift vertically or horizontally across the board. There were different strategies one would use, and they would lead to over a million different outcomes of the game. There would always be the same amount of pieces on each side when the game began and, by the end, many were defeated on the sidelines. The king piece would be the figurine to protect, and it was the job of all the other pieces to make sure he never fell.

But there was one thing that Wren loved most about the game. It wasn't the strategizing and sneaky maneuvering of the pieces, which Wren was sure she'd be good at, or the satisfying feeling of defeating the smaller figurines before the large ones, which Wren also knew she'd take too seriously.

It was the fact that the game of chess was made to protect the king, but the queen had all the power.

"Get out." From his throne, Kiran ordered the rest of the crowd away from them with a simple wave of his hand. They split immediately, moving back into the crowd with disappointed grumbles. When they were all dispersed, the king drew his attention back to Wren. She saw his green eyes sparkle like a real gem before he said, "You've changed since the last time I saw you."

"And what do you think of me now?" Wren asked, gesturing down at herself. She knew she was striking in her uniform, both frightening and beautiful. When she had constructed it, she made sure the fabrics hit every curve of her and yet still could make her look like a nightmare come to real life.

It was beauty in panic, and that was how she liked it.

"I think that you've become what they've made you," Kiran remarked, leaning further back into his chair. He took the smoking device in his hand and bit it between his teeth, sucking in smoke before spitting it back out into his hand. This time, the purple substance barely made it to Wren before she brushed it away from her face.

"So, what am I?" Wren was baiting him, subtly tilting her chin downwards so he could see the gleam of her rifle scope above her hood. Kiran laughed and opened his mouth to respond, but Artemis interrupted instead.

"A puppet." She spat, examining Wren up and down. Her arms remained crossed over her chest. Between her fingers now, Wren saw the glimmer of a small knife tucked carefully into her palm.

"You say that like you haven't become the same thing." Wren snickered. It was obvious from the way the girl stood next to Kiran's throne that she still did whatever he told her, including fighting in the pit. The recent scars and scabs all over her body told Wren at least that much.

"I haven't." Artemis countered, her top lip curling to reveal a straight line of gleaming teeth. Wren remembered her smiling at her all those years ago in the pit. It didn't scare her then, and it didn't scare her now.

"Last time I was here, I remember you were doing his bidding." Wren jerked her chin towards Kiran, who was watching their exchange with beaded eyes. "Tell me, are you not still fighting in that arena?"

Artemis narrowed her eyes. "Last time you were here, it was because you betrayed us. I didn't think you had the backbone to actually come back."

"I'm standing here, aren't I?"

"Regrettably."

"Ah," Kiran sighed, closing his eyes for a moment as if he were reveling in a happy memory. "I remember the good times when you two used to run around the city trying to best each other. I could never seem to completely wash the blood off my floor."

"I've moved on." Wren directed her attention back to Kiran as he chuckled to himself.

"I've noticed." His eyes moved past Wren and to Briar behind her. "Dancing with the son of the Supreme Leader, now, are we?"

Wren grit her teeth. "Much better than what I used to do for you."

"You think that running around the palace instead of the city is an upgrade?"

"It's better than anything you could've ever given me." Wren knew she hit home with the blow. Despite their complicated history, Kiran was with Wren for years before she left and became the Phantom. It was a giant web of lies and deception, but weaved into it was a bond deeper than Wren would've liked to admit.

"Yet you always come back." Kiran sneered, unwilling to let his guard down as he deflected her attack.

"Not by choice."

"The rebels sent you again, did they?" Kiran tittered, tapping his device on the arm of his metal throne. "Well, tell them to hurry and give me my next payment. I want to make some renovations."

After Wren had fought in the pit for a few years under Kiran's watch, the Rising Sun had hunted her down to take her back. She was one of their best soldiers being put to waste in the city. To Wren's dismay, they were insistent on freeing her from her punishment, so much so that they arranged monthly payments to Kiran to keep his mouth shut about what happened. They wanted her back badly, and not just because her brother claimed he missed her.

They needed an inside person in Raedon, one that could use their training to become a complete ghost under the Republic's watchful eyes. Henceforth, the Phantom.

"I'm not sure how much worse this place can get." Wren looked from side to side. The amphitheater, so dark she could barely see the dirty surfaces beneath her feet, flared around her. Half of her didn't want to know what she was stepping on or smelling.

"Be careful when you're insulting my livelihood." Kiran snapped. "This was the place you came back to when you had nowhere else to go."

"This is not a livelihood. This is criminal activity that could get you executed."

"Going to tattle?" Artemis scoffed. Wren knew she was only continuing to argue because she knew Kiran was considering whatever Wren wanted without her having to tell him anything. They both knew that he couldn't resist a good game when he saw it, no matter who offered it to him.

Wren tilted her head from side to side as if she was considering it. "I wasn't thinking about it, but I'd be happy to give the Republic your name instead of his."

The girl's jaw tightened. "You wouldn't dare."

"Oh, I'm not so sure." Wren grinned underneath her mask. "I'm quite the risk taker."

"You don't say." Kiran tossed his smoking device to Wren. She caught it in one hand. "I've heard the rumors over the years. The nameless, faceless assassin haunting Raedon. You've built yourself quite the high platform."

"I hope she falls off." Artemis snickered maliciously.

"If you've heard of me from all the way down here, I must be doing something right," Wren said, ignoring Artemis's comment. She brought the device up to her mask and took a deep breath. The smoke traveled quickly through the small, embedded holes in the fabric. The taste of it was what Wren would describe as guilt and regret. When she finished, she felt the sting of the drug traveling out of her nose. She tossed the device back to Kiran. Next to him, Artemis rolled her eyes and scoffed. The drugs traveling back and forth between her and Kiran was a first step towards getting what she wanted.

"Of course," Kiran said, continuing to tap the device against his chair. The way he looked at Wren was like an observer watching a creature in a cage. "But I still like the girl you were when you worked for me."

Wren schooled her face into a blank stare, even though the mask covered any expression she had. "I killed her a long time ago." Wren Sitara was dead from the moment she tore the Republic barcode from her skin.

"I noticed. But who's to say I'm not allowed to be disappointed?"

"I'm not." Artemis inserted herself again. It was obvious to Wren that she didn't enjoy being excluded from her and Kiran's side jeers. She glared at Kiran from the side of her eye. "Cowards don't belong here."

Wren refused to give Artemis the attention she wanted. "Then you should've come with me, Artemis."

"I remember it was my knife to your throat all those times in the pit."

"Then you'll remember who ended up winning."

Artemis's hand reached for another knife in her belt. Wren's own unclipped the holster of her gun. She could grab it and pull the trigger faster than Artemis could throw her knife.

"Save it, both of you." Kiran stopped them, although Wren saw he wasn't too keen on his decision. "Blood is messy and firearms are against my rules."

Wren waited until Artemis pocketed her weapons to put back her gun.

"But if we're walking down memory lane and mine serves me right, I remember the only reason you ever visit me is when you want something." Kiran hummed from his throne. "So, what is it? We both know you didn't come here for a little get-together, smoke, and chat. Your debt is currently being paid off and we're even." He inhaled another breath from his device and puffed it, only this time the smoke formed a purple ring. It floated towards Wren, but before it could reach her, she cut through it with a swing of her arm.

"I need the help of people who know the city best." She told him, now completely ignoring Artemis. She kept rolling her eyes and scoffing every time Wren opened her mouth, and it was becoming excruciatingly annoying.

"You've come to the right place." Kiran opened his arms and gestured to the amphitheater surrounding them. If Wren listened closely enough, she could hear the rattle of bargaining chips being tossed around. The next fight hadn't even started yet and people were already throwing their money away.

"There are central powering stations around the city." She explained. "I need your runners to cause a blackout when the order comes."

"What makes you think we'll help you?" Artemis couldn't hold herself back. Annoyed, Wren held up a hand instead of fully responding to the girl.

"Shut up or next time you open your mouth, you'll find yourself tongueless." She didn't need to look at Artemis to know she was already hissing and recoiling into her small corner of shadow.

"As much as I would enjoy watching that," Kiran sucked in an entranced breath through his teeth, "I will accept your deal. But I want one thing."

"I would've assumed nothing different." Wren's heart dropped even though this was what she expected from him. There was a price to pay for everything that came from Kiran. "What do you want?"

Kiran's emerald eyes simmered as his lips spread into a wide, lazy grin. His gaze danced giddily from Wren to the caged pit in the center of the arena. Wren felt her chest hollowing out as she followed his eyes.

The jingle of betting chips being tossed around grew louder in her ears.

They were betting on her.

When Wren turned to face Kiran again, she found him staring at her as he twisted the smoking device in his hand. "One more thing."

Wren didn't respond. Instead, she watched Kiran look sideways at Artemis and lean over the side of his throne. He let his lips tauntingly graze the girl's neck as he whispered in her ear. His voice was quiet, but Wren knew he wanted her to hear it.

"Fight like the good old days." he smiled against Artemis's skin. Wren felt a pit in her stomach as memories of her past in the arena overran her mind.

Artemis nodded her head as Kiran recoiled back into his seat. She twirled one of her knives in her hand, stepping towards Wren. She stopped at the assassin's side. The lights flashing around them lit up her eyes like an iridescent fire.

"I haven't fought a coward in a long time." She said, Her voice slithered under Wren's skin. "This should be fun."

Wren didn't respond as Artemis moved past her shoulder and vanished into the crowd behind her.

From his throne, Kiran threw the smoking device to Wren one last time. As she caught it, his hoarse voice rattled through her ears like a knife scraping through flesh.

"Make it a performance worthy of my help, little ghost."

Being the stupid creatures they were, humans believed that technology would take over their world and kill them all.

That would've never been the case because idiocy would've gotten to them before the robots did. Throughout history, technology has always been a form of success. First, it was the invention of the ever-famous lightbulb. Then, it was the telephone, allowing two people to communicate across a certain amount of space. Next came advancements in science and data collecting. After that, technological transformations in the inventions of our daily lives changed the way humans looked at everything around us.

The gears, literally, in our minds worked differently, spin faster and tick louder than ever before.

Then it was a race to see who would create the best technology; and faster. Advancements surfaced one after the other, all competing against each other to help humanity improve more than the others.

Everyone aspired to be the best, to *have* the best. Money circulated and lives were changed because of a certain wired circuit or a motherboard that had one small adjustment to make a camera zoom in clearer.

Technology not only improved society but protected it. Retinal and face scans were invented. Heat signatures and fingerprint scanning allowed for tighter and more restricted access to certain things, keeping confidential information truly confidential. It kept phones locked and digital accounts sealed until the true user, identified by their access codes and scans, wanted to gain control of their assets.

But when humanity thrives for too long, doubt must come to cut it down.

What would happen if the artificial intelligence system gained control of everything humanity had put inside of it? What if all the passwords, security codes, fingerprints, retinal scans, heat signatures, and facial recognition records were used against society?

Only that was impossible. A human cannot create another brain by simply *giving* it information. It needed to be constructed and nurtured like a true human mind, not one made from circuits and programmed spaces.

They had put so much trust into a digital being that could eventually put an end to them by metaphorically and ironically cutting a wire.

-An excerpt of the first Supreme Leader's journal, extracted from the Archives of the Imperial Republic of Raedon

Chapter Twenty

"Fortis cadere potest sed non potest cedere."
-The strong may fall but cannot yield.

Briar was used to people surrounding him. He liked it when his father's court looked at him as he walked through the throne room or danced with a girl at parties. Although he'd never been the best dancer or the most graceful when simply walking, Briar always knew that he was being watched. It gave him an excuse to act out.

But this time, Briar wasn't the only one coming up with schemes and misbehaving. He was surrounded by an entire group of people who seemed to do just that for their livelihood.

"This place is amazing." Briar laughed, still feeling the sensation of the eye drops causing trouble in his mind.

Where was he? Whatever. He didn't care.

What was he doing here? He didn't care about that either. He couldn't seem to think of a reason to care about much of anything right now.

Where was Ebony? Oh well. She could handle herself.

The lights around him continued to flash. Some of them were in special shapes, like lasers or grids moving around on the floor. There was music playing around them in a style that Briar had never heard before; was this what people in Polaris listened to? Briar didn't get the chance to listen to much music in the palace. Either he was zoning out on the classical sounds his father insisted on playing, or he was covering his ears to avoid listening to anything at all.

The group surrounding Briar continued to babble. They had invited him to seats further away from Kiran Sabik, the man Ebony continued talking to as Briar took in the space around him. Whenever Briar tried to look over the blaring crowd, the group around him always seemed to engage him in a new topic of conversation. Even though Briar was always interested in the people around him, he couldn't help but think one thing; Ebony had been speaking with Kiran and the other girl for a while. What were they talking about? Was Ebony alright?

Never mind. Briar couldn't bring himself to care.

Kiran's friends never seemed to stop talking or huffing smoke from their multicolored devices. After each sentence, they seemed to inhale whatever the colorful fumes were. Briar didn't have one of his own, but when he breathed it in second hand, he felt all of his senses heightened. Or maybe they were decreasing. Either way, it felt better than he'd imagined.

"You ever try 'em?"

One of the younger boys behind him tapped his shoulder. Briar turned around, unable to fully hear the rest of what he was saying over the music. He simply nodded his head, and the boy nodded back with a wild smile, shoving the small device into Briar's hand. When he turned back around again to inspect the small gadget, he found another boy next to him modeling how to use it.

The boy brought the top of his device to his mouth and took in a long inhale. When he couldn't breathe in anymore, he removed the device from his mouth and blew out. Briar was amazed to find an orange-colored smoke blowing out of both his nose and his mouth as he smiled. It even ran out of his mouth in between his uneven teeth.

Briar tried it next, mimicking the rest of the group. He felt the edges of his vision becoming blurry with the prospect of more chemicals, but he didn't care. What would it feel like? What would it taste like?

There was only one way to find out.

Briar didn't seem to be able to stop himself as he put the device to his mouth and breathed in. All at once, he tasted something sweet and fruity, smelled something tangy, and felt a rush of adrenaline race through his blood. He inhaled until he couldn't anymore and breathed out, the feeling of a tingling cold running through his nose as smoke escaped his nostrils.

"Good, 'eh?" The man next to him encouraged Briar to do it again by lifting the device in Briar's hand to his mouth. Briar couldn't do anything but comply.

Only this time, when Briar inhaled the substance, he felt the device being slapped away from his hands.

"I thought I told you not to take anything you were offered."

When Briar looked up, he found Ebony standing above him. His mouth immediately split into a lopsided smile as he reached for her arms, pulling her to sit down with him.

"This place is amazing," He told her, blinking furiously as Ebony resisted his pull. She scowled at him, and Briar realized that it was his voice that had turned breathy.

"Don't take anything else." She told him, yanking her arm out of his hand. Briar could tell she was trying her hardest to keep herself from slapping the boy next to him, who had shown him how to use the device. "You're high."

Briar pouted. "I saw you smoking over there in that corner with him." His hand lazily pointed to where Kiran sat, the man curiously watching the two of them with suspicion looming in his eyes.

"I'm an adult." Ebony snapped.

"I-" Briar protested but halted.

Ebony was taking off her rifle.

She handled it with such care; her gloved hands moving fluidly across the parts as she unloaded and pocketed the ammunition. Then she extended her arm and put it in Briar's hands without a word.

Briar felt the cold metal of the scope and the smoothness of the long barrel. He looked down at the weapon in his hands, still feeling the warmth of where Ebony's hands had touched it. Instantly, panic set into Briar's heart, overriding any drug in his system.

Ebony never gave up her rifle.

Briar felt his senses coming back to him like fire being washed over with water. His head snapped back up to look at Ebony, only he found her still gazing at the rifle with a distant look in her eyes.

"Ebony?" He asked, suddenly standing from the bleachers. The group around him seemed to have become uninterested in him and didn't stop Briar this time. He felt woozy, and the world spun around him.

Ebony's eyes remained downward as she took the firearm out of her belt, too.

"What did you do?" Briar asked again, clutching the rifle tighter. Something in his chest was capsizing. "What did you do?"

He repeated it over and over again, but Ebony refused to respond until she finally lifted her chin, her turquoise eyes locking with his.

Something in her irises shifted as she said, "Don't watch."

Before Briar could grab her arm to pull her back and ask what she meant by it, she was dragged away by the crowd.

We were the killers of our world.
It is so easy for us to not think about the future
when we know that we won't be living in it. It is
because of simple-minded people we do not care
about the sustainability of our planet. Earth could
only withstand so much abuse.
And we were bloody monsters.
The world before the sun imploded left us with
only a certain amount of the planet that could carry
the number of people Raedon would grow to have.
It had beaten Earth down to a pulp, using it until it
couldn't be used anymore. Of course, the sun
played into that role by decimating life, drying up
water, and poisoning the air, but not as much as
humanity did in its own way.
Wasting resources on unnecessary things. Spilling
oils into the oceans and allowing chemicals to waft
into the air. Throwing trash around like it would
simply disappear. And it disappeared, only to
reappear somewhere else to kill us later.
They did this to themselves.
Thankfully, Raedon fixes all the mistakes of the
past.

-An excerpt of the first Supreme Leader's
journal, extracted from the Archives of the
Imperial Republic of Raedon

Chapter Twenty-One

"Si non flecto voluntatem coeli movebo gehennam."
-If I do bend the will of heaven, I will move hell.

There were six rules for Kiran's arena.

1. Don't kill your opponent too quickly; People want a show, it's why they're there.
2. No firearms. Just know that the weapon you pick will either cost you the win or help you obtain it.
3. Place your bets before the fight begins. Cheaters are thrown out and banned for life.
4. A sixth of the winnings go to the victor to use however they see fit.
5. The fighters are under no requirements to have previous experience; you must rely on what you already know or nothing at all.
6. Killing is on the table.

Wren was no stranger to following these rules. She'd done it for years when she was indebted to Kiran and knew that the words were so deeply engraved into her mind that she could recite them all backward in ten seconds. These numbered commandments had kept her alive for the duration of time she spent in the underground arena.

But the girl who fought as Kiran's pet died when the ghostly assassin was born. As the Phantom, Wren wanted to add one more rule to the list.

7. All those who fight against the Phantom must be prepared to fall at her hand. Any resistance will be met with the force of Raedon's most notorious killer herself.

Wren marched through the amphitheater, following one of Kiran's runners towards the heart of the arena. Around her, she felt people reaching for her from the bleachers; grabbing at her legendary uniform just to get a feel of how the fabric ran underneath their fingers. Wren allowed them to do it as she kept walking, knowing that this was the closest she'd ever been to anyone without killing them afterward.

The blaring music synced with the rhythm of Wren's thundering heart. It fuzzed in and out of focus in her ears, creating a staccato beat that somehow kept her moving. The strobing lights around the arena moved to be her flashing spotlight, following her so that people wouldn't lose track of the assassin on her way toward the pit. She could hear the Phantom's name being roared around the stands, filling the entire space with the booming echo of her famous presence.

In the pit, Wren would truly be dead. The person who would stand in her place tonight was the Phantom, moving like a predator to kill the prey she had been longing to defeat.

Kiran's runner stopped five paces ahead of Wren. He opened the cage by lifting a latch, the metal bars squeaking with rust and age. When she passed him, he lowered his chin to avoid meeting her eyes. Wren could feel the fear radiating off of him as she stepped into the spot-lit pit, listening to the bellowing of the crowd as she faced them with open arms.

If it was a performance that Kiran wanted, it was a performance that she would give him.

Wren made it to the center of the pit and gazed around herself. The spectators outside of the cage were pounding on the bars and reaching their arms through the metal to touch her. They were feet away from even grazing her, but yet they still tried, bending their bodies in miraculous ways to get closer. The pit smelled like blood, old and new, infused into the floor and splattered onto the bars around her.

Wren remembered every aspect of the ring well. She spent years of her life inside of it trying to dig herself back out. But now that she had fallen in again, Wren didn't know if she ever wanted to leave. It was the bloodlust and the adrenaline from victory that pumped through her veins and made Wren sure that she made the right decision to leave it all behind.

Just because a monster was born in a cage didn't mean it was confined forever.

Suddenly, a tremor shook the arena like a quake moving through the earth. Wren didn't have to look behind her to know that Artemis had finally entered the pit. She could feel the girl's footsteps vibrating on the ground. She was walking around the perimeter, letting the people who were reaching for Wren grab her instead. That was all fine with Wren; they couldn't reach the best, so they had to grapple at mediocrity. Applause rang through the cavernous space and only grew louder when Artemis eventually stopped her pursuit, meeting Wren in the center of the pit.

Artemis glowered straight into Wren's turquoise eyes, infesting them with her wrathful disease. Her hands flexed hungrily at her sides.

"You never belonged here." She said, her voice grating against Wren's ears like a serrated knife. But the assassin smiled regardless, feeling the corners of her lips flickering upwards beneath her mask.

"My title as reigning champion disagrees with you."

"Not for long." Artemis spat. "It's easy for you to be confident until I pull the floor out from underneath your feet."

"And it's easy for me to look at you, knowing that I'll beat you just like I did the last time I was here." Wren's excitement flared like the embers of a small flame.

"I doubt that."

"Don't doubt me."

Artemis chuckled devilishly as she turned over her shoulder and strutted towards the perimeter of the mat again. Wren did the same thing so that they were on opposite sides of the ring. There were no rules how people could fight; dirty or with honor, was up to you. But when Artemis and Wren had battled repeatedly years ago, they'd always kept the same distance away from each other in the very beginning. It left the center of the ring open for whoever had the guts to attack first.

Like Kiran said, the good old days.

When Wren turned around again, Artemis was already lunging across the ring. She met Wren on the other side in five long steps, letting her fist fly towards Wren's jaw. Before the blow could hit her, though, Wren caught it in her gloved palm and shoved Artemis backwards. The girl stumbled and

Wren kicked her further back, planting the heel of her boot on the fighter's abdomen, and pushed.

Artemis reared. She didn't stay down for long, attacking again. She was hungrier this time. Wren allowed her to advance, moving backward in the ring with quick feet until she felt the bars at her back. When Artemis flung her fist through the air again, she ducked to the side and allowed the girl's knuckles to meet the steel bars. Artemis screamed in rage, jabbing her knee up to slam into Wren's nose.

The assassin growled, hooking her arms into the bars as she swung her legs forward and out to propel Artemis away from her. Cheers rang from around the amphitheater as Wren separated herself from the perimeter of the cage, allowing Artemis to regain her footing. When she did, they both resumed their places on the outside of the ring. This time, Wren moved first and circled her like a beast battling for the last scrap of prey.

"You made a mistake coming back here." Blood dripped from the corner of Artemis's mouth. A drop leaked until it became too long and splattered to the floor beneath her boots. Wren's nose was bleeding underneath her mask. The thick, metallic smell to it was almost unbearable.

"I don't make mistakes," Wren said back, regaining her stature.

"You do now." Artemis's hand moved slyly towards her belt, where Wren found a collection of small throwing knives. Her fingers played with the silver hilts of the weapons, teasing the assassin when they hit the light and glared. "Once I'm finished with you, I'll shred the boy and send his head back to the palace where it belongs."

At the mention of Briar, she bared her teeth. "You won't make it out of this ring alive."

"Even if I don't, I'll make sure he doesn't either." Artemis smiled. Her teeth were wet with gleaming crimson. "It's no mystery who he is. Maybe I'll do the rebels a favor just this once." She finally let her fingers rest on a small knife on the end of her collection. They twirled and, in an instant, she was throwing them, not towards Wren, but tauntingly tossing them up and down. Her threat glistened on the blade like polish on the silver surface.

"You'd have to get to him over my dead body."

Artemis grinned. "I can arrange that."

The assassin pounced. She ran for Artemis, meeting her on the other side of the ring. The fighter was ready for her, already throwing punches and swinging her knife to defend herself. Wren allowed Artemis's fist to make contact with the side of her jaw, but twisted around her back when the second one came. She jammed her elbow into Artemis's ribs and kicked the back of her knees. The girl roared as her leg buckled, falling right into Wren's awaiting fist.

The crowd filling the amphitheater erupted when Artemis struggled to rise. Wren didn't attack again. She wanted Artemis on her feet for what she had planned next. She knew Kiran wouldn't allow her to leave this arena with both her life and a deal in her pocket without spilling a little blood beforehand.

And to do that, Wren needed Artemis angrier than she ever had been before.

So, when Artemis rose to her knees and lifted herself onto her feet, Wren lunged forward with an obvious maneuver. It allowed Artemis to hook her foot onto Wren's leg and trip her, dragging her knife across the assassin's forearm as she fell. Wren felt the searing pain of the injury as she held out her hands to catch her on the floor. Artemis was gaining control before Wren hit the floor, grabbing the assassin by the top of her hood and turning her on her back. She sat on Wren's chest, pushing the air from her lungs.

"Imagine the look on his face when you die right before his eyes." Artemis traced small, delicate patterns on Wren's neck with her knife. The blade never pierced the skin, but sent a cold shiver through the assassin's spine. Artemis pinned Wren's arms down with her boots. She felt her heels digging into her wrists, painfully wringing out feeling from her fingers. Wren grunted, blinking in the spotlight shining down on them.

Wren had told Briar not to watch. As she felt hundreds of eyes on her, she knew that he was amongst them. He was surely seeing her on the ground now, gripping tightly onto her rifle. He would watch her bleed, watch her as a knife was pressed into her throat.

"You're pathetic." Artemis spat and as she spoke, a splatter of blood from her mouth sprayed Wren in the face. Wren didn't allow herself to flinch, feeling the heated warmth of the substance and allowing it to simmer into her skin. Artemis licked the front of her teeth, pressing the point of the knife against the side of Wren's neck. The amphitheater around them climaxed and Artemis cackled.

The Phantom grinned back.

Artemis's smile suddenly vanished.

Wren used every inch of force in her body to slam her forehead against the top of Artemis's nose. She flipped the girl over, feeling the floor shake under the impact of their bodies. She crawled onto Artemis and held her forehead to the ground, allowing the blooming blotch of red and purple sprouting in the center of her face to be hit by the spotlight and seen by the entire arena. Wren didn't wait for the girl to catch her breath. She used the eruption of the surrounding crowd as motivation as she let her fist fly, finally snapping Artemis's nose.

Artemis screamed. Wren hit her again. She heard the amphitheater around them howl with pleasure at the sight. Wren's gloves were dripping crimson as she took them away from Artemis's face. She whimpered beneath Wren as she stood, wiping a spray of blood from the outside of her mask. When Artemis saw the assassin above her, she struggled. Wren stopped her with a boot planted in the center of her chest.

She pressed down and felt the breath escaping from Artemis's lungs. She wheezed, clawing at the sole of the Phantom's perfectly white boot.

"Please!" She gasped, choking on air that wasn't there.

"Remember this when you choose to underestimate me again." Wren pressed down again, curling her hands into fists to keep herself from shattering the girl completely.

"There's a special place in hell for you." Artemis coughed, then spat blood across the top of Wren's boot.

The Phantom looked down at the splatter of scarlet with narrowed eyes, listening as the entire amphitheater went silent to hear her response. She leaned down, resting her elbows on her knees, watching the terror coalescing in the pit of Artemis's eyes.

"I *am* hell."

The moment her boot lifted from Artemis's chest, the girl rolled sideways and heaved breath back into her lungs. Wren waited for a moment, wanting to see if she would face the assassin again. When she remained on her side, curled into herself, and shaking violently, Wren turned away from her.

As the assassin walked away from the center of the pit, she looked to the spot in the crowd where she knew Kiran was watching. The blood that was spilled on the ground of the arena was still drying as she left it, listening to the echoes of the crowd exploding around her.

Wren winked at Kiran, smiling through the tang of blood on her mask.

The Phantom followed no rules but her own.

She was the queen of chess, after all.

It is a harsh reality, but one that we must face. Authors were the writers of books that brought humans to new worlds they'd never seen before. Worlds that were impossible to exist anywhere on the planet, filled with creatures and magics that were also just as impossible. The literature allowed them to imagine holding a flaming sword whilst riding on a glittering white horse down to the valley of war to save the day. It authorized the belief of humans being able to do anything they wanted if only they could dream it.

Dreaming was a drug.

They were all addicts.

No, a person could not gallop on a steed holding a sword without falling off and breaking a bone. No, a person could not wield magic that allowed them to transform into different shapes or hold fire at their fingertips. Those kinds of nonsense stories belonged in the head, where the problem began. In the head, dreams could be stomped out before a human could think it could ever become a reality for them.

Because even in those stories filled with mighty heroes and powerful creatures, there was always a greater evil.

No story is ever truly good, and no life is ever horrible enough to want to escape.

The world before our eyes is the only thing we have left. It would be a misuse of our second chance if

we filled our time with looking beyond our wildest
dreams and ignored what was truly in front of us.
Wake up.
No heroes are coming to save you.

-An excerpt of the first Supreme Leader's
journal, extracted from the Archives of the
Imperial Republic of Raedon

Chapter Twenty-Two

"Dum spiro, spero."
-While I breathe, I hope.

Watching the Phantom in the arena was like nothing Briar had ever seen before. It was like watching a performance, only this show involved weapons, drugs, and a lot more blood.

Briar couldn't erase the images of Ebony from his mind. He didn't want to. She moved with a lethal grace he'd never seen in anyone. She was like ink dipped into water, fluidly transitioning from one dance move to the other. She never hesitated, not even when she took a few hits herself. She was always guessing what her opponent would do next and was always ten steps ahead of the game than Briar thought she was.

The Phantom wasn't putting on a performance; she *was* the performance.

Briar sat on the railing of his balcony, looking into the city from above. He braced his hands on the metal beside him, letting his feet dangle in the open air. His eyes traced the path he and the Phantom took on the way to the underground arena, all the way from the entrance to the slums to the corner shop where they'd escaped into the walls. Briar had never been somewhere where he felt both an adrenaline rush and the sudden urge to leave before; he didn't know if that was a bad thing or a good one.

Watching Ebony in the ring made his heart skip a few beats. He could still feel his hands gripping the barrel of her rifle as he watched her disappear into the crowd. The next time he saw her, her knuckles were wet with blood and she was winking at someone distant in the crowd. When Briar followed her eyeline, he saw her looking at the man sitting on the throne in the far corner of the amphitheater. Kiran, Briar remembered his name to be. He swore he saw a small nod of satisfaction and a grin on the man's face as Ebony shrugged out of the ring. Then she came to retrieve Briar, completely passing Kiran's throne, whose eyes were trained on her back the entire time.

Ebony didn't speak to Briar for the rest of the way back to Sanctum Palace.

Briar glanced over his shoulder at the open balcony doors behind him. Ebony was inside his room now, most likely in his bathroom. He hadn't seen the damage done to her in the underground arena; they left too quickly for him to ask about it. But Briar had a lot of things to ask her about that night and he certainly wasn't going to start with, "Are you okay?".

What had Ebony been doing in the amphitheater in the first place? What did she need to negotiate with Kiran just to end up ignoring him on her way out? Was it a way to show everyone that the Phantom hadn't gone soft because she was dealing with some misfit prince from the palace?

The jingle of silver betting chips interrupted Briar's thoughts. He twisted his neck backward again, seeing Ebony wordlessly closing the doors to his room behind her as she walked up to the railing. She'd dropped the bag of her winnings at the base of the iron rails before gracefully hoisting herself up next to Briar.

Briar had never seen her skin without the white mask overtop. In civilian clothing, she was smaller and more delicate than when she was padded with her ivory fabrics. Without her mask, Briar would see the downward tilt to the corners of her lips and the unusual sunken look to her cheeks. There was a spray of blood across the side of her face; she must've missed it when she had been cleaning up the rest of her injuries. There was an array of small cuts around her jaw from where she was hit, blooming with tiny blue bruises. Her turquoise eyes shone brighter under the stars, and Briar couldn't seem to drag his eyes away from them.

"You can have them," Ebony said, yanking Briar back to reality. She had placed a bag of medical supplies on the railing in between them.

"What?"

"The winnings." She looked down at the sack of metal chips. "I don't need them."

"Oh." Was all Briar could bring himself to say. Ebony pulled out supplies from the medical kit like she did when they were stuck in the safe point together. She grabbed the same materials except for the stitching threads and needles. Briar noticed a jagged cut along her forearm, lightly doused with blood from where the girl in the arena had split her skin with her knife. Briar didn't know the unfamiliar fighter; he had only seen her talking with Ebony and Kiran before she went into the arena.

But what he did know was that for some reason he couldn't explain, he wanted her dead for even thinking about touching Ebony.

Briar looked sideways at the assassin sitting silently beside him. How was she so calm? She had just done drugs, entered a pit fight, beat another girl up, and won that fight all in one night. Briar assumed she would at least gloat a little bit, seeing that she won the crowd over and everyone betted on her before she even threw the first punch.

"I don't know what I would use them for," Briar told her, looking back at the winnings.

Ebony shrugged, still not looking at him. Her back was curved and hunched over; she usually sat tall whenever she was around anyone else. It was like she was trying to hide herself from him. "You could pay your father back for all the money you lost in the gambling halls."

Briar didn't respond. Ebony didn't say anything either, as she pulled out a package of cleansing wipes. She brought one up to her face and began to gently dab the cuts on her jaw.

"I didn't realize you cared so much." He swayed on the rail, watching her hands work cautiously across her skin. Ebony chuckled, but it was an empty sound and looked like it hurt her to do so. He turned away from Ebony, still listening to her wince as she met the disinfectant with her ripped skin. She had never been so raw before him, so willing to hiss every time her skin burned because of her injuries.

"Why did you go to the arena?"

Ebony paused, her hand halfway between getting another wipe from the kit and her face. She was hesitating, pressing her lips together as she thought of how to respond. Briar didn't think it was such a complicated question, but she was so adamant about not telling him before; why would she tell him now?

"I had to pay off a debt from a long time ago." She went back to cleaning her wounds. When Briar glanced sideways at her again, he saw a hollow look in the pit of her eyes. He could tell she was thinking about the fight. The blood on her discarded gloves wasn't hers, and neither was the splatter of crimson across her cheek. Ebony didn't seem to realize it was still there.

When Briar watched the Phantom in the arena, it was like she couldn't stop herself. She was hurting and still was, but it was like a kind of drug that made her feel empowered by it. Briar could've sworn he heard the breaking of the other girl's nose from up in the stands. He also saw the assassin smile after she did it.

But that wasn't Ebony. That was the Phantom.

"Did you have a history with Kiran?"

"Something like that." She responded solemnly. Her mind was ticking faster than Briar saw it in the fighting ring. Was it all that hard to talk to him? Or maybe it was because she was concocting lies to tell him.

"It was before you became the Phantom, wasn't it?" Briar held onto the railing tighter. He knew he wouldn't fall, not with Ebony here. But he felt a pounding sensation in his chest that made him feel like there might be the slightest chance he would throw himself off purposefully if Ebony told him she wanted him to.

"Yes." Her responses were small and simple, nothing like the insults she usually spat at him during their banter.

"Does Kiran know who you are?" Briar asked. He knew Ebony wasn't the Phantom's real name. No one knew who she was; that's why she was nameless and faceless. Well, not anymore. Not to Briar.

"He does." Ebony nodded her head.

"Why hasn't he told anyone?"

"You ask a lot of questions." Ebony gave him a thin-lipped smile. She still didn't look at him. It made Briar's feeling of jumping off the balcony increase.

"It was only five." He countered, counting them in his head.

Ebony's jaw ticked as if she finally felt the drying blood on her cheek. She reached up with an ungloved hand to touch it, bringing it back down to inspect the small flakes of red on her fingers. Briar heard her steep inhale as she instantly scraped the side of her face with her nails, disregarding the angry red lines they left when she did so.

"Here," Briar reached for her hand, and for a moment, he didn't think Ebony would let him touch her. But miraculously she did, and Briar pulled her hand away from her face, grabbing another disinfectant wipe to clean the rest of the blood from her cheek. Her skin was warm underneath his own and he wondered how long it had been since someone else's skin had touched hers. There wasn't much left of the blood after she'd scratched it away, but Briar felt that there was enough to start lightly dabbing on the small spot left untouched by her nails. He was gentler than he'd expected himself to be, wiping away the spray until all that was left was her freckled cheek underneath his fingers.

Briar sat there for a while, static and unable to take his hand away until Ebony flinched and inclined her head away from his hand. Briar brought the cloth down, biting the inside of his cheek as he tucked it into his hand and curled his fingers into a fist. When he built up the courage to look at Ebony again, Briar could see the small lines of her face crinkling in confusion.

"I know you told me not to watch, but I — "

"I know."

Briar swallowed. He wanted to touch her hand again, to tell her that she didn't have to be afraid of telling him the truth. He didn't want her to hesitate when she spoke to him or have to conceal herself from whatever she was running from.

But instead of reaching for her, Briar said, "I didn't know what to think of you when you were fighting the other girl. Or when you snapped her nose."

Something in Ebony's expression told Briar that she didn't know what to think of herself either.

"I did what I had to do." She finally answered him, even though he hadn't asked her to. Her voice sounded like it had been forcibly carved out of her throat.

"She was going to kill you?"

"Yes."

"But you didn't kill her for it." Briar couldn't keep his eyes off of her. "Why?"

Ebony didn't respond. Instead, she knocked the bag of medical supplies off the railing and sat in their spot while they fell to the ground behind them. She was so close that Briar could feel her warmth against the side of his body. His breath hitched when she leaned even closer, practically putting her head on his shoulder as she pointed a finger toward the center of the sky beyond them.

"The sun used to be right there." She told him. Briar's chest contracted and he fought with every bone in his body to look at the sky instead of Ebony. "It was a giant ball of gas and flames like those stars." She continued, moving her finger to different clusters of stars. "People used to call each sol cycle the 'daytime' when the sun was in the sky. Then it would switch places with the moon. Then it would be night."

"Ebony --" Briar knew she was deflecting.

"There were times between the day and night that people called sunrises and sunsets. The sky would change colors."

"It sounds beautiful," Briar admitted. He'd never seen a sky that wasn't pitch black and dotted with stars. It seemed impossible, but when he heard Ebony speak about it, he knew differently.

"It was." She breathed.

"How do you know?"

"Because I can see it." She replied. Sensing Briar's confusion, she nudged his shoulder with her own. "Close your eyes. I'll show you."

Ignoring the flames sparking in his arm, Briar did as he was told. His vision went black, and he could only feel Ebony sitting beside him, listening as she told him what to do.

"Picture a bright blue sky." She instructed.

Briar pictured a blue like the lights on the interior of Sanctum Palace. No, not bright enough. Instead, he focused on the color of Ebony's eyes. A crushing turquoise sky, more beautiful than anything he'd ever seen in his life.

"Now think about the color pink. Then some yellow." Ebony's voice drifted through his ears as Briar's mind painted the scene. "And maybe some oranges."

"I don't think -- "

"Stop thinking. Just imagine it."

Briar did.

The sky was the purest blue he could think of, fading into pink and then yellow and then orange. There was a sun over the horizon, a large frame of bright golden light that illuminated the sky. He imagined the light shining off of the city skyscrapers, creating dazzling rays of flaxen beams that reached them on the balcony. He imagined a soft breeze he would never be able to feel and clouds that he would never be able to see. He imagined the warmth of the gleaming sun heating his face and coloring his skin a golden color.

He couldn't just see it. He could *feel* it.

"Open your eyes."

Briar's eyelids peeled. He didn't know how long he had been sitting there, watching the sunrise dawn in his mind. He didn't know what Ebony had seen, or if she was creating her vivid picture in her mind. He didn't know that the sky could be so dark after he'd imagined it being so light. All Briar knew was that when he opened his eyes, he found Ebony staring into them.

"Did you see it?" She asked him, and he wordlessly nodded.

"How did you know what it looked like?"

"I've heard stories." She shrugged, and her shoulder brushed his arm again. "Pieced the parts together well enough."

Better than *well enough*, Briar thought. But he didn't say it. Instead, he asked, "What else have you heard of?"

Ebony tilted her head to the side, thinking for a moment. Then, her lips split into a smile as she leaned into him again. "Oceans."

"Excuse me?"

Ebony sighed and tucked both of her hands beneath her legs. She swung her feet forward and backward, pushing off the iron rails for momentum when she needed to. "Raedon used to be an ocean. It was a giant body of water that was salty and a more vibrant color of blue than you could ever imagine."

Briar doubted that. He was sure he could imagine the brightest blue in the world. But despite that, he couldn't bring himself not to listen to Ebony as she talked. The way she spoke about these things was so passionate and interesting that he couldn't help himself from being passionate and interested in it, too.

"The saltwater would extend over millions of miles in between continents and go deeper and deeper the further people went down. The water would become so dark that there had to be lights guiding the way of those who explored the depths."

Briar looked around the city. Polaris was one of the bordering districts to the edge of the deep valley it was constructed in. Was the balcony they were sitting on that deep underwater all those millions of years ago?

"How many oceans were there?" he felt his interest beginning to peak.

"I don't know," Ebony said again, but she didn't seem concerned about what she didn't know. Instead, she was focused on what she seemed to dream about. "The oceans had waves that curled over one another and tides that rose onto things called beaches. The tides would be cohesive with the moon."

"What the hell is a beach?" Briar thought it sounded more like a curse he'd shouted at many of his father's court members a few times.

"They're like little spits of land covered in sand. It was grainy like salt and brown like chocolate."

"Chocolate salt doesn't sound appealing." Briar brushed a hand through his hair. "Although, waves sound much more interesting."

"Then imagine something like clouds," Ebony suggested. "Rain fell from them like teardrops from the sky."

"The sky would cry?"

"No, I said, *like* teardrops from the sky." She corrected him. Briar hummed and nodded his head. He knew that there was acid rain in the time shortly after the sun imploded. That must've been before any of the clouds disappeared and the teardrop rain was diseased with some sort of radiation.

"Rain and sun grew plants. But not the mutant ones that we grow food from now. These plants just," She paused to let out a small sigh. "Grew."

"What's the point of them just being there if they don't have some kind of use?" Briar couldn't imagine something sprouting from the ground that wasn't one of Raedon's engineered plants to provide them with food and oxygen.

"They didn't have to have a use." Ebony insisted, defending the extinct plants. "They were beautiful, and that was all they needed to be."

"Right." Briar didn't know how to imagine useless plants like he imagined the sunrises.

Ebony didn't speak after that. She continued to look into the city, the neon lights from the skyscrapers reflecting in her eyes like stars in the blackness of her pupils. When Briar looked into the real sky, he saw the stars blinking back at him.

For once, they were not laughing. They were *listening*.

"You still haven't answered my question. Why didn't you kill that other girl?"

Ebony's hands tightened around the rail. Briar was tempted to reach for them.

"You were there." Her voice was small, and for the first time, afraid. "I didn't want you to see me the way I saw myself."

In her eyes, Briar could see that very fear curling inside her.

"I do see you," Briar told her. "But not as a monster."

"You think that?"

"No." Briar shook his head as his hand moved to unclasp hers from the railing. Ebony's skin heated underneath his fingers and her eyes rose to meet his. Briar swore he saw small bits of stardust inside of them as he smiled.

"I know that."

Humanity used to be so fickle in how they celebrated.

A "holiday" was an expanse of time devoted to commemorating one momentous moment in history. The birth of a holy child, for example. The scaring away of spirits with masks and afterward devouring sweets once the work had been done. The shimmying of a fat man down a chimney once every year.

But did it ever occur to society that their revelry was more wasteful than it was truly celebratory? The birthing of a child is no small feat, not even with the medicines and advancements in the Imperial Republic. Yet why were there streamers hung in the halls and plants decorated in honor of one small baby boy? Why would children pounce on other children to scare them out of their wits and take their candy? And why, pray tell, would anyone want a fat man scooting down their chimney in the dead of night, reading a list of names and addresses, and leaving mysterious presents underneath towering green plants?

I will tell you why.

Because humankind used to believe in faith. They truly believed that celebrating an event in history would bring them good fortune and a good year ahead. Yet even before the sun imploded and whilst these revelries were popular, there was science to prove that no child born on a certain date held any speculation as to what happened in the

world or that there was no point in bullying other
children out of their fun.
Wasteful was what it was.
And what was a waste before the sun imploded
was immediately illuminated in Raedon.
The Lunar Inception is a ten sol cycle celebration in
the Imperial Republic, meant to give society a break
from their regular lives to honor the rebirth of our
world after a struggle.
Nothing was more memorable than the
achievement of perfection.

-An excerpt of the first Supreme Leader's
journal, extracted from the Archives of the
Imperial Republic of Raedon

Chapter Twenty-Three

"Ex favilla nos resurgemus."
-We will rise from the embers.

The Lunar Inception was a celebration in Raedon that literally meant, "the beginning of the night". It commemorated the implosion of the sun and the rising of Raedon from its ashes. Well, metaphorical ashes because when the sun's radiation wave hit Earth, nothing was left behind.

On the first sol of the celebration, the Supreme Leader hosts a party with his most elite guests. Those consisted of his court members, close friends, Advisors, and anyone deemed important enough to see him in the flesh instead of on the television screen. On the second to ninth sol cycles, the rest of Raedon celebrates. They host parties of their own in their homes and it's the only time of the year when people are excused from their occupations and school for eight sol cycles. Then, on the tenth sol, the final party, the Supreme Leader, hosts the largest function of all; a ball.

The next sol would mark the first sol of the Inception.

On her way to the training room, Wren had spotted more than the normal number of servants bustling down the halls.

In their arms, they held decorations, ribbons, silks, and banners with Raedon colors. Wren knew they wouldn't be put up during the sol cycle; they'd be hung in the night while everyone else was sleeping, almost as if they miraculously appeared.

Surprisingly, Wren had nothing against the Lunar Inception. Well, except for the fireworks display on the night of the tenth sol. She thought it was a total waste of resources to launch colorful explosives into the sky when they could be used for better things, like rigging a trap to go off when the Supreme Leader walked under it. Other than that, everything that was celebrated on the holiday was true; the sun did, in fact, implode and Raedon did, in fact, rise from nothing. She supposed it was a good cause for a party because without Raedon, and as much as she hated to admit it, they'd all be dead.

"Bloody hell." Briar cursed in front of her.

Wren's attention snapped back to reality. In front of her, Briar adjusted his grip on the firearm. He held it out in front of him, squinting at the target twenty yards from where he stood. Every time his finger moved to the trigger, the unsteadiness of his hands crushed his aim. Then he would have to start over, making the shooting of a simple weapon that should've taken him five seconds, an affair that lasted thirty minutes instead.

This sol Wren had regrettably backed away from hand-to-hand combat. Now looking back on it, she realized that fighting Briar would have been a more effective use of her time. She believed that her original idea of teaching him to shoot was brilliant; she'd had enough of fighting against a useless opponent, and she was sure that Briar had had enough of getting hit in the nose, especially after watching her crush Artemis's. So, when he walked in this morning to meet her, she'd tossed him a gun and ushered him toward a target. At first, he was confused. He didn't know how to load the ammunition without jamming it. Apparently, he'd never shot a firearm before, and it made Wren a little bit disgusted.

Didn't everyone know how to shoot a gun?

Obviously not, because Briar was so lousy, Wren had forced herself to look away every time he tried to make the shot. A bullet hadn't even struck the target yet, and Wren was already immensely bored. It was only twenty yards; she didn't see why this was so problematic for him.

"Put it down." Wren sighed and rounded his shoulder. Briar did as he was told, his arms hanging slack by his sides.

Wren shoved him over with a hand, pulling her gun out with the other and firing it all in one second. The echo rang through the room and when they both looked at the target, they found a bullet hole piercing the dead center of the middle ring.

"I could've done that." Briar instantly said, crossing his arms in front of his chest. His gun still hung from his index finger, a mistake Wren hoped he'd come to regret when he accidentally pulled the trigger and shot his foot.

That would've brought her the laugh she needed.

"Right." Wren rolled her eyes when he didn't injure himself. She holstered her gun again.

"Just out of curiosity though," Briar began, "how did you do that without aiming?"

"Muscle memory. My body knows the position it has to be in when shooting from different distances. Twenty yards is a bit more relaxed than forty and that is more relaxed than sixty." She explained. When she glanced at Briar, he was mouthing her words back to her to try and understand. Wren waited for him to finish and when he did, he looked up at her with an even more perplexed expression.

"I've had a lot of practice." She said instead, then stepped to the side to allow Briar to line up with the target again.

"I would have that too if you'd just let me shoot the gun for once."

"There's no point in practicing if you're going to do it wrong every time." Wren spat back. "Get back into your stance."

Briar planted his feet wide on the ground and brought up his arms, aiming at the target. Wren had to pause and mentally prepare herself for the torture of simply teaching him how to stand before she crossed his back to reach his other side.

She touched his arms lightly, feeling his skin heat beneath her gloves. "Loosen your grip." She bit out, trying to keep herself from chuckling. "You're not shanking someone, you're shooting them."

"I've never shanked anyone in my life," Briar responded, keeping his arms loose as he squinted at the target.

"I find that surprising."

She moved in front of him to glance at his position from a different angle. Briar instantly took his finger off the trigger.

"Shouldn't you be standing behind me, not in front of me?" He asked, peeking around the side of the weapon at her.

"You won't shoot me." She said calmly. Truthfully, she wasn't worried that he would hurt her. Even if he wanted to, his aim was so lousy he'd probably end up firing at the ceiling before being able to reload and kill her.

Briar grumbled something under his breath, but Wren ignored it as she stepped forward. Now, her forehead was practically pressing against the barrel of the gun as she reached for his hands.

"Is this what they call déjà vu?" Briar commented as she shifted his fingers around the grip of the weapon. He allowed her to touch him, adjusting him until he held the firearm right.

She remembered the feeling of his hand entrapping hers on the balcony. It made her cheeks flush, but her mask covered her emotion for her.

"If your grip is too tight, the force of the bullet will cause you to aim wrong." She told him, stepping back once she finished and trying to ignore the blooming feeling in her stomach. Briar nodded, his throat bobbing. Then Wren moved to reach for his shoulders, pressing them down with the palms of her hands.

She realized too late that he was also blushing.

"Relax your shoulders." She said, coughing to hide her snicker.

"Are you laughing at me?" Briar sneered, peering over his shoulder at her.

"Eyes on the target." Wren snapped.

"I'm the one with the gun here."

"Then shoot it sometime, will you?"

The shot echoed off the platinum walls. Wren lifted herself to her toes and looked over Briar's shoulder at the target. There was a new bullet hole in the upper right corner of the outer ring. It was nowhere near perfect, but he'd managed to reach mediocre.

With her help, of course.

Briar's lips broke into a smile. He spun around on his heel, twirling the gun in his hand. "The Phantom can take today off. A new assassin just stepped in."

"You could never," Wren argued, although she wasn't mad at him for insulting her like she always was when he made fun of her.

"I just did."

"Barely." Wren jerked her chin towards the target. "The only reason you were able to do that was because of *this* assassin's help." She jabbed a thumb towards her chest.

"You should have more faith in me."

"I'll have faith in you when you stop swinging that thing around." Wren grabbed the weapon from his hands. "You're going to shoot me."

Briar shrugged, and his smile widened. "Good. Maybe after that, you'll realize that I don't need you around here and you can skip off to somewhere else in Raedon and bother some other unfortunate soul with your attitude."

"I do not skip." Wren blanched. "And my attitude isn't the one that needs adjusting."

Briar's eyes narrowed, but Wren could tell he wasn't truly angry with her. Not this time, at least. "The world would be a much better place if you and your scowl left it alone."

Wren couldn't help but roll her eyes as she swiveled around on her heel, unloading the gun and placing it on a table behind them. When she turned back around, she found Briar pointing at her rifle leaning against the side of the table.

"I want to shoot that."

"No." Wren scoffed, picking up the rifle.

"Why not?" Briar sounded offended.

"You won't be able to," Wren explained. "It requires accuracy; something you clearly don't have very much of."

"Oh, please." Briar grabbed for the rifle, but Wren pulled it away from him. "I've never seen you shoot that thing. How do I know you're not rusty?"

Wren snarled, feeling her upper lip curl. She didn't know why her heart chose that moment to begin beating twice its normal speed, but she knew that she didn't enjoy the feeling. She also didn't like the overwhelming sense of pride washing over her, encouraging her to prove him wrong.

The Phantom was known for sharpshooting; it was how she took out most of her targets. She was supposed to be a ghost, invisible to the eye, which also meant being invisible to all the monitors placed around Raedon. The Republic had cameras stationed around all seven districts, making sure that every citizen was following their assigned protocols and doing what they were supposed to be doing. So, when the assassin wanted to take a minor break from publicity and being on news footage, sometimes she would simply aim her scope through a window and pull the trigger. It was much simpler and her preferred method of getting things done.

"Fine." She turned away and slung the rifle over her shoulder. Briar chuckled from behind her as she walked away, approaching one of the climbing ropes attached to the rafters of the domed ceiling. Wren grabbed it with firm hands, gracefully thrusting herself upwards until she reached the rafter. Then she pulled herself up, her head almost touching the glass-domed roof above her.

She spotted Briar still looking at her, now stepping aside so she had a clear shot at the target. He crossed his arms again and he was leaning against the table, shaking his head as if to tell her that he knew she couldn't do it.

Wren smiled, knowing that she could.

Wren ignored Briar and took off her rifle. She set it against her shoulder and loaded only one bullet; she didn't need two when her first shot would be nothing less than perfect. Wren took a deep breath, lowering her face so that she could peer through the scope. She saw the target immediately, exhaling slowly as she allowed her finger to retract on the trigger.

The shot rang through the room louder than a regular bullet. Wren didn't need to look at the target to know she'd hit exactly where she wanted.

Briar cursed colorfully, looking from the target to Wren, now lowering herself from the rafter and sliding down the rope. He watched her with his mouth hanging open as she approached him, planting her rifle at her feet and leaning on it like a cane.

"How did-" Briar began, but Wren interrupted him.

"I can't teach you how to shoot it, but I can tell you how to spot one." She took out a cloth from her pocket and began to shine her scope. It wasn't dirty, but it was a habit she'd gotten used to doing. "You can always spot a sniper by the gleam of their scope."

"Why is that?"

Wren ran the cloth over the cold metal again, watching it shine in the white lights. "A sharpshooter's proudest piece of equipment is their scope."

Saying that we are all born the same is ridiculous. Yes, we are all human. Yes, we look different from each other. Yes, we are all born onto the same platform and status.

But that does not mean that we are equal.

No two people are equal because no two people are the same. Some humans are simply better at certain things than others. Smarter, more intelligent in different areas. But being skilled in one aspect does not mean that you are equal to someone else. It means you are better than them.

It is our choice if we advance ourselves. Some are born with assets and others have to work hard to earn them. But no matter how we are born and with what skills we possess, we make our own decisions and choose how high we rise.

No one is going to do it for you. It is up to us to determine where we belong in society.

Do not expect that since we are all born human, we are equal.

-An excerpt of the first Supreme Leader's journal, extracted from the Archives of the Imperial Republic of Raedon

Chapter Twenty-Four

"Invictus maneo."
-I remain unconquered.

Briar's favorite holiday was the Lunar Inception because of one rule; there were no rules.

Sure, he wasn't allowed to murder hundreds of people like the beloved Phantom watching him at all times, but none of those kinds of activities appealed to Briar the way other things did. He would rather get drunk on as much wine as he could and talk to as many girls as he could fit into his bursting schedule than embark on a killing spree with his favorite babysitter.

Which is why, when Briar woke up that sol and dressed in his revelry finest of black velvet decorated with silver thread, he ran straight for the ballroom. As he roamed the hallways, he could already feel the liveliness of partying sparking in his veins. Servants were walking around with baskets in their hands, carrying banners and silks of purple and black. When Briar arrived in the ballroom, his excitement only ignited into true flames.

There were three levels to the ballroom; the dance floor, what Briar called the talking floor, and the Supreme Leader's dais. The center of the ballroom was the lowest level, usually used for dancing and surrounded by small steps that led upwards to the talking floor. The talking floor was normally where Briar congregated with members of the court, specifically the girls who had been staring at him all night. This time, though, the second level of the ballroom had been set up with long tables lined with black and purple cloth. The obsidian marble floor would be filled with guests on both floors soon enough, and the tables adorned with food. The third and final level was smaller than the other two but had a table as well, meant for the Supreme Leader, the Captain of the Guard, other important members of the court whose names Briar didn't care to remember, and of course Briar himself.

Decorated in the purple and black embellishments Briar had seen earlier, the space looked more regal than he'd ever seen it before. The silks that were once in the process of being ironed now lined the walls in a transparent shine. The banners with the Raedon seal, two crossing swords, and three crowning stars that Briar saw being stitched were now draped across the iron rafters like honey from a spoon. Briar could barely see the domed ceiling looking out at the stars from beneath them.

The doors to the ballroom now turned into the feast room, he supposed, opened for guests not long after Briar himself arrived. He was immediately swept away in the celebration. No one would be sitting at the tables until his father arrived, Briar knew, but that was no excuse to not pass by them and occasionally sneak a delicacy from one of the trays covered by silver domes when he wanted to. He meandered his way throughout the entire room like a needle stitching thread, weaving in and out of conversations on different levels of the room. When he was tired of one thing, he switched to another. When he was sick of hearing the same conversation about court drama that he always listened to, he jumped over to a group of girls who had been waiting for him to notice them in the corner.

"Are you enjoying the party?" One of the girls asked him when he joined them. They were all wearing fine dresses of bright colors in the most expensive Raedon fashions, but this girl had chosen differently. She wore a striking black colored gown that reached the floor in long shimmering curtains. The jewels lining her neck in a collar had immediately caught his attention as he approached them.

"I am now," Briar responded with another sip from his glass. He didn't bother counting how many cups of the bubbling sensation he'd had, but he was completely in control of himself, regardless. "But not as much as I'm enjoying this champagne." He held up the glass for her to see, even though she had one in her hand as well. All the girls giggled.

There was a girl in an unusual cream-colored dress standing next to the girl in black. She wore no jewelry, and her cinnamon-colored hair was left alone to cascade down the length of her back. She reminded Briar of Ebony dressed in her ivory uniform. Although looking up and down at the girl before him, Briar knew that Ebony looked better in the color than the girl ever did. She looked positively green against the paleness of her garment, and Briar knew Ebony would've never laughed at the comment he just made.

Noticing his stare, the girl in white smiled at him. Her teeth were perfectly even. "Your uniform looks lovely." She told him.

"Thank you," Briar responded with a grin of his own, taking a swig from his glass. "Your dress makes you look sick."

The girl gasped and put a hand to her chest as if appalled that Briar would say such a thing. But instead of apologizing, which didn't have an appeal because he did nothing wrong, Briar simply shrugged and finished his glass of champagne, handing it over to an awaiting servant before fully turning to the girl in black.

He reached to tilt her chin up with the tips of his fingers and flashed her a charming smile that he knew would cause Ebony to vomit. "I'll see you soon."

She blushed profusely while the rest of the girls shot her looks of reproach and disgust. Some of them were still laughing about the previous comment he made. Briar let his fingers fall from her face as he turned around on the heel of his boot, roaming deeper into the room to find another cluster of awaiting fun.

As the celebration continued, Briar allowed himself to be served one glass of champagne after another. He was almost positive that his father had assigned a certain servant to give him the drinks because he'd seen the boy pouring the alcohol into the glass at a slightly lower volume than all the others and adding water to it as well. Nevertheless, Briar couldn't bring himself to care. He seemed to think that if he drank enough before his father arrived, he could avoid speaking to him for the rest of the party.

That was proved wrong when the small layer of music being played from the corner of the room stopped. Briar forced himself to keep his eye-rolling in check as he swiveled his head towards the grand doors on the other end of the hall like everyone else. The girls he had been talking to were standing behind him, straightening their gowns and fluffing their hair. Briar scoffed, pretending to gag at their efforts.

When the doors opened, the Supreme Leader marched through the crowd with a crown of silver and black diamonds resting on the top of his head. Following closely behind him was the Captain of the Guard, her hand placed gently on the holster of her gun. Advisor Sonnen and Achlys were also there, trailed by two of the other head Advisors on Briar's father's council. Briar made it a point to ignore Achlys as the guests split for their entrance, parting like a rift to allow them to pass through. He took a large swig of champagne as his father neared him, only slightly inclining his chin while the rest of the guests nearly fell to the floor in the presence of the Supreme Leader.

Briar had forgotten he was supposed to meet his father outside of the ballroom before they entered. There was a missing spot next to Quinn Vega where he should've been walking, but Briar felt that the attraction of the party was too much for him to handle and let the responsibility slip from his mind. He was positive he'd be scolded but the price of it was worth the fun he'd had before his father stomped on his good time.

When the Supreme Leader and Quinn finally reached the stairs to the third-floor dais on the other end of the room, everyone resumed their positions on the main floor. Briar's father rounded the table and Quinn followed him as usual.

The Supreme Leader took his seat in the center of the table, lowering himself into a silver-decorated chair that resembled his throne in the throne room. Quinn sat to his left, leaving space for Briar when he would eventually be forced to join them on the high dais. Achlys and Advisor Sonnen were on the other side of the table. Good, Briar thought, because if Achlys had been seated next to him, he would've never attended the celebration.

When everything had begun as usual, Briar turned back around to continue speaking with the girls but found an empty marble floor where they used to be.

"What the-" He began, spinning around himself in a circle. When his eyes surfed the end of the room, Briar found his father looking directly at him while wagging a finger in his direction. Briar cursed under his breath and gave his champagne to a random guest walking past him. The man didn't complain as Briar wormed his way through the crowd, swearing under his breath. People cleared a path for him as soon as they saw who he was, instantly backing away another five feet when they heard the vulgar words escaping his lips. It allowed him to reach the dais easier than he would've enjoyed, storming up the stairs and not bothering to bow his head again when he reached the top.

"What?" He snapped, pulling his chair out from under the table and collapsing into it. He crossed his arms in front of his chest and slouched down so far that only his shoulder blades were touching the back of the seat. On his other side, Quinn ignored him.

"What did I tell you about the champagne?" Dorin Atlas said in a low voice.

"You told me that I could have as much as I wanted because this is a party and the one time I actually get to have fun," Briar spoke in a normal volume because he didn't care if anyone heard him and his father arguing. Maybe that would give them something better to talk about than the court gossip that continuously bored him to the point of near death.

"That is not what I said." the Supreme Leader ground his teeth together in annoyance.

"Then I forget." Briar sneered. "Please enlighten me."

"Don't get smart with me, boy." Briar's father's lip curled. "The only reason you are here is because the Phantom is as well. If she wasn't watching you, I would've locked you in your room."

Briar coughed and under his breath said, "You mean prison?"

Beside him, Quinn's eyes glimmered, and her shoulders bounced with silent laughter. Briar was amused that she found him so entertaining until her eyes swept the ballroom again. What was she looking for? An invitation to talk to someone other than his father? Briar would've searched the deep depths of hell for a request that would allow him to escape the Supreme Leader's monotonous drawl.

His father didn't notice the Captain as he said, "If that is what you want to call safety, then yes." He rolled his shoulders and looked out into the ballroom. He, too, was scanning the crowd for something.

Briar might not have known the Phantom as well as she'd led him to believe, but he knew one thing; she wouldn't be caught dead roaming the ballroom like a regular guest. She'd rather be up in the rafters with her rifle, hidden perfectly by the silks and banners. Briar could almost imagine her scope pointed directly at him so she could watch him at all times without losing him in the crowd like he lost the guards assigned to watch him at the last party his father hosted.

Briar bit his lip and scolded himself. No, how could he be so gullible? The Phantom wouldn't watch him out of everyone in this ballroom. He should've known better than that. She'd probably have her eyes on the most important members of the party, like the Supreme Leader's Advisors or someone worth saving from potential rebel threats. Lord knew she would rather take her eyes off of him and have him get shot than miss watching the chocolate fountains finally melt into molten goop.

But even with those thoughts in mind, Briar couldn't keep himself from glancing up at the rafters that supported the glass-domed ceiling. When he did, he saw only stars. Their friend was not here tonight.

But even though the Phantom was a whisper in the air, Briar could still feel the memory of her in his mind's eye. He remembered their latest lesson together, how she'd touched his arms and his shoulders to adjust his grip on the gun. Then she showed him her rifle, telling him about the scope and the importance of every piece of equipment she owned after that. She spoke to him like he'd never been spoken to before; he wasn't being scolded or reprimanded or ignored. He was simply being talked to.

It was an experience that Briar was not accustomed to feeling. He couldn't tell if he enjoyed the sensation or despised it because of the sudden fluttering in his stomach. Maybe he'd have to attend another lesson just to test his theory out.

"Our dear friend informed me that you've been excelling in your combat training." Briar snapped out of his haze when he realized his father was still talking to him. It didn't take long for him to realize that their "friend" was the Phantom. Briar blushed.

"I don't see why you would expect anything less from me." Briar lifted his chin, forcing the fluttering in his stomach to be replaced by pride. He smothered his smug expression into a tight-lipped frown.

"I expected you to resist." The Supreme Leader admitted with a small shrug. It was a casual gesture that Briar was not used to seeing on his father. "Cooperating has never been one of your strengths." Briar looked sideways and found the corners of his father's lips tilting up in a small smile. "I am proud of you."

Briar's blood curdled at the words. His mouth would've fallen open if his lips weren't already sewn shut.

He was proud of Briar? When was the last time he'd heard those words come out of his father's mouth? Certainly not in a long time, maybe even years.

"T-" Briar hesitated. He hadn't thanked his father for anything in a while, either. "Thank you."

The Supreme Leader nodded his head in recognition, continuing to look over the guests. The musicians in the corner had begun to play their melodic music again as guests began to circulate and find their seats at the tables. Briar remembered the promise he made to see the girl in the black dress later and saw her sitting next to a few other men his age. Normally, Briar would've felt jealous, but all he seemed to be able to think about now was suffocating the unpredicted smile fighting to appear on his lips.

But the pride was short-lived when he heard a small whistle come from down the table. Briar rolled his eyes, ignoring the small sound and hoping that it wouldn't bother him again. Unfortunately, Achlys was as persistent as he was annoying. He whistled again, and this time leaned forward, looking past his father to meet his eyes.

Before his former friend could talk, though, Briar flashed him a vulgar gesture and winked. From beneath the table, the Supreme Leader stomped on Briar's foot in response. But he didn't care, partly because he'd gotten the last word he didn't have when they'd argued in person and partly because it simply felt like the right thing to do.

Did that make him a passive-aggressive person? Probably.

Did Briar care? No.

From beside him and quickly recovered from his foot-stomping, the Supreme Leader stood from his seat and all the heads in the room turned in his direction. The cameras and news reporters sitting in the corners straightened, training their lenses and listening devices on Briar's father. Briar himself took the opportunity to wink at a few of the girls he'd spotted when wandering, but hadn't gotten the time to talk to before he was summoned to his father's side. They giggled back at him but quickly stopped themselves with a hand to their mouth, their cheeks blooming red when they realized they were in the line of the cameras.

Briar's knee bounced under the table. He couldn't find the words to describe how bored he was, so instead he opted to roll his eyes every few seconds to make sure the rest of the Republic watching the televised speech knew that he was as turned off as they were.

"Failure was a word to describe the opposite of what we know as success. It was used when people lost when they hadn't achieved the unachievable. It was an inevitable thing, destruction, defeat, and omission. But standing in front of you now proves that wrong. The sun imploded and left Earth in ashes. It was a devastating conquering of fate over our people. Out of those ashes, Raedon rose. Calling this a 'fresh start' would be an abuse of our lengthy suffering. Nor do we call this 'learning from the past'. This is the future. We, all as one, are the future."

Clapping arose from the ballroom that drew Briar back to reality. He realized he was the only one not applauding his father's speech and instantly joined in, nodding his head as if he had been listening the entire time when really, he was mainly focused on the servants filing in behind their table with glasses of champagne on their trays. In the mists of the ovation, they leaned in between the seats and set the glasses on the tables by their stems. The liquid inside was bubbly, but not the same ivory color as it normally was. It was dark and shadowy, like the night sky.

When the applause ended, the Supreme Leader opened his arms in an invitation, inviting his court to eat. Instantly, silver platters and trays were uncovered in the center of the tables. Fumes of roast meat and flavorful spices rose into the air. Briar couldn't help himself, instantly diving into the potatoes placed in front of him. He obliged his hunger, filling his plate with everything stationed in front of him and more. When he finished his first glass of midnight champagne, a serving girl rounded his shoulder with another bottle. She looked familiar; the braids scattered through her hair swinging as she leaned towards the table. She picked up his glass and stopped pouring the champagne when it was halfway to the top of the glass. Before she could set it down again, Briar stopped her.

"Fill it to the top." He ordered and watched as the young girl blushed and obeyed. Her gray eyes widened when she looked sideways at the Captain, her gaze quickly flickering back to Briar. When she had finished, Briar flashed her a charming smile and watched as she retreated to the kitchens, turning feverishly red.

Beside him, Quinn helped herself to healthy amount of each dish, respectfully placing her napkin on her lap. She barely spoke to the high-ranking soldier next to her, as if what he had to say held no interest. Her copper hair was coiled in a braid around her head like a crown, but Briar suspected it was put out of her face for convenience rather than beauty. She was good to look at; he had to admit, especially in her tight-fitting uniform. But in all the years Briar had known the Captain, he'd always assumed that she had no interest in things like that. Things like *him*. She was quiet as she usually was, but not inattentive. It was almost as if she was waiting for someone.

Briar took a wild guess and assumed that they were waiting for the same famous assassin.

Where was the Phantom? Why hadn't she come to the celebration? What was deemed more important than one of the largest social events in Raedon? Briar wanted to believe that she had a valuable reason when suddenly, a thought flew through his mind.

Was she celebrating with someone else?

No, Briar thought and shoved the idea away. Ebony was an assassin; she didn't hang around with random people.

She wasn't the kind to celebrate something like this, especially when she seemed hell-bent on disagreeing with everything the Republic stood for. But even when he had assured himself over and over again, Briar couldn't help but keep his eyes searching around the room for a glint of white amongst the rest.

Unsuccessful and feeling the sense of failure his father had spoken about, Briar stabbed the greens piled on his plate and chewed them harshly. They tasted horrible; he never liked vegetables. He hoped that dessert would come sooner rather than later, but towards the end of the main meal of the doors on the other end of the ballroom opened, a soldier marching through the room rather than servants with dessert trays.

How disappointing.

No one paid him any attention as he marched through the center of the room, his pace hastening with each fumbled step. It caught Quinn's attention before anyone else's at their high table, and soon enough, the soldier was standing directly in front of the Supreme Leader.

"Sir." The soldier bowed his head to Briar's father. Briar was in the middle of spitting the rest of his greens out into a napkin when the Supreme Leader leaned forward, allowing the guard to speak into his ear. His words were hushed and fast, so fast that Briar barely heard anything before his father's face turned to stone.

His voice was on the verge of trembling as he said, "Let her in."

Briar's heart skipped as the soldier turned around, signaling to the others near the door to open it as commanded. Reluctantly, the four soldiers standing guard at the end of the hall reached for the enormous handles, cranking open the platinum doors to reveal a white figure waiting outside in the hallway.

As soon as the doors parted, she entered. The Phantom marched quickly, catching the attention of everyone as she passed. The room turned utterly silent; she had that sort of effect on people. Briar felt a lump forming in his throat, both from seeing Ebony in her uniform again when he couldn't get the memory of her *out* of it, out of his mind and also because she looked positively terrifying. Her silver rifle shined brighter than ever before, almost as if she'd layered on fifteen coats of polish instead of the usual five. Her mask was strapped to her face and the small train of her uniform billowed slightly behind her, revealing rows of silver knives like teeth on a beast. Even though Briar had spoken with the assassin on multiple accounts, suffered a few too many targeted insults, seen her without her uniform, and been punched by her, he still felt a tremor go through the room as she marched onto the dais, approaching the high table.

Still, she neglected to bow and made her way up the stairs. Briar kept staring at her eyes, willing the turquoise irises to flicker his way. As if he summoned them to him with sheer will, the Phantom blinked as she ascended the steps, her eyes casually sliding across the table until they met his. Even though Briar knew that wherever the Phantom went, trouble followed, he couldn't help the sly smile spreading onto his lips.

But as soon as it happened, it was gone. Rather than approaching the Supreme Leader, Ebony turned her attention beside Briar, towards the Captain of the Guard.

Amid the silence, her eyes wandered around Quinn's plate, her fingers twitching at her sides.

"It's poisoned."

Quinn blanched. The two of them, along with the entire ballroom, were looking at the glass of midnight champagne placed before the Captain's plate.

"What are you talking about?" Quinn snapped, her top lip curling.

Even Briar's father seemed to hold his breath, watching the exchange with a careful glare. Ebony didn't seem to mind and, in fact, seemed to ignore everyone in the room except for the Captain.

"The drink has been poisoned."

"That's ridiculous." The Captain bit out, inspecting the stemmed glass. She hadn't taken a single sip, as far as Briar knew. The bubbling liquid was bubbling as it should've been, and the color of it was the same as the rest of theirs. "All of our food is tested."

Instead of responding to her, Ebony turned on her heels to face the soldier still standing in front of the Supreme Leader. Her shoulders rolled confidently, and Briar knew she must've been smiling underneath her mask. The soldier's throat bobbed when she met his stare, and Briar couldn't help but feel jealous even though he knew what was coming next for the poor guard.

"Drink it." Ebony's finger whipped towards the glass.

The soldier's mouth opened but closed again as if there was something he wanted to say but couldn't bring himself to do it. Briar had a few ideas in mind, like, 'No, I'd rather not be poisoned to death on this fine eve of celebration. Choose someone else'. But instead of the soldier pointing out another that could try the drink in his stead, he stepped forward with shaking hands and lifted the glass by the stem. They all watched as he shakily brought the rim of the glass to his lips, tilting his head back and letting the liquid pour through his thin lips.

A collective intake of breath echoed around the room as they waited for him to drop dead in front of them all. But he didn't collapse. His shoulders tightened for a moment, fearful of the effects of the supposed poison, but relaxed once he realized there was nothing wrong with him.

"Is this how you choose to win your attention now?" Quinn glared at Ebony through the fire burning in her eyes.

"I do not *win* anything." Ebony hissed back.

"Then what is all of this about?"

"I found an extra worker exiting the servants' quarters today." She began to explain, and instantly, a million questions flared behind Briar's mind. "When I looked through the records, no new employee had been added to the list in the past year." Quinn bit her cheek as Briar leaned forward to listen closer. "Instead of coming to the celebration tonight, I followed the extra servant into the kitchens and watched him assist with the making of the meal until it came time to bring out the toast. He dipped a small silver skewer into the drink meant for the Captain."

"How did you know the drink was destined for me? My soldier is fine." Quinn questioned her, something Briar knew Ebony was not used to. Yet she took the suspicion with grace, instead tilting her head as if simply bored with their conversation.

"Poisoning the Supreme Leader or his son would have no effect in the long run. Taking out their court members one at a time, unraveling it like a thread, would mean weakening the Republic faster." Briar let out a slow, disappointed breath. She hadn't even mentioned his *name*. "You are just as much of a target for the Rising Sun as the rest of them."

Briar noticed how she didn't say *us*. It was like she knew that she was untouchable.

Briar's chest warmed at the thought; *he* had touched her.

"That's impossible." Quinn battled, determined to prove the Phantom wrong. "All of our food and drink is tested and checked for poisons. Nothing gets past it."

"Until now."

When the words left Ebony's mouth, Briar felt his heart skip more beats than it should've. The ballroom remained utterly silent around them; everyone was waiting for them to finish, if not to continue eating, but to run and escape. Briar felt like running; he'd been drinking glasses of champagne all night. What if he was also poisoned and simply didn't know it yet? No, Briar thought to himself. Ebony said he would not be a target of the Rising Sun. He was safe for now.

"Thallium poisoning is undetectable in food." Ebony's eyes were pinned on the glass. Her sentences were long and drawn out, like she knew she was taunting everyone in the room, including him. "It has no color, no odor, and no taste. It's easily bypassed. It's a toxin made under the eyes of the Republic, handed out by dealers in the city scrounging for whatever money is left. It would've been easy for someone to get some, only harder for them to remain as undetected as the poison itself."

Just as the words fled her lips, the soldier beside her coughed. Briar's head snapped to him. He knew he shouldn't have been as excited as he was as the soldier's hands had traveled up to his throat and his eyes widened, the veins in his forehead now popping blue. He began to cough more violently, leaning over to heave a full breath into his lungs. Only nothing came. His skin turned scarlet from the lack of air, transitioning into purple in an instant. He grabbed onto the edge of the table, attempting to support himself. But it was no use. Briar's mouth hung open as the soldier fell to his knees, twitching on the marble floor before them.

Then his attention whipped to Ebony, casually looking down at the dying man at her feet.

How magnificent.

"Guards!" Quinn had already jumped out of her seat, ordering her soldiers to come and retrieve their colleague. The guests around the room panicked, breaking away from their tables and glasses of champagne. Beside him, Briar's father sat in his chair, white-knuckling the arms of the seat as he listened to the sounds of choking from beneath the table.

Soldiers climbed the dais, but Ebony held out her hand.

"He's dead." She confirmed. Indeed, the sputtering sounds had stopped.

Quinn glanced at the Phantom. In her eyes, Briar couldn't tell if she was thanking Ebony, or telling her that she didn't trust her. Either way, Briar knew that it was some shared language that he'd never be able to interpret. Only that he wished he had known the dialect as well.

"Find the traitor and kill him." Dorin stood from his chair as well, finally speaking after being stone silent for so long. The soldiers immediately did as he commanded, beginning to rush back down the dais and towards the doors on the other end of the hall.

"I've already dealt with it," Ebony told the Supreme Leader. A part of Briar wanted to ask how she did it; how did she know everything before it happened?

But he had waited too long. The Phantom was already turning on her heel and stalking down the dais, following after the soldiers looking for someone Briar knew would surely be a ghost by now.

If there was a God, why did he not save us?
If there was a prophet, why didn't he think to remember us?
If there was a holy being above ourselves, why did he forget about us in our time of most desperate need?

Before the sun imploded, there were over 4,000 belief systems titled, "religions". Each religion had its own set of beliefs, like a mechanical kit for how to behave to achieve the maximum benefits of life. Many religions believed in one god, while multiple others put their faith in three or four. All higher beings looked different, and some were even connected. They each had stories about their origins, telling tales of how each belief came to be in a specific region of the world.

But if there were so many of these beings looking down on us, why did the world end?

Was it their plan to destroy us all along? Was it their primary goal to use us like puppets in a game until our effectiveness ran out? Were they simply playing with us like toys until they realized they had done too much damage to reverse?

The answer is simple; there is no higher being. If there was, we would have been brought to their holy kingdom instead of abandoned to survive on the scraps of what was left after the sun imploded.

We would have been taken care of, fed until our bellies were full, and bathed with the most lavish of

soap, until all the sin and ugliness of Earth had
been scrubbed from our bodies.
But that did not happen.
We were not saved, and in fact, we saved ourselves.
So, the question I pose is this;
Are we not gods ourselves?

-An excerpt of the first Supreme Leader's
journal, extracted from the Archives of the
Imperial Republic of Raedon

Chapter Twenty-Five

"Si vis pacem, para bellum."
-If you want peace, prepare for war.

The Phantom never slept. She was in a constant state of insomnia and although it might've been seen as a weakness to be tired, Wren saw it as a strength. If she was tired, she'd have to work harder to get things done. Her eyes were never closed, save for blinking, of course, and her nerves were always alert and on edge. It seemed to be the requirement to fit the part of Raedon's most notorious assassin; do not sleep because you never know when you'll need to strike next. It didn't matter if she'd completed a job for the rebels or saved Briar from them, either way, she couldn't bring herself to close her eyes.

But the Phantom certainly wouldn't be getting any sleep that night; especially after the stunt she'd just pulled in the ballroom.

Giddy with excitement, Wren was practically skipping down the corridors. She passed by soldiers running towards the ballroom, winking at them, and shooting finger guns at their backs as they scrambled to assemble with their Captain after what had just happened. Wren cackled as she walked, her exhilaration seeping from her like sprinkling magical fairy dust on the ground. The soldiers kept their eyes downcast when they passed her, almost as if the Phantom was the angel of death rather than a pretty fairy.

In some ways, Wren supposed she was.

When Wren reached the doors to her chambers, she was met with the peak of her excitement. Her plan had worked; Quinn believed that she was going to be poisoned and solidified Wren's spot in Polaris. She could still see the faces of the guests in the ballroom, their mouths practically hanging open when the soldier dropped dead by her feet. Even Nova had played her part well; slipping poison into the Captain's drink just before it was served in the ballroom. She even poured some champagne into Briar's cup to throw suspicion off of herself.

And, oh god.

Briar's face!

It was the best thing Wren had seen in years. He was shocked, utterly shocked, by what she had pulled and even more so when she left him sitting there, watching her as she left the ballroom. It was a night that no one would ever forget, and not only did it cause a spectacle that would put the Phantom in the news next sol, but would also ensure that Wren stayed at Sanctum Palace for longer.

If the Captain of the Guard almost dying and Wren saving her didn't explain why the Phantom was needed, she didn't know what would.

Twisting the knob of the door, Wren sauntered into her chambers. But her eagerness suddenly faded when she realized something was wrong; someone had been in here while she was at the feast.

Wren slowly paced into the center of the room. She was silent; not even the sound of her breath made a noise. She kept the lights off in case her attacker was still there; turning them on would alert them. Although, it wasn't a bad idea to catch them off guard. They would scurry out from whatever hole they managed to find themselves in right into her awaiting arms. But as Wren moved towards the back of her room, assured that the rest of the space was empty, the gun she'd pulled out for protection was immediately holstered.

"Tired of your grubby dungeon dwelling, I see." She mocked, looking straight into the dark corner of her room between her bed and the wall. "Subtle, as always. Although I should teach you about the flare factor if you're going to try and sneak up on me like that."

Eden Sitara stepped out of the shadows, meeting the assassin by the edge of the bed.

"Took you long enough to find me." Eden jeered.

"Where's the red scarf?" She asked, surveying him up and down. He had no Rising Sun insignia anywhere on him. His civilian uniform was armed with weapons, just as it was the last time Wren had seen him. His expression was daunting and sharp as it always was, and he formally tucked his arms behind his back. It was something that Eden was used to doing when he addressed the Commanders back in Novus, but here, Wren simply found it irritating.

"It would've given me away."

"Oh, of course." Wren faked sincerity, rolling her eyes. "Because sneaking into Sanctum Palace on one of the busiest nights of the year wouldn't get you killed, either."

"Busy, for sure." Eden nodded curtly. "I've been hearing soldiers running around for a while now. I'm assuming you had something to do with it?"

"Partly." Wren licked the top row of her teeth and ended the motion with a sly smile.

"Be careful how you play your cards, sister," Eden warned. "You could end up as dead as me if you get caught."

"Don't play noble." Wren snapped. "You could've gotten yourself killed even coming here tonight. Who's to say those soldiers you've heard stomping around aren't looking for you?"

"They aren't." When Wren cast a skeptical gaze, he explained, "Nova doesn't just work for you. I told her to roam the halls and signal if anyone was coming our way."

"You put our lives in the hands of a sticky-fingered novice?" Wren blanched.

"My hands are not sticky." A radio cracked somewhere on Eden's person as Nova responded from somewhere else in the palace.

"You're right," Wren replied to the radio. "They're just clumsy."

"Trust me." Nova pleaded, and Wren could hear the longing in her voice through the crackling of the technology. "I've got this."

Wren didn't doubt that; not after the girl had proved herself to the assassin during the feast. Her plan went off without a hitch, partly because Nova was there as well.

"Go back to making sure we don't get killed. And be careful." Wren told her, and Eden halfway smiled at the sincerity in her voice. Wren replaced it with anger as soon as the radio turned off. "If you're lonely and wanted an invitation to the party, all you had to do was ask."

Eden growled. The corners of the assassin's lips tugged upwards, but her smile vanished when she saw her brother's expression. He was looking down at the ground, any hint of kindness from moments before vanishing. Now, he looked much more skeletal in his civilian uniform than he ever had before. Wren had always known she was the better-looking of the two, but why was Eden so stiff that night? It should've been her first warning to back off and let him get to his point, but instead, Wren had a little bit more fun than what was warranted for that situation.

"I don't want to go to a stupid party that celebrates the birth of a tyrant political system." Eden voiced strongly. It only confirmed what Wren had been thinking; it would be a mistake to take him to any social function because all he would do is talk about how screwed up Raedon was and recruit new rebels.

Wren paid no attention to him as she went on. "No, you're right. They don't allow traitors past the front doors."

"Pay attention."

"Although I'm sure you could sneak in and hide under the table." She laughed and clapped her hands together like an excited child. "Maybe they'll be nice enough to spoon-feed you under the tablecloths!"

"Wren, focus." Eden slapped her hands away from each other. Before she could reach up to hit him back, Eden was already speaking again. "There's something you need to know."

"So, why did you summon me here this time?" She asked instead of listening, leaning against the plated silver wall to her left. "Did the Rising Sun finally decide that paying Kiran is much more trouble than I'm worth?"

Eden sighed. Wren could tell he was suppressing something from her. "The Command in Novus is shifting. A new Commander is claiming that he has Sun Searcher blood and should take the place of one of the others."

"Meaning Rheas is in danger of being replaced?" Wren schooled her initial dumbfounded expression into a face that matched the sincerity of Eden's. Commander Rheas had been one of the top Generals in Novus when Wren was still training there. He even saw to some of her lessons himself. Wren didn't admire the man as much as her brother did, but never before had his position in the Rising Sun been questioned so severely.

"Yes." Eden was clearly hit personally by this attack on his beloved idol. But even though Wren had been making fun of his relationship with the Commander for years, she knew that Rheas was somewhat of the father Eden never had.

"Why didn't this new Commander step forward sooner?" Wren asked. Sun Searchers were the founders of Novus; without them, the rebels would've been based in Raedon and most likely caught before they were ever able to make any difference in the world.

"He's not a Commander yet," Eden spat. "No one knows where he came from, but he's rallied enough rebels to make his case to the other leaders."

"What case?" Wren found herself unintentionally steering off a cliff. A new Commander in Novus meant new orders for her in Raedon. What would he do? Would he be in favor of her continuing to be the Phantom and doing jobs for the rebels or would he detach her from them entirely, leaving her at the mercy of Kiran and all the information he had about her real identity and where she came from?

Wren didn't enjoy being out of control; her fate was in the hands of a man she'd never met before, probably one who valued his gain more than her life.

"The rebels uniting behind him don't want to wait any longer," Eden confirmed, stepping into the center of the cellar to meet Wren. "They're choosing to strike now."

"That doesn't make any sense." Wren countered, beginning to feel the tension spreading from her brother to her. "It's too soon. You just attacked the palace. If the advances become too close to each other, people will suspect things about where you're getting your help from."

"Meaning you?"

"Meaning the people around Polaris who keep orchestrating your chaos for you." Wren snapped. It was becoming clear to her that Eden had not arranged this meetings like he had the others. He had been ordered to talk to her that night.

The question was, what did they want from her this time?

"The tenth sol of the Lunar Inception is drawing closer." Eden uncrossed his arms. In the darkness of the bedroom, Wren thought he looked more like one of the Commanders rather than one of their Captains. "The Rising Sun thinks that this is as good a time as any to make their move."

"What are you saying?"

"The kill order came from the Commanders with the support of almost all of Novus behind it," Eden explained. "Everyone is expecting you to follow through. We have to obey the commands."

"What was the order?" Wren's voice was hollow.

Somehow, she already knew.

"There is a special kind of ammunition you'll need, but you already know where to find it." Eden laid it out for her like one of his plans. Only this wasn't a train raid to hurt the Republic; this would surely kill it.

"How will you do it?"

"I won't be the one killing him, Wren." Eden stepped closer to her. Not to comfort her, but to make sure that she knew what he wanted from her.

What the rebels wanted from her.

"You will."

The Rising Sun was calling in the order; Briar Atlas was no longer an asset.

He was a target.

I want to make one thing abundantly clear to the people of Raedon.

The only reason they are alive is because of *me*. The only reason their food hasn't run out is because of the programs I put in place to increase spending on nutrition research. The only reason they still have water is because of the rationing system I have drafted. The only reason the Republic has not fallen into anarchy is because of the laws I've put into place to keep society controlled.

The only reason they have their very *lives* is because of me.

Yet they dare defy me?

I held a speech this sol cycle in the square. I was surrounded by the remaining few hundred humans whose ancestors survived the implosion of the sun.

They were not just people to me; they were my allies. If one of them had eaten an extra food ration, my parents would've starved, and I would've never become the Supreme Leader. If one of them drank a single drop of water from another bottle, I would've never existed.

I trusted that they saw me the way I saw them; as family.

But would a sibling try to kill me?

They lunged from the crowd in an attempt to wring my neck. Thankfully, my guards standing beside me apprehended him before the tips of his fingers could lock on my skin. There was only one who tried to kill me, but that did not empty my mind of one horrible thought.

If there was one, there were others.

How many more of them thought of me as a totalitarian rather than a just leader? How many of them blamed me, however innocent I am, for the murder of their forefathers and humanity itself?

How many more of them believed that I had planned everything out; I was the Supreme Leader, the highest position of power in the Imperial Republic of Raedon.

Who's to say I didn't put myself there without the proper processes?

The answer is no, I didn't. But the fact of the attack remains.

How many more are going to rebel?

-An excerpt of the first Supreme Leader's journal, extracted from the Archives of the Imperial Republic of Raedon

Chapter Twenty-Six

"Nullum malum est beatus."
-No evil is blessed.

"Well, this was fun." Briar's chair jerked out from underneath the table as he stood. The entire dais was still silent as the rest of the ballroom unfolded into layers of chaos. Some guests were on the floor, trying to hack up their meals in fear that they too had been poisoned. Others were comforting each other, and even more were screaming at the guards, demanding to be let out of the palace at once. The soldiers, under Quinn's command, had kept everyone inside the room; no one was safe, and everyone was a suspect. Could a rebel have been one of the guests at their party? Could they be hiding in plain sight, keeping themselves concealed under court gossip and wonderings while causing utter chaos when no one was looking?

Briar didn't think it was such a bad idea; to create a mask of deception to disguise themselves behind it. He wasn't a master of planning and secret court maneuvers himself, but he knew that if he were a rebel, hiding in plain sight would've been the first thing he thought of. It was sneaky, and even more impressive than simply marching through the front door with a red scarf tied to his face like the Rising Sun did when they attacked the castle.

Whoever orchestrated this was cunning, and unfortunately for the Republic, seriously good at what they did.

Beside him and still in shock, Quinn Vega held a hand to her chest and breathed in. Briar had never seen her so out of place before but somehow, he found it comforting; he wasn't the only one who felt like they needed to vomit.

So, before he could put his sickness out on display for all of the guests to see, Briar rounded his chair and swept himself away from the table. Only, he didn't get as far as two feet before a firm hand grabbed his wrist and yanked him backward.

"Do not go anywhere." The Supreme Leader's face was cold. He hadn't said anything when Ebony revealed the poison in his Captain's drink; perhaps he was too shocked himself. But that didn't stop Briar from pulling his wrist out of his father's hand.

"I'm fine." He said. "Poisoning me would have no effect in the long run, remember?" Briar parroted what Ebony had said and passed behind his father's throne.

"Briar!" The Supreme Leader shouted after him, but he was already stalking away from the table and practically leaping down the dais. He would've liked to tell himself that he was leaving the ballroom for one reason only; he was about to be sick and didn't want anyone else to see it, especially the girls he'd promised to meet later. But in his chest, he felt a blooming sense of eagerness; he wanted to talk to Ebony.

He didn't know about what yet, but he knew that he needed to speak with her immediately. Not once did she spit an insult at him. Briar thought that he should've felt relieved that she chose not to embarrass him in front of all of Raedon, but instead, he found a cold pit where that amusement should've been. He wanted her to taunt him and he wanted to fight back.

Briar weaved his way through the panicked guests and towards the doors at the end of the hall. Soldiers were creating a barrier around them; entrapping them in so none had the chance to leave. But when Briar approached, despite hearing his father still shouting after him and most likely stomping off the dais to follow him as well, Briar scooted past the wall of soldiers and slipped into the hallway. Once he shut the doors behind him, he found peaceful silence greeting him. But he couldn't wait a moment longer. There were only two options, two pathways down the hall. He didn't know which one Ebony had picked so he chose the left side, jogging around the corner and into the next corridor. She wasn't there either, but Briar kept going, determined to find the Phantom before she disappeared for good.

He would go to her room first. He'd never seen her there, not even hearing her mention the place, but he decided that was a good place to start.

Passing by the wall of windows on his right side, Briar winked at the stars and told them to wish him good luck. He'd need it. Racing towards her chambers and passing by multiple squadrons of soldiers running towards the ballroom, Briar navigated his way through the palace. He assumed her room was near the guest wing; although perhaps she was kept in the dungeon for all the suspicion she tossed onto herself.

Briar chuckled to himself as he reached the wing, searching the hallways until he found the right door. Oddly, no soldiers were standing outside. He assumed there would be, seeing as the world's most dangerous person was behind the very doors he was approaching at that moment.

Briar placed his hand on the knob, hesitating slightly.

Was this a good idea?

Yes. Probably. Maybe. No.

Wait, yes.

Briar rolled his shoulders. If everything went according to his plan, which it should, this would all work. First, he would walk inside and find her unloading her weapons. Then, he would ask her how she knew about the poison in the cup even though she'd already explained it to him and the rest of Raedon in the ballroom. Then, she would tell him exactly how she did it, and by that point, Briar would be even more amazed at her than he already was. Eventually, they'd reach the point in their conversation where they were close together, just like they were that night on the balcony. Except Ebony wasn't beat up and Briar hadn't just *watched* her get beat up. Then, at that moment when everything was going perfectly, he would --

Briar froze.

Were there voices coming from inside the room?

Without thinking, he turned the knob and pushed the door. The platinum hinges split immediately, and Briar's eyes adjusted to the darkness of the bedroom. He could only see the open doors of the balcony and Ebony standing by the rail.

She was frozen for a moment with her back facing Briar.

"Did you just push someone off the balcony?" Briar asked, taking a step further into the bedroom and pointing at the railing. The Phantom had yet to move, save for the small breath she took as she turned around.

"Of course not."

"Because that seems like something you would do," Briar told her, his finger dancing around the area of the balcony.

"Come closer and you'll find out." Ebony wasn't smiling, nor was she joking.

"I thought I heard voices." Briar approached the open double doors and looked around the chamber behind him. It was dark, silent, and empty except for them. Or at least he hoped.

"No." She snapped. "I was talking to myself."

"Why did you leave the ballroom? Just because someone died doesn't mean the party's over." Briar asked, trying to veer back to his plan. He hadn't been able to ask about how she knew about the servant, so he supposed he skipped to step two. Or was it step three? "There's still a ton of champagne waiting for us."

Ebony stared at him underneath her hood with beady eyes instead of her crushing turquoise ones. Her posture was rigid, and not in her usual way that reminded Briar of a beast prepared for an attack. Her jaw ticked below her mask as if she was grinding her teeth together to keep herself from saying something she wanted to scream. Beneath the white fabric, Briar could imagine her pressing her lips together to form a straight line of self-restraint across her face. He could still feel the warmth on his skin from when he held her hand on the balcony, but it was no longer as inviting as it had been that night. It was burning this time, like a wildfire spitting flames onto his skin.

He didn't enjoy the feeling.

"If there's a party," Ebony bit out, "you should go back to it."

"And you should come with me." Briar bounced on the balls of his feet. Ebony looked past his shoulder like she was looking at the celebration itself. The doors to the bedroom had closed behind him, leaving them both in the darkness. There was something that reminded him of anguish buried in the pit of her eyes, something at the time Briar was too confused to see.

"I have somewhere to be." She took in a breath sharper than her knives.

"I'll come with you." Briar grinned.

"Not this time."

"You always have somewhere to be," Briar complained and lightly tapped the side of her arm. He meant it to be a comforting sort of touch but instead Ebony glared at where his hand met her arm as he said, "You've let me trail behind on one of your other adventures. I didn't get into too much trouble." That was an utter lie. "I remember it was *you* who looked like she was going to shoot someone in the head. And besides, it's the Lunar Inception; there's no work tonight."

"Those rules don't apply to me."

"None do." Briar smiled but it faded when Ebony's expression darkened.

"Go back where you belong, Briar." There was desperation in her voice when she said it that time. Like she was begging for him to leave her alone.

Briar felt something digging at his chest. "I left to find *you*." He told her, taking a step closer to fill the space in between them. "I wanted to talk to you."

"We talked." Briar heard the strain in her voice. She was refusing to look at him and ended up staring at the inside of her hood instead. "I have to go."

"Wait!" Briar yelped when she had begun to take a step past him. "What's going on? Why are you so insistent on leaving?"

"I never belonged here in the first place." Her voice was hollow. She looked hollow; the parts of her face Briar could see over her mask were pale and her expression was tight.

He wanted to reach for the ivory disguise and take it off. He wanted to see her face, to see *her*. But Briar knew that any attempt to touch her like he had the night of Kiran's arena would end with him being tossed off the balcony as well.

"What's that supposed to mean?" Briar felt something inside him beginning to falter but he wouldn't let it throw him off; whatever it was. "You're the Phantom. You belong everywhere."

"Why aren't you afraid of me!" Ebony screeched. Briar fell back, stumbling as the fault in him cracked. She was staring at him now, fury mixing with confusion as their eyes met.

"Why would I be afraid of you?" Briar noticed how heavily she was breathing. How her fingers flexed at her sides like she was trying not to hurl a fist at his face.

"Because you just said it!" She cried out. "I'm the Phantom! You should be terrified to even look at me!"

But he was looking at her now, right in the eyes, as he wanted to all night. He felt something hot slash across his chest. That pain, that hurt rattling through her voice, shook him to his core, deeper than anything ever had before.

"But I'm not afraid of you," he told her, thinking about taking another step closer but deciding against it. "I-"

"Why not?" The assassin howled, thrashing her hands at her sides. "What makes you so different from everyone else? What is so special about you that makes you exempt from fear?" She was looking him up and down as if truly trying to see into his genetic makeup, searching for the cure that allowed him to be immune to her.

"I'm afraid of things," Briar admitted, "but none of them are you."

"Then tell me what they are because I cannot go on being something less than a monster."

Briar was on the verge of collapsing in on himself. He wanted to fall on the ground before her and beg her to see reason; beg her to see that she was wrong.

"Why are you so determined to be a monster?"

For the first time, Ebony hesitated. Then she said, "Because if I'm not a monster, what am I?"

"You're the one who told me about the oceans. You told me about the sunsets and the sunrises. You helped me *see* them." Briar could still see his imagined sky behind his eyes; The oranges and pinks and blues with the sun grazing the horizon.

Ebony didn't see the same things as he did. Instead, she seemed to be looking at a completely different picture. "It would be better if you forgot I said any of that."

"What?" Briar didn't know what was happening; what was going wrong. All he knew was that he wanted it to stop. Immediately. "Why?"

"Because this isn't how things are supposed to go." She was frustrated now, breathing heavier like it was a chore rather than a natural habit. Her shoulders were rising and falling at a rapid pace when Briar looked into her eyes again. She wasn't crying.

She was seething.

"I didn't come here to fill your head with useless delusions. I came here to make sure you don't die before you become the Supreme Leader."

"But I'm right here." Briar gestured down at himself. "I'm not dead and you've been doing your job. And those weren't delusions or lies."

She scoffed and shook her head slowly. "I'm a good liar, remember?"

"No. You're Ebony." Briar assured her, placing his hands on both of her shoulders. "Not the Phantom. Just Ebony."

"Don't you get it?" She spat, shoving him away with her hands against his chest. He was afraid that for a moment, she would feel how fast his heart was beating. If it was beating at all, anymore. "Ebony isn't my real name, Briar. She's something I made up, just like the rest of them."

Briar knew what she was talking about. Her masks: the different identities she wore all around Raedon. She never repeated a name or a lie. It was her job to remain under the Republic's radar. But for one moment, one small fraction of a second, Briar wished that she would strip off all her false identities and show him who she was.

"To keep yourself hidden?" Briar felt something close to tears swimming beneath his eyes.

"To keep others away."

Others like him.

But Briar was determined to be something other than everyone else. "Not me," he told her. "Not this time. You won't push me away like you've separated yourself from everything else." He shook his head and swallowed the lump forming in his throat. Then he repeated, "No."

"You don't know me," Ebony insisted. "You don't know anything about me."

In some ways, Briar knew that she was right. No, he didn't know the Phantom. He knew the illusion she created for herself. He knew Ebony. But why wasn't that good enough?

"Why is that a flaw?"

"Briar." The Phantom's voice finally split like the ground in an earthquake. He felt it deep in his core, like a knife reaching the center of his heart and pulling it out of his chest. "There aren't supposed to be flaws in Raedon."

"That doesn't mean there aren't."

Her eyes were shining with a glaze he'd never imagined he'd see on her. She was shielding herself from him, hiding behind a wall like she was afraid of him.

Briar felt his mouth opening again, but before he could say anything to convince her further, Ebony pressed on. "I am who I am, and you are who you've always been, Briar." She said his name like a stranger. Like they'd never met before. Like she hadn't protected him when a rebel held a knife to his throat. Like she hadn't shielded him with her body while she was injured. Like the moments they shared on his balcony never happened.

"I won't be afraid of you, Ebony." Briar's brow crinkled. He was losing. "Not like everyone else is."

"Don't call me that."

"I'm not scared of you."

"Maybe you should be."

"Ebony -- " Briar began, but she stopped him.

"I told you not to call me that."

Briar felt a single tear slide down the left side of his face. He flinched like a bullet had struck him through the heart. And in some ways, he supposed it did.

"Then what is your name?"

Ebony blinked. Once, twice.

"The Phantom."

Briar didn't know how much longer he stood there on the balcony, only that the Phantom left him in the company of the stars, watching as her ivory figure slowly slipped away into the night.

Researching humans is one of the most complex
things another human could ever do.
If not, the most.
Humans, as creatures of our environment, function
in ways that are unique to our being. It is
complicated to create a general term for what
humanity is because there is no one word to
describe us all perfectly.
Well, until the sun imploded. Then it became
obvious that all humans were failures.
However, the ways each of our minds move and
function to adapt to new situations and conditions
are extraordinary. Humanity went from thinking
that they could be alive for another thirty years
until they died of old age to huddling against a wall
in their house, hugging their knees, and knowing
that those moments were their last. The actions we
as humans take to bend to our new environment
and circumstances greatly affect how others see us
as well, and from there, a reaction of responding
actions follows.
It is like lighting a match and beginning a fire.
Studying the human brain and the responses it has
to different situations allows scientists to gain
further knowledge of how to improve. That is how,
after hundreds of studies, tests, and records,
Raedon became perfect.
Not all humans think one thing is perfect, but the
least we can do to change that is change them to
make them *think perfectly.*

-An excerpt of the first Supreme Leader's
journal, extracted from the Archives of the
Imperial Republic of Raedon

Chapter Twenty-Seven

"Non omnes me morientur."
-Not all of me shall die.

The Phantom questioning herself was like choosing potassium cyanide over ricin to poison someone. It just never happened.

She was always sure of where she needed to be and what she needed to do there. Being prepared for anything to happen was part of who the ghostly assassin was; she'd never been caught by the Supreme Leader until she wanted to be and even then, she still managed to undermine him in the deadliest way possible. She was an improviser and a good one. Catching the Phantom off guard would've been her second most fear if she had any.

But the first would've been emotion.

The Phantom was Raedon's most notorious killer. She was the Angel of Death, the white cloud of smoke looming over a victim in their final moments. She'd never felt sorry for any one of her targets because she knew that no matter who they were, the world would be a better place without them. That was, until now, when she had her scope set on Briar Atlas.

There aren't supposed to be flaws in Raedon.

It was true. Raedon was made to be perfect. There were no diseases, no pain, no war. Nothing should've gone wrong; no flaws should've been made. Yet here she was, the Phantom, an outcast amongst a society of people who were born to fit in. She and Briar were too different. Wren had been forced to dig herself out of hole after hole to survive, while Briar merely had to dodge a few poorly aimed bullets. He had no idea what it was like to fight for himself every moment of his life like Wren did, but even then, she couldn't bring herself to truly disagree with him.

Wren *had* felt something inside of her when she sat next to him on the balcony. She'd never felt it before and while she kept telling herself that she didn't like the feeling, it was just another lie. The Phantom was a good liar, as she had told Briar. But Wren had been caught up in too many false images of herself to know when she was telling the truth, or just spitting out another one of her fake scenarios to trick someone else.

But the Phantom had gotten her this far. She wouldn't let the ghostly assassin fail her now, not after everything she's done to get there.

Wren peered over the edge of the skyscraper, looking downwards at the long steel bars and glass windows making up each of the floors beneath her. The neon city lights reflected on the glass, almost like they were challenging the stars themselves. Wren blinked at its beauty and pulled her hood further onto her forehead. The streets were empty and still, like a hibernating beast during its downtime. There wasn't a single speck of movement from below, and that was how Wren liked it.

There would be no witnesses tonight.

Making sure her rifle was secured to her back, the Phantom leaped off the rooftop.

She was only falling for five seconds before she landed in a graceful roll on a balcony ten floors beneath the penthouse. Then she hoisted herself over the railing and did it again, falling from veranda to veranda like a drop of water from a fountain. She kept going until she was on the bottom floors, finally jumping down to the main street.

Wren's boots barely made a sound as she landed. She looked to both sides of the road before crossing. One never knew when there'd be a hitman with a gun waiting for her to cross, is what Eden would always tell her. She supposed it was a good piece of advice for someone who was in actual danger of being killed for rebel sympathizing. But for her, it didn't matter. No one would dare step within five feet of her, much less aim a gun at her head.

Besides, she would shoot them first.

When Wren finally made it to the opposite sidewalk, she found herself face-to-face with a small pawn shop. The walls were made of rundown metal material, but they weren't complete garbage. The lights out front were neon, but not as bright as everywhere else in Polaris. There was an 'open' sign flickering in the middle of a pair of windows on the left side of the door. Through the glass, Wren could see small shelves of useless baubles and jewelry.

The entire street was like this, a line between the slums and the normal city. The lights didn't flicker, but they weren't as colorful as the rest. There was running water, heating, and air conditioning, but it sometimes malfunctioned. It was the gray area between the black and white sides of Polaris, and the perfect location for her to get what she wanted.

Wren stepped up to the door and placed her hand on the handle. She looked around the street before pulling it and strolling inside, hearing the small chime of a bell as the door closed behind her.

The interior was small. The walls were painted royal blue and doused with gold and black framed paintings. The outer perimeter of the space was lined with glass cases and cabinets, filled with trinkets and other little knick-knacks that seemed completely normal for a pawnshop of this size. There were curtains on the windows that were ironed perfectly, the colorful fringe on the end just reaching the floor. The lights were golden colored and dim, but still functional. There seemed to be nothing out of place; Calder Cardea was always organized.

As she stepped into the center of the room, Wren was immediately welcomed with the smell of jasmine. She took in a small whiff and smiled at the peaceful scent, knowing that the only reason Cal kept the air smelling so nice was that the jasmine hid the smell of chemicals underneath the shop.

Wren crossed the room until she met the display case in front of a small red velvet curtain leading towards the back rooms. She took a moment to inspect her surroundings; no cameras, listening devices, or thermal signature machines. Good. When she was finished, she reached across the glass to ring the silver bell on the corner of the cabinet.

Not a moment after her finger left the cold surface, the velvet curtain in front of her split.

Calder Cardea looked the same as he did when Wren had walked into his shop on her first mission in Polaris. He was tall and muscular, towering feet above the crown of her head. His full pink lips spread into a wide smile the moment his chocolate eyes met hers from across the way, closing the distance between them with two large steps. Cal spread his arms wide and leaned against the corners of the case, leaning into Wren so that their noses were only inches apart. He smelled of stronger jasmine.

"What can I get for you, lovely?" His uncut golden hair fell into his face in a way that made Wren want to brush it away herself. His freckled cheeks scrunched as he grinned at her.

"Good to see you again, Cal." Wren didn't back away from him. Erasing any memory of the previous events that night, she allowed herself to get closer. It only made his face glow brighter, his perfectly straight teeth showing through his smirk.

"I knew you would visit me eventually," Cal tucked his elbows into his chest and leaned on the glass case to place his chin in his palms. He peered at Wren through his long black eyelashes, batting them like a schoolchild getting the attention of the girl they liked. "You never seemed to be able to stray far from me."

"You read my mind," Wren responded sweetly, drizzling honey into her voice.

Years ago, when Wren had become the Phantom, she was assigned her first assignment in Polaris. She was to kill members of an elitist group trying to cheat their way onto a seat in the Supreme Leader's council. At the time, Briar's father had just begun to serve his time, but he was young and inexperienced. He didn't know the workings of the court, and the Rising Sun predicted that by the time he learned it would be too late.

So, they'd sent the Phantom to knock off a few of the higher members of the group. She needed a weapon that wasn't trackable by any Raedon forces; it was to be a silent assassination with no ties to her or the rebels. Almost as if it had happened by pure mistake. Wren had been told there was a dealer already in Polaris, stationed in the city just for this reason. He made weapons that Raedon hadn't yet; untraceable ammunition, poison, and other lethal methods.

It was where she learned how to make the thallium poisoning for Quinn's drink to teach Nova. She needed the Captain and the rest of Raedon to see how valuable the Phantom was to Raedon.

The Phantom went to Cal before either of them knew who the other was. She was just beginning to make herself known in Raedon and was spreading her disease to Polaris when she met him in his small pawn shop, asking in code for the poison she needed for the assassination. He'd told her about it, even taught her how to make it on her own if she ever needed to get out of a tough situation. Wren knew that she was too good to get herself into trouble again, not after the mistakes she'd already made. But she listened anyway and ended up having to keep coming back to Calder for more lessons on poisons in her arsenal and weapons he'd made just for her.

Eventually, Wren finished the job and separated herself from Cal. She took weapons with her, including the knives she had hidden in the sleeves of her uniform at that very moment. She didn't pay for them, but she knew that Cal didn't mind. At the moment, he would've given her his entire operation if she asked him to. Wren was sure that he would still do that now, even after how she left him all those years ago.

In front of her, Cal scrunched his nose and stood up straight again. He began to walk slowly to his right, dragging a finger across the top of the display cases until he stopped above an aquamarine gemstone bracelet.

"I think you'd like this one," he said, tapping the glass without taking his gaze off of her. "It would match your eyes."

He moved on, drawing her attention to a brooch that was carved from gold and lined with pearls. "This would go well with your skin."

"I prefer silver," Wren said. Cal's eyes flickered up to the scope of her rifle, shining platinum in his dim golden lights. The corners of his mouth flickered, and his eyes sparkled.

"Of course." he nodded his head in agreement. "Then perhaps this?" His finger was now above a necklace made from glass beads. The craftsmanship on each of the circular pieces was so fine that Wren knew Cal had carved them himself.

"I appreciate it, but that's not why I'm here." She told him.

Before she could blink, Cal reached across the counter and grabbed her forearm. It wasn't a demanding grip, but rather a light, gentle touch that Wren couldn't help but obey. He pulled her arm across the glass display towards him, running his fingers over the fabric.

"Did you remodel this?" He already knew the answer, but Wren humored him for the sake of getting what she wanted.

"I did." She said proudly and saw a flash of pride cross Cal's face.

"This fabric is expensive," he told her, running his finger on the inside of the sleeve. His skin was warm against hers, but she didn't allow the chill running up her spine past her middle vertebrae. No one had come in contact with her skin in a long time. Only one other person would dare try, and she let him that night on the balcony. "You must've stolen it like the knives hidden inside."

Wren pulled her arm back and saw the small tick in Cal's jaw as he debated pulling it back. "You always had an eye for borrowed things."

"Borrowed and never returned, you mean?" he snickered but wasn't mad at her. He never was and never could be.

"You'll get them back over my dead body." Wren grinned and felt the cold blades through the thin fabric holding them inside her sleeves.

"I am never getting them back, am I?" Cal laughed, unable to look anywhere but Wren's eyes. She shook her head and looked at him through her eyelashes. She blinked extra for him, reminding him of what it felt like when she looked at him all those years ago when she first met him. They stared at each other like that for a few moments before Cal was able to pull himself back into reality.

"You are lovely, aren't you?" He couldn't help the finger that traced Wren's neck until it reached her masked chin, tugging at the bottom.

Wren obeyed and reached inside her hood to unclip it. She took it off with ease, knowing that Cal would have her take it off, eventually. She never used to wear it around him, but she couldn't deny herself the pleasure of taunting him just a little bit more.

"I think you mean deadly, darling." She purred, lifting her chin so his finger fell from her skin. He huffed out a disappointed exhale.

"Of course." He said breathily, turning around his shoulder and walking back towards the velvet curtain where they started. Wren followed him until they reached a small gate, which he politely unlocked and opened for her, gesturing for her to follow him.

Cal parted the velvet curtain for the both of them to reveal a thin hallway leading into a workroom behind the main shop. It was an even smaller space than the first and filled with workbenches and closets that Wren guessed were stuffed with jewelry and trinkets that had no use to Cal. There were a few carving materials and leather working tools set out on the table, but Wren knew that they were only for when regular people walked into his shop. No one but the rebels knew what he was hiding beneath the glass cases and gold brooches.

Cal led Wren past the tables and through the maze of random boxes and crates until they came upon a large wooden closet in the very back of the room. Cal couldn't help but glance over his shoulder at Wren and smile as he tugged on the door, opening it to reveal a spiraling staircase built where the clothes would normally be hanging. Cal allowed Wren to go first this time. She'd been down here millions of times before; it was the real operation behind the mask of the pawnshop.

Cal was not a jeweler or even a repairer of broken things. He was a weapons manufacturer for the Rising Sun.

The room beneath the stairs was lit with electric blue lights that were too bright to even think about flickering. The walls were lined with shelves and racks of weapons of all kinds: knives, firearms, crossbows, axes, and spears. There was a table in the very center of the room, occupied with different kinds of ammunition and blades from different weapons. Cal even had two different firearms dismantled and was now assembling them with parts from the other.

"Welcome back," Cal opened his arms from behind her, walking around the room until he met her on the other side of the table. "No need to give you the tour, you already know the place well enough."

It was true, she did. Wren had been here hundreds of times for ammunition and different weapons to use in her assassinations. Cal's specialty was cross-engineering separate contraptions to make them completely untraceable. He would design a firearm that would shoot a bullet the speed of a machine gun but had the ammunition of a small handgun. It confused any weapon tracking systems the Republic had and made anything that Cal supplied completely impossible to find.

It was what Wren liked most about his weapons. They were invisible, just like her.

Wren wandered over to a rack of knives, They were displayed and shined to perfection, all of them having been tested and tinkered with by Cal himself. When Wren used to visit him regularly, he would show her how to use every single one of his contraptions. Once one of his weapons was used in the field, it couldn't be used again. At least, not in the same way. Cal would have to take it apart and rebuild it with different pieces so that it stayed untraceable. The good thing about that was that Cal never seemed to run out of ideas or weapons to splice together.

Wren's eyes danced across the knives until she reached a blank spot on one of the shelves. She pointed to it and spun on her heel, finding Cal already looking at what she was motioning to.

"Where'd this one go?" She asked, but already felt the answer pressing against her thigh in one of her hidden pockets.

"I'm saving that spot for when you return it." He said, licking the top row of his teeth. "That was my favorite, you know."

Wren nodded and turned back to the shelf. The knife she took was her favorite, too. It was a switchblade with knives on both sides of the hilt. The grip fit perfectly in her hand as if it was designed especially for her, and Wren wouldn't be surprised if it was. But the best part about the weapon wasn't the ways she could hold it; it was the blade itself. The tips of the two knives were made from one metal, while the sides were made from serrated and jagged steel. No side of the blade was completely the same as the other, almost like a fingerprint. So, no matter where Wren used it, it looked like she'd used a different knife each time.

Wren had never told anyone about that knife, as she did with her rifle. She kept it hidden away, close to her at all times.

Wren looked away from the knives and moved onto a rack of spears. One was electric and had an iron tip; that would kill a person in an instant. Wren had always admired Cal's ability to think about things differently than others; she didn't know anyone else in Raedon or Novus who could think of making nun chucks that swung like metal maces and had electric tips to shock whatever they touched.

"I know why you're here." Cal finally said, still standing by the table and watching her roam. "The Rising Sun finally gave you the order."

"I can't be here because I like to talk to you?" Wren turned over her shoulder and slowly strolled back to the table. She hid her sour expression with a sly grin. She planted her hands on the corner like Cal had done on the glass cabinet upstairs.

"We both know that you like to do other things rather than talk," he said with a sly smile, and Wren could see his fingers jerking at his sides.

Wren hummed. "Then you know what I need from you."

"I know what *I* want from you. And maybe what you want from me." Cal cast her a crooked smile and Wren returned it with a wink.

"Later." She said to him, standing up straight.

"Fine." he pouted but couldn't stop himself from chuckling. "Be that way."

Wren ignored him as he turned away from her. She peeked over his shoulder as he wandered towards a rack of ammunition. He fumbled with the rows of golden and silver cases before reaching towards the back of the shelf to pull out a small black box sealed with a fingerprint latch.

Cal carried it back to the table and placed the box in front of Wren. He nodded towards it. "Your fingerprint is already installed."

"How did you get my fingerprint?" She asked suspiciously, pulling the latch closer to her.

"You used to come here all the time, remember?" Wren could hear the disappointment that he tried to hide in his voice as he said it. It sent a pang of guilt through her chest, but she temporarily ignored it as she removed her white glove and pressed her thumb against the cold glass surface of the lock.

She felt a small tingle against her skin before the latch clicked. When she opened the box, she found two pure white bullets secured in black velvet inside.

"They are one of a kind," Cal described, mesmerized by his creation. "Personalized for your rifle and untraceable by any Raedon forces. The fastest flying bullet I've ever made."

"All this for me?" Wren asked, picking up one of the bullets from the velvet. It was smooth in her fingers, but cold. She feared that if she put too much pressure on it, it would break in her palm. Delicate, but utterly deadly.

"Anything for you."

Wren's eyes snapped up to his and for a moment, she longed to reach across the table and brush a strand of golden hair from his eyes. She missed the time they'd spent together, but she knew that if they got too close, it would only damage them both over time.

The Phantom wasn't allowed to get close to anyone. It was her poison creation, one that she'd mixed especially for herself.

"The craftsmanship is impeccable." She told Cal, ignoring his comment. He wasn't hurt by it, rather understood why she did so.

He shrugged casually. "I don't fool around with things like this."

"Why are there two?" Wren inspected the other bullet, still lying idle in the velvet.

Ahead of her, Cal smirked. "In case you miss."

"I don't miss."

Wren carefully placed the bullet back into the case and closed it. When she did, she heard the latch lock again until she needed to open it once more. Then she tucked the small box into the pocket of her uniform, making sure there were no identifiable bumps to be seen from the outside.

"Thank you." She said, rolling her shoulders backward to crank out the ache blooming between them. When she turned around again, she found Cal's hand wrapping around her arm and twisting her to face him. He was standing on her side of the table now, so close to her that her nose almost touched the bottom of his chin. His warm breath slid down her face and made her skin dance.

She had to look up to look into his eyes as he said, "Are you going to leave without paying me?"

"The rebels should've already paid you for your service." She responded.

Cal's jaw ticked. "You know what I mean."

"I do." Wren hissed. "But that's not how things are anymore."

She saw Cal's eyes dim slightly, but he didn't show it on the rest of his face. "I know you miss me, lovely."

Wren didn't respond, even though she knew he was right. She did miss the comfort of always having someone to come back to when she was finished with a job. Cal was a comfort to her, a known place she could go when she needed a place to be that wasn't the blood-soaked house of one of her victims. But she also knew that as the Phantom, comfort like that wasn't available to her anymore.

There were no safety nets large enough to catch her when she fell as often as she did.

Wren licked her lips and looped an arm around Cal's neck. She pulled him closer, but instead of meeting his mouth, she slid her lips across the side of his face until she reached his ear.

His breath caught.

"You always fall for the same tricks." She whispered against his skin.

She felt him smile against her cheek. "Can you blame me for trying, lovely?"

Wren pulled away and smiled at him, winking once more before finally spinning on her heel and ascending the spiraling stairs once more. Cal didn't follow her as she entered the main room of the pawnshop again, clipping on her mask and sliding on her gloves before exiting through the front door. The bell above the door still echoed behind her as she crossed the street, disappearing into an alleyway before beginning to climb to the top of the skyscrapers once more.

When she was at the top, Wren forced herself to not look at the shop one last time. She walked to the edge of the building until she balanced on the edge, leaping across to the next rooftop and landing masterfully on two balanced feet. She traveled across the city without looking back, knowing that if she did, she wouldn't be able to move on.

Finally, far enough away, Wren pulled out the black box and sat down on the edge of a skyscraper. Her legs dangled above the city as she held the case in her hands, inspecting the craftsmanship of the fingerprint latch.

She had always felt the most comfortable in the sky.

Wren belonged in the folds of the world that were unseen by regular eyes. She fit best in the open air, standing on the edges of the rooftops of the skyscrapers in the cities. She was always close enough to feel like she could hold the stars yet far enough away to keep them yearning for her very touch. The assassin knew that this was her place. With a clear mind, the open sky never seemed so beautiful.

But now, holding onto the very thing that would end Briar's life, everything around her seemed to shrivel like a dying organism before her eyes.

It was a mistake to tell Briar about the oceans and blue skies. It only made them think that they could do something that they could never actually do. She was Wren Sitara, a member of the Rising Sun rebels. She was the Phantom, the ghost killer who was feared by everyone who heard her legendary name. She was Ebony, a soldier hired to protect the Supreme Leader's son at all costs.

There could no longer be three of her. The lines between them had become too blurred for Wren to see, and it was her fault alone that she had let it become that way. There was a difference between what she could do and what she wanted to do. There was no option for her anymore; she'd been wearing a mask for so long that she forgot who she was behind it. Briar had seen a glimpse of who she was, and it was a mistake.

In nine sols, Briar would be dead, and Raedon would fall into the hands of the Rising Sun. The Phantom would pull the trigger and Wren Sitara would lead the rebels into the palace.

Ebony had no place in those plans.

As far as Wren knew, she was dead.

A man can yearn for peace but still find himself in the center of the bloodiest battles.

In the time before the sun imploded, war seemed to be inevitable. The powerful battled against the powerless in a never-ending cycle of struggle and misery. It was an arms race, a sprint to see who could come up with the most gruesome technology to defeat the enemy while everyone else sat idly in their temporary safety, nervously biting their nails in anticipation of what would come next. Proxy wars were fought on behalf of higher powers, and even then, the violence raged on for what seemed like a lifetime. Some wars lasted a mere 38 minutes and others that unfolded into 781 years of bloodshed.

People fought for what they called freedom, only to end up in the hands of another totalitarian dictator. They fought against their leadership and revolted against the control that was being set upon them. But what they did not realize, as foolish human beings, was that control was exactly what they needed to cease fire.

There needed to be a hand to stir the pot, to sway the outcome of all wars. They would never end if nothing had stopped them. It would be constant death, constant bloodshed, constant loss of millions of the same people fighting for what they believed was right.

And at the moment, everything felt right.

Now, looking back at it, it's clear that everything
was wrong.

-An excerpt of the first Supreme Leader's
journal, extracted from the Archives of the
Imperial Republic of Raedon

Chapter Twenty-Eight

"Sumus quod sumus."
-We are what we are.

The tenth night of the Lunar Inception had arrived.

Wren moved like a machine. She did not blink, she barely breathed. The only sound that came from her was the clicking of ammunition into place as she wordlessly loaded her gun.

Her hood had been secured to the crown of her head. Her mask was tied onto the lower half of her face, leaving no skin but the thin line of her eyes uncovered. She'd pulled on her gloves the moment she began to armor herself with weapons; fingerprints would get her killed.

The Phantom had no time to get killed tonight.

Behind her, Nova stood silently with her hands folded behind her back. She watched in fear as the assassin mechanically checked the ammunition on all of her weapons and tested each dagger point until it was deemed sharp enough for her liking. Her gray eyes wandered around the expanse of Wren's uniform, watching the folds of the fabric contract and stretch as the assassin continued to silently move in the darkness.

Wren had summoned Nova to her room before the celebrations of the night began. She had drilled a plan into the girl's mind so deep it might've been a chip installed into the back of her neck. Wren supplied her with weapons as well; she might not be able to use them as efficiently as the assassin could, but Wren was counting on Nova being able to defend herself to make it out alive. Wren herself was stuffing knives wherever she could fit them on her person, up her sleeves, in her belt, in the interior of her boots. Anywhere she could hide a weapon, she did.

"Where are you going?" Nova squeaked. She was so quiet Wren had almost missed it.

"Do you remember what I told you?"

"Yes." She lifted herself to her toes and peered over Wren's shoulder. "But-"

"Tell me," Wren ordered, reaching across the table to pick up an extra line of ammunition. She stuffed it into her belt and then covered that with her white armor.

"But-"

"Tell me, Nova."

She swallowed. "I'll be in the west wing; near the point the rebels will use to enter the palace. Away from the ballroom." She repeated exactly what Wren had told her.

"What will you do there?" The assassin tucked a small throwing knife into the inside of her boot. Then another in the other shoe.

"Wait." Nova's voice shook. "I'll wait for Eden Sitara and my sister to find me once you tell them where I'm hiding."

"Good." Wren nodded her head slightly. Nova did not yet know that Eden was Wren's brother; or that they were related at all. "Good. Stay there. Don't come out for anyone except the Captain or your sister."

"I-" Nova's breath hitched. "I know."

"Do not hesitate, Nova," Wren said over her shoulder. Her voice was colder than the shadows curling in the dark corners of the bedroom. "Hesitation will get you killed."

"I know." She said again, and Wren heard her walking closer until she was beside her, watching the assassin feverishly sharpen dagger after dagger. Her midnight hair was swept into a single braid, swinging down the length of her back. Her servant's uniform had been abandoned for a regular citizen's outfit; it would help her blend in once Eden retrieved her and escaped from the palace. She watched in marvel for a few moments, the reflection of the silver knives shining in her gray eyes.

"Where are you going?" Nova repeated.

Wren hesitated as she tested the point of her dagger. It dug into her finger too hard, and she felt blood spilling underneath her glove.

"I have a job to do." She bit back, clenching her teeth together as she jabbed the knife in Nova's direction. She held it out for a few moments as Nova nervously glanced at the knife before lightly pulling it from Wren's fingers. She twisted it around in her hands, her eyes glazing over the cool surface of the weapon.

"You're going to kill him, aren't you?"

The container of ammunition in Wren's hand jostled as she clamped her fingers around it. Her eyes wandered to her rifle, sitting between her and Nova and leaning on the side of the table. Nova's eyes scraped the surface of the weapon.

"I'm not stupid." Nova let her hand fall with the dagger. "I saw you pack the bullets into the case. They're white, aren't they? You got them when you disappeared the other night after hiding Eden below the balcony, didn't you?"

"Nova -- "

"Tell me!"

Her breath cracked when she heard the echo of her voice bouncing from the walls. Wren's eyes slid up to hers, abandoning the container of ammunition by her side.

"Yes." There was a fault forming on the edge of her voice. Nova's lip quivered.

"Why?" It was not a question. It was a demand.

"Because I have orders." Wren's breath curled around her nose underneath her mask. She smelled her bloody lies, but didn't dare to cringe at them.

"Why do you follow orders you know are wrong?" Nova's chest expanded, holding her breath until Wren slowly responded.

"Who are they wrong to?" She set her jaw, cinching her teeth together until her gums were black and blue. "I work for the Rising Sun, not the Republic."

"You told me that you don't work for anyone."

"This is different." Wren snapped, flames dripping from her tongue. "You know what needs to be done."

"Why?" Another demand.

Another hesitation.

"I'm not going to explain this to you, Nova."

"Because you don't think I can handle it or because you don't know the answer?" Her voice rose and echoed off the platinum walls louder than before. She did not flinch at the volume.

Wren didn't respond.

She didn't know why she dragged herself around Raedon to serve the same rebels who had abused her abilities and exploited her strength. She did not understand the lust within her, the monster that surfaced every time she saw even the smallest drop of crimson blood. She didn't know what would happen if she let that monster loose, let it take control of her.

For the first time in her entire life, Wren did not know the answer.

"I won't let you kill him."

Wren blinked. Nova stared at her through stormy, gray eyes. The assassin watched as tears flooded the wells of her face, dripping down the sides of her cheeks and pooling in the curves of her lips.

The assassin stepped forward, close enough to Nova now that when she raised it to look at Wren's face, her chin almost touched the bottom of her neck. She smelled the fatality rolling off her like coils of smoke rising from a fire.

"You will not *let* me do anything."

"Don't do it." Nova choked out. She sidestepped Wren and stood defiantly in the center of the room, directly between her and the door. Her throat bobbed.

"Get out of my way," Wren warned.

"No." Nova balled her hands into fists at her sides. "You're not leaving this room until you promise me that he will come out of this alive."

The Phantom did not make promises she couldn't keep.

Wren shook her head. "I can't."

"Promise me."

"No."

"Swear it to me."

"No!" Wren thrashed, throwing herself at Nova. The girl jumped back, just out of the reach of Wren's claws. The assassin's breath was running ragged from her lungs now, her hands shaking at her sides as she reigned in her control. In front of her, Nova's eyes widened as she stared at her in horror, bracing herself for the next attack with small, wavering steps on the balls of her feet.

"Get out of my way or I will move you myself."

Nova lifted her chin, the corners of her lips threatening to betray her. "Go ahead. Try."

Wren hesitated.

She waited. She did not want to hurt Nova. She was just a child, a pawn in all of this. She did not belong in Wren and the Rising Sun's crossfire, and they both knew it. She had been sent to Polaris as a trial, a way for the rebels to test her in the field. She wasn't supposed to be a part of the plan and now that she was, Wren couldn't stand to see her hurt.

But she would rather hurt Nova herself than see her fall into the hands of the Republic.

"Don't make me do this."

"No one is making you do anything."

Wren attacked. She was too fast for Nova this time, capturing her in a headlock and dragging her down to the ground. She squirmed in Wren's pin as the assassin held her in her arms, the knobs of her spine digging into Wren's lap as she resisted. Wren tightened her elbow around Nova's neck, listening as she gasped for air.

"He has to die," Wren whispered in her ear. Nova clawed at her forearm, gulping air into her lungs like a tether to consciousness. Her vision was already going dark. Once she was unconscious, Wren would take her to the safe point where Eden would find her.

"Don't." Nova coughed, the sound of her voice smothered by another wave of choking as Wren squeezed harder, feeling Nova begin to weaken in her hands. There was a pain in every inch of her voice, the hurt of betrayal as she watched Wren above her. Her body was going limp, the blue veins in her forehead popping. The hands clawing at Wren's arm had fallen, now gently twitching on the cold floor. Wren looked down at the girl, a single tear slipping from her gray eyes.

"Don't kill him."

Don't do this to yourself.

It was already done.

"I'm sorry, Nova."

No one is ever truly free.

Freedom, like many things, is an illusion. From freedom comes humankind believing that they can do whatever they want. It allows them to think that there are no consequences or repercussions for their wrongdoings. It plants a seed in their mind that sprouts into a dangerous plant, one whose leaves sprinkle on the ground and leave their imprint. Bad ideas, horrible ideas that cause the downfall of society. How could anything be wrong in a world of freedom?

I'll tell you what can go wrong.

No one would be able to control themselves. They will want more and more on top of that. They will become greedy monsters, grabbing fistfuls of whatever they want because they can say four simple words that explain it all: *because I want to.* We all want to do things. But when the fog clears, there are prices to pay for everything we corrupt. One of those prices was the implosion of a yellow star in a bright blue sky. Our greed brought on the end of the world. But the Imperial Republic of Raedon will not allow the same to happen to our second chance.

Call it freedom with limits if you must, but limits are what keep us alive.

Because if there was no control, we'd all turn into the monsters we convinced ourselves had died during the implosion.

-An excerpt of the first Supreme Leader's
journal, extracted from the Archives of the
Imperial Republic of Raedon

Chapter Twenty-Nine

Briar's glass had remained full the entire party.

It was a tragedy having a servant come up to him with a fresh jug of wine just for Briar to have to tell them to go away; his cup was always as full as it had been when he picked it up off of a random table. As he walked behind his father and Advisor Sonnen, he twirled the glass stem in his hands. He could feel sweat pooling underneath his fingertips. It was taking a great deal of effort to keep his lips away from the rim of the glass. He wanted to make sure that he was awake and alert should anything happen; should *anyone* happen.

The Phantom was bound to make an appearance. She couldn't help herself; every time there was a public event or cameras in the room, she pulled a stunt that had all eyes on her. First, it had been saving the Supreme Leader at the speech and then it had been stopping Quinn from drinking poisoned champagne. Even though multiple people had warned Briar to stay away from the Phantom, which was a suggestion he was going to ignore once he saw her, he couldn't help but rise to his toes every time he saw a glimmer of white out of the corner of his eye.

It was never her, though; he must've been having hallucinations from the lack of wine he was consuming. But Briar had survived until the age of sixteen before he took his first sip of champagne. If younger Briar could do it, so could he.

"Beautiful night, perfect for a firework display." one of the Advisors commented. They were standing in a huddle with the Supreme Leader and Briar by his side. He had been following his father around the ballroom the entire night, forced into conversations that were so incredibly dull that Briar had considered turning and running away for the sake of causing a scene.

"Every night is beautiful in Raedon." Another Advisor said, obviously trying to upstage the other. Next to him, the Supreme Leader chuckled falsely and threw his head back. Briar held his tongue until it bled.

Briar disagreed. The tenth night of the Lunar Inception was always his favorite; the decorations were strung perfectly through the rafters, the music was flawlessly tuned, and the food was effortlessly cooked. Even the domed glass ceiling above their heads had been hoisted open, allowing the night sky to be seen through the layers of surrounding silks. The fireworks display would begin soon, and guests were already huddled in groups in excitement, waiting to watch and comment on the pretty colors. Truthfully, Briar was looking forward to it too, but he would've much rather watched them when he knew the Phantom was standing behind him marveling at the same display.

"Both are right, yet I favor one answer more than the other." Briar's father chuckled, slightly tilting his head towards both Advisors. They sank their mouths into their glasses as another spoke, this one older than the rest.

Briar thought he looked like a shriveled grape more than a man.

"I've seen the recent articles." He said, his voice so scratchy and hoarse, Briar imagined him swallowing pebbles before he came to the celebration. "It won't be long until you've stepped into your father's shoes and become the center of the Republic. We will follow you like we have revolved around your father."

Briar pasted a thin smile onto his lips even though his body was aching to reach across the way and slap the Advisor. This was the exact kind of conversation that he was trying to avoid, but it seemed virtually *unavoidable* as he was walking around with a group of politicians.

"Yes." The Supreme Leader responded for Briar. "My son will be the next Supreme Leader of Raedon, and I am sure he will continue to follow the same path as I have."

Briar clenched his teeth together.

"I see," Advisor Sonnen voiced, and behind him Achlys's attention spiked. Briar ignored him, as usual. He had to admit, he was becoming quite talented at neglecting his old friend. "Are you planning on creating new programs to enhance the number of soldiers in the military?"

"Or perhaps continue to improve the amount of energy used throughout the Republic?" A second Advisor added before Briar could respond.

"What about looking at the statistics of the population?

"Or perhaps funding new projects that promote reserving resources?"

Briar blinked.

No, no, no, and he had no idea what reserving resources would look like.

So, no.

"Sure." He smiled again, swallowing down the reproach bubbling in his throat. He'd just gotten here, and the Advisors were already planning on digging their claws into him to try and make him the perfect puppet to manipulate. Briar was not a master puppeteer himself, but he certainly didn't want to be tied to strings for the rest of his life.

"I'd like to remind you that the only reason he will ascend to my position is if I perish." The Supreme Leader chortled jokingly, but in his eyes, Briar couldn't help but see a small flash of sadness.

Around him, the Advisors erupted into laughter about something Briar's father had said. Briar had realized he'd zoned out for the remainder of the conversation but smiled regardless, feeling the heavy pat on his back as his father roared with laughter.

They were laughing at *him*.

"Wha -- " Briar began to ask when something flashed in the corner of his eye. He whipped around himself, blinking in the white lights on the perimeter of the room. Confusion bubbled beneath his skin as his eyes surfed the crowd.

He'd just seen her. How could she have disappeared so quickly?

"Excuse me," Briar muttered to the Advisors, handing one of them his glass as he weaved through the crowd. Now his hands were sweating as he wiped them on his shirt, frantically searching the ballroom for-

There!

"Ebony!" Briar swerved in between a couple and dodged another.

There she was, the Phantom.

Briar couldn't see her face; her hood was obstructing his view. Her uniform was pressed to perfection, with the interior lined with silver blades. Her rifle was strapped to the knobs of her spine, the scope twinkling in the light as she moved. Her shoulders were set in a straight line and her hands were clenched in focus. Her boots paced the floor quickly, moving fluidly through and around groups of people toward the other end of the ballroom. Briar saw the tip of her ivory mask poking out from the fabric of her hood, shifting ever so slightly as she walked, as if she was talking to someone.

The odd thing was, there was no one walking with her.

It was strange the way no one turned to look at her as she passed; she truly was invisible to them. There was not a single gasp of fear as she moved through the guests, gracefully slipping in and out of shadows. Like a ghost.

In one moment, Briar's eyes were transfixed on the assassin. In the next, he bolted after her before she could slip through his fingers again.

"Ebony!" Briar shouted her name again. He was back on the balcony after the first night of the Lunar Inception, running after the Phantom before her interruption of the feast. She was doing it again; that annoying ignoring Briar habit that she seemed to be developing. Only this habit was on purpose. And it bothered Briar more than anything.

Why was she running away from him?

Then he saw it again, the small movement of her mask as her chin bobbed. She was talking to someone; an invisible someone. Perhaps she had gone mad, and she was hearing voices in her head. Briar heard himself in his head all the time; sometimes he told himself that what he was planning was a bad idea and other times he was trying to convince himself to do the exact thing that the other version of him told him was a bad idea.

It wasn't often that Briar agreed with the former rather than the ladder.

But no, that couldn't be it. Ebony was not arguing with herself; she would never do something as time-wasting as that. She was always right, or at least she convinced Briar that she was.

So then, who was she speaking to?

And why wasn't it Briar?

The Phantom was too far away now; she had already begun to sink into the folds of people, surrounded by disguises who had no idea they were even shielding the assassin. Briar stopped in his tracks as if his feet had been involuntarily stuck to the floor.

He watched the Phantom vanish into thin air, becoming nothing more than an ivory brush of momentary smoke.

We are all born into nothingness. We have no privilege, no reputation. We have no skill or passion. For the first few moments of our lives, we do not even have a name.

All until we open our eyes for the first time and the progression of human life begins. We learn how to function our legs and walk. We hear sounds more clearly. We learn how to speak, and we teach ourselves how to read and write. We use our fundamental abilities to discover new properties in ourselves and new values to seek out in partners and friends. We observe everything, down to the very core of the planet. There is not one thing that goes unnoticed by our eyes.

Well, all until we face the harsh reality that no, we are not innocent creatures.

We are not born with clean spirits; we have a guilty conscience to pay for our sins of the past. There is blood on our hands, an invisible stamp on all fingerprints that marks our mistakes. We have sentenced billions to death to save hundreds. We have closed off our doors and allowed millions more to die from poisonous air and toxic radiation. We are not innocent, but we were strong enough to convince ourselves otherwise.

Because what would humanity be like if we remembered the souls that were lost like personal wounds on our bodies? Who would we have become if we did not forget our past in order to achieve the future?

Perfection does not come from nothing.
And strength does not come from being wholly
innocent, either.

-An excerpt of the first Supreme Leader's
journal, extracted from the Archives of the
Imperial Republic of Raedon

Chapter Thirty

"Ad quod iuga non possum sergere?"
-To what heights can I not rise?

In the Raedon Archives, a Worldkiller was described as an existing dilemma that led to the downfall of society before the sun imploded.

Problems like fighting a war under a flag of false peace. Plague spreading through the land accompanied by its sisters, famine, and hunger. The slaughter of millions and the ascension of only hundreds. Handing unfair balances of power to the most corrupt individuals known to humankind. Causing the downfall of thousands of empires and murdering billions.

But that night, the Archives would permanently change.

Because tonight, the Phantom would forever be known as a Worldkiller.

The assassin had heard Briar Atlas call her name. She had ignored him as she continued pacing towards the end of the room, locking her eyes on a small door hidden behind a curtain of sheer silk. It led upwards towards a hidden balcony above the ballroom just below the glass ceiling, which had been unfolded to reveal the open sky above.

Normally, the balcony was used for musicians to create soft music that mysteriously floated over the guests who were oblivious to where it was coming from. But tonight, only one song will be sung from the hidden terrace.

Wren would call it the "Ballad of A Fractured Republic".

And she would make it a masterpiece to remember.

The stars twinkling above the open dome watched her with steady gazes, blinking as they followed her path through the ballroom. They didn't speak to her this time; either because they wouldn't question the fate they had predicted was coming towards Raedon or because they were scared, truly frightened about what the assassin was about to pull off. Not a single guest turned their heads to glance at her, nor did they whisper gossip like they usually did. The party didn't stop abruptly like it had the last time she interrupted an event. It went on as usual as murmurs of the upcoming fireworks display that was about to begin.

Wren weaved in between the crowd like a sewing needle threading through soft fabric until she reached the corner of the room. Looking behind her before slipping underneath the deep purple silk, Wren escaped into the secret passage and mounted the stairs. They were steep and thin, and her body barely fit in between the walls of the winding staircase. How the hell did instruments and choruses fit up here?

"Wren," Eden's voice rang from her ear cuff as she curved up the steps. She could hear the warning in his voice. He was already in position with his team, waiting in locations around the outside of the palace for the rebels to make their move.

"Hang on." She bit out, approaching the top of the passageway. There was a small platinum door that she pressed her hand onto, popping open at her touch like one of the safe points throughout the rest of the palace. When she ducked beneath the doorframe and walked into the space, Wren soon realized that this was a better position than she could've imagined.

It was empty and small, but not cramped, and just large enough to fit her body once she situated herself with her rifle. The ceiling was low enough that if she stood the full way, her hood would just barely graze the platinum walls around her. Wren stepped into the center of the passageway and kneeled, swinging her rifle over her shoulder. There were thin railings along the entire third wall like a grate that passed air to different rooms. From her perch, she could see the entire ballroom perfectly.

"Get into position," Eden ordered from her ear again. "The rebels are getting closer to the power lines."

Everything was falling into place. The Rising Sun would cut the power after she'd made the shot from the hidden balcony. It would cause havoc, of course, and also secure a period when the guard on the palace was down and the rebels could storm the stronghold. It had been Wren's idea, after all, to carry out the plan during the fireworks display. A loud shot from her rifle would be disguised until Briar fell.

But it only gave her minutes, maybe even less, to escape.

Once she made it out of the ballroom and through the line of incoming rebels, she would find Nova in her hiding spot along with Eden and his team. The attack would die down and the rebels would take hold of Polaris. The Rising Sun would gain control of the capital of Raedon and the Republic would fall into the hands of the very rising dawn they had ignored for far too long.

"We have one chance to succeed. Take the shot and don't miss." Eden continued as Wren took slow, steady breaths. She could not allow herself to be nervous; a single moment of hesitation would kill both her and any attempt the rebels had to take over Polaris. Besides, this was what she was made for. This is why she created the Phantom.

Every revolution had to begin with a spark.

Luckily for the Rising Sun, Wren had previously become a pyromaniac.

"I never miss," Wren growled in response, planting her rifle in front of her. She adjusted her position so the back of the weapon rested snugly against the crook of her shoulder and neck. She peered through the scope once and readjusted; she needed a clear shot.

From the ballroom below, the Supreme Leader had summoned the attention of his guests with a small clinking of his champagne glass. All eyes turned to him, the room becoming almost silent.

"It is an honor to stand in front of the Republic tonight, holding a glass before me to salute the one thing that Raedon has succeeded in achieving above all else; perfection." Dorin Atlas's voice boomed over the entire room, echoing off the walls. It rang in Wren's ears the loudest of all as she peered through her scope, reaching toward the shining silver device to adjust the sight of the weapon. She rotated it until the miniscule clicking had stopped and her vision through the glass was crystal clear.

"There used to be an old saying that described perfection as the result of something called practice. One would work hard over some time and eventually obtain their success with one final push." The Supreme Leader chuckled, and his shoulders bounced happily. "Well, my friends, I'd say we've had plenty of practice."

Not taking her eyes off Dorin through her scope, Wren reached down into her pocket. She felt the cold white bullets against her gloves, but only selected one to load into her rifle with a heavy snap of metal.

One bullet for one perfect shot.

"There is not a moment that goes by that I do not dwell on the mistakes of the past and thank our forefathers that we have made it to the future. There is not a moment where I am not proud to say that we have become the exception in the laws of destiny. The Republic has defied nature and built us a new reality. We have resisted mortality and diseased deaths. We have confronted war by standing together in unbending unity. We have faced our past and have forgotten what it was like to be flawed."

Wren carefully moved her aim to Briar, standing beside his father and the other Advisors. His uniform was pristine and clean, crafted from midnight black fabric embellished with silver stars. His hands were tucked neatly behind his back, and his chest rose and fell in steady motions. His face was ticking as if he was battling everything the Supreme Leader was saying, countering it in his mind, but not with his lips. There were unspoken words in his eyes that Wren could see, the smallest fractions of resistance shining in the center of his dilated pupils.

"Are you in position?" Eden asked, speaking over the Supreme Leader as he resumed his speech. His tone was clipped and tense, as if he was watching the ballroom through binoculars. By now, the rebels had infiltrated the power system and were waiting for his call.

And he was waiting for hers.

"Yes," Wren responded, shifting her shoulders to smother the ache throbbing in her chest. Her heartstrings were shuddering with the speed of her hammering heart, causing her entire body to shake uncontrollably.

"Five." Eden began counting down.

Briar shifted on his feet, nodding his head to what his father was saying.

"Four."

Wren's finger lifted to the trigger of the rifle. The center of her scope danced around Briar's chest. He blinked, squeezing his eyes shut for a moment.

"Three."

The Supreme Leader smiled. "So, as I was saying, it is an honor to stand in front of the Republic tonight, holding my glass before me to ask one question."

"Two."

The Supreme Leader lifted his glass.

"To what heights can we not rise?"

Briar Atlas turned his head, his eyes rising to the balcony as the shine of the Phantom's scope caught his attention through a crack in the wall.

"One."

A purple firework fractured in the sky.

Wren pulled the trigger, and the entire world went dark.

To be loyal is to be brave. To be brave is to be loyal.
They go hand in hand.
One who dares to stand up for what is right is loyal
to the cause that they believe in. One who fights for
what they think is right has the bravery to be loyal.
It is a symbiotic relationship between two
intangible things. You cannot hold bravery in the
palm of your hand, but you know it is there in other
people. You can see it in their eyes before they
march into battle, the sheer determination of valor.
Nor can you hold loyalty, but simply standing by
the side of a leader marks you as a patriot to their
cause.
It is important to have loyalty and bravery in
today's world. While there are no wars to fight, we
battle internally each day. When one is not happy,
the rest are not happy. We then must pinpoint the
problem and solve it, making sure that discomfort
towards a certain situation never occurs again. We
look to our leaders for the right answers, faithful to
their decisions. We are reliable and trustworthy.
That is why society will not die.
We value each other. We fight for each other.
But like with all balanced relationships, there must
be a warning. Because once trust is broken, it
cannot be earned back.

-An excerpt of the first Supreme Leader's
journal, extracted from the Archives of the
Imperial Republic of Raedon

Chapter Thirty-One

"Ego te provoco."
-I challenge you.

For a fraction of a second, there was peace.

The lights had gone out. The rifle aimed towards Briar Atlas's heart was empty.

The assassin released a breath, feeling her trembling index finger still pressed against the trigger of the weapon. Her brother in her ear did not speak a word; all she could hear were the echoes of his breath as he waited to see the result. The entire world seemed to be waiting, stilled for a moment as they stood by, tracing the tip of her rifle, where a streak of smoke was still rolling from the barrel. The assassin's eyes didn't move from the line of her scope, waiting until the lights came back on to see the destruction she had created in one split moment of hesitance.

What had she done?

A scream erupted from the silence.

A firework ruptured in the sky.

A glass bottle broke as it was knocked from a table.

Another scream.

More fireworks.

The lights flickered back on and in the small window of clarity, the Phantom saw the result of her decision; the Supreme Leader had been shot in the heart. Beside him, Briar Atlas had disappeared.

Chaos overtook the ballroom. Guests stampeded towards the doors, tripping over one another to escape whatever was waiting for them in the next wave of darkness. Soldiers in black uniforms spread through the room like ink leaking into paper, swerving through the crowds to regain organization. The assassin did not spot Quinn Vega; her fiery head of hair had vanished amongst the rest. The Advisors who stood around the Supreme Leader now kneeled next to his body, lifting his lifeless limbs in an attempt to help him escape. But it was no use; he was dead from the moment the Phantom had made her decision. Fireworks continued to light up the sky, illuminating the ballroom during the moments of temporary darkness from the blackout. No one could tell what was a firework and what was a gunshot.

All until the doors burst open, and the Rising Sun stormed into the ballroom.

Wren took that as her cue to withdraw. There was no time to process what she had done or think about the consequences; she'd be gone by the time everything had played out. Another whisper on the lips of history, a Worldkiller responsible for the downfall of Supreme Leader Dorin Atlas and the Imperial Republic of Raedon.

Standing in the passage and swinging her still smoking rifle back over her shoulder, Wren dashed across the balcony and threw open the door to the stairs. The lights were still flickering throughout Sanctum Palace, strobing white and blue as she ducked her head to avoid becoming blinded by them. Her legs never moved so fast; pounding against the steps until she made it to the second door. She reached to her hip and pulled out a firearm, loading the weapon with a tight click before clasping it in both hands and kicking open the door.

What had she done?

Wren couldn't see a thing; the Rising Sun had thrown smoke grenades into the ballroom. Gunshots rang from all sides of the room and screams shattered any hope Wren had of hearing her way through the havoc. She saw both the shadows of party guests and the dark figures of the rebels, dressed in makeshift black uniforms from torn fabrics and dyed clothing. The only ounce of color on them was a blood red scarf, tied around their arms or their heads with the picture of the golden rising sun in the corner. They looked like wraiths, creatures of the darkness that only appeared in nightmares. Pinned to the lower halves of their faces, the rebel's masks obstructed the view of any facial recognition cameras throughout the palace. They held weapons against guests' throats, knives, firearms, and thin cords like ropes.

This was not a part of the plan; the rebels were supposed to infiltrate the palace and hold everyone inside hostage. They weren't supposed to murder anyone!

A firework exploded, reminding Wren that she was standing in the middle of the chaos. Gripping her gun tightly in her hands, she sprinted across the length of the floor. Her hood rippled behind her, and she could feel the tips of her knives poking into her uniform. Her heated breath trapped inside her mask curled up her nose, smelling of the exact fear she was supposed to be inflicting on other people, not the other way around.

Blinking in the white smoke, Wren spotted a rebel racing towards her. Their black uniform came into shape as her red hair whipped like the crack of a storm behind her.

No, not a rebel.

Quinn Vega.

The Captain barreled towards the assassin, roaring with rage as she sliced her sword across Wren's chest. Wren ducked quickly, the blade barely missing the skin of her abdomen. Her boots slid across the floor with the momentum of the attack, and she watched as Quinn twisted her sword around her arm.

"I knew it was you." The Captain circled Wren, fire dancing in the center of her eyes. Wren followed her as she moved, her hands inching closer to her thighs as she pulled out a knife from her belt. "I knew it from the moment they let you inside these walls."

"Then why did you let me live?" Wren taunted, flourishing her hands to taunt the woman. She was in no mood for games, but she needed time. It would be impossible to cross the ballroom through the smoke and layers of guests to make it to the other side in time to find Eden and his team, and hopefully Nova on the way. "Or did you simply figure out that I couldn't be killed?"

"You are not immortal, Phantom." Quinn shook her head, baring her teeth. "As much as you defy death, you bleed the same red as the rest of us."

Wren had always wanted to battle the Captain. Now was her chance.

"Wanna bet?"

Quinn hurled herself at Wren, raising her sword to jam it into the assassin's temple. Wren moved swiftly on her feet, twirling out of the Captain's range, and kicking her in the back with the heel of her boot. Howling, Quinn whipped back around and threw her sword at Wren, slicing her upper arm open as the blade flew by.

"Do you believe me now?" Quinn jeered, weaponless but still jerking her chin mockingly in Wren's direction. Indeed, she had begun to bleed. Crimson blood was leaking from the wound and spilling down the white arm of her uniform.

"I may not be immortal, Captain," Wren snarled, lifting her arm with the gun, and pointing it at Quinn. "But neither are you. And a bullet is sure as hell faster than a sword."

Her finger locked on the trigger.

The gun clicked; her ammunition was jammed.

"Is that it?" Quinn sneered, unsheathing a knife from her belt. Cursing her incompetence, Wren threw the gun aside with a clatter.

She had brought a malfunctioning gun to a knife fight.

Perfect.

Wren threw her first knife, replacing it with another before it hit her target. Quinn dodged the dagger with masterful skill; of course, she did, she'd been trained in one of Xadon's military academies. She had risen in their ranks to the position of Captain of the Guard; how could she not dodge a simple knife? She was a machine, functioning on the highest level of lethality there was for a human being.

Alas, the Phantom was not human.

Wren felt the anger pooling in her veins as she ran towards Quinn, locking her aim on the Captain's heart. She dodged again, only to fall into Wren's awaiting fist, slamming into her nose. Quinn reared, wiping a hand across her face, and bringing a bloody trail with it. She jabbed at

Wren's ribs. The assassin caught her wrist before the knife could make contact. She twisted out of Wren's grip and found herself locked in her arms instead, forced to abandon her knife as she clawed at the assassin's arm for breath.

"This is what it feels like to die," Wren hissed in her ear.

"You will be the only one dying tonight." Quinn's palm slammed behind her head and into Wren's face. The border of her mask jerked into the assassin's nose, and she could feel the fracture deep within the nerves of her face. Screaming in rage, Wren's arms went limp around the Captain and she escaped, taking one of the Phantom's knives from her belt with her.

Blood poured down the bottom half of Wren's face, pooling in the curves of her mouth. She could taste the metallic warmth seeping into the cracks of her lips, the tangy taste of it burning her tongue as she took a step away from Quinn. The Captain was bleeding as well, gripping her neck as she hauled air back into her lungs. They were both oblivious to the chaos around them; the fireworks still booming, the grenades still exploding.

Quinn looked up at the assassin through her eyelashes, barely blinking as if Wren would disappear if she did. Her sword was gone and so was her gun, both of them lost during the duel. Kicked to some unknown spot on the floor, the gun Wren had tossed aside had most likely been trampled on and lost amongst the crowd.

The Captain's bloody nostrils flared. "A murderer like you does not deserve the glory of killing the Supreme Leader." Her face contorted into a twisted hate, one that told Wren that she would do everything within her power to make sure the Phantom died at her hand.

Wren cocked her head to the side, her lip twitching with a kind of crazed amusement. "And a Captain like you does not deserve the honor of killing me."

The Phantom lunged. Quinn had seen the knife that was headed straight for her head, the one that Wren had made sure she'd seen the glint of when they'd been speaking. But what she did not realize was that blade was simply meant to be a diversion.

A shot rang through the room as the Captain of the Guard fell to her knees, the bullet from Wren's gun sinking deep beneath the skin of her thigh.

Quinn's arms wrapped around Wren's torso as she slowly collapsed onto the ground, bending below the level of the assassin's knees as she howled in pain, gripping her leg. Blood leaked through her fingers as she screamed, her entire body trembling in rage.

The Phantom holstered her gun and leaned over the Captain, pulling her head up by her hair. The assassin lowered herself to the Captain's ear, her voice grating like shards of glass scraping skin.

"The Republic will be *mine*." She rasped and disappeared into the smoke.

Saying that you have the moral right to do something is plain ignorance.

No one person has the *right* to do something another doesn't. That is called being a hypocrite, and there were too many of those in the world before the sun imploded. Saying that you can do one thing when another can't do the same thing is hypocritical. Acting against someone and becoming upset when they take action back is hypocritical. You are born with the same amount of status as everyone else, and it is your job to figure out how high you will rise. Working hard will allow you to succeed whilst doing nothing will cause your life to look accordingly. Just because one person has risen higher than you have does not mean that you should be risen to that same platform as well.

Earning and deserving are two different things. We earn what we have, and we deserve nothing more.

Humanity used to say that every action had an opposite and equal reaction.

For once, they might have been right.

-An excerpt of the first Supreme Leader's journal, extracted from the Archives of the Imperial Republic of Raedon

Chapter Thirty-Two

"Fata volentem ducit et invitam trahit."
-*Fate leads the willing and drags the unwilling.*

This was not how Briar imagined dying.

There were supposed to be golden chariots coming down from the night to bring him to whatever world was beyond this one. There were supposed to be celebrations on the sol he was born, hell maybe even a holiday named after him. The stars were supposed to welcome him with open arms, toasting champagne as he joined them as a legend in the sky. He was supposed to go peacefully but dramatically; in his sleep with gold draped over his head like a halo would do just fine. Anything would be just fine as long as he wasn't gagged, tied up, and being dragged somewhere by the scruff of his neck.

Oh, wait. He was.

The rebels were dragging him away from the ballroom. There were three, no four, of them behind Briar shouting orders to each other over the blare of gunshots and fireworks in the distance. The first, a man with hair so deep it looked blue, was the one who held onto Briar by the back of his collar. His rough knuckles occasionally bit into the back of

Briar's neck and caused him to kick in retaliation, only to be hit on the side of the head by a woman with a mask over her face and golden hair spilling down her shoulders in curly waves. The third was another woman, her mask torn halfway across her face as she screamed at another, a dark-haired man who seemed to lead them down the length of the corridors.

Briar had recognized their uniforms the moment the lights flickered back to life, and he found himself being ripped from his father's side. They were clearly rebels if the binding and gagging didn't already give it away. Their uniforms were torn as if they'd gone through a shredder and somehow came out alive. They held various pieces of equipment, some of it looked entirely improvised while others were intentional. Firearms, knives, small grenades, tool belts and trinkets. There were masks tied around each of their faces and no matter how many times Briar cranked his neck to peer backward at them, he never got the chance to see who they were.

Not that he would recognize any of them. Briar Atlas did many things in moments of panic, but one of them was not making friends with people who were more likely to kill him than invite him out for a fun night of gambling.

Briar struggled with every ounce of his strength against his restraints. His hands were bound behind his back in a way that made his shoulders bend to the point of near dislocation. His feet had been left unbound, but from the hurried way the rebels moved down the corridors, they'd most likely given up trying to bind him and instead focused more on the escaping part of their plan. Tied so tightly around his head, the gag split into the corners of his lips. He could feel blood pooling into his mouth; there was also some dripping from the ever-growing wound on his temple from whenever the blond woman hit him in response to his panic.

"Where the hell is she?" The dark-haired man roared from behind Briar, the gun in his hands still firing at guards running towards them that Briar could not see. The edges of his vision had begun to blacken, like an oncoming wave of smoke around a fire. There was a ringing in his ears, constantly blaring louder as each grenade exploded and each firework snapped. He could not think straight or properly, or maybe even at all. Everything seemed to blur together, like the entire world was pausing and Briar was the only one left moving.

As he bucked against the rebel dragging him along, a hard surface came crashing down on his temple. Then came the realization that slammed into him like running into a wall of pure stone.

The Supreme Leader was dead.

Briar did not remember, could not remember, what had happened. Nothing was clear; it was like he was looking at his memories through a pane of warped glass. Sounds morphed together, and images became fuzzy and contorted. The last words of his father's speech had been emptied from his mind as if they were liquid and, when his head was shoved to the side, leaked out of one ear. There were smiling faces from the crowd, then a firework popping in the sky. Then --

Then Briar remembered.

The gleam of the Phantom's scope had caught him in the eye just before the lights went out and the first firework lit up the sky. No, not a firework.

A gunshot.

The Phantom had killed the Supreme Leader.

Ebony had assassinated Briar's father.

Briar choked on the blood leaking into his mouth. It burned his throat, singed his tongue, and rotted his teeth. He could not breathe; he could barely even see or hear anything. The hallway around them shifted, spinning as if it was being sucked into a black hole and they were all about to fall into the abyss of nothing.

Screaming as they turned another corner, heading to somewhere far away from the ballroom, Briar kicked his legs out in front of him, trying to gain traction on the floor and slow the rebels' escape. They would not kill him, not when they had just murdered his father. Blood gathered on his temple and spilled down the side of his head, creating a path of crimson scars down his face. Tears streamed down the sides of his cheeks as he screeched through his gag, his pleas for help coming out as nothing but gasping and moaning.

A boot came down on Briar's ribs, sending a streak of pain through his abdomen.

"Shut up or I will shoot you before the Commanders have the chance to." It came from the dark-haired man above him, the one shouting the orders to the rest. Over his mask, Briar could see the stern expression on his face and the determination flaring in his dark brown eyes. His forehead was creased with frustration and his gaze constantly flickered from Briar to a point down the hall as if he was waiting for someone to join them.

He groaned, wishing he had his hands to fight back as he curled onto his side, continuing to be dragged away. The floor burned at his scraped skin, sending scorching pain through his entire body.

"She should be here by now!" The blond rebel shouted to the leader. She held her gun in front of her as she ran backward with them, guarding their weakest point against soldiers who came for them from the end of the corridor. She raised her gun again and fired, hitting a Raedon soldier directly in the chest. "We need to leave, Eden!"

"No!" The leader, Eden, shouted back. "The Commanders might have given the rest of them different orders but for now you are under my command! We wait until we cannot anymore!"

"Our time is running out, mate!" The blue-haired man behind Briar yelled back. He'd begun to drag Briar slower as if he was also waiting for this person and giving Eden the benefit of the doubt. "She did her job, now we've got to do ours!"

All four of them, including the second woman who had yet to speak and only worriedly glanced down the corridor, turned towards the end of the hall. In that moment, Briar mustered the strength to do the same.

A white figure dashed out from behind the corner, sprinting with all the power her legs could gather. The Phantom's uniform was stained with red, blood leaking from a wound on her shoulder and from beneath her cracked mask. Her weapons had been abandoned, most of them at least, save for the silver rifle hanging limply from her back and the gun she held in her hands, her finger still on the trigger but not pulling it.

"Ebony!" Briar screamed, but again it came out as a muffled sound.

Thank you, he wanted to say, finally releasing a full breath. The Phantom was coming to save him. She was going to kill the rebels and take him back to somewhere safe, somewhere free of the Rising Sun. It wouldn't matter that he had seen her scope on the hidden balcony because she was simply watching him; her hand couldn't have been on the trigger. She would protect him until everything was secure again and then bully him about saving his ass for the second time. And he would let her because Ebony would've saved him from dying to the same rebels who assassinated his father.

But as Ebony got closer, Briar's breath drew to a complete stop. She was holstering her gun, not shooting it. She was slowing her pace, not gaining momentum to throw herself at Briar's attackers. She was not untying his restraints or taking down the rebels. Their entire group had seemed to stop, waiting for Ebony to meet them.

"What the hell happened in there?" Eden approached Ebony before she had the chance to speak. She was wincing from simply breathing. Her eyes hurriedly danced around their group until she found Briar, only looking at him for a few seconds before turning back to Eden.

What she said next was inaudible, and so was Eden's angered reply. Ebony flinched when she spoke, the wound on her arm bleeding even more.

"Don't you understand?" Eden argued, his arms lashing. "The Commanders will kill you for doing this! Do you have any idea the magnitude of the mistake — "

At that moment, Briar's vision blurred and his ears rang. Everything was falling into place, but it was all in the wrong places.

The Phantom was working with the Rising Sun. No, not just working with them.

She was a rebel.

Ahead of him, Ebony continued to argue with Eden as the other three rebels looked around nervously. The blond continued to hold her gun in front of her, preparing for an attack from both ends of the corner. The silent woman with dark hair did the same, her eyes picking apart every aspect of the corridors, looking for a way to escape. The blue-haired man gripped Briar tighter, even though he didn't have the strength to fight, but it didn't matter.

Ebony's eyes flickered towards him as she argued with Eden. Both of them raised their voices, but Briar still couldn't hear; all of his senses were being drowned out by pure panic. Her expression above the bridge of her mask was contorted in worry, her face turning pale against the dark blood stamping her skin.

"We don't have time for this," The man holding Briar broke the barrier of his hearing. The thrashing sounds of the attack slammed back into him like a wave of heat from a sudden fire.

"He's right." The blond shouted over a gunshot ringing from some place near to their corridor. "They're catching up and if we don't leave soon, we'll never leave at all."

Both Ebony and Eden paused, glaring at each other. Eden stood tall in his black uniform, but Ebony stood taller despite her wounds. The scarlet splattering on her ivory uniform matched the red of the Rising Sun's flag tied to Eden's arm. She muttered something under her breath to the rebel, shaking her head as she did so. Eden firmly shook his back, a silent battle between the two of them that no one else seemed to decipher.

"You owe me this, after everything I've done for you." Ebony's voice was so cold, freezing all the blood in Briar's veins. "Get out of here."

"I will never forgive you for this," Eden warned, but he wasn't making a threat. He was telling her to come with them; to escape with the Rising Sun.

But Briar, all of them, knew from the moment she turned the corner that the Phantom would not come home, wherever that was.

"I do not deserve your forgiveness," Ebony countered, and then she was turning to Briar.

The Phantom took a step towards him and knelt by his side, the pain of his gag and the sting of his tears flooding back the moment he closed his eyes, waiting for her hands to hold his head and press his forehead against hers. He waited for her to apologize to him, waited for the tears to fall down her eyes when she realized she had been wrong about him.

Instead, she grabbed his chin with her gloved hand, raising it to meet hers.

"You made it so easy."

Time halted around them.

"What?" Briar choked between labored breaths.

"You were weak, and you were wounded." She sneered through the cracks of her mask. "You were naïve and foolish to think that you could love me."

"Ebony — " Briar cried her false name, tears falling down his face.

"The name for what I am didn't exist." The Phantom's fingers curled around his chin, lowering to grab his neck. She squeezed, suffocating the air from his lungs. "So, I came up with my own."

She held his neck for a moment in her hands, wringing the life out of his body. But it only lasted a moment before her clawed hands slipped from his face and she stood by his side, looking down on him as he shook his head, begging her not to leave.

"Please," he sobbed through the gag. "Please don't — "

"You wanted to see me, Briar?" The Phantom's eyes gleamed with wrath as she showed her open palms to him. "Here I am."

The sound of marching punctured his ears.

Quinn Vega, followed by a legion of shadowed soldiers, stormed around the corner of the corridor. The Captain's leg was oozing with blood, her skin soaked with crimson and battered by battle. She limped on her good leg, staggering forward like a demented beast towards them.

No.

Briar struggled with all the remaining strength in his body. From the core of his heart and the marrow in his bones, he kicked. He tore his teeth through the fabric, splitting his lips. He bucked against the ropes tied around his wrists, not caring about the blinding pain it brought to his shoulders. The Phantom was already becoming a blur in the distance, a white figure in the silver hallway, confronted by an army of darkness.

As he was dragged away, the assassin glimpsed at Briar one last time, her brilliant eyes aflame with chaos.

Then, as if the world itself had been cleaved apart, Briar's vision blackened.

We were tired of wanting impossible things.
So, we made them possible.
We were told that humanity would die within the first few minutes of radiation that destroyed the world.
Yet here we are.
We were told that humanity would only last ten years inside the Atlas 1078 before all life on Earth died.
We were told that once humans rose out of the ground again and built our new society, we would tear it down again. We would destroy ourselves like we have destroyed the world, over and over again. We were killers, bloodthirsty animals.
But we do not repeat history; we learn from it.
We do not make the same mistakes man did before the sun imploded because of what we have seen ourselves doing to the world. We have made the change to improve when everything else has been degraded and decimated.
We have picked up the broken pieces of our fractured world and refused to remain shattered.
We were told that perfection was an illusion.
Yet here we are.

-An excerpt of the first Supreme Leader's journal, extracted from the Archives of the Imperial Republic of Raedon

Chapter Thirty-Three

Wren needed Briar to hate her.

She needed him to see the fury in her eyes, the uncontrollable terror that she had made him believe was inside her. She needed him to see the monster let out of its cage, raging in her eyes. He needed to see the surrounding destruction, feel the burn of the fire surrounding Sanctum Palace in its grasp. He needed to hear the screams of horror and the gunshots that followed, wincing as every bullet hit innocent skin. He needed to taste the blood, the thickness of the gore, and know that deep down, they all had blood on their hands.

Because the fracture in Raedon was already marrow-deep; all they had to do now was break the bone.

The Phantom turned around. The legion of Raedon soldiers had surrounded her, entrapping her in a circle of darkness with no holes to escape. Their guns were drawn, their shoulders pressed tightly together to ensure the strength of their barrier. She was one lone star in the galaxy of shadows, awaiting the void that would finally suck her up into eternal black.

The Phantom could not leave with the Rising Sun. It was her or Briar, and she had made her choice. The Republic would not settle for neither; they demanded payment for the chaos raging around them. And who better to have than the root of the problems herself?

The soldiers parted at the helm, allowing Quinn Vega to limp into the ring with the Phantom. The Captain's armor had been torn off and the skin below it was torn and raw. She smiled at the assassin, the front of her teeth stained red.

"You have a heart as cold as ice, Phantom." She snarled, blood leaking from her nose and pooling in the curve of her lip. "I bet it shatters like glass."

The heel of the Captain's boot connected with the assassin's ribs, knocking her backward into a pile of awaiting soldiers. Wren allowed herself to be shoved. They pushed her forward again, into Quinn's curled fists. She sunk her knuckles into the assassin's face, fracturing her mask in a clean split down the center. The middle knobs of her spine screamed as boots connected with her back, pushing her into an elbow that ripped her skin as her tooth speared through her lip. A knife sliced across her forehead, a searing cut of fire that burned away any shred of defiance the assassin had left. The tips of their metal shoes slammed into the backs of her knees, forcing her to the ground.

Quinn leaned down, grabbing the back of the assassin's hood and forcing her into a level stare with the Captain.

"Raedon's most notorious assassin." Quinn laughed, but her grip on the back of the assassin's head was not gentle. "Society killed the sun once, but now it is you that has obliterated our Supreme Leader. What are they to call you now, on your knees before death?"

Wren Sitara smiled through the cracks in her mask, peering up at Quinn through the gore spilling into her eyes. The Captain moved her grip to her chin, her fingers digging into Wren's jaw. Her nails bit into her skin, but Wren refused to flinch as Quinn leaned forward, blood spraying from her lips.

"Tell me your name!"

The Phantom laughed, a sound that echoed through the world like the crack of an imploding sun.

"Starkiller."

By the law of the Imperial Republic of Raedon, set
forth by the Supreme Leader and his cabinet of
twelve elected Advisors, any act of insurgency or
resistance to the constitutions of the land is
addressed by:
Execution by firing squad.

-An excerpt of the first Supreme Leader's
journal, extracted from the Archives of the
Imperial Republic of Raedon

Amelia Arvie is an up-and-coming author from Pennsylvania who uses her work to transport readers into a captivating world of intrigue, strong female characters, and plot twists. Her interests focus on young adult novels that take imagination to new levels and allow readers to escape from one reality into another.